THE
MINDBREAKER
ANNIHILATION
MARINA EPLEY

The Final Book in
THE MIND BREAKER Trilogy

PART 1

CHAPTER 1

I can vividly see her in my dreams. She's standing right in front of me, all decked out in camo, long red hair flowing over her shoulders. Kitty. I still don't know whether she's dead or alive. She moves her lips, trying to tell me something, but I can't comprehend a single word.

I wake up, disappointed and confused. I can't understand whether I'm having telepathic visions, or my imagination is working in overdrive.

Perhaps Kitty along with the rest of my friends are goners. Maybe I just don't want to accept their deaths.

It's early morning and dim light seeps through the window blinds. I hear the sounds of gunfire and high-pitched voices coming from outside. Feeling troubled and lonely, I stagger to the sink to wash my face with cold water. I put on my Retaliation uniform, approach the window and take a cautious glimpse out into the prison yard.

The main gates of the Death Camp open as military trucks pull in, carrying several dozen freshly captured non-breakers. A handful of guards dressed in camo uniforms identical to mine command the prisoners to line up along a wall. The fresh inmates obediently execute the order. I make out a few old people and little kids amongst them. I'm sure they've committed no real crime and their only guilt lies in being non-breakers. The guards open fire and I watch silently as the inmates fall.

One of the soldiers notices me and salutes, believing me to be his commander. They all look on me as some sort of hero and living legend, the one who assassinated all the leaders of our former government and took over the country. The thought makes me sick.

The truth is, I'm nothing more than a prisoner here. My captors transported me to the Death Camp 3 weeks ago, when my condition finally stabilized. This place used to be the largest Elimination prison in the Republic, designed specifically for terminating captured mind breakers. Now, it's used as Retaliation headquarters and a place where breakers terminate ordinary humans 24/7. There's little difference to me.

I'm living in quarters once occupied by an Elimination executive. It reminds me of a cheap motel room furnished with a bed, TV, table and a couple of chairs. It contains a small closet and bathroom as well. The door is permanently locked, and guards always follow me any time I'm allowed to leave this room. Except for the transport from the hospital, I haven't been outside for a full 4 months.

That changes tomorrow. I'm determined to escape, no matter how hard it may prove to be. I must return to Kitty as I promised. Assuming she's still alive, that is.

Tomorrow my captors will transport me to the Retaliation parade in the capital. This is going to be my first real opportunity for escape. So I have to find a way and get rid of the blocking collar around my neck, which prevents the ability for hypnosis. Luckily, I know someone who may help with this particular task.

The door opens at 7 AM sharp and a young girl with long red hair strolls in. Her eyes are unnaturally green, so I suspect she's being forced to wear contact lenses. She claims to be sixteen, the same age as Kitty, but I can bet she's closer to twelve. Kitty looks much younger than her actual age, and this girl is obviously intended to be her replacement. She's dressed in a white mini-dress and wears high heels, moving along somewhat unsteadily. A tray with my breakfast is clutched in her small hands.

"Good morning, Rex!" the girl exclaims, stretching her lips into a well-trained smile. "I was missing you so badly."

"Hi Chelsey," I say, forcing a grin. "I've been missing you too."

Maintaining the same frozen smile, Chelsey marches across the room and places the tray on the table.

"Breakfast is served," she announces cheerfully, then approaches and wraps her arms around my neck. She performs the same annoying ritual every morning. After an awkward kiss on my cheek, she asks, "So you were thinking of me?"

"Night and day," I answer.

Normally, I have to lie, but not today. I've spent plenty of time recently trying to figure out how to turn Chelsey against Retaliation.

She giggles, motions to the tray and suggests, "Please eat."

I begin eating my breakfast, although I have no real appetite. Chelsey leaves me alone for a while, standing by the window and gazing into the prison yard. She must not realize I'm paying any attention to what she's doing, because her face suddenly loses its beaming expression. Her eyes become distant and sad, and her smile fades. And for a split second I believe I may actually see the true Chelsey, a real human being, not a pretentious doll. The realism lasts only a moment. Chelsey catches my wary gaze and quickly curls her lips back into an artificial grin.

I smile back at her.

Chelsey and I have a very complicated relationship.

Guardian sent her to me after delivering the despairing news about Kitty's death. I was faking clinical depression in order to make Retaliation believe I had no fight left in me. They sent Chelsey, looking disturbingly similar to Kitty and vigorously pretending to be in love with me. She was supposed to become an amusement, a little trade-off for my agreeing to cooperate. I assume I could do whatever I like with Chelsey. But mostly, I've just wanted to kick her out of my room and yell at her to never come back. I didn't, because I had to make my captors think they had ultimate control over me. I needed a way to lower their guard to make an escape more feasible. So I've been playing along with this girl, pretending to be interested.

I used to strongly dislike her. I was disgusted at the fact that someone so young and innocent-looking could also be that manipulative. I tried to catch Chelsey in her lies. I made her repeat the same stories about her family, school and time spent in Elimination prison over and over. I wanted to find any inconsistencies, some small details she'd forgotten. But Chelsey never made the tiniest mistake, her lies being stunningly accurate and consistent. And soon my resentment gave way to a deepening respect. I had to admit she was a great actress, a calculating and headstrong girl.

Recently, I started to suspect that Chelsey might be as much a victim here as myself. I finally began to realize that my captors likely forced her to play this game. We could be in the same boat, each having been reduced from independent human beings into Guardian's puppets. And just possibly, I could dare to obtain Chelsey's help in my escape.

I still don't know anything for certain though. I wish to utilize Chelsey in my plans, but how can I trust this girl? There's always a possibility that she's spying on me, willingly cooperating with my captors. So I have to be careful and find proof of her reliability first.

After I finish breakfast, Chelsey offers to watch TV with me. I agree because I need to buy some time to think. I haven't quite decided what I should do with her. How can I snap Chelsey out of her pretentious mode?

I sit in a chair in front of the TV, pretending to watch the news. Chelsey approaches and plops down on my lap, placing her head on my shoulder. I envision myself grabbing Chelsey and shaking her, demanding she quit pretending. I remain motionless, just watching the news.

Currently, there's only one channel available, the one taken over by the so-called Army of Justice. Newly hired correspondents proudly report on cities and towns being liberated by breakers. They show unsettling images of burning buildings and piles upon piles of mutilated human corpses. They've been broadcasting similar videos for a few weeks now. The entire country seems to be collapsing with hundreds of innocent people being killed every day.

Breaker journalists report that only a few outlaw groups of Elimination officers are still holding a large city on the eastern coast. The Army of Justice will soon break their miserable resistance as the Elimination troops have very little ammo or manpower left at their disposal. This worries me. As soon as the city falls, Guardian will have complete control over the country, and there will be nothing to stop him.

The journalists also make sure to pay respect to my legend. They briefly tell of my days being incarcerated in an Elimination prison, and the riot I initiated. This is where truth ends and the lie begins. A further report covers several acts of terror I supposedly organized, burning children alive in schools and bedridden patients in hospitals. They describe how I took over the Death Camp and assassinated the leaders of the former government. Right now, I'm apparently leading the Army of Justice eastward to destroy Elimination. I'm said to be a fine example and inspiration for all breakers.

It takes all my self-control not to smash the TV.

I turn off the news and sit in silence for a while. Chelsey yawns, closing her eyes in boredom. She used to be stiff and alert in my presence, but now seems very relaxed. After all, I've never done anything provocative nor threatened her in any way.

Maybe I should just scare Chelsey out of her mind, so that she'd be more terrified of me than she is of Guardian? Maybe she'll confess her lies in this scenario? I decide to give it a try, although I'm not quite sure this is even possible. I've never met anybody as intimidating as Guardian, but hopefully my reputation will help. I am much older than Chelsey, having recently turned 19 and look even older.

"Will you be attending tomorrow's parade, Chelsey?" I begin.

She looks up at me sleepily.

"I don't know yet," she answers. "I'm hoping they'll let me go there with you. I'll be missing you terribly, if we have to spend the day apart."

I sigh. She's repeating the same old stuff as always. I'm getting really tired with this nonsense.

"Why do you love me so much, Chelsey?" I ask boldly.

"Well," Chelsey utters, momentarily confused. "You're very nice... and tall," she pauses, struggling now. "And handsome."

Having spoken, Chelsey frowns slightly, probably realizing she's overdoing it a bit. Considering the fresh scar from the bullet I took in my face, the handsome part is really farfetched.

"I'm a bad person, Chelsey," I say. "You've heard what they say in the news about me. I've killed hundreds of innocent people. What do you think about that?"

It doesn't trouble Chelsey for a split second.

"You've done things to liberate mind breakers," she answers. "You saved all of us. The only people you killed were our enemies, ordinary humans. I admire you a lot and think you're nothing less than a hero."

I look deeply into her eyes, trying to find a speck of truth in them. Is this what she really believes? Sometimes I truly wish I could read her thoughts. But reading thoughts is no more than a silly myth about breakers. Telepathy doesn't work this way.

Chelsey smiles from ear to ear.

"Tell me the truth, Chelsey," I say. "Are you scared of me?"

I place my hands around her neck. I have to try and knock her off balance. I need to make Chelsey panic and lose her hero worship attitude.

"No, why would I be?" she answers. She is still smiling, but I feel her stiffen.

"I'm a killer, Chelsey," I say calmly, and I'm not lying. "You know that."

"I don't care," she counters.

"So how far are you ready to go?" I ask.

"Just as far as I have to," Chelsey states.

I'm not sure what to do next. I hate threatening her, although I feel like I have no choice but push harder. I have to crack Chelsey and find out whether she's a friend or not.

"Alright then," I say. "Let's see."

I grab Chelsey by her shoulders, dragging her forcefully toward the bed. She lets out a surprised sob, but doesn't dare protest, remaining as passive as a rag doll. I throw her onto the bed and get on top of her, pinning both of her arms down. She becomes silent but doesn't try to put up any resistance. Kitty would already be clawing, biting and kicking, should anybody risk violating her in such a manner.

"Aren't you scared now?" I ask, feeling somewhat silly.

Come on, I think, show me the real Chelsey. Admit that you hate me.

"Why would I be?" she repeats.

I can feel her body shaking from fear. Her eyes are distant and empty now, but her lips are still stretched in the same stubborn grin.

I give up. She's much tougher than I thought.

"Damn it," I say calmly. "Just stop pretending already. I know everything."

This is when her gaze becomes fearful and she stops smiling.

"Know what?" she asks.

"You know exactly what," I say. "You're pretending to have a crush on me and I'm pretending not to realize that you're pretending. It's exhausting, Chelsey. Let's just quit all that."

Chelsey is quiet, staring at me in utter horror now.

"I can read all your thoughts," I lie. "You know I'm a telepath. So just stop pretending."

She swallows hard and whispers, "I can't."

"Why?"

"He'll simply kill me, if I do."

"Is Guardian forcing you to entertain me?"

She nods.

"It's alright," I say softly, releasing her.

Chelsey sits on the edge of the bed beside me, adjusting her dress with shaky hands. Large tears stream down her face.

"I'm sorry," she mutters. "Please don't be angry with me. He made me do it. He said he'd tear me into pieces, explode my head if I disobeyed. You know he can really do it. Please, don't tell anybody that I've failed in my job. And please forgive me... I just want to survive."

Her voice cracks. Chelsey covers her face, crying silently. Seeing her in so much despair just breaks my heart. At the same time I'm still not sure whether I can trust her.

"It's okay, there's nothing to forgive," I say, making my voice sound gentle. "I'm not angry with you. And I won't tell anybody anything."

"When... When did you learn that I was pretending?" Chelsey asks.

"The first moment I saw you," I explain.

"My goodness," she sobs, turning away. "I feel so stupid."

"Chelsey, do they keep your relatives hostage here?" I ask carefully.

"No," she says. "I haven't seen my parents since Elimination captured me. I don't know where they are. As I told you before."

She did, but I couldn't know what was true or a lie. I remain quiet for a few minutes, thinking everything over one last time. Maybe Chelsey is just putting on another act. But I'm really sick with perceiving everybody as being my enemy. I have to start taking chances at some point.

"Chelsey, listen to me very carefully," I say, touching her shoulder. She looks up at me. "You're a smart girl and must realize I'm a prisoner here too. You and I are in the same boat. Guardian is holding me here against my will, but soon I'll be getting out of this place. I may be able to take you along with me. It's very dangerous though, and only you can decide how much risk you're willing to take. So how far are you willing to go to regain your freedom?"

Chelsey's eyes widen. She asks in a conspiratorial whisper, "Have you been able to contact your friends? Are they still alive?"

"Sorry, but I can't tell you that," I answer coldly.

"I won't rat you out. I swear I hate Guardian as much as you. So you can trust me."

"Just answer my question, Chelsey. Are you in?"

She hesitates, thinking, then asks, "What will I have to do?"

"I need to get this thing deactivated by tomorrow," I answer, pointing at my blocking collar. "You think you can steal the control key?"

"I'm not sure," Chelsey says. "I know where they keep the keys, but I'm not allowed to that area. And should they catch me, I'll be in really big trouble."

"Chelsey, I'm getting out of here with or without your help," I say. "I can't make this decision for you and I can't force you to help me. But you should really think about what Guardian and his people have done to you and all the other prisoners. Do you want to be free or remain somebody's amusement? Just think about it."

Chelsey frowns, still hesitating, then her expression becomes decisive.

"I'll do it," she says. "I'll steal the control key. I always play dumb around the guards anyway, so they don't take me seriously. I don't think they'll pay much attention to what I'm doing."

"I believe in you," I say. "You're a good little actress and you're really brave."

"Thank you," she utters, smiling slightly. This is a different kind of smile, shy and sincere. I begin feeling guilty for making Chelsey risk her life for me.

"Please don't leave me behind," she begs. "I'll bring you the key. I'll do anything you ask. Only help me get out of this place. I hate it here. I can't stand all this killing and hearing all the cries all the time and…" She pauses, taking in a breath. "They wanted to make me a guard at first, and have me execute prisoners. I refused and they beat me really badly. They kept me in solitary with no food or light for a few days and I thought I'd go crazy. And then Guardian arrived." Chelsey shivers at her painful memories. "He raised me up into the air to the very ceiling, then turned me upside down. He promised to break every single bone in my body if I didn't agree to entertain you. And I knew he'd do it, I could feel it. It was just…"

She closes her eyes, becoming quiet. I let her recover. I still remember Guardian throwing me across the room and smashing me into a wall.

"Okay," Chelsey says, getting to her feet. "I'd better go now. I have work to do." She grins happily and adds, studying my face, "You're different from what I first thought."

Her words send a chill down my spine. I remember Christina saying almost the same things about me a few hours before she was shot. I get an image of little Lena leading me through prison passageways, helping to hunt down our enemies. A few minutes later she was dead. I become really worried that something bad may now happen to Chelsey. I seem to endanger anyone coming into close contact with me.

"Chelsey, if anything goes wrong, anything at all, stop immediately," I say. "Please be careful and don't get caught. I promise to take you with me, even if you don't bring that key."

"I want to help," she interrupts. "I hate Guardian and want to do something to get back at him. And don't worry. I won't get caught."

She knocks on the door and guards let her out of the room. I remain motionless for a few more minutes, thinking. I can't understand whether I'm correct in trusting this girl. What if she rats me out, reporting my intentions to Guardian? What if he decides I'm too resistant and not worth the trouble? He'd probably simply waste me in that case.

The sounds of rifle fire outside become louder. I hear another scream. My head begins aching. I groan and lie down on the bed, pressing my left ear tightly against the pillow. This way I can't hear much of anything.

I spend the rest of the day worrying and having doubts. I try to contact Kitty again, but don't succeed. I feel ashamed for using Chelsey to help me escape. She's already been used and abused by Elimination and Guardian, and here I am, talking her into risking her life. At the same time, I can easily imagine Chelsey marching straight to Guardian and telling him about my plans. And if even she doesn't rat me out and does bring the key, what then? What exactly am I going to do tomorrow? How am I going to fight my way out past a few dozen guards?

An opening door makes me turn around. A short thin man with gray hair walks in. He's in his late fifties, but his face is youngish-looking.

He always wears a dark business suit and tie. In spite of my best effort, I become nervous.

"Good evening, my friend," the man says softly. He has an overly soft voice and is always excessively polite. Nobody knows his real name, but he calls himself Guardian. He's the very one who's destroyed the country and ruined my life.

"Good evening, sir," I answer.

"Are you excited about tomorrow's parade?" he asks, watching me warily.

"Very excited, sir," I assure him. "It will be great to finally meet the breakers we've liberated."

"You're a bad liar, Rex," Guardian says. "Do you really think I don't know you're plotting an escape?"

I hold my breath. Chelsey must have ratted me out. I don't have time to become disappointed or angry. The next moment a chair rises abruptly into the air. It flies across the room and smashes into the wall just inches above my head, splintering into many pieces.

He's going to kill me, I realize.

CHAPTER 2

I freeze, sitting on the edge of the bed. I know I can't put him under or fight with him in any way. All I can do is to try and conceal my frustration.

"I have to admit I'm a bit disappointed, my friend," Guardian says. "I've given you everything a human being could ever hope for. From an average boy, I've developed you into a national hero. I've molded you into the primary commander of my army. And after everything I've done, you're ungrateful enough to continue plotting against me. Behavior I find very disrespectful."

"I'm not plotting anything, sir," I answer.

I work hard on showing no emotion.

"I'm afraid you still don't fully realize who I am," Guardian says. "Telekinesis is not the only ability I possess. I'm also a strong telepath who can read your mind." He pauses, letting his words sink in. "I'm inside your head now and know well what you're thinking," he adds.

The next moment an invisible force grabs me and throws me against the floor. The tremendous impact knocks my breath out of my lungs. I'm dragged across the room and slammed into a wall. Pain pierces my body. I hear Guardian laughing. I know I can't fight back, but instinctively begin swinging my arms and kicking at the air. I'm trying to fight off whatever is holding me. Nothing works. I'm totally defenseless. Still tightly pressing me against the wall, he raises me up to the ceiling.

I gasp for air. My head begins spinning. I've been tortured and beaten many times before, but nothing comes close to this experience. It's something indescribable and surreal, like something straight out of a horror movie or really bad dream.

"Do you really think you're so unique or special?" I hear Guardian's voice below. "You're nothing unless I will it. Completely worthless. I can easily find a suitable replacement. Level 4 breakers are not such a rare breed. So you should feel very lucky I chose you solely based on propaganda considerations. Serving me is the only purpose in life you now have."

I want to yell at him to go to hell, but something squeezes at my throat, cutting off my air. An enormous invisible weight presses against my entire body. I can't breathe.

"Give up any hopes of ever escaping from here," Guardian says. "All your friends are dead, and nobody will be coming to rescue you this time."

The strong grip on my throat tightens. My vision darkens. He's not human, I think in horror, no human being can possess such power, nobody at all.

"I could easily kill you," Guardian says, relishing in my predicament. "I can explode your head or smash you into a bloody pulp against the wall. You'll have to completely submit and give up any further thoughts of resistance if you wish to continue to survive."

I momentarily lose consciousness. He drops me to the floor. I land hard and lie unmoving for a few seconds, recovering my senses. My neck hurts.

"I'll kill you along with everybody you love or care about should you choose to disobey again," Guardian adds, still smiling.

I look up at him with hatred and disgust.

"You've already killed everybody I love and care about," I counter.

"What about that sweet little girl whose company you seem to enjoy so much?" he asks. "What's her name? You do like her, don't you?"

"She's all right," I answer.

"You wouldn't wish anything bad to happen to her, would you?" he continues. "I'm sure you care deeply about her well-being. Chelsey is a very nice and obedient little thing. You can be sure I'll skin her alive while you watch, should you attempt anything off hand during tomorrow's parade."

I don't say anything. I suddenly realize Guardian must be bluffing. He can't read my thoughts, otherwise he'd be aware about my plot with Chelsey. He's just trying to intimidate me, to make sure I've given up on any thoughts of escape. And Chelsey hasn't ratted me out. I'd be already dead if she had.

"Are you all right?" Guardian asks mockingly. "You look a little pale. Getting some fresh air tomorrow might do you some good."

What a jerk, I think angrily.

"You don't need to be scared," Guardian says. "I'm not threatening you. It was just a little sample of what could happen, should you forget your place."

"I get it, sir," I say.

He thinks for a moment.

"You still feel sympathetic toward ordinary people, don't you?" he asks.

"I despise all non-breakers, sir," I answer readily. "They're a lower race and don't deserve to be living as equals."

I have no idea whether he's buying what I'm saying or not.

"Breakers are a significantly superior race," Guardian agrees. "Non-breakers are like cave dwellers in comparison. Everything happening today is simply the logical result of our evolution. Breakers must rule the world and dominate humanity as the higher species. Our time is now. Ordinary humans must become subservient, else be killed."

He pauses, waiting for my response.

"You're absolutely right, sir," I answer. What else can I say?

Guardian approaches the window and stares out into the yard. I remain on the floor, tensed for another possible attack. I feel like a cornered rabbit trapped in a cage with a hungry wolf. One false move and it will be dinner time.

"I've saved the breaker race," Guardian says. "Without me, breakers would continue being hunted by Elimination, resorting to hiding and living fearfully in the shadows. You may think I'm too violent or even evil, with the blood of thousands of breakers on my hands. But you must also realize the sacrifice was necessary to force breakers into action. I didn't have another option, but to take everything under my control. What else could I have done, burdened with such responsibilities? I'm the only level 5 breaker in existence. How else might I achieve my potential and fulfill my destiny? It is my fate to dominate this world."

"I get it, sir," I repeat. "I only can't understand why you need me."

"I prefer to remain in the shadows," he explains. "I perceive the world as a grand stage and everything that happens is like a play. My role is not to be an actor in this play. I'm the director. I'm offering you the leading role along with an opportunity to provide inspiration for breakers. This role can be delivered by others should you perform poorly. I can always find new actors."

"I see clearly now," I say.

"I'm pleased you finally understand," he answers, heading toward the door.

"Sir, I do have one small request," I say. "I'd like for Chelsey to be permitted to attend tomorrow's parade. I believe some fresh air might be good for her, too."

He gives me a long look, then nods with an understanding smile.

"You're truly enjoying my little gift, aren't you?" he asks. "I personally chose her for you. Does she treat you well and meet your needs?"

"Chelsey exceeds all expectations," I answer honestly.

Guardian grins.

"Good. She'll be permitted to attend the tomorrow's parade with you," he adds, exiting the room.

I give a finger to the closing door. It's all I can do for now.

I slowly get to my feet, overcoming the pain in my aching muscles. My throat hurts and I'm dizzy from a lack of oxygen. I walk into the bathroom and check my reflection in the mirror. I have darkening purple bruises all over my neck.

I return to the room and sit down on the bed, but can't keep still. I approach the window, taking a glance outside. I see a now familiar scene, guards in camo beating and shooting down groups of defenseless prisoners. I turn away and begin pacing the floor.

Chelsey hasn't ratted me out, but where the heck is she? What is taking her so long? I can't stop worrying. What if the guards have caught her in a restricted area?

I feel ashamed. I've likely just sent a twelve-year-old girl straight to her doom. The guards would execute Chelsey for such a violation of rules. Disobedience in any form is punishable by death in this joint.

When I can't stand it anymore, I knock on the door. A guard opens up, asking what the hell I need.

"Do you know where Chelsey is?" I ask.

"Getting lonely in there, hero?" he asks, holding his rifle on me.

"Very lonely," I answer. "Where is she?"

"No idea," he answers, slamming the door in my face.

"Jerk," I say, and continue pacing the room.

I think of Guardian's words concerning my deceased friends. I wonder whether he spoke the truth. What if Kitty and everybody else are really dead? What if the certainty of her death was too much for me to handle and led me into creating false hopes? What if I'm just trapped in my own overly optimistic illusion?

Chelsey finally returns around midnight.

"What happened?" I ask hurriedly, looking her over.

She doesn't answer. Smiling, she raises up a small metallic object over her head. The key.

"Amazing," I whisper. "You did it."

"I did!" Chelsey exclaims. "I stole the control key!"

She lets out a short laugh and runs toward me, spreading her arms into a tight hug. She almost chokes the life out of me.

"I had to wait forever until it was safe," Chelsey gushes. "Those stupid guards never noticed anything. Gosh, I wish you could have seen me. I was invisible. I was like a ninja. Oh, I'm so excited! I can't wait to get out of this place."

"You did great, Chelsey," I say. "I'm so proud of you!"

She finally releases me from the bear hug and begins jumping around the room.

"Freedom! Freedom!" she repeats happily. I don't recognize this side of her.

"Chelsey, calm down," I say. "We gotta keep cool."

But she can't help herself. She continues jumping around and giggling. Her excitement becomes contagious, and I begin feeling wired and anxious as well. I start laughing along with her. I realize that we may finally get a chance to escape. The thought of freedom can be intoxicating.

I spend the next several minutes trying to bring Chelsey back to her senses. I decide to make her sit down on the bed and practice deep breathing exercises.

"Calm down," I repeat. "Just breathe in and out. Slowly."

I demonstrate the technique for her, taking in a deep breath. Chelsey shrieks, falling onto her back and laughing. Her eyes begin tearing.

"Please, stop already," she begs. "You're killing me."

"Gosh, Chelsey," I exclaim. "Get control of yourself."

Exhausted, she finally calms down.

"Do you know how to use this thing?" she asks, holding the key up to her face.

"No, I don't," I admit. "How about you?"

"No clue," Chelsey sighs.

We both stare at the strange remote control key, passing it back and forth and turning it every way. It has several buttons. I press a few.

"Did it work?" Chelsey asks.

"I can't tell if it deactivated the collar yet," I answer. "I guess, we'll find out tomorrow."

"We need to check it somehow," she says. "I know how. I'm just a level 1 breaker. You can easily hypnotize me, can't you?"

I probably can, although I'm really uncomfortable with the idea. Chelsey looks at me expectantly. She's right. We have to know whether my collar has been deactivated before tomorrow.

"Have you ever been hypnotized before?" I ask.

"No," Chelsey answers.

"It can be very unpleasant," I warn.

She shrugs.

"All right then," I agree, concentrating. I haven't practiced hypnosis since the time of my capture. As I direct my thoughts toward Chelsey, an intense pain envelops my head. It's more painful than usual.

Obviously, it works. I can almost physically sense the moment I capture her mind. Chelsey must be a very weak breaker, because I don't feel any resistance. Her face relaxes, losing all expression. Her eyes become glazed and unfocused. My blocking collar is definitely deactivated.

The second I realize this I stop the hypnosis.

"Wake up," I say, shaking her. "Hey, come back. Can you hear me?"

Chelsey snaps from her trance, staring at me in a near panic. I know exactly what she's going through.

"Did it work?" she asks in an unsteady voice. I nod.

It's getting very late and time for Chelsey to leave. She lingers, looking at me with hesitation.

"I'm afraid the guards may discover the control key missing," she finally says. "If Guardian learns about this, he'll become really angry." She pauses, lowering her eyes, then asks shyly, "May I stay till morning? I'm just really scared. I know you can't protect me from Guardian. But being with you makes it less scary somehow."

"Sure," I say. "Of course, you can stay."

"But where will I sleep?" she wonders. "There's only one bed."

She nervously looks at me, her expression almost fearful again.

"Yeah, but look at this nice comfortable chair," I answer. "I'm sure you'll be very comfortable sleeping in it."

Smiling, she kicks off her shoes and settles down in the chair. It's too small for her to stretch out so she curls up into an uncomfortable half-sitting position. I switch the light off and crawl into bed, feeling somewhat guilty. Maybe it should be me sleeping in the chair or on the floor? I finally decide what the heck. It's my bed and I still have work to do, trying to contact Kitty.

I close my eyes and concentrate on Kitty's image. I can draw her in my mind in perfect detail, but can't feel any connection. The first few weeks after my capture, I was getting very strong visions and even managed to telepathically exchange messages with her. Then for some inexplicable reason our connection faded.

I concentrate harder, refusing to give up. Find me, I project my thoughts, answer me. Can you hear me, Kitty?

Nothing. It's just not happening. Either I suck at telepathy or Kitty is dead.

"Rex, are you asleep?" Chelsey whispers.

"No."

"Are you trying to contact your friends?"

"Why do you ask, Chelsey? Just go to sleep. Tomorrow is an important day."

"Can you really use telekinesis?" she wonders. "They lie about that, don't they?"

"I can't use telekinesis," I say, getting annoyed. "Now try to get some sleep."

Chelsey becomes quiet. She turns a few times in her chair, being too anxious to sleep. I have to admit I'm still wired as well.

"Rex," Chelsey whispers again.

"What?"

"Are you still awake?"

I groan and raise my head, looking at the electronic clock on the table.

"Gosh, Chelsey, it's 3 AM," I say. "We need to be well-rested for tomorrow."

"If they catch us tomorrow, Guardian might spare your life," Chelsey says. "You're a telepath and memory reader. But I'm a weak breaker, about as common as dirt. Guardian says I'm worthless. He'll kill me if we fail tomorrow."

"We won't fail," I assure her, although I really don't know. "And Guardian thinks that everybody is worthless, except himself. We shouldn't care what he says."

"I'd rather be dead anyway, than spend one more day in this prison," she adds.

I keep silent for a few minutes, thinking. I feel deeply sorry for Chelsey. She has gone through too much for somebody her age.

"Becoming dead is the worst thing that can happen to you," I say. "As long as you're breathing, you can fight."

I hear her sigh sadly.

"The worst thing is when somebody you love dies," Chelsey answers. "I haven't seen my parents since my capture. I don't know whether or not they're still alive. But if they're dead, it's my fault. Elimination could have killed them because I'm a breaker."

Chelsey stops talking, pretending to sleep. I remain awake for a long time. I imagine the aircraft with Kitty, Marian and Rebecca aboard crashing during take-off. No survivors. I get an image of my friend Jessie bleeding in my arms. I remember Holtzmann holding his crippled hand with two missing fingers, blood still spilling onto the floor.

Chelsey may be right. Losing somebody you love and care about is far worse than your own death. If my Kitty is dead, I'm certainly the one to blame. Her blood would be on my hands, and I would have no reason to continue living.

I close my eyes and will myself to sleep.

***

"Rex, wake up! I hear them coming!"

Somebody is shaking me. I wake up in a panic, taking a quick look around. I see Chelsey standing by the bed, wearing only her underwear. Her dress is lying on the floor.

"What the heck?" I ask.

"Let me in," she whispers, hurriedly climbing under the blanket and stretching out beside me. "Hold me. And pretend to be asleep."

She places her head on the pillow and closes her eyes. I hear voices in the corridor. I finally get it. I put an arm around Chelsey, pretending to sleep. Chelsey spending a night in the chair might raise unwanted suspicions.

Hammer along with four guards enter.

"Time to get ready for the big parade, hero," he says loudly.

Chelsey sits up, rubbing her eyes and yawning.

"Is it morning already?" she mumbles. "I didn't get enough sleep."

Hammer looks at me with unhidden disgust. I grin. I don't really care what Hammer thinks.

The guards hold their rifles ready, while Chelsey and I dress.

"Is all this really necessary?" I ask Hammer, motioning to the barrels pointed my direction. "Are you really so frightened of me?"

"Shut up," he growls. "And hurry it up. We're running late."

I finish dressing as slowly as possible. Hammer and I are longtime enemies. He attempted to kill Kitty and I once before, then later helped Guardian capture me.

Hammer and his guards lead us into a spacious room with several chairs and a large mirror. I see more well-armed recruits around. Guardian stands aside wearing a satisfied grin. We greet each other. Chelsey waves to him, smiling widely. She holds my hand tightly, yet her fingers still tremble. I squeeze her hand back slightly in support.

The guards present me with a general's uniform along with a peaked hat and bulletproof vest. They also place an eye patch over my right eye. I take a quick glance at myself in the mirror, feeling like a complete idiot. The bullet tore an optic nerve and subsequently left my right eye permanently blind, but all the damage is internal. The patch isn't necessary, although

Guardian apparently has a different opinion on the matter. I'm wearing this patch and uniform in all the posters containing my image.

"You look very charismatic," Guardian comments.

I don't answer.

A chubby middle-aged woman in camo brings a red mini-dress for Chelsey. She has Chelsey change her clothes right in front of everybody. Then the woman braids Chelsey's hair and covers her face with a thick layer of makeup.

"You're very pretty now," the woman compliments.

Chelsey doesn't protest, wearing the same icy smile and now closely resembling a doll. I suddenly remember her lying beneath me, all stiff and putting up no resistance. I become worried. The guards won't let us slip away without a fight. How can I be sure Chelsey won't simply freeze up, when faced with danger? Today, we'll both need to be strong.

Hammer, along with a few guards, escort us out to a waiting helicopter. Guardian doesn't follow. He wants to stay in the shadows and won't participate in a parade.

Chelsey clutches my hand the entire trip to the capital. I realize that I'll soon find out the truth concerning Kitty. If nobody shows up to help me escape, then she's dead. I'm not sure I can face that possibility. I close my eyes and try to relax, fighting a growing anxiety.

"I hope you won't try anything stupid during the parade," Hammer says. "Guardian would be very disappointed. He'd order you to be shot."

I can be sure Hammer is asking me to give him a reason. He wants to take my place and lead the Army of Justice. He's obsessed about leadership.

The helicopter lands alongside a long black limousine too closely resembling a hearse. We're ordered to get in. We spend the last part of the trip surrounded by armed guards. They're obviously not taking any chances. The limo moves incredibly slowly as a crowd of people stand in the way. Two military trucks drive ahead of us to clear the road, and two SUVs follow behind to complete our procession.

We finally make it to the central square of the city. Hammer leads us inside an old historical building. We walk through a few passageways, climb up a screeching staircase and wind up on the balcony of the third floor. I squint into the blinding sunshine. Yelling and whistling on the street below is deafening. The entire square is filled with shouting people. All breakers. Some wear Retaliation camo and others are dressed in civilian clothing. They all raise their arms, holding posters and shouting out slogans.

It's overwhelming.

A guard shoves a barrel into my back.

"Wave to them," he commands.

Chelsey and I begin waving at the crowd. I anxiously scan the surroundings. Four guards stand directly behind us, holding rifles. The people below shout out my name. I wait for something to happen, although I'm not sure what exactly to expect. I just have a strange feeling that something will happen. Or maybe my imagination is working overtime. Maybe I will never escape Guardian's hold.

A few long minutes pass without anything happening. I begin losing hope.

Chelsey looks over at me, worried.

Suddenly, a building explodes on the other side of the square.

CHAPTER 3

I flinch, momentarily startled. I watch as thick black clouds of smoke pour from the building. The people below fall silent for a few seconds, turning their heads in the direction of the explosion.

What the heck was that? A terrorist attack? Some kind of diversion?

My confusion lasts only for a moment. I turn just in time to land a hard punch into the guard's face. He staggers backwards. Two other guards lunge at me, grabbing my arms, and begin dragging me back inside the building. I instinctively project my thoughts, hoping to use hypnosis. It doesn't work. These guards are far too resistant. Guardian knew whom he should send to escort me.

A rifle fires and one guard falls dead, a large bloody hole between his eyes. Jessie. That must be Jessie...who else could score such a perfect headshot? Perhaps she's alive and well after all, and has come to help.

I punch the remaining guard in the gut. He doubles over, and I bring a knee up straight into his face. As he's going down, I add a hard kick in the head for good measure, knocking him out cold. Yet another guard approaches, training a rifle on me. Another gunshot and he collapses across the floor.

I turn to see Chelsey struggling against a big guard. He's dragging her back inside the building. Chelsey bites and claws at the guy, but he's far too strong for her. I rush in closer, throwing a heavy punch from way down low, delivering a solid blow into his jaw. His head jerks backward as he releases Chelsey. I grab his face and slam him against the wall. I improve my grip on his head, and begin smashing it repeatedly against the wall until his legs give and he collapses.

Chelsey screams. Additional guards have entered the balcony. The mystery shooter brings a couple more down, but there are just too many.

I grab Chelsey's hand and begin climbing over the balcony's railing. This may be the only chance we have. I project my thoughts toward the people below us, directing them to catch us. We can't worry how dangerous it is at the moment or what injures we might sustain. There's no option left to avoid recapture, but to jump the three floors down.

We quickly go over the railing and free fall. There's a momentary sensation of weightlessness and then we crash onto the people below. A quick thud of impact mixed with the crunching sound of bones breaking. Sharp pain shoots throughout my body. I can't move or even breathe for a few moments, lying across a pile of bodies. I look to my left and see Chelsey outstretched beside me. We stare blankly at each other, both still stunned and disoriented from our fall. She's first to scramble to her feet.

"Let's go!" she yells, pulling me up.

I shake off my stupor, getting up. The guards on the balcony open fire. I hunker down, believing at first they're trying to hit us. But they're firing at the rooftops of the nearby buildings. They must be attempting to take out the sniper. If that shooter actually is Jessie, they will have their hands full.

I grab Chelsey's wrist, pushing through the quickly dispersing crowd. I shove and elbow anybody standing in our way. We need to distance ourselves from any pursuit. More guards begin exiting the building onto the street, searching for us. As soon as they get a visual, they fire warning shots above our heads. Chelsey screams, hunkering down lower. I can't hypnotize these guards, but the people in the crowd are not so immune to my hypnosis. I project my thoughts, directing them to attack the guards. They're terrorists, I repeat in my mind, and they're trying to kill you.

I hear sounds of fighting breaking out behind us. Neither of us bother to look back.

A second explosion shatters windows nearby. More people begin running in a panic. The crowd pulls us forward. If we don't go with the flow, we'll be trampled. Chelsey stumbles several times, but continues moving. Her eyes are frantic and she's gasping for air. I'm out of breath as well. The unfortunate who fall are being stomped into the concrete. I bump into somebody and almost lose my balance. Chelsey sobs as she runs behind.

We finally make our way out of the crowd. We sprint across a street only to run smack into three guards.

"Freeze!" they yell, opening fire above our heads. Chelsey shrieks, pulling her hand away from me and staggering backward. I fling my arms up in surrender, standing motionless and projecting my thoughts toward the guards. I put all my effort into the hypnosis. My head feels ready to explode from the pain.

The three guards slow their approach, staring at me in confusion. Their eyes are foggy and unfocused. I reach for the rifle of the nearest guard, but another grabs me from behind. The still fully alert guard puts me in a tight bear hug and begins attempting to lift me into the air. I secure his wrist, holding it tightly. I take a quick step forward and roll in a quick somersault, sending the guard flying over me. He lands hard onto his back on the concrete and lies unmoving, his eyes wide open and glazed. I elbow him into the face.

"Watch out!" Chelsey screams.

Another guard charges into me from the right. I didn't see him because of a blind spot on that side. I wind up on my back, with the big guy mounted on top of me. I cover as he begins slamming the butt of his rifle at my head. I can't knock him off me and can't even strike back as the attack is too vicious. He's attempting to smash my skull. The three hypnotized guards are still standing in a daze. I direct my thoughts toward them, hoping to make them shoot down my attacker. They don't react, I'm too weak.

As I'm struggling with the guard, Chelsey takes a handgun from a downed soldier, aims it at my attacker and squeezes the trigger. Nothing happens. She probably doesn't know how to take the safety off. Chelsey stares at the gun, screams in frustration and slams the gun into the guard's head. He swings his rifle around at Chelsey. I reach for his face with both hands, jabbing my thumbs deeply into his eyes. The guard cries out in pain, jerking backward and firing his rifle. Chelsey drops flat on the concrete, covering her head. I kick the guard off of me, grab up his fallen rifle and fire off a round straight into his face. A circle of blood stains the street as his head bounces off the pavement.

"Behind you!" Chelsey yells.

I turn and fire at the approaching guards, grab Chelsey's hand and we take off running again. She's still carrying the handgun she took from a downed guard. We move as fast as possible, but can't shake our pursuers. Chelsey has kicked off her shoes, jogging barefoot ahead of me now.

A military SUV cuts us off. Tinted windows roll down and a few rifle barrels extend outward in our direction. The gunmen open fire as I tackle Chelsey to the ground, shielding her. I aim my rifle at the SUV, firing a few rounds. I can't tell if I hit anything because my vision is poor. I project my thoughts toward the driver, but don't know if that will work.

Something happens. The SUV abruptly accelerates, driving across the street and passing within a few feet of us. It collides into the nearest building with violent force, smashing into the front and recoiling backward. I get a thought that it's about to explode, and we're too close. But it doesn't explode, just rolls several feet backward and becomes still. Nobody emerges from the vehicle. I scramble to my feet, yanking up Chelsey, and we take off again.

The guards behind continue their pursuit. I hear a blare of the sirens coming in the distance. I realize that they'll soon recapture us. We can't move fast enough as we're both too beaten up and exhausted to keep running. Chelsey is limping now. My head is swirling and I can't think straight.

We turn a corner, running into a new squad of guards blocking the street.

"Freeze!" they command, training rifles on us. "Drop your weapons!"

We can't go back because of the guards still on our tail. And I don't dare to open fire as our enemies look a little too willing to shoot us down.

I project my thoughts toward the guards standing in our way. They're still holding their rifles on us, but their expressions change, becoming meaningless. We jog between them. I hear the footsteps of our pursuers getting closer behind.

"Fire!" I command.

The guards execute my request, shooting into the guards still coming. Chelsey and I run further, leaving the gunfire behind. A large helicopter flies above our heads. I raise my rifle, firing a few rounds. The helicopter ascends.

Suddenly, a van speeds toward us, then comes to a sudden stop. I prepare to shoot, but as the back door opens I see Kitty. She's dressed in camo and armed with an assault rifle. She waves her arm, yelling, "Get in!"

My heart skips a beat. She's alive. It wasn't just my imagination.

I grab Chelsey's hand, running as fast as possible. Chelsey is gasping, but manages to keep up. Kitty fires at our remaining pursuers. They kneel and return fire. The space around the van quickly fills with loud shouting and flying lead. The last several yards between us and the van seem to last forever, but Chelsey and I somehow manage to avoid being shot. We sprawl inside on the floor in near complete exhaustion.

"Drive!" Kitty commands.

The van leaps forward. I sit on the floor with my eyes closed, waiting for my dizziness to fade. Chelsey coughs somewhere nearby. I'm totally drained. My heart pounds heavily in my chest and my head aches. We're free is the only thought swirling in my mind. We're free, we have escaped.

"Rex! Can you hear me? Are you injured?"

I open my eyes and see a thin girl with short black hair bending over me. She's holding a sniper rifle. Jessie!

"I'm all right," I say, smiling broadly. "I've been through worse, I guess."

"Welcome back," she answers, grinning.

I suppress a strong desire to squeeze her in a big hug. Instead, we quickly shake hands. Jessie picks up her rifle and hurries to assist Kitty. Kitty is busy tossing grenades at our stubborn pursuers through the opened door of the van. We must have a few vehicles on our tail now. I stare at her in shock, hardly recognizing her. I've seen Kitty during a gunfight before, but she seems more violent now. I don't know what to think about that.

Jessie fires her rifle at our pursuers. Chelsey sits beside me, holding my hand and sobbing. A tall young guy in camo assists Jessie and Kitty, reloading rifles and lining up grenades. I've never seen him before.

Kitty and Jessie finally lower their weapons.

"We've lost them!" Kitty exclaims.

"The helicopter," Jessie says. "We can't bring it down." She glances at the young recruit. "Your turn," she adds.

The guy nods, his expression becoming determined. He stares at me and salutes, saying, "It's an honor to meet you, sir!"

He takes my rifle and moves closer to the door. The van slows abruptly. Only now I realize that the recruit is wearing a uniform almost identical to mine. He has an eye patch over his right eye. His hair is dark and he's about my size. I suddenly understand.

"No! Don't!" I yell.

It's too late. The van stops for a moment and the guy jumps out, running off. The vehicle moves forward.

"They'll kill him!" I shout. "Stop the van!"

I hurl myself toward the door, but Jessie grabs my shirt. I push her away.

"They'll capture him," I say. "As soon as they realize it's not me, they'll put him down."

"Shut up and keep down, idiot," Jessie growls. "He volunteered for this mission. He agreed to divert their attention so we could rescue you."

"Why?!" I exclaim. "How can my life be more important than his?"

"You're needed for a special project," Jessie answers curtly.

"What project?" I ask.

She ignores my question.

"Those suckers bought it," Kitty reports. "We've lost the helicopter. It's following him."

"Good," Jessie sighs.

They shut the door.

Exhausted, I sit on the floor, staring off into space. My mind is blank. I close my eyes, overwhelmed by exhaustion and frustration. I'm sick of causing the deaths of innocent people. I don't want any human sacrifices on my behalf. But people continue dying no matter what I do or where I go. It's always the same and there's no escaping it.

I shake off the disturbing thoughts, open my eyes and see Kitty sitting in front of me, smiling slightly. I can't worry about the deceased any longer. I don't care about anything else because here she is, only a few feet away, alive and unharmed. We're together again and I couldn't possibly wish for more.

"Rex," Kitty mutters.

I stretch my arms for her. Kitty gasps and throws herself toward me, falling into my arms. I hold her tightly, enjoying her warmth. I was missing her so badly. Kitty kisses my face and lips, crying. She's no longer the tough ruthless fighter, but my sweet needy girl once again. And I couldn't be happier.

"Rex, my love," Kitty utters. "I was going crazy without you. I thought I'd never see you again. Are you all right? Did they hurt you?" She doesn't give me a chance to answer. "Who the heck is this?" Kitty asks, looking suspiciously at Chelsey.

Chelsey's expression becomes fearful.

"Kitty, this is Chelsey," I answer as if it will explain everything.

"I don't believe it!" Kitty exclaims. "You're only away from me 4 months and there's already some kind of Chelsey." She trains the barrel of her rifle on the girl. "Get away from him!"

Chelsey hurriedly crawls away to the opposite side of the van. Jessie approaches her, wrapping her arms around Chelsey.

"It's all right," Jessie says in a soft voice. "You're safe now."

"Kitty, Chelsey is my friend and…" I begin.

"Oh, just be quiet," Kitty groans, holding me tighter. "You're mine. I own you. Nobody else can have you." She suddenly starts crying again. "I really thought I'd lost you forever."

"I was trying to reach you in my mind," I say. "I was sending messages."

"I know," she utters. "I saw you in my visions and that's how we found you today. I tried to tell you about our rescue plan. Couldn't you see me?"

"I wasn't sure what I saw," I answer.

"This new scar on your face," Kitty says. "Is that where the bullet hit you? How did it happen?"

"Guards shot me," I lie. I'm not ready to admit the truth of what really happened. It's too painful and ugly. She doesn't need to know about that.

"You… you have only one eye now?" she asks carefully.

I realize that I'm still wearing an eye patch.

"Don't worry, my eye is all right," I say, taking the patch off. "You see? It's perfectly fine. It's just blind."

"Oh no!" Kitty exclaims, covering her mouth.

"It's okay," I say. "Vision in this eye was always kind of blurry anyway."

I smile broadly, not mentioning about my right ear being deaf as well. I don't want Kitty feeling any sadness or pity toward me.

"Are we together with Oliver's group now?" I ask, changing the subject.

"That's correct," Jessie answers. She's still holding Chelsey in her arms. The girl seems more relaxed being held. "We currently reside in the southeast, close to the shore," Jessie continues. "Many of Oliver's breakers left and joined Guardian's force. Stinking traitors! Guardian hasn't destroyed our group yet only because he still hopes that we'll soon join him."

I nod, thinking over her words. I doubt Oliver's breakers can fight successfully against Guardian's army. Most of them are not real soldiers, but civilians trying to protect themselves and their families.

I hesitate, then ask, "Is Marian still alive?"

"She's all right," Kitty answers.

"And Rebecca?"

"Your Rebecca is fine," Kitty says, rolling her eyes. "She's taking care of the kids in our camp. And she's also Holtzmann's assistant."

"Holtzmann? Is he in our group too?"

"Of course. Who do you think built the bomb to level the post office and divert attention?"

My jaw drops. I remember Professor Egbert Holtzmann, a young sickly guy, eloquent speaker, and more than a little crazy. He never hurt a fly in his life. I can't possibly imagine him creating bombs to blow things up.

"Egbert knows a lot of useful things," Kitty continues. "He's not only an expert in functions of the human brain, but is also proficient in chemistry and other weird sciences. He knows how to make bombs and Molotov cocktails and… What? Why are you looking at me like that?" Kitty begins laughing. "Oh come on. We didn't kill anybody. The post office was completely empty. In case you've forgotten, today is Sunday. And the bomb was a fake. It just produced a lot of noise and smoke like a firecracker. You'd have to be sitting directly on top of it to get injured."

I look at Kitty with pause.

"Yeah, Egbert is really cool," Kitty concludes. "We're lucky to have such a great scientist on our side."

"Jess, what project were you talking about?" I ask. "Is it another one of Holtzmann's experiments?"

"That's right," she admits. "And you're the star attraction."

"Oh great," I groan. "What's he planning to make me do this time?"

"Nothing too special, darling," Kitty answers, looking into my eyes. "You're only being required to help save the world."

CHAPTER 4

"What are you talking about?!" I exclaim.

Kitty chuckles at my reaction.

"Holtzmann believes you're a key for saving humanity," she adds.

"Well, humanity is doomed in that case," I answer. "I've no idea how to go about saving this messed up world."

"Leave all the details to the professor," Kitty assures. "He'll let you know exactly what you need to do."

I sigh. What else could I expect from Holtzmann? He has always been obsessed about saving mankind and stopping the war between ordinary humans and breakers. Unfortunately, I don't see how I fit into any of his crazy schemes.

"Could you at least describe my part in the future mission?" I ask.

"If I tried to explain, it would just come out sounding stupid," Kitty answers.

I begin to protest, but Kitty refuses to continue the subject.

Our van begins to slow and comes to a complete stop.

"Time to switch vehicles," Jessie announces.

We get out. A grinning Victor climbs out from behind the driver's seat. He greets me warmly as he checks his pockets for pills. He fishes out a few and quickly swallows. I wonder whose bright idea it was to make Victor the driver. I'm surprised we all haven't already perished in a fiery car crash.

We leave the van behind, and begin walking toward a bridge. This part of the city seems deserted. We pass a couple of burned out houses and notice old weathered posters littering the street, advertising the need to kill breakers.

A large black SUV sits waiting under the bridge. A short teen in camo stands beside it, armed with an Elimination rifle. I recognize Dave. He may look like a harmless kid, but he's a well-trained killer.

"Welcome back, sir!" Dave blurts out upon seeing me. I extend my hand, expecting a handshake. Instead, Dave wraps me in a hug, saying how happy he is that I've returned. He approaches Kitty and also hugs her, asking whether everything went according to plan during the rescue.

"Everything went great," Kitty answers.

"High five!" Dave exclaims and Kitty slaps his palm, laughing excitedly.

I silently watch their interaction, remembering Jack.

"Hello there. Are you a breaker too?" Dave greets Chelsey. "I'm Dave. I'm from Elimination, but I've nothing against breakers whatsoever."

Chelsey looks Dave over, obviously a bit suspicious with his overt friendliness.

"Let's get moving," Jessie says. "Guardian's killers are still out there lest you've forgotten."

Dave hurriedly opens the door of the SUV. Jessie, Kitty, Chelsey and I all cram into the backseat, barely fitting in. Kitty has to practically sit on my lap, although doing so seems to please her. Victor settles in up front as Dave gets behind the steering wheel.

We drive by a group of travelers walking solemnly along the road. They carry heavy backpacks filled with their possessions and all wear the same hopeless expressions on their faces. These must be ordinary humans fleeing from blood-lusting breakers. They had to leave their homes and lives behind in order to save themselves. Now homeless and hunted, they're staggering through the country in a desperate search for food and shelter. The situation has changed into the polar opposite of the way things were before. Breakers hunt and kill ordinary humans with the same eagerness and ferocity that Elimination used to hunt and kill breakers. It's depressing how we're all the rotten same inside.

My head begins aching.

It's getting dark as we arrive at a large old farmhouse stuck in the middle of nowhere. The SUV stops at the front porch. We get out and I see a tall scrawny guy in his late twenties, with a long nose and crazy eyes. Holtzmann. I was worried he would never recover after being tortured in the Death Camp, but the professor seems fine. He's wearing a baggy camo uniform and even has a holstered handgun. Probably not loaded, knowing him.

Holtzmann quickly greets us, mumbling something about the importance of preventing apocalypse. I notice his left hand with two missing fingers.

"I'm sorry you had to go through that, professor," I say.

"No worries, my friend," Holtzmann answers. "I've adapted nicely."

He turns to face Chelsey.

"I see you've brought an additional guest," he says, smiling. "Good evening, young lady. I presume you to be a breaker as well. I'm Professor Egbert Holtzmann, the lead scientist at Oliver's camp. I'd be thrilled to include you in my ongoing studies."

"I'm only a level 1 breaker," Chelsey mumbles, clearly embarrassed by all the attention. "I'd be worthless to study."

"Oh contraire, my little friend!" Holtzmann exclaims. "It's been my observation that personally exclusive features exist in each subject. I'm certain we'll discover some unique attributes in you as well."

Chelsey gazes at the professor with a mixed expression of fascination and fear.

"C'mon, Holtzmann," I sigh. "Give her a break."

He leads us inside the house. Oliver's camp is too far away so we'll shelter here for the night. It's only recently abandoned and looters haven't messed up the place yet.

Holtzmann helps unlock the blocking collar around my neck. He knows how because these things were his invention. During supper, I briefly explain the situation in the Death Camp, answering Holtzmann's questions about Guardian.

"He can not only move but cause objects to explode by telekinesis," I say. "And he's obviously a very strong hypnotist. But I don't believe he's a good telepath. He wasn't able to read my mind."

"Very interesting indeed," Holtzmann comments.

"And Guardian has a large number of breakers following him," I continue. "Maybe a few thousand by now."

"Guardian," Kitty says, frowning. "The name doesn't fit too well. We should call him something else, something nasty and evil."

"Lucifer," Dave offers.

"Perfect!" Kitty exclaims. "Lucy for short. What can we call his Army of Justice?"

"The Army of Injustice?" Dave suggests.

Kitty becomes euphoric. I watch as they chuckle and wink at each other. I haven't quite figured out what to think about that.

"Tell me about your new project, professor," I say. "What are you up to now?"

"You're too exhausted at the moment to be holding such an important conversation," he answers flatly.

"Come on," I complain. "I'm fine. Just tell me."

Holtzmann refuses to explain anything further till morning. I give up. It's no use arguing with this crazy scientist. He has to be one of the most stubborn people I've ever met.

After supper, Kitty grabs my hand, leading me into another room. We sit on a mattress, looking each other over and holding hands. Kitty has a big smile across her face. Her eyes are somewhat playful.

"Kitty, tell me more about the project," I demand.

"Gosh, Rex!" Kitty blurts out. "You haven't seen me for 4 months and Holtzmann's project is all you can think about? Stop with the questions and just hold me!"

She moves closer and I hold her tightly, burying my face in her soft hair. I still can't completely believe she's really here with me again.

"You've changed," she states, gazing at me. "You look different, almost like a stranger." She sighs sadly. "I'll never let you leave me again. You and I belong together. We always have."

She suddenly averts her gaze, blushing.

"Well," she begins. "I feel like I have to remind you about one of our conversations. Right before Elimination captured you, you said you loved me. Is that still true?"

"Of course it's true, Kitty," I answer.

Her smile becomes wider.

"So you love me as a friend?" Kitty asks.

"More," I answer.

"You love me as your sister?"

"Much more," I repeat.

Kitty lets out a quiet sob, putting her hands on my shoulders and looking right into my eyes.

"I don't believe you, Rex," she states. "You'll have to prove it. Right here. Right now. While we're still alive."

"All right," I say.

Kitty shrieks happily and kisses me deeply. It feels strange at first, because I used to only see her as a close friend or even relative. But her warm kiss helps me to quickly overcome any doubts. I finally accept the fact that we belong together. And I know I won't ever love anybody nearly as much as I love Kitty. She's my whole world.

***

Afterward, we lie in bed in silence, gently holding each other. Kitty lays her head on my chest, gazing at me.

"Know what?" she says. "Lucifer will definitely try to kill you. Your escape must have made him really angry."

It takes a few seconds to comprehend what she's just said.

"It's not so easy to kill me," I answer.

"We should go ahead and kill him first," Kitty suggests.

I think on her words. Guardian is a strong enemy, easily the strongest one we've ever faced.

"I'm not sure how we might go about it," I say.

"Holtzmann," Kitty says. "He knows how to take him out. This is what his project is all about. And that's the reason why I have to ask you for something."

"What?"

Kitty sits up, looking at me seriously. Her expression is troubled. She grips my hand tightly.

"Promise to trust and believe in me, Rex," she pleads.

"Of course I trust you and believe in you, Kitty," I answer, feeling nervous now. There's something almost desperate in her eyes.

"I mean it, Rex," Kitty says. "You have to trust me. You have to believe that I'm capable of much more than you think. I'm a tough fighter too."

Now I'm really worried. I can't understand what she's hinting at yet, but I suspect it's not going to be something I'd approve.

"Kitty…" I begin.

"Just promise me, please," Kitty begs.

"All right," I say. "I promise. I trust and believe in you. But I'd truly like to know what this is all about."

"You'll learn soon enough."

We share a few more moments of silence. Kitty's expression remains uneasy. Something must be really bothering her.

"I need to talk to you about Dave," she finally admits. "And I don't want you to become jealous."

"I'm listening," I say, calmly.

"No! Don't make such a face. Dave and I are just friends. Really good friends."

Her admission is already getting interesting. Kitty used to hate Elimination officers.

"There's this girl he's secretly in love with," Kitty adds, smiling. "Only he doesn't know how he should approach her."

I roll my eyes.

"Stop making faces, this is very serious!" Kitty exclaims. "He's in love with Jessie. What? Why are you laughing? He's crazy about Jessie, but he's intimidated by her."

"I can't say I blame him for that," I admit, trying not to laugh.

"We have to help Dave," Kitty says. "You're Jessie's good friend and so maybe could influence her. So when you talk to Jessie, you should always remember to say something nice about Dave."

"Kitty, please don't involve me in all that stuff," I say.

"You're just jealous," Kitty groans. "And it's me who should be the jealous one. You've brought this Chelsey girl along."

"Come on," I say. "Chelsey is just a kid and…"

"I'm just teasing you, silly!" Kitty interrupts, giggling. "I told you I was receiving visions. I know how she helped you to steal the control key." She pauses, giving me a strange look. "I'm also aware of who it was that really shot you," she adds quietly. "You don't need to lie about that."

I don't say anything. Kitty lies back down beside me, seemingly sad now.

"How's Marian?" I ask. "Is she doing all right?"

"She seems fine. But she's a little strange. You know, like there's something off with her."

I keep quiet, thinking. I know exactly what Kitty is trying to say.

"She's run away from camp a few times, but then always returned," Kitty continues. "She's constantly smiling and laughing, but never seems truly happy. I thought I'd hate her, because I can't stand your loving anybody else besides me. But I can't hate Marian. She reminds me of you in so many ways. And she's so beautiful. I wish I could be more like her."

"That's silly, Kitty," I say.

"You don't understand," Kitty sighs. "Your sister is perfect. I've never seen anybody as beautiful as her."

Kitty places her head on my shoulder and is soon asleep. I remain awake for a long time. I lie motionless, thinking about Marian. There is definitely something off with her. I remember her screaming and clawing at me. I remember feeling her resentment and then sudden change to affection. I don't know whether I can help her. But what I do know is that I'm not going to betray my sister a second time. No matter what, I won't give up on Marian.

I close my eyes, finally drifting off.

***

I suffer several hours of light nervous sleep, waking every twenty minutes. I dream about staggering through the long dark passageways of the Death Camp. I have to step over lifeless bodies spread across the floor. I can smell freshly spilled blood and the stench of death hanging in the air. It's overwhelming. I'm desperately looking for a way out. But no matter where I go, I always wind up in the same small windowless cell. Emily sits on the floor, holding a small red-haired girl in her arms.

"Don't leave me here!" the girl screams.

I grab her hand, pulling her away from Emily. But our mother has a strong grip.

"She's mine!" Emily yells. "You can't have her!"

She raises a handgun and shoots me in the face.

I finally give up on trying to sleep. It's already dawn. I sit up, blankly staring into space. I can still hear Emily's hateful voice echoing inside my head.

I put on my uniform, taking a long look at Kitty peacefully sleeping. She never seems to suffer bad dreams. I tuck in the blanket covering her and kiss her lightly on the forehead. Kitty mutters something incoherent. I smile as I leave the room.

I find Jessie and Chelsey having breakfast in the kitchen. Chelsey is chowing down on a sandwich. I grab a seat at the table, joining them. Jessie fishes out a package of cookies, beef jerky and more sandwiches from a backpack. We eat in silence for a while. I watch Jessie.

"What?" she asks, noticing my gaze.

"I'm just happy you're okay, Jess," I say truthfully. "I thought you were dead."

She snorts.

"Well, it was a close one," she says, pulling up her t-shirt. A rough red scar runs across her midsection.

"Gosh, Jess," I breathe out. "I'm so sorry."

"It's not your fault," Jessie grins, pulling her shirt back down. "I gotta learn how to make myself a smaller target."

Chelsey pats me on the shoulder to garner my attention, then quickly leans in, putting her face close to mine.

"Have you noticed anything different about me?" she asks. "Can you see?"

"See what?"

"My eyes! They're not green. They're gray. I've gotten rid of my contact lenses."

"Oh, very cool," I say, finally taking notice.

"Thank you for getting me out of the Death Camp," Chelsey adds, smiling. "I'm so happy to be free again."

"Me too," I answer. "And I'm the one who should be thankful. You helped me escape." I notice a handgun on the table, the one Chelsey took from a downed guard. I take it and show Chelsey how to switch the safety off. "It's your trophy now. Jess can teach you to shoot later."

"Thanks," Chelsey whispers, turning the gun in her hands.

"That's about right, Rex," Jessie groans. "Go ahead and teach a little girl how to use a gun."

"Come on Jess," I say, a little surprised by her reaction. "You probably learned how to shoot before you could walk."

"That doesn't necessarily make it right," she sighs.

Soon Holtzmann and Dave join us. I notice that Holtzmann is wearing three wristwatches.

"What's that, professor?" I ask. "Another experiment?"

"This is my newest innovation," Holtzmann answers proudly. "I use the alarm of this watch to let me know when I should take my medicine," he says, pointing at a watch. "The second one signals when I'm supposed to receive my meals. And the third one controls my sleep schedule. This way Rebecca doesn't have to constantly assist me."

I don't say anything. Egbert is crazy.

"You're a genius, professor," Dave compliments.

"Thank you," Holtzmann answers, then looks at me. "Rex, do you think you're ready to discuss your role in my new project?"

"I've been ready since yesterday," I answer.

"Very well then," Holtzmann says. "Let me start by refreshing your memory concerning the classifications used to differentiate various levels of mind breaker abilities."

"I remember it," I say, but Holtzmann isn't listening.

"The first level is the most common," he begins. "It consists of the ability to hypnotize ordinary humans having low resistance to hypnosis. The second level allows breakers to utilize additional psychic power over more resistant types and even manipulate one another. The third level features an uncommon ability to read memories, while fourth level breakers possess the additional gift of telepathy."

Holtzmann pauses as his left eye begins twitching annoyingly.

"As I've stated in our previous conversation, this classification scale is informal," he continues. "I have always been certain there would be other levels identified at some point in the future. And it happens I was correct. The current leader of this renegade group of breakers, this so-called Guardian, is a level 5. This level features a unique ability for telekinesis. Level 5 is an outlier phenomena, previously undocumented within modern science. And I believe he'll become the individual to drive humankind into total extinction. Neither breakers nor ordinary humans will survive this war, taking our current population issues under consideration."

"So what can we do about it?" I ask.

Holtzmann hesitates a few seconds, then says, "Rex, you probably realize that I place a high value on human life and have little tolerance for violence. Unfortunately, I have to make an exception to principle in this case. I simply don't see any other choice available, but to terminate him. His army of breakers will never surrender as long as they have him as leader. And Guardian is a powerful manipulator who can always recruit new soldiers to serve his cause. We must assassinate him to preserve humanity."

"I have no problem with the idea, professor," I say. "I just don't see how we can kill him. He can stop bullets midflight. I'm not convinced a bomb would even be effective against him."

"It probably wouldn't work," Holtzmann agrees. "His assassination requires an entirely different approach."

It's odd to hear the gentle professor speak about killing.

"Let me tell you about some experiments I was forced to conduct in the Death Camp," he continues. "Guardian kept me alive only because he needed to develop a method to increase the psychic abilities of his soldiers. I was able to create a unique drug which can alter the level of a mind breaker. After my work was complete, Guardian intended to terminate me as he realized I was the only scientist who might develop an effective strategy for his assassination. But he was too slow. You and your friends liberated me before he deemed my death necessary." Holtzmann pauses again, taking a deep breath. His hands are somewhat shaky. "To assassinate Guardian, it is necessary to use the drug I developed, and create another level 5 breaker who at least in theory would be able to terminate him."

"Sounds good to me," I say. "So what's the problem?"

"There are multiple problems to overcome. I can't recreate the drug as I don't have the requisite chemicals or equipment," Holtzmann explains. "We'll have to acquire the drug from the research facility in the Death Camp."

Great, I think gloomily. I've barely escaped from that slaughter house and now I'll have to return.

"Secondly, the drug itself is highly toxic," the professor adds. "Even a small amount has severe side effects on the immune system. Increasing level 1 to level 2 requires a very minimal dosage, which carries a decreased risk for health. Altering level 2 into level 3 becomes more dangerous as a higher amount of the drug is necessary. Alteration to the fourth level carries an increased risk up to fatality. And we'll have to use even higher dosages to alter a level 4 breaker into a level 5. Doing so could possibly even kill the subject within a few hours of the injection time."

"So what's your solution, professor?" I ask.

"We'll use two subjects, who can act together as one, and divide the dosage," Holtzmann says. "I'll need a powerful and highly experienced telepath to become the Alpha subject in my experiment. This breaker will perform the major role, ultimately developing the ability for telekinesis and assassinating Guardian. The Beta subject will mostly assist, performing a smaller role..."

"Wait a minute, Holtzmann," I interrupt. "I do have strong telepathic abilities, but I'm not a very experienced telepath. I still struggle to use my abilities."

"You surely do," I hear Kitty say. "But Holtzmann wasn't referring to you."

I turn around and see Kitty entering the room. She slowly approaches and sits on my lap.

"It's me, darling," she says, curling her lips into a sweet smile. "I'm to be the Alpha subject in this project, and I'll assassinate Guardian. Your job is to help me."

CHAPTER 5

"No way!" I blurt out. "You can't do it. I won't let you take part in something that dangerous."

Kitty's smile disappears and she jumps down off my lap.

"I knew you'd say that!" she shouts accusingly. "Nothing ever changes with you, Rex!"

She takes a seat across the table, looking over at me angrily.

"Kitty, this is just too risky," I say. "I don't want you to be injected with some kind of toxic drug and then try to kill Guardian. This whole idea sounds like a suicide mission. That's not exactly the type of thing I would wish for anybody."

"There it is!" Kitty groans. "You're just being envious! You want to be the Alpha subject, but I'm the stronger telepath."

"Stop it, Kitty!" I answer, raising my voice. "I don't care to be any kind of subject. All I really hope for is to keep you safe and alive."

"I can't listen to any more of this nonsense!" she exclaims, covering her ears.

"Rex, we'd be conducting the administration of the drug under close medical supervision," Holtzmann mutters. "I can reasonably assure you that dividing the dosage between two subjects will greatly decrease the risk for both and…"

"Kitty won't become a subject in your crazy experiments," I growl at him. "I'll never agree to that."

Kitty's face turns pink as she begins crying. Holtzmann shakes his fists in the air, demanding me to help him prevent the coming apocalypse. I become angry as I ever have, because I finally realize in addition to the considerable danger involved, there's lots of conspiracy going on around me. Kitty knew I wouldn't approve of her participation in this dangerous mission. Holtzmann and Jessie must have been aware of this fact as well. But nobody chose to tell me anything. They were all stalling for time, refusing to explain anything till morning. And I suddenly wonder whether this is the real reason why Kitty was behaving so sweet and loving towards me. Was she trying to manipulate me into letting her participate in Holtzmann's project? Was she just trying to comfort me and improve my mood? It makes me furious. I'm sick and tired of being manipulated. I don't want to become anybody's puppet ever again.

We quarrel with one another for a good twenty minutes. Chelsey silently watches with a terrified expression. Dave lowers his head, sitting still as possible. A yawning Victor enters the room, takes one look at the unfolding scene and hurriedly takes his leave. Only Jessie doesn't seem to care, eating her sandwich with an expression of outright boredom.

"Stop this madness!" Holtzmann finally barks. "We must save humanity!"

"I don't care about humanity," I answer. "I care more about Kitty's safety. Why does she have to become your primary subject, Holtzmann? Can't you find another telepath?"

"Kitty is currently the most advanced telepath we have," Holtzmann explains. "Additionally, she has a strong emotional and telepathic connection with you, Rex. And I need my Alpha and Beta subjects to have a solid connection to be able to synchronize their actions and work as one, otherwise the strategy simply can't be successful. You and Kitty are perfectly compatible matches for this project."

"Kitty's safety is more important for me than your project," I persist.

"Listen to him, he doesn't even try to understand," Kitty groans. "Rex, why don't you ever believe in me?"

"I don't want you risking your life," I answer.

"Why do I always have to do only what you want?" Kitty asks. "I'm sick and tired with your over-controlling ways. Sometimes it seems you're a lot like Guardian. He wants to keep everybody under his control too. But I can make my own decisions. And I choose to become the Alpha subject in Holtzmann's project, and help save the world!"

I'm getting really frustrated with her.

"Fine," I say, getting up. "You do whatever you please, Kitty. But count me out. I won't willingly participate in something that may very well kill you."

I head toward the door.

"Rex!" Holtzmann calls. "Your participation is absolutely necessary as well. The plan requires two telepaths to be successful."

"Sorry, but I just don't give a damn," I answer, exiting the room.

I walk outside and sit on the front porch. I can still hear Kitty's accusations inside my head. Is there any truth in her words? Am I really over-controlling?

Something else bothers me even more. I really didn't like Kitty comparing me to Guardian. I despise and hate that monster who tortures and kills the innocent and now threatens all of humanity. But I can't stop wondering why he chose me for a leadership role. He explained that his choice was entirely coincidental. He needed a strong level 4 breaker and there I was. My staged execution gained me popularity amongst rebellious breakers. But I now question whether these were the only reasons why he picked me.

What if he saw some kind of familiarity in me? Do I really have the same desire for control and violence?

I ponder on the thought for a while. I sense there's something truly wrong with me. I easily adapted to my new life, becoming a killer. I've certainly taken many lives since, although I did so mostly in self-defense and defending those whom I love. But the thought of killing those people never so much as bothered me.

Could it be that I'm just as cruel as Guardian? Would I ever willingly accept the idea of becoming the leader of his army?

I shake my head, trying to straighten out my thoughts. No, I'm not Guardian. I'm nothing like him. I don't wish to become anybody's leader. I only want to keep Kitty safe and alive. She's still young and vulnerable. She doesn't fully realize what she's getting herself into. And should anything happen to her, I'd never forgive myself.

Kitty walks outside and sits beside me, smiling shyly.

"I'm very sorry for what I said," she utters. "I didn't mean to hurt you. Don't be angry. But please agree to participate in the project to help save the world."

"No," I answer curtly.

Kitty gently touches my hand.

"Does your no really mean no?" she asks. "Or does it mean you'll resist a little more and then agree?"

"No means no, Kitty," I answer, getting annoyed.

"Don't be so stubborn," Kitty pleads. "Just give me a kiss."

She leans in closer toward me, but I stop her short.

"It won't work, Kitty," I say. "You don't have to continue trying so hard."

Kitty stares at me in surprise. Her eyes darken. She slowly gets to her feet, taking a few steps away.

"Is that what you really think of me?" she sobs quietly. "You don't truly know me then. And I guess you don't even care to know the real me."

I don't say anything.

"Why can't you believe in me, Rex?" Kitty asks, as a tear begins rolling down her cheek. "You promised to believe in me and you lied. You still think I'm a helpless girl who can't fight or protect herself. But that's not who I've been for a long time. What do I have to do to prove myself to you? I've already saved you from the Death Camp. Isn't that enough? I've been on dangerous missions before and did many risky things, but never once got hurt. So why do you refuse to believe I could kill Guardian? Do you believe I'm not good enough?"

Kitty's voice quivers. She gasps, covering her face. I know she's hurting. I can almost feel her pain. But I remain quiet. Nothing I might say would change Kitty's mind.

"If we don't kill Guardian, he'll be coming after us," Kitty promises. "I can't let him kill you, Rex. You always think you need to protect me. But in reality it's me who needs to protect you, because it's always you getting shot or captured. But I won't let it happen to you again. And if needed, I'll happily give my life for you. I'd die for you, Rex. I really mean that."

Her words stab through me like a sharp knife.

"Don't talk that way, Kitty!" I demand. "I don't ever want to hear you speak about dying again."

Her lips tremble.

"You've already died for me once," she utters. "Someday, I might need to return that little favor."

I just look at her with exasperation.

Kitty turns around and walks back inside the house, crying bitterly. My heart aches for her. I remain on the porch, thinking. I don't want anybody to ever have to die for me again, especially Kitty. Unfortunately, she doesn't seem to understand this simple fact.

A few minutes later Chelsey walks outside and stands in front of me.

"Rex, you need to agree to take part in the project," she proclaims. "And you have to let Kitty become Holtzmann's subject. She's a very strong breaker."

I take a deep breath. It's unbelievable. Now they've sent Chelsey to work on me.

"I thought we agreed to quit playing these games, missy," I remind her.

"I'm not playing games," she argues. "I hate Guardian, wish him dead and this is the only way to do it."

"Go back inside the house," I command.

Chelsey sighs, leaving me alone.

Next comes Jessie. She sits down beside me, smoking a cigarette.

"I won't change my mind, Jess," I growl.

"I just came out to smoke," she answers.

"Kitty doesn't understand what Guardian is capable of," I continue. "I can't let her confront him. He's a monster."

"Can you just let me smoke in peace?" Jessie groans.

I become silent.

"Anyway, what do you think about all this mess, Jess?" I tiredly ask.

"I'd like to gun down Guardian myself, but I'm not a strong enough breaker to get close enough," Jessie sighs. "My bullets won't hurt him. It's a shame because he's the one giving the orders to murder breakers and their relatives. Perhaps he didn't pull the trigger of the gun that killed my parents, but their blood is on his hands anyway. I definitely want to see him dead."

I nod in understanding. Jessie looks away, gazing at the horizon.

I think more on Kitty's words. If she is right, Guardian will soon be coming after us. I suddenly remember his vicious promise. He told me he'd kill everybody I love or care about, should I ever disobey. I don't doubt that a bit. So how can I stop him? What choice do I really have besides becoming a subject in Holtzmann's crazy experiment?

I sigh. No choice as usual.

"Fine," I say. "I'll do it. But only because I believe it's the only way to protect Kitty and the rest of you."

Jessie rolls her eyes at me.

"I still don't think you can even protect yourself," she mumbles.

I frown at her.

I return to the kitchen and take a seat at the table in front of Kitty and Holtzmann. The professor looks at me expectantly, his left eye twitching. Kitty turns away, pretending to ignore me.

"All right, I will agree to become the Beta subject in your project conditionally," I say to the professor. "The moment I decide that it's too dangerous, we'll stop. I mean it, Holtzmann. One word and it ends."

"I believe we can agree to that," Holtzmann answers, smiling.

Kitty expels a sob and hurls herself toward me, wrapping her arms around my neck.

"I knew you'd come around!" she exclaims. "I knew you'd agree at some point! I love you so much!"

She plops down on my lap, kissing my face, becoming all sweet and loving again.

"Enough, Kitty," I say, trying to slow her down. She doesn't care. And I can never seem to remain angry with her for too long.

"We'll become Holtzmann's psycho team," she says, laughing happily.

"Psychic team," the professor corrects.

"Whatever," Kitty answers.

Jessie and Victor join our discussion. A major problem is that Oliver's group no longer has any financial support. They now have only very limited amounts of ammo, food and transportation. Also, the so-called Army of Justice considerately outnumber Oliver's recruits. Guardian will undoubtedly send his troops to attack the camp as soon as he realizes Oliver's breakers are not joining his force. Not to mention, stealing the drug from the Death Camp will require an aircraft and a few dozen well-armed and well-trained soldiers. And on top of everything else, Kitty and I will need medical supervision during the administration of the drug, and Holtzmann will have to perform multiple tests requiring special equipment.

"So what are you getting at?" I ask, becoming suspicious again. I feel like they're withholding more information from me.

Holtzmann hesitates for a few moments, then says, "As you are aware, Elimination soldiers are still holding a large city along the eastern seaboard. The information regarding these holdouts is only partially correct. As it happens, the number of Elimination officers are higher and their resources larger than Guardian wants his recruits to believe."

I understand what he's about to suggest.

"Please don't tell me we'll have to cooperate with Elimination again," I say. "There has to be another way."

"There's no other way," he answers. "Oliver's group and Elimination have a common enemy. We have to combine efforts in fighting Guardian's forces. It is also an opportunity to develop trust between ordinary humans and breakers. We'll have to go to war together and afterward quickly learn how to coexist in peace."

"Elimination will likely just kill us at the get go," I state.

"No, they won't," Dave disagrees. "You may have forgotten I'm an Elimination officer. I'll do my best to explain to other officers the fact that not all breakers are their enemies. I'm sure they'll understand."

He flashes a wide enthusiastic smile. I suddenly think about Chase, Marcus and other Elimination guards who were helping us. And Frank... I still can't overcome my doubts.

"Elimination believes me to be a terrorist," I remind everybody.

"They also believe you're the leader of all mind breakers," Holtzmann counters. "You do have some authority, Rex."

I hesitate. I remember Captain Wheeler slamming the butt of his rifle into my head. I remember being drowned in a barrel of mop water. I think about Dr. Carrel approaching me with a drill, determined to put holes in my skull with no anesthetic. Elimination has done plenty of horrible things to me. They even forced me to work for them, turning me against my own kind. I don't know whether I can ever forgive that. But I also realize that we do have a common enemy now. And I know that not all Elimination officers are haters. Most of them are just brainwashed.

Everybody looks at me, waiting for my answer.

"All right," I sigh. "We don't seem to have much of a choice."

It doesn't take long for me to start wondering whether I'm going to regret this decision. I have a strong hunch that nothing good will ever come out from cooperating with Elimination. I can only hope I'm wrong.

***

We arrive at Oliver's camp in the evening. There's a few dozen excited recruits to greet us, and I spend a good half an hour shaking hands and answering questions about my time in the Death Camp. The young recruits perceive me as a battle tested hero. I don't know what to do about that.

An attractive girl in camo with long dark hair pushes through the crowd. She approaches me, smiling shyly and nervously fidgeting with her glasses.

"Welcome back, Rex," she softly says.

"Happy to see you, Rebecca," I answer, shaking her hand.

Kitty lets out a small groan, which I pretend not to notice. I want to give Rebecca a big warm hug, but I'm afraid it would be too awkward. I'm still a little uncomfortable around her. I felt there was something between us back in the Elimination facility. But then everything was over before it ever really had a chance to begin. I don't know what Rebecca thinks about my relationship with Kitty. And I still remember trying to kiss Rebecca before. It was embarrassing.

Rebecca hovers around her cousin Holtzmann, worrying whether he took his medicine and when he last ate. The professor patiently answers all her questions, although I pick up on some small irritation in his voice.

We leave Chelsey with Rebecca and head toward Oliver's tent. The camp is currently located on the edge of a dense wooded area and provides shelter for over six hundred breakers along with their non-breaker relatives. I take a look around, noticing many young teens wearing camo and carrying guns. Things must have really gotten bad if Oliver has resorted to recruiting children as soldiers.

We walk between numerous tents and finally locate Oliver. He's a tall broad-shouldered guy with an intimidating appearance, but he is also one of the most decent and kind people I've ever met.

We greet one another. After my short story about the Death Camp and Guardian, I explain Holtzmann's project and the need for joining

Elimination. Oliver remains silent for a long time, then says, "I don't think it's a good idea."

I secretly agree with Oliver, but remain quiet.

"This is the only way to stop the war," Holtzmann states. "Elimination isn't our enemy. The organization was created strictly as a defense mechanism charged with protecting society from criminals who possess breaker abilities. Guardian has transformed Elimination into a mechanism for performing the mass genocide of breakers. I believe we can and will change that."

"What exactly are you planning to do?" Oliver asks. "Are you going to just march into an Elimination prison and offer your services? They'll shoot you on sight."

"That's a distinct possibility," Holtzmann admits. "This is the primary reason we need a squad of your soldiers to provide support during negotiations."

Oliver seems astonished by the professor.

"I won't authorize a mission with those kind of risks," he says. "I won't needlessly send my soldiers to their deaths. Elimination has killed thousands of breakers. They've been hunting us for years. We can't just forget everything that's happened."

Holtzmann looks over at me, and I say uneasily, "Oliver, breakers and Elimination can't continue to survive hating and killing each other. We all have to learn how to forgive and coexist."

My words sound unconvincing, even to me.

"Do you really believe in all that crap?" Oliver asks, grinning.

I really don't. I'm not certain what to believe anymore. I no longer trust even my own judgement. I've been tricked and manipulated into terrible mistakes too many times before. But I do know that if there's one single person in this world who knows how to stop the war, it's Holtzmann. So I choose to believe in him.

"Elimination has never been our true enemy," I say. "Guardian controlled the former government and Elimination. He's always been the enemy behind the curtain. And if we don't assassinate him, he'll come after us. Your group won't be able to take on his army on your own. If we don't cooperate with Elimination, we'll all end up dead. Think about it carefully, Oliver."

"Why don't we just let Guardian's army and Elimination exterminate each other?" he asks.

"Guardian won't stop until all ordinary people are enslaved or dead," I counter. "You always wanted to protect the innocent regardless of their being breakers or non-breakers. We now have a chance to save thousands of people from certain doom."

Oliver takes a minute to think over my words.

"I'm not willing to help Elimination," he says. "They'll never accept breakers. They'll always hunt and kill us."

"Professor Holtzmann, Rex and I all used to work for Elimination," Dave proclaims. "We'll speak to the officers and explain to them how breakers are allies, not enemies."

Oliver remains silent for a long moment, then asks me, "You used to work for Elimination?"

I nod. That's not something I'm proud of. Oliver offers no comment.

"I still won't approve this mission," he finally repeats. "And I prohibit you and your team from so much as contacting Elimination. That's a direct order. Our group has nothing to do with those murderers. We shouldn't get involved in this war, but instead keep a low profile and mind our own business."

Holtzmann, Dave and I argue a bit more, but Oliver refuses to continue the discussion. We leave, walking through the camp in silence.

"This situation is unacceptable," the professor mutters. "We have to convince him to change his mind. We need approval for this mission."

"It's useless, Holtzmann," I say. "Oliver won't agree to contact Elimination, and I can't blame him."

Jessie and I exchange glances. I can bet we're thinking about the same thing.

"We'll just have to ignore Oliver's order," I say. "We'll take a truck and leave before sunrise."

"I never cared much for his orders anyway," Jessie states, smiling.

CHAPTER 6

"I can't recommend contacting Elimination without a reliable support group," Holtzmann protests. "Otherwise, this could be too risky."

"I'll take that risk," I answer. "Elimination has been trying to kill me as long as I can remember anyway. So who else is in with Jess and I?"

"I'm with you guys!" Dave exclaims, smiling excitedly. "I can't wait to meet my brother. I'm sure he's there defending the city. We can help you with any negotiations."

I suddenly think that his brother may be long gone by now. I don't articulate the thought.

"I'm in," Victor says. "I've worked for Elimination before, and they provide better meds than I'm finding around this place. So why not try working for them again?"

Victor is one of the best hypnotists and memory readers amongst known mind breakers. Elimination forced him to scan prisoner memories every single day. This led Victor to lose part of his own personality in other people's memories, and created severe flashbacks. He now has to use drugs to block his afflictions. I'm certain Victor's abilities will come in handy during our mission, although I still have trust issues concerning his tendency to switch sides.

"What about you, professor?" I ask Holtzmann. "You may be better off remaining in camp. This mission will likely be a hard one."

"My participation is absolutely unavoidable," Holtzmann answers, although his voice doesn't sound too confident. "I'm still a respected scientist and possibly have a chance to influence Elimination."

"All right then," I say. "We'll pack some food and ammo, and borrow an SUV before sunrise. How long will it take to get there?"

"One or two days," Kitty answers, letting out a short laugh. "I'm so excited! I can't wait to leave this camp!"

"Wait a minute, Kitty," I say. "You're not going anywhere. It's too dangerous."

"Of course," she sighs. "Here he goes again."

Jessie clears up her throat and says, "Rex, Kitty is more than enough qualified for this type of mission."

"Elimination could just kill us on sight," I snap. "Kitty is staying inside the camp. That's a direct order."

Jessie grins. "Rex, I'm sure you're aware that you've been away for four months now. You may not be aware of the fact that you're no longer the leader of our team."

"Oh really?" I ask, becoming angry. "Who's leading us then?"

"That would be me," Jessie answers. "And I authorize Kitty's participation in this mission."

We stare at each other silently. Jessie easily takes my gaze.

"Fine then!" I say. "If nobody cares about my opinion, then I'm out. You may do whatever you please."

I turn and leave, walking toward the edge of the camp.

"Rex, wait!" I hear Kitty call after me.

"Leave him alone," Jessie commands.

Kitty doesn't follow. It's good because I don't want anybody's company at the moment. I need to spend some time alone.

I reach the edge of camp and walk a little further into the woods. I sit on the ground under a large tree, closing my eyes and resting. I wonder why I really became so irritated with the idea of Jessie being the leader of our team. I've never really cared about leadership. And Jessie is one of the few people I fully trust. She's always been at my side, and helped Kitty and I during our darkest hours. So maybe all my anger is just a result of the strain over the last several days. Or to be more correct, the last several months.

I take a deep breath of the cool autumn air. I sit motionless, just enjoying the silence. It seems unusual to hear no rifle fire or anguished cries. The evening is very peaceful and it brings back a soothing image of the life I had before. I can still remember myself being an average law abiding citizen, holding down an ordinary job and having modest hopes and dreams. It's been almost a year since my life went off the rails and all the crazy stuff started to happen. I now wonder whether or not we'll ever be able to return to a normal life. Maybe I've grown too accustomed to all the fighting and killing. Maybe it's already too late for me to go back.

"Are you all right?" somebody asks from behind.

I turn to see Rebecca standing a few feet away.

"I'm fine," I lie. "Just resting."

She sits down beside me and suddenly gives me a tight hug. I'm quite surprised because Rebecca is a very shy girl.

"I'm so happy you've returned," she utters. "I was worried for you."

I'm not sure how to respond to her unexpected affection.

"Thank you," I reply.

Rebecca moves away a little and gazes at me, smiling kindly.

"Rex, I don't want us to have any misunderstanding," she begins. "I like you, and our relationship is very important to me." She pauses, blushing. I become really uneasy. "I'm not sure how to tell you this," Rebecca continues. "So I'll just say it. I just want you to know that you don't need to feel guilty. Everything is fine, and I'm very happy for you and Kitty. You two have always belonged together. I knew it from the moment I saw her, and I never wanted to come between you." Rebecca pauses, averting her eyes. "You'll always be a really good friend for me," she adds, seemingly embarrassed.

"Thank you, Rebecca," I repeat. "You're a great friend, too."

"And as your friend, I'd like to ask you for a favor," she says. "Egbert told me about his idea to contact Elimination. It seems very dangerous to me and I worry for him. I'd really like for Egbert to remain inside the camp this time."

I instantly understand Rebecca is concerned about Holtzmann's safety just as I'm worried for Kitty.

"I'm no longer the leader of the team," I say. "I don't make the decisions."

"You still have some influence on Jessie and Egbert," Rebecca protests. "I'm sure they'll listen to you."

"We actually do need your cousin on this mission," I answer. "He may help to persuade the Elimination commanders on not killing us."

Rebecca gives me a worried look, her expression being close to utter despair.

"I'm so afraid he'll get hurt," she mutters. "Egbert needs his medicine and he can't defend himself. Even the stress during this mission may seriously damage his health."

"Rebecca, I'll make sure Holtzmann is all right," I say.

"You don't understand," she utters sadly. "Egbert is very sick. I don't want him to risk his life."

I understand Rebecca better than she knows, but Holtzmann's participation is really necessary in this project.

"Holtzmann is a grown man and can choose what's best for himself," I answer. "You should stop treating him like an invalid, Rebecca. He seems to be doing much better than when I saw him last."

"He hasn't suffered any fits for a while," she agrees. "Egbert thinks that the fresh air and interaction with people have helped improve his condition." She becomes quiet for a few moments, then adds with pain in her voice, "Egbert believes himself a burden, and is growing resentful of my care. But whom else can I take care of? He's the only relative I have left. Everybody else in our family is now gone. I won't survive should anything happen to Egbert. I've already lost too many loved ones."

Rebecca's voice breaks. She turns away, hiding her tears. I feel deeply sorry for her.

"It's gonna be all right," I say softly.

She doesn't answer. We share a few moments of silence. I suddenly become worried.

"How are you doing here, Rebecca?" I ask carefully. "Do you like being in Oliver's camp?"

Rebecca shrugs, smiling slightly.

"Everybody is very nice to me," she answers. "But I don't feel I belong here. I'm not a breaker and can't really be too useful."

"We don't care around here who's a breaker or who's not," I protest. "And I've heard that you've been very helpful."

"I'm not a good fighter," she says. "Should Guardian attack the camp, I'd be useless." Her cheeks blush again and she adds, "I've never even killed anybody. I've learned how to shoot, but I don't believe I'd be able to kill."

Rebecca seems embarrassed.

"Anyone can kill when it comes right down to it," I say. "But it's good that you haven't had to do so. You should be proud of that."

Rebecca shrugs.

"Good luck on your mission," she says. "And please, do look after Egbert."

She pats me on the shoulder and leaves. I remain under the tree, thinking over our conversation. I wonder what kind of world we're living in, if Rebecca is so embarrassed about the fact of not being a killer. That's just plain wrong.

It's getting late. I should probably go check on Marian. I haven't seen her for so long, but am still not ready enough for the encounter. I don't know how she'll react to me. Will she hug me or start clawing at my face?

I finally get up and work my way around the camp, searching for my sister. I soon come upon a group of young girls in camo, chatting around a small campfire. I stop several yards short. The prettiest girl in the group, with long bleached hair, notices me and motions the others to leave. She's obviously the leader here as everybody promptly executes her request. Being left alone, she picks up an old book from the ground and pretends to be reading. I take a deep breath and walk toward her, stopping a few feet away.

"Hey Marian," I say. "It's me."

"I can see that," she answers coldly.

"How is it going?" I ask. "You doing all right?"

"I'm doing perfectly fine," she mutters.

I'm not sure how to continue the conversation. Marian intently stares into her book, ignoring me.

"What are you reading?" I wonder.

Marian rolls her eyes, shutting the book.

"What do you care?" she asks. "Do I now have to report to you on what I read?"

"I'm just trying to talk to you," I answer defensively. "I haven't seen you for so long."

"I don't want to talk," Marian counters.

I'm stunned by her aggressive attitude.

"What's wrong, Marian?" I ask.

She throws the book to the ground and jumps to her feet.

"Don't act like you don't understand me!" she yells. "I know very well what you've got on your mind."

I simply stare at her, still not fully believing she's my sister. Marian is only fifteen, but looks closer to my age, very tall and fully grown. We're almost the same height.

"I've no idea what you're talking about," I say.

"You always hated mom," Marian answers accusingly. "You wanted to hurt her, and you finally did. I know you killed her. And now you've returned to kill me!"

I get the sensation of being punched straight into the gut. I take another deep breath and remind myself to stay calm.

"How can you believe such nonsense?" I ask. "Come on, Marian. I know you remember me better than that."

"Get away from me," she says. "Go now or I'll start screaming."

I can't believe my ears. What's going on with her? Why is she acting this way?

"Marian," I begin saying, taking a step toward her.

My sister screams. I freeze, unsure how to react. We look at each other. Her eyes are wide open and filled with terror.

"What the hell?" I ask.

She suddenly pulls a knife.

"Don't come any closer," she threatens.

I stare at the long sharp blade. Marian's hand is trembling slightly. I get a sudden flashback of Emily pointing the gun at me.

"Put the knife down, Marian," I say carefully. "We wouldn't want anybody to get hurt."

"Or what? What will you do if I don't follow your command? Will you kill me like you killed mom?"

I'm really getting tired of this nonsense.

I take a quick step toward my sister, tightly grabbing her wrists. She lets out another terrified shriek as she tries to yank her arms away. I take the knife and toss it to the ground. Marian covers her face with her free hand, as if I'm about to hit her.

"Listen to me very carefully," I say slowly. "I didn't kill Emily. I'd never do anything like that, and you know it. I tried to save her and she shot me in the face for my effort. She wanted to shoot me a second time, but some Elimination guards brought her down. If you don't believe me, go ask Kitty. She saw everything through her visions and will confirm my words."

"Liar!" Marian screams. "You're a stinking liar! You're a filthy breaker! I hate you!"

Her accusations sound painfully familiar. I can't stand it. I release her wrist and begin walking away.

"Why can't you just leave me alone?!" Marian yells behind me. "What do you need from me?!"

I stop, facing her.

"You're an orphan, Marian," I answer. "I'm your legal guardian and responsible for you."

She snarls, picks up the book and throws it at me. I duck. The book flies by a few inches above my head.

"Go to hell!" my sister shouts.

I leave, disappointed and angry.

***

I wander aimlessly through the camp, trying to stop thinking about her hateful words. I can't understand why my sister is acting in such a spiteful manner. What happened to the sweet little girl who used to be my best friend? I try to bring back her image from memory. I make myself envision the giggling five-year-old who loved listening to my bedtime stories, always wanting to run away to some magical land. The image lasts only for a few seconds before fading. All I can think about is the vicious stranger who now has only resentment toward me. I'm not too sure I'll be able to handle her.

I find myself sitting alone under the tree, remembering my mother. I recall her throwing me against the wall. I remember her slapping me around and calling me a filthy breaker. I remember how desperately I was trying to understand what it was I'd done wrong.

I realize that my sister has become just like our mother. I also know that it's partly my doing. If I didn't leave Marian alone with Emily, she'd probably be a different person now. I can only wonder what all my sister had to go through.

I shake off the memories. I have a strange suspicion that Marian was putting on some sort of act. She was fishing for some kind of reaction from me. But what exactly was she trying to accomplish? Was she testing me or just being obnoxious? I think it over and decide it doesn't really make any difference. All I realize is that my sister hates me, and I don't have a clue what to do about it.

***

"You look so sad," Kitty say softly, approaching me. "Is it your sister?"

Kitty's a telepath, I remind myself. I nod.

"She doesn't like you very much," Kitty states.

"No, she sure doesn't," I admit.

"But she likes me."

"Everybody likes you, Kitty."

"Oh sure," she groans, rolling her eyes. "Especially Lucy and Hammer. I imagine they're both secretly in love with me."

I don't answer, still thinking about Marian.

"It's getting late," Kitty says. "We should get some sleep before the mission." She pauses, stretching her lips into a sweet smile. "You'll be going on the mission with us, won't you?"

"Of course I will," I sigh.

"Good!" Kitty shrieks joyfully, grabbing my hand and leading me further into the camp.

We wind up lying on a blanket inside the tent, with me gently holding Kitty.

"I saw you and Rebecca through a vision," she suddenly states. "Goodness, she's so freaking nice. It really makes it hard to hate her."

"You've got no reason to hate Rebecca," I say tiredly.

"I know," Kitty answers. "I'm just being mean and selfish, because that's how I am. I can't even understand why you love me. I'm not exactly a good girl."

I open my mouth to protest, but Kitty stops me.

"I know what you're about to say," she says. "I'm such a nice and sweet girl whom everybody adores. That's how you always see me. But I'm afraid it's just an illusion you've created in your mind and fell in love with." Kitty sighs. "I truly wish you could know and accept the real me."

I don't know how to answer, so I remain quiet.

"You still don't want me to take part in Holtzmann's project, do you?" Kitty asks.

"No, I don't want risk losing you," I answer.

"Don't raise your voice at me, Rex," she says, frowning.

"I'm not…" I begin to protest but break off upon noticing her angry stare. "Am I?"

"Can't you hear?" Kitty asks.

I actually can't. Sometimes I don't realize how loudly I speak because of my deaf ear.

"Sorry," I whisper.

"Rex, you're acting really strange," Kitty states, giving me a kiss. "Let's get some sleep. We have to leave in a few hours."

She cuddles up close to me, falling instantly asleep. I remain awake for a long time.

***

I dream about disfigured corpses hanging from trees. I see blackened faces with empty eye sockets. These are the usual nightmares I've now grown accustomed to.

I wake up, feeling unrested and drowsy. Kitty is still asleep, holding me tightly. I carefully remove her arm and crawl outside. The sky is dark, and the night air cold and fresh. I see Jessie walking toward me, carrying two rifles.

"I've come to wake you," she quietly says, plopping down beside me. "It's about time to leave. You're going with us, aren't you?"

"Do I really have a choice?" I ask.

Jessie smirks. She lights a cigarette, takes a few deep drags, and then passes it to me. I smoke, becoming somewhat dizzy. I'm not really used to nicotine.

"I was a little surprised you agreed to join Elimination," I say.

"I want to see Guardian dead, whatever the cost," Jessie answers, getting to her feet. "Well, it's go time, hero. Let's wake Kitty."

I don't like Jessie calling me a hero. It brings unpleasant associations. I wake Kitty, and we walk cautiously toward the area with parked vehicles. Holtzmann, Victor and Dave are already waiting there. The professor has a haunted look on his face.

We pick out a large SUV with a full tank of gas. Dave gets behind the wheel, and Victor helps him start the engine without the need for a key. We drive along a narrow road toward the edge of the camp.

A squad of the young recruits block our way, holding their rifles ready. Dave slows down to a complete stop, looking at Jessie with hesitation.

"Rex, go talk to those kids," Jessie commands.

I get outside.

"Let's not do this, guys," I say to the recruits. "We're leaving and you won't be able to stop us."

The recruits exchange glances. I doubt they'd be willing to gun down their hero, although I really don't want to find out the hard way.

"We're under Oliver's orders to stop you, sir," the leader says unconvincingly.

"I'm tired with these suckers," Jessie groans. "Let's just drive away."

I get back inside the SUV.

"Go," Jessie commands.

"Yes, ma'am," Dave answers readily and begins driving slowly toward the recruits. They fire a few rounds into the air, hurriedly moving out of our way. We leave the camp, driving toward the city far away held by Elimination.

I'm not sure where this adventure may lead.

CHAPTER 7

We travel late into the night, passing through devastated sections of the country.

"Are you with us, Rex?" Kitty asks, snapping me out of my unhappy thoughts. "Come back to me."

"I'm right here," I answer. "What were you saying?"

"I was telling you how I helped to provide for Oliver's group," Kitty answers. "The recruits and I would go on missions to rob stores in the nearest towns for food and ammo. We also did some breaker style hunting. We hypnotized any deer and rabbits we came across in the woods."

Holtzmann also shares his thoughts concerning life in the camp.

"It's been a unique experience," he says. "As a scientist I'm infinitely grateful for such an exclusive opportunity to study breakers in their natural environment. As the lead scientist in camp, I've received Oliver's permission to observe and test any breaker in his group."

"And the only scientist," Jessie comments.

"That doesn't diminish the importance of my role," Holtzmann counters, "but rather increases it."

"It's an honor to work with you, professor," Dave says with respect. "If we had a hundred scientists in the camp, you'd still be our top scientist anyway."

"Thank you," Holtzmann answers. "I happen to concur fully with your insightful opinion."

I can't stop from grinning, although I totally agree with them both.

A moment later, I hear a loud bursting sound as our SUV goes into a crazy spin. Kitty cries out, grabbing hold of my jacket for balance. I realize our tires must have gone flat. I doubt it's accidental. The SUV swerves off the road, but Dave manages to safely steer us between the ruins. We stop only a few inches away from the wall of a half-destroyed building. I hear voices outside and take a cautious glimpse out the window. It's too dark to see a damn thing.

"It's an ambush," Jessie warns. "Get out. Hurry!"

We all grab our weapons and exit the vehicle, stumbling in ankle-deep ash. Jessie leads, heading toward the ruins. I aim my rifle into the pitch black darkness, ready to shoot anything coming in sight.

"Where did they go?" I hear voices coming from the SUV we've just left.

I take a look back and make out a few dozen dark figures surrounding our vehicle. I don't think they are Elimination. They must be Guardian's soldiers sent to recapture me.

"How did they learn of our location?" Dave whispers.

I shush him to be quiet. Staying obscured is our only chance to remain free.

The soldiers shine flashlights, searching for us. I realize they might possibly follow our tracks through the ash. Jessie leads us further inside the ruins, changing direction several times.

We jog through long crumbling passageways and finally conceal ourselves in a dark nook of a dilapidated building. It's very quiet and I get a small hope that we've shaken our pursuit. A couple more silent minutes pass, then we hear footsteps approaching. We take off again, trying to maintain a safe distance. Kitty grips my hand tightly, leading me forward. It's so dark I can't see where I'm stepping.

Flashlights continue slicing through the darkness. We take cover as soldiers pass by only several yards away.

"Rex! Come on out, we know you're here!"

I recognize Hammer's voice.

"Come on," he yells. "You have nothing to fear. Guardian just sent me to speak to you."

He pauses, waiting for my response. I get a strong desire to yell something back at him. I remain quiet, listening.

"I have an order to bring you in alive!" Hammer shouts. "Guardian still believes in you, Rex. You should stop resisting and accept your fate."

I can be sure he's lying. It's just a ploy to make me reveal our location.

"Let me help you," Hammer groans. "Let's quit these silly games. You know who you are. You're a breaker and belong with us. It's time to go home. We're not your enemy."

Such a bad liar. I'm certain he'll try to put a bullet between my eyes the first chance he gets.

"Guardian will give you more freedom," Hammer promises. "You don't have to be a prisoner. You only need to do as you're told. Just think what you're turning down. You can have whatever you wish. You can even bring Kitty along, no problem. We can always use more strong telepaths."

I remain silent. Jessie watches me with an alarmed expression. Is she really having doubts about me? I thought she knew me better than that.

"Kitty, we need strong fighters like you!" Hammer continues. "You're welcome to join us."

Kitty snarls, and I barely manage to cover her mouth before she shouts something back. I put a finger to my lips, signaling her to keep quiet. Kitty rolls her eyes, looking very angry.

"Jessie! Are you there as well?" Hammer continues. "You did an impressive job killing those guards during the parade. Our army needs good snipers. Guardian would be pleased to have you on our side."

Jessie remains unfazed. She approaches me, whispering something. I turn my head, directing my good ear to her.

"I saw their trucks further back on the road," she whispers. "We need to steal one."

I hadn't noticed any trucks, but I can't see well in the darkness.

"We'll need a distraction," Jessie says.

I understand her instantly.

"It's gotta be me," I whisper. "I'm their main target."

"Professor Holtzmann!" Hammer yells. "Guardian is ready to make an exception for such a valuable scientist like you. We'll spare your life as well."

"Draw their attention away, while we take a truck," Jessie instructs. "Then head toward the road. We'll try to cover you."

"Victor!" Hammer continues. "We can always find a spot for experienced hypnotists and memory readers!"

I become tensed, watching Victor suspiciously. He remains oblivious to Hammer's words, but I still don't fully trust him.

"I'm going with you, Rex," Kitty whispers. "I'm not letting you go anywhere without me."

I want to protest, but Kitty looks too determined. I doubt I can change her mind, and we don't have time for any argument.

"All right," I agree.

She tightly grips my hand, leading me off into the darkness. Kitty has much better night vision than I do. We distance ourselves from our group and wait a few moments. I aim my rifle at the sound of Hammer's voice. He still continues his idle attempts to sweet-talk our team into joining Guardian.

"Come get some!" I yell loudly, pulling the trigger and hoping to hit Hammer.

"Take him!" he commands.

I hear footsteps and voices fast approaching. Kitty and I run between the crumbling walls. She leads the way, firmly clutching my hand and pulling me forward. I jog, staring straight ahead and trying not to stumble. I feel disoriented. Without Kitty's guidance, I'd be entirely lost in the darkness.

A soldier suddenly charges into me, grabbing my rifle with both hands. I hadn't seen him coming. I swing my arm around, hitting him in the face as hard as I can. My fist stings. The soldier's head bounces to the side, but he doesn't release my rifle. Another guard grabs me from behind, wrapping his arms around me. I sway my head backward, head-butting him, as I simultaneously kick the first guard into the knee. He comes back with a haymaker that I just manage to slip. I hear Kitty struggling with a third guard somewhere nearby.

I punch the guard gripping my rifle again. A solid blow right into his temple. He silently goes down, sprawling in the ash. I grab the wrist of the second soldier, throwing him to the ground. He lands on his side. Anger fills me and I smash the butt of my rifle into his head until he stops moving. I truly hope he's dead.

"He's over here!" somebody yells.

Another soldier lunges at me and we both hit the ground, sinking into the deep ash. He winds up on top, tightly gripping my arm and twisting it. Kitty emerges from the darkness, jumping on the soldier's back. I notice a small blade flashing in her hand. She slits his throat with one smooth motion. The soldier lets out a wheezing noise as blood spills from his neck. His body collapses. I push him off, scrambling back to my feet.

"Get them! They're right over there!" Hammer commands.

I grab Kitty's hand, running as fast as I can. A couple dozen soldiers chase after us. Now that they are all aware of our location, there's no longer any need in trying to remain concealed. I fire my rifle as I run. They open up as well, aiming above our heads.

As we approach the road, I finally see four military trucks parked along the side. Several bodies lie unmoving in ash. A few guards stand motionless, limply holding their rifles. They obviously see us, but don't react. I realize they're deeply under. I increase my speed, running toward them.

"Here!" Jessie yells, standing at the back of a truck. She aims her rifle into our pursuers. Dave comes out from the front of the vehicle, firing his weapon. While they provide cover, Kitty and I jog between hypnotized guards and climb inside the truck.

"Fire!" Victor commands.

Gunfire fills the space behind us. I take a brief look outside to see the hypnotized guards shooting at our pursuers. Victor and Jessie hop inside the truck and the vehicle abruptly leaps forward. Dave must be driving. I sit motionless on the floor, taking a moment to rest. My head is still spinning. I look around and see a pale-faced Holtzmann crouching in the corner. His eye is twitching, but he seems stable enough. Kitty is right beside me, wiping off her knife.

"They won't be able to follow us anytime soon," Jessie says. "We cut the tires on the other trucks."

She smiles broadly and I smile back. I still can't believe we've slipped away.

"You're hurt," Kitty utters, gently taking my hand. My knuckles are bloody.

"It's okay," I say.

She kisses my hand, muttering something. I have a flashback of her cutting the guard's throat without mercy. It's somewhat disturbing. I've known for a while now that Kitty can be a vicious killer, but haven't fully reconciled the fact yet.

***

Several hours later I stand beside the parked truck, staring off into the distance. I try to make out any Elimination checkpoints, but can see only outlines of the city across the field. It's early morning and a thick veil of fog blocks visibility. I'm feeling nervous, but do my best to remain calm.

An anxious Holtzmann paces around the truck, mumbling something about apocalypse. Kitty and Dave sit napping, side by side.

I finally see Victor and Jessie walking back toward us. As they approach, Jessie says, "We were right. There's a checkpoint at the city border. We counted twelve Elimination guards."

"Are you completely sure about this idea?" Victor suddenly asks me.

I'm not sure about anything, but I nod.

"We should split up," Jessie suggests.

"Holtzmann, Dave and I will contact Elimination," I offer. "You, Victor and Kitty provide backup."

"No way!" Kitty exclaims, immediately waking up and scrambling to her feet. "I want to come with you!"

"Kitty, we need a telepath to monitor the contact group," Jessie says. "You're staying behind. That's a direct order."

Kitty frowns, turning away disappointed. Jessie winks at me.

Holtzmann, Dave and I begin walking toward the checkpoint. The professor leads the way, acting as a human shield. Soon, multiple guards move to block the road. They raise their rifles and we immediately raise our arms, staring down at the numerous barrels pointed our direction. I feel really uncomfortable, having no weapon. We left our rifles back at the truck, as a gunfight here isn't amongst our objectives.

"Halt!" a guard commands. "Identify yourself!"

"I'm Professor Egbert Holtzmann!" Holtzmann yells.

"Hold your fire!" the commander orders the officers.

I realize they've obviously recognized Holtzmann. I identify myself, proclaiming that we've arrived to offer our full cooperation. A long pause follows, then all the guards come for me.

They approach quickly, holding their rifles ready and barking commands. I drop flat to the ground, spread-eagled, covering my head. I know they believe I'm a terrorist, the very one who has destroyed the country. I can't understand why they haven't shot me yet.

Dave begins explaining that he's an Elimination officer as well, but the guards aren't listening. They throw him to the ground, securing his arms behind his back. A now gasping Holtzmann shakes his fists in the air, demanding them to stop this madness. The guards gently lead him away, treating him as if he's a freed hostage. Somebody puts a knee on the back of my neck while roughly handcuffing me.

I work hard on giving no reaction, although my blood is boiling. I deny an almost overwhelming desire to fight back. I can probably hypnotize some of the guards, but it wouldn't serve our purpose. I have to be obedient and cooperative.

Two guards grab my arms, forcefully dragging me closer to the checkpoint. I don't try to resist. They place a hood over my head and throw me inside a transport vehicle.

"Don't move, breaker," a guard growls, shoving a barrel of his rifle into my face.

I see it's gonna be difficult to persuade these jerks on not killing me.

We drive for half an hour before the vehicle stops and the guards lead me outside. I wind up locked inside a prison cell, still wearing a hood over my head. Nobody has bothered to remove my handcuffs. I remain alone like this for a long while, recalling my first time in an Elimination prison. I can't believe I have to go through this all over again.

I vividly remember the sadistic Captain Wheeler and Warden Browning. I wonder whom I will have to deal with this time.

I finally hear the screeching of the door sliding open. I become tense, readying myself for anything. Somebody approaches and removes the hood from my head. I look up and see a tall Elimination officer in his mid-twenties.

"You're an idiot," he says.

"Hi Chase," I answer. "Nice to see you too."

"What the hell are you doing here, breaker? Why did you turn yourself in?"

It's a really good question.

"I've come to offer my full cooperation," I answer. "This is what Elimination always wanted from me, right?"

Chase takes a moment to think.

"You've gotta be kidding," he says. "You do realize that you're currently the most wanted criminal in the country, don't you? You've long since received a second death sentence."

"Tell me something new," I answer, smirking.

"What game are you playing?" he asks.

"No games this time. I simply want to cooperate."

"I don't believe you. You're always plotting something, breaker."

I realize that Chase is glaring at me with outright hatred. His voice sounds aggressive. It's confusing because I thought we were friends.

"What are you talking about?" I ask.

"You manipulated me into helping you destroy the Death Camp," he answers. "You involved me in the killing of Elimination executives and then you assassinated the leaders of our government. I don't trust a word you're saying."

I stare at him in shock. "Is that what you really believe, Chase?"

"I don't know what to believe," he answers. "I only know that you're nothing but trouble."

I wonder why Elimination didn't execute Chase as a traitor. Do they even know about him helping me destroy the Death Camp?

He keeps quiet for a while, then asks, "I've heard your gang was still holding Rebecca hostage. Is she all right?"

"We're not a gang, Chase," I answer. "Rebecca is with us by her own free will. And yes, she's fine. She's helping to take care of kids in the camp."

I don't think he believes me.

"Did you really get shot in the face?" he asks.

I nod.

"Let me guess, no brain damage," he continues. "So I was right, you're brainless. There's simply nothing to damage, otherwise you'd be dead."

I don't say anything.

"Major Vogel will arrive soon to interrogate you," he adds. "So you'd better think of what you're going to say."

"Who's Vogel?" I ask.

"The current commander."

"Another Wheeler?"

Chase grins.

"Major Vogel is not only smarter but much more dangerous than Wheeler," he answers. "So let me give you some free advice. Don't even try playing any mind games, because there's no way you'll win."

Chase leaves me to my thoughts, locking the door behind. I lie down on the floor. I think about my coming encounter with Vogel. I haven't decided how I should act yet.

The majority of the regular guards are just brainwashed, but their commanders are typically of the sadistic killer variety. They genuinely enjoy torturing and killing mind breakers. I doubt this Vogel is any different. Most likely he's as bad as Captain Wheeler, or if Chase is correct, possibly even worse.

I close my eyes, forcing myself to relax. The strain of the last days and lack of sleep finally hit me, and I pass out almost instantly. I watch helplessly as Guardian's recruits gun down unarmed prisoners in my dreams.

The next thing I know, somebody is shoving the barrel of his gun into my shoulder.

"Wake up, breaker," Chase commands. "It's show time."

I sit up, gazing around sleepily. My head is foggy and I'm a little disoriented. I see Chase holding his weapon on me. A tall thin woman in her late forties stands beside him, looking at me with a sort of detached curiosity. She's wearing Elimination black and has a holstered handgun.

"Good morning, Rex," she says in a soft voice. "I'm Major Erica Vogel. And I need to hear a really good reason why I should continue keeping you alive."

CHAPTER 8

Major Erica Vogel. I have to admit to being a little confused. I've never heard of female officers in Elimination, but they obviously made an exception for this particular lady. And I think I can make a pretty good guess as to why.

There's something about her that already reminds me of Wheeler. She has the similar polished appearance and hardened eyes of a cold-blooded killer. I can easily imagine her pressing a gun to my head.

I grin, trying to appear friendly and calm.

"I've come here to offer my full cooperation," I say. "Elimination and breakers will be needing to combine efforts in a war against a very strong common enemy. Is that a good enough reason for starters, major?"

I realize my words sound stupid. Unfortunately, it's the best stuff I can come up with on the fly.

Vogel returns my smile, answering, "Very interesting. I have to admit I was quite surprised by your sudden decision to turn yourself in. How can you be so certain I won't just order your execution?"

"Elimination needs me alive," I insist.

Vogel watches me warily, still wearing the same artificial smile. She suddenly looks at Chase holding the rifle on me and says, "Chase, that won't be necessary."

Chase lowers his weapon.

"And remove his handcuffs," she adds. "He looks awfully uncomfortable in those."

"Yes, ma'am," Chase answers, executing her request.

I think I know what she's doing. Vogel is showing me she's not the slightest bit intimidated or threatened by me and can even free my hands. She's role playing the good cop, attempting to make me more cooperative. Not a bad effort, but it won't work on me.

"I've studied your personal file," Vogel says. "You have an impressive list of crimes, considering your age."

I recall the file states I'm twenty three.

"My crimes were exaggerated," I answer.

"You're only nineteen, aren't you?" she asks.

"That's correct," I admit.

"Shall I call you Rex or Alex?"

I look at her, doing my best to conceal my surprise. How the heck does she know my real name?

"I prefer Rex," I say.

"Very well, Rex," she continues. "So please, tell me the real reason for your contacting Elimination."

I take a deep breath and repeat what I'd said earlier, adding information about Holtzmann's plan to assassinate Guardian.

"Who's Guardian?" Vogel interrupts.

"You really don't know?" I ask.

"Answer the question."

Her voice sounds soft, but I sense a hidden menace behind her polite manners. I begin telling her about Guardian. I don't really believe she has zero information concerning her most dangerous enemy. Vogel really must be playing some sort of game with me.

"Your explanation contradicts information we have," Vogel states after I finish speaking. "According to my sources, you assassinated the leaders of government and subsequently attempted to take over the country. You're a level 5 breaker with an ability for telekinesis."

I just stare at her.

"You've additionally committed several acts of terrorism," she continues. "And you sent your army of breakers on missions to kill ordinary humans."

I take another deep breath, calming myself. I'm so sick with all the false accusations.

"Your information is bad," I answer. "But I believe you already realize that."

Vogel smiles kindly.

"I'm more than willing to hear your side of the story," she says. "Please, continue."

I start telling my story from the very beginning. I explain how I revealed my breaker abilities, trying to stop a bank robbery almost a year ago. I tell her how Elimination captured me and made me go through the horror of a fake lethal injection without informing me that it was fake. How I tried to help Elimination catch a terrorist group of breakers and was tricked into capturing the wrong guys. I tell how I attempted to fix my mistakes by initiating the prison riot and freeing all the prisoners. I finish with how I became Guardian's puppet and was forced into destroying the Death Camp.

It's a very long and complicated story. I've no idea whether Vogel believes me or not.

"Your version sounds a little farfetched," she finally says after a long pause. "I'm quite sure that you're lying."

Her face reveals no emotion, and I can't imagine what she's thinking. Does she really think I'm a terrorist? I doubt it. She'd have already ordered me shot in that case.

"I'm not lying," I answer.

"Why would Warden Browning organize acts of terror against ordinary humans?" Vogel asks.

"He needed to increase his budget for building new prisons," I explain patiently. "He also wanted to manipulate the government into allowing for the total scanning of the entire population for breaker abilities. Those acts of terror helped him accomplish all of that."

"Didn't he realize it would lead to war?" Vogel wonders.

"I believe war was his end goal," I answer. "Browning could have been controlled by Guardian."

"Could you repeat the exact role Guardian played in all this?"

I obediently repeat my story about meeting Guardian and his evil plan to destroy the world as we know it, killing or enslaving all ordinary humans. Vogel listens without any expression on her face. She seems bored. Chase stands beside her, watching me carefully. He obviously doesn't trust me.

"So you want me to believe that everything that's happening right now is the doing of one single individual?" Vogel asks after my explanation.

"That's correct," I answer. "Guardian is responsible for this war and the genocide of ordinary humans."

"And you hope to assassinate him."

"Yes ma'am, with your assistance of course."

"And how exactly are you planning to do that?"

This is getting ridiculous. I'm having to explain everything to this lady over and over. I hide my frustration, telling her again about Holtzmann's project.

"Did you kill Browning?" Vogel suddenly asks.

"He committed suicide," I answer.

"Did you kill Captain Wheeler?"

"I took part in that."

Vogel remains quiet for a few moments.

"We used to work together," she says.

Great, I think, she's also Wheeler's friend.

"Did Wheeler also work for Guardian?" she asks.

"I don't believe so," I answer. "He genuinely hated breakers and seemed to enjoy hurting and killing them."

"Of course he did," Vogel says with a grin. "It was his job. He was an Elimination officer and I must say very efficient at his job."

I'm coming really close to hating this lady.

"Elimination was never supposed to execute innocent breakers," I counter. "Guardian transformed Elimination from peaceful organization into a mechanism for genocide."

"Yours isn't a traditional view on Elimination," Vogel comments. "So could you please explain how you happened to come to such a conclusion?"

I begin telling my story all over again. After I finish my explanation, Vogel demands me to repeat everything one more time. She follows up with multiple questions. She asks what floor Carrel's lab was on and refuses to believe it when I can't remember. She wants to hear the details of Lena's and Jimmy's capture, which I can't offer. She expresses doubts of my being able to survive an entire night in a freezing well. She disbelieves the fact I managed to locate Drake's group through telepathic visions. Her inquiry lasts for what seems like a really long time, wearing me down.

I finally become exhausted and annoyed with this pointless interrogation. I realize that Vogel is just trying the same thing with me that I did with Chelsey. She has me repeating my story in order to catch any mistakes. I no longer think Vogel is interested in hearing the truth from me. She's just trying to see what kind of person I am. She wants to see how I'll react to her repeated questions. Vogel must be curious whether I'll become angry and refuse to speak to her. Will I lose my temper and attack her or maybe begin begging her to spare my life?

I'm sick with playing these games.

"Listen, major. I believe you have all the information about everything that's happened," I say. "You know I haven't committed the crimes I've been accused of, otherwise you'd have already ordered me shot. And I also believe you realize there's no other way for Elimination and breakers to possibly win this war against Guardian, except through cooperation. So let's just quit wasting time. I'm sitting here before you, offering our full support. Take it or leave it. It's really that simple."

My statement seems to amuse Vogel.

"Chase advised me that you're nothing but trouble," she says. "So why would I want to cooperate with you?"

Damn Chase, I think angrily.

"I didn't come here to make any trouble for Elimination this time," I answer. "I really came to help you."

"Don't you feel somewhat like a traitor, betraying your own kind?" she asks with a smile.

For a moment I'm truly afraid I may lose self-control and say something offhand. But I realize I can't allow myself that luxury.

"No, I'm just trying to protect innocent people," I answer sincerely.

Vogel takes a moment to think.

"Chase, do you believe Elimination should cooperate with breakers?" she suddenly asks.

Chase looks caught off-guard. He begins mumbling something incoherent.

"Officer Chase, I've requested your opinion," Vogel says in a firm voice. "Speak clearly, please."

Chase hesitates, then answers unsurely, "We can't trust breakers, ma'am. They're our natural enemies."

I wonder what this is all about. I don't think Vogel is really interested in hearing Chase's opinion. He's just a regular officer.

"You'll be soon informed of my decision," she says before leaving.

Left alone, I try to rest and collect my thoughts. Her interrogation has worn me completely out. My head aches, and I feel edgy. I wonder whether Vogel will order my execution after all.

I also think about her calling me a traitor. There might be some grain of truth in her words. Maybe I actually don't know where I stand or to what side in this war I belong. Everything has become too complex. I can no longer easily understand what's right or what's not.

I stretch out on the floor, closing my eyes. I need to get as much rest as I can in preparation for whatever lies ahead.

***

I awaken to Officer Marcus entering the cell, a big grin spread across his face. He looks similar to his younger brother, Dave, and is friendly in the same way. He once helped my team escape from Elimination.

Marcus greets me, shaking my hand and asking how I'm doing.

"I've been through worse," I answer.

"Dave and Holtzmann filled me in on everything," Marcus says. "I'm glad you finally came around. We really need as much help as we can get. We don't have enough manpower to adequately defend the city."

"Where are the professor and Dave now?" I ask. "Are they all right?"

"They're fine," he assures. "Vogel is interrogating them as we speak."

I feel sympathy for Holtzmann and Dave.

"Vogel," I say. "Tell me about her. Where does she come from?"

"She saved the organization," Marcus blurts out. "Elimination would be utterly destroyed by now, if it wasn't for her. All the other executives were either killed or had simply run off. It was a big mess. Breakers were constantly attacking us, killing everybody they could. We never received any instructions because all the high ranking executives were already dead. Nobody left to lead us. Then riots broke out in prisons all over the country. We lost our financial support and all communication. It was total chaos."

Marcus pauses, his expression gloomy. These recent memories must be painful for him. I wonder how many fellow officers he's had to watch die in this war.

"And then Vogel arrived," he continues. "She assumed leadership as a higher ranking officer and organized the resistance, defending this city."

"So she's actually the current leader of Elimination," I conclude.

"Elimination officially no longer exists," Marcus sighs. "There's only a thousand officers remaining to defend this city. That's all we have. We don't even get paid anymore."

"Why haven't you left then?" I ask.

Marcus looks at me in astonishment.

"We must protect ordinary citizens from breakers," he answers simply. I nod, understanding him well enough.

"How did Vogel survive during the prison riot?" I wonder.

"Vogel wasn't on duty at that time," Marcus answers. "I heard she was hospitalized. I don't know any details."

"You think she'll order me shot?" I ask.

"Nah," Marcus says, laughing. "I think she likes you."

I'm not so confident about that, but don't argue. After Marcus leaves, I wonder why he was permitted to pay me a visit. It must be against Elimination's protocol. I'm also curious as to why I'm not wearing a blocking collar. Something feels wrong. Or have things become so messed up that nobody worries about rules?

Chase enters the cell. I become somewhat anxious, not knowing what kind of news he's about to deliver.

"I've no idea how you do it, breaker," he says.

"Do what?

"Manage to survive. Come on, Vogel wants to see you. She's agreed to cooperate."

I follow Chase out into the corridor. He no longer holds his rifle on me, but still appears very alert in my presence.

"So, what's your real agenda, breaker?" he asks as we walk.

"There's no hidden agenda, Chase," I answer tiredly. "I just want to take out Guardian and need your help to do it."

"I don't trust you," he says. "I think you're working for Guardian. I think he sent you to assassinate Vogel."

"Chase, I thought you were smarter than that," I say.

"Well, you'd best not try anything," he warns. "Vogel is used to dealing with much more dangerous breakers than you. Remember Roger? Her squad captured his entire gang. Like to know what the other officers call her? Crocodile. Because she's like a cold-blooded reptile. She has ice water running through her veins and she'll readily bite off your head should you ever decide to go up against her."

"Nice to know," I comment. "But don't worry, Chase, I'm not planning to assassinate your commander this time."

I meet Vogel in her office, and she announces her decision to cooperate. I don't completely buy her friendly attitude. I wonder how many innocent breakers this kind-looking lady has eliminated over her career.

"What's your personal angle, Rex?" she asks. "I mean, besides terminating Guardian and protecting the people you love. What do you want for your cooperation?"

"I want vindication," I answer. "I'd like all false charges against me dropped. And I want Elimination to become what it was originally designed to be."

"Deal," Vogel says, extending her hand.

I hesitate for a moment, then firmly shake her cold hand.

Vogel sends out a few officers to pick up Kitty, Jessie and Victor. Chase brings me lunch, along with a black Elimination uniform.

"Looks like you work for us now," he comments.

Later, our team meets with Vogel to discuss the details of our cooperation. Chase and Marcus are allowed to take part in the discourse as well. Holtzmann and I try to persuade Vogel on providing us with an aircraft and support group for the mission. She refuses, stating Elimination currently has very limited resources. They have only a few transport aircraft with no missiles. Neither is she willing to send her officers in to directly attack the Death Camp. Holtzmann insists on the importance of obtaining the drug, but Vogel isn't the type of a person you can really argue with. She answers that breakers first must earn Elimination's trust, and only then demand the minimum necessary resources. Holtzmann finally gives up the argument, seemingly distressed. Jessie remains silent and indifferent during the entire discussion. She watches Vogel with obvious resentment, smoking a cigarette.

Vogel agrees to send transport aircraft to relocate Oliver's group into the city.

"Are you completely sure Oliver's breakers will agree to cooperate with Elimination?" she asks.

"Oliver didn't initially approve of the idea," I answer, "but I think I'll be able to change his mind. He's a sensible man and will understand what has to be done."

"So let me get this right," Vogel says. "You claim that you're not the leader of this group of breakers, but the leader follows your commands."

"Well, we don't exactly have a strict structure," I mutter.

Jessie approaches me after the meeting.

"So what's your opinion about Miss Elimination?" she asks.

"I don't think I like her," I say. "She reminds me of Wheeler somehow."

"You realize where all this cooperation will lead, don't you?" Jessie says. "Elimination will use us to fight Guardian's army, and then they'll only have to get rid of the rest of us. I don't believe breakers and Elimination will ever become equal partners. That's just one of Holtzmann's delusions." She pauses, staring me in the eye. "When our work is done, Vogel will attempt to kill you along with Oliver's breakers."

"I don't doubt that a bit," I agree.

"Then you understand what we'll have to do," Jessie says.

I nod, saying, "You and I will have to get her first, before she has a chance to get us."

CHAPTER 9

"Do you realize what you and your team have done?" Oliver asks. "You disobeyed a direct order and not only contacted Elimination, but delivered them right here to our doorstep."

"We did what we had to, Oliver," I answer.

"I thought I could trust you, Rex," he says. "I thought we were on the same side."

"Listen Oliver..."

"I don't want to waste my time listening to more of your sorry excuses," Oliver interrupts. "Go back to your Elimination friends and tell them to get the hell out of my camp."

He points toward the Elimination transport aircraft landed across the field. Several officers in black stand around it, warily gazing over the camp.

"Elimination doesn't even officially exist any longer," I say. "There's only a thousand brave ex-soldiers defending the city, a last line of defense from Guardian's forces. We gotta help them."

I'm sure Oliver realizes this, but he's not willing to give in easily. We argue for a long time. It's getting late and the sky begins to darken. The officers in black patiently wait by the aircraft. My team wanders around close by, not eager to join our discussion. Holtzmann and Dave had offered to help persuade Oliver, but I turned them down. I don't want a small disagreement with Oliver to escalate into a huge fight, which could be

92

unavoidable should the overly excitable Dave and unstable Holtzmann join in.

"Your group doesn't have any support," I say, trying to sound reasonable. "Elimination can provide us with ammo, food and shelter. They currently reside inside a large secure prison. It has enough space for every member of your camp."

"Are you suggesting my people voluntarily relocate inside a prison?!" Oliver exclaims.

"C'mon," I sigh. "You know what I mean. They won't lock us up. And it beats living in a tent. Winter is coming and it's gonna get cold soon."

"We're better off freezing to death than going to prison!"

The argument continues late into the night, but we finally come to an agreement to give Elimination a chance.

The next day all members of Oliver's camp relocate to the current Elimination headquarters. Everybody receives a new black uniform, ammo and proceeds to their cells. I find the situation almost ridiculous. We all did our best to avoid capture and incarceration, and are now willingly marching inside a former high security prison. I can't help feeling cornered. A strange sensation of impending doom and wrongness settles over me.

I carefully observe as Elimination guards watch the breakers pass by. Oliver's recruits trade suspicious glances with their former enemies. Everybody is edgy, and it seems that the slightest spark could start a disaster. One wrong move or insult might be enough to begin a brutal gunfight.

Surprisingly, nothing extraordinary happens during the relocation. No fights break out, and Oliver's breakers safely settle into their new home. Vogel personally supervises the entire procedure, warmly greeting the new arrivals at the entrance. I can bet she ordered the officers not to show any signs of aggression. Nobody dares to break her command.

I remain convinced Vogel plans to kill all of Oliver's breakers right after Kitty and I assassinate Guardian. Vogel won't have any reason to keep us alive afterward. I suspect she's really no different from Wheeler or Browning. So we'll have to take her out first. But I'm not certain how Jessie and I should go about doing so. We can't just attack Vogel right out in the open. We'll have to make it look like an accident, otherwise a thousand Elimination officers will immediately be after us.

Thoughts of killing Vogel constantly swirl in my mind. She catches my gaze and offers a gracious smile. I quickly return a grin, feigning friendliness.

A raging crowd of crazed journalists arrive outside the prison's walls the same evening. Vogel and Oliver hold a long press-conference explaining the new relationship between Elimination and breakers. They smile and shake hands for the cameras. I remain inside the building, not willing to become the center of attention. I'm equally sick with being a public enemy as I am a national hero. All I want now is to restore my reputation, and then keep a low profile.

Unfortunately, the journalists outside don't seem to care what I want. The next morning newspapers carry indignant articles about Vogel selling out the city to breakers. They predict the coming mass murders of innocent residents, and even come up with a few indecent caricatures of Vogel and myself. In most pictures she's either sitting on my lap or passionately kissing me, while the ruins of the city burn in flames behind us. There's no mention of Oliver in any article. The journalists have completely ignored him.

My jaw drops as I stare at one artist's rendition of our relationship.

"I really don't know what to say," I finally mutter.

Kitty and Dave snicker, looking at the caricatures. They perceive everything as a joke, but I realize there's nothing funny about the situation. Unfortunately, I soon happen to be proven correct.

Within an hour, a crowd of furious residents gather at the prison walls. Angry people demand all breakers to leave the city at once, shouting hateful slogans with some even throwing stones. I hear the sound of shattering glass. We have to back away from the windows. Vogel sends a squad of officers out to deal with the protestors. The officers set a perimeter between the crowd and prison entrance, and manage to calm people down a little. I can still hear some shouting, but at least no more stones are flying into the windows.

"Looks like we'll also have to fight an informational war," Vogel says. "Chase, you will form a special team to monitor the city media."

Chase looks dumbfounded.

Vogel also instructs him to write a series of articles about me, describing my story from my first capture up to the current moment. It should help my reputation as well as hopefully begin to establish some trust between ordinary humans and breakers.

The next day Chase rages over her instructions for a solid ten minutes.

"She always gives me the strangest orders," he complains. "Working with Wheeler was so much simpler. I just needed to capture breakers, follow commands and always answer "yes, sir." That was good and fine, but Vogel doesn't like things to be so simple. She makes me deal with a lot more paperwork. She always demands to know what I think about one thing or another, and then becomes angry if my opinion contradicts hers. As if it really matters to her what I think. I'm only a soldier and nobody pays me for thinking." Chase pauses, frowning. "Well actually, I'm currently not getting any salary at all," he adds. "And now Vogel wants me to write these stupid articles only because she somehow learned that I once wanted to obtain a degree in journalism. I think she just hates me. This must be her way of torturing me."

I can't help from laughing. Chase groans, opening a notebook. He came to my quarters to listen to my story, as if he hadn't already heard enough during my interrogation.

"You're like a real reporter," I comment.

"I haven't written anything since high school," Chase sighs.

He still seems alerted in my presence, but his once hateful attitude has changed. Although Chase obviously doesn't trust me too far, he has at least stopped with his accusations.

I patiently repeat my story, trying to separate truth from fiction. Chase listens attentively, taking notes without commenting. He remains quiet, thinking, long after I'm finished.

"All right, breaker," he finally says. "I still don't fully believe you, but let's just consider the possibility that everything you say is true. How can you willingly cooperate with us, after all Elimination has done to you?"

"I just don't see any other way," I answer.

"You don't really believe Holtzmann's fairy tale about everybody living in peace and all that, do you?" Chase asks.

"I do happen to believe Holtzmann," I say.

"You must be as insane as he is," he concludes.

"Still better than being a hater," I counter.

"I don't hate breakers," he protests. "I just don't feel safe around them. Breakers will always represent a danger to ordinary humans."

"So will other ordinary humans," I answer. "There's local police to deal with ordinary criminals. And so there should be Elimination to capture and prosecute criminal breakers. I've got no problem with that. I just think you shouldn't bother innocent law abiding breakers."

"Elimination no longer bothers any breakers at all," Chase offers. "All we're trying to do these days is protect the city. We have enough food and ammo for approximately four months. As soon as we run out of resources, this war will be over. I doubt we'll be able to hold on till next spring."

Chase's facts about Elimination's resources have me worried. I didn't realize things had gotten so bad. I meet with Vogel to discuss the current situation.

"What are we going to do after we run out of food and ammo?" I ask directly.

"There won't be any after," she answers with a half-smile. "We have to defeat Guardian before next spring. We must recruit new soldiers. I'm sure there's a good number of breakers concealing themselves in this city. They now have no reason to fear Elimination. We should recruit them, as well as any other resistant people. Request for Oliver to organize that. I'll send some officers to assist him."

"New recruits won't have any combat skills," I protest.

"We'll organize a training center," Vogel suggests.

"I don't know, major," I grumble. "We'll have two or three thousand soldiers at best. And Guardian has breakers from all over the country."

"Most breakers aren't too eager to join his forces," she says. "They're leaving their homes and concealing themselves the same as ordinary citizens. I'm certain you're well aware of this fact. So why continue to argue?"

I wonder about that myself. I secretly agree with all Vogel's suggestions, but deep down feel hostile and aggressive toward her. I can't stop thinking that soon one of us will have to kill the other. And perhaps Vogel will manage to succeed where Wheeler failed.

She remains calm during our entire conversation. Nothing seems to disturb this cold-blooded professional.

"We should also arrange to have some of Oliver's breakers join Guardian's force," she offers. "We need eyes in the enemy's camp. Can you suggest any candidates for this type of job?"

I can't, but I certainly know someone who'd be able to select and train future spies.

The same day I approach Victor, announcing his promotion as director of our new intelligence group.

"I don't believe I'm the best choice for the job," he objects.

"C'mon Victor," I say. "Nobody else knows how to switch sides and spy around as well as you."

"Did you just call me a snitch?" Victor asks, grinning.

"You obviously have some unique talents for adapting to the situation and obtaining needed information," I reply. "You should coach others here how to do that. We really need you to lead our intelligence department."

"Elimination doesn't even have such a department."

"You will create one. Everybody believes in you."

Victor thinks on my words and suddenly says, "I do want to help. I'm just not sure how wise it is to give me a lot of responsibility."

I sense something different in his attitude, some guilt or unease in his expression.

"What's that all about?" I ask.

"Remember when I told you I felt like somebody wiped my memories?" Victor asks. "Like something told me to join Elimination to spy on them? What if it was Guardian? What if I knew about him right from the beginning and joined his side of my own free will? He might have wiped my memories so that I couldn't reveal any information about him. I can't stop thinking that. I know I'm not exactly a good person. But could I really be that bad? What would it mean if everything I suspect about myself happened to be true?"

Victor glances at me in utter desperation. I've never seen him like this before.

"Well," I say. "It would certainly mean that you have even more experience in spying than we originally thought. You need to become director of our intelligence."

"Is that all you've got to say?" Victor asks.

"What more do you expect me to say?"

"Do you really think I can be ever forgiven for everything I've done?"

I realize Victor is going through some sort of personal crisis. Unfortunately, we have no time for that.

"You can't even remember what all you've done," I say. "But if you have to make amends, this is your big chance. Pull yourself together, Victor. We all have to do our best to have a chance to win this war."

Victor seems unconvinced, but agrees to try organizing the spy department. I'm sure he'll be a huge success.

The next several weeks Elimination along with Oliver's breakers set up recruiting offices around the city. Chase's squad comes up with a series of propaganda articles, encouraging all resistant people and concealed breakers to join the city defense. The effort lends to a surprising result, and Elimination manages to recruit more people than originally expected. The officers send them straight to our training center, where Jessie, Dave and Marcus along with other instructors teach marksmanship and basic combat skills.

We soon form city patrols consisting of Elimination officers, Oliver's breakers and freshly recruited resistant residents of the city. Although I persist how doing so might lead to unavoidable conflicts, Vogel believes the mixed patrols will help develop trust between ordinary humans and breakers. I secretly agree with her.

Holtzmann offers to create a group of telepaths to monitor our enemies. Vogel gives her approval, and the professor begins testing all available breakers for telepathic abilities. He works day and night, organizing his new team and coaching his subjects. Rebecca assists in his work, although Holtzmann appears to be growing resentful of her care. She ultimately decides to find a new occupation.

"I've volunteered for work in the northeastern refugee center," Rebecca tells me. "Plenty of residents in that section lost their homes during airstrikes. The center's workers provide them with food and shelter. I will be working with the kids there. What do you think?"

"I think it's a wonderful idea," I say. "I'm sure you'll be a great help."

Holtzmann requests Kitty and I to join his team of telepaths, but we manage to always stay too busy to assist with that mess. Spending hours in a dark room making countless attempts to locate our enemies just seems plain boring. And I'm sure Holtzmann has enough telepaths without our help. Instead, we join the city patrols, walking along the city's streets at night. Our squad consists of several Elimination soldiers and Dave. The first few nights the officers are somewhat standoffish toward us, but their attitudes soon change. Kitty is of course the one to break the ice. She's simply too innocent-looking and sweet to be perceived as an enemy. The Elimination officers can't help themselves from being friendly toward her. She asks them about the breakers they've fought and captured. The officers share a few stories, and I tell them about our battle against Roger's gang in return. We come to agree that not all breakers are evil and not all Elimination officers are sadistic and mean. We soon become friends.

But I always keep in mind that everything can change in a moment's notice. These same officers would quickly put a bullet in my head, should Vogel ever command.

Marian remains resentful towards me. She avoids me whenever she can. We don't exchange a single word for days at a time. Whenever I enter her room, she always pretends to be asleep or reading. I don't know what I should do about that. I'm hesitant to force any further interaction because doing so would almost certainly lead to an ugly fight. At the same time I'd like to establish a better relationship with my sister. And I refuse to believe Marian is actually scared of me.

One occasion Marian starts a fight with a recently recruited girl. She viciously scratches at her face, aiming for her eyes. The officers drag my sister away, taking her straight to me. We soon end up shouting at one another. I demand an explanation why she attacked that girl.

"I don't have to explain anything to you!" she yells furiously.

I repeat my request, and Marian begins cussing at me. I've heard some rough talk before, but I've never heard anything so obscene and dirty coming from a fifteen-year-old girl. Marian takes a cautious step backward, gazing at me and waiting for my reaction. I'm not sure how to react. I take a deep breath and calmly say, "Marian, I don't ever want to hear that kind of language from you again."

"Or what?" she asks, grinning.

"Or I'll wash out your mouth with soap."

"I'm not a kid," Marian says, frowning. "You wouldn't dare do that with me."

"Don't try me," I warn.

I expect my sister to scream something outrageous or even attack me, but she hesitates. There must be something in my voice or expression that prevents her from throwing further insults.

"Just leave me alone," she utters tiredly.

I start losing hope of rebuilding any type of relationship with her. She is simply too violent and wild to deal with. Maybe I shouldn't continue holding onto the past, and simply give up on her? But how can I leave her completely alone when I'm the only relative she has left?

On another occasion passing by her room, I hear girlish giggling and whispering. I can't help from sneaking a glance through the half-opened door. I see Kitty sitting on the bed, a delighted smile spreading across her face. Marian is braiding Kitty's hair, quietly telling her something. They look happy and act like best friends.

I suddenly feel gratitude toward my sister. Kitty never had anyone to braid her hair and do other girly stuff. So I'm really glad my sister chose to become Kitty's friend. Maybe Marian isn't as bad or mean tempered as she tries to come off?

The next evening our team along with Chase and Marcus meet for supper. We all reside in a separate section of the prison which used to serve as living quarters for high ranking officers. Although the rooms somehow remind me of my confinement at the Death Camp, they're still larger and more comfortable than regular prison cells. We prefer to dine separately from the others.

Marian and Kitty sit together next to me. My sister seems to have a whole different attitude tonight. She winks at me, offering a slight smile.

Chuckling, Kitty says, "Marian and I know how to establish trust between Elimination and breakers. Are you guys ready to hear this?" She pauses, exchanging a sly glance with my sister. "Oliver and Vogel should get married and show everybody how to coexist in peace by example."

Everybody bursts out laughing.

"No way!" Jessie groans. "We can't condemn Oliver to a lifelong torture."

"Everybody has to make sacrifices in this war," Kitty protests.

"It's too much of a sacrifice," I say.

We joke and laugh for a while, then Marcus suddenly says, "Vogel was previously married. She's a widow."

"What happened to her husband?" Kitty asks. "Did she bite off his head?"

"He died from cancer a year ago," Marcus answers. I recall his mother also died from the same disease. "Vogel's husband worked for Elimination, although he was just a regular officer," Marcus continues. "I've heard they were happily married for more than twenty years."

"That's too bad," Jessie says.

The room becomes uncomfortably quiet. Nobody feels like joking and laughing anymore. Although Vogel is at the core an enemy, I still feel some sympathy. We've all lost people we loved.

"Her son also died a few months back," Marcus adds. "Breakers killed him when all this mess first began. He was about your age." He motions toward me.

I don't know what to say. I wonder how Vogel is even able to go on living. She doesn't seem broken or even the slightest bit depressed.

"How about a change of subject?" Kitty exclaims. "I've been recently thinking about who I should become in the future. So, I wanted to hear your thoughts on the topic. Victor, who do you wanna become after the war?"

"Working in a drug store would be nice," Victor answers.

"Very clever," Kitty comments. "What about you, Jess?"

"A bartender," Jessie answers. "That's what I did before all this crazy stuff started."

"Yeah, I remember," Kitty says. "But it seems boring. You should remain a sniper."

Jessie snorts. She must be getting fed up with all this fighting and killing.

"Who do you want to become when you grow up, Chase?" Kitty asks, smiling widely. "A journalist?"

"A nobody," Chase answers tiredly. "But I'm afraid I won't ever get the chance."

"No way we're letting you out," Kitty mocks. "What about you two?" she asks Marcus and Dave. "Who do you want to be?"

"Elimination officers!" the brothers answer at the same time, with no hesitation.

"Marian?" Kitty asks.

I stop eating, now listening carefully. It may be my opportunity to learn something new about my sister. I know almost nothing about her.

"Well, let me think," Marian says, looking up at the ceiling. "I guess I could become just about anybody. My IQ score is much higher than average. So I could potentially become a doctor or lawyer. But that's all nonsense of course." She lets out a playful laugh. "I imagine I'll wind up becoming an exotic dancer."

Kitty starts giggling. Victor holds up a thumb.

"Why?" I ask.

"Because I'm pretty enough," my sister simply says. "And I like dancing."

"There are other kinds of dancing in the world," I say.

"You mean like ballet or something?" Marian rolls her eyes. "You must be kidding. I'm already too old to start learning that stuff. And nobody watches ballet dancers anyway."

"I watched ballet once when I was a kid," Dave interjects unexpectedly. "Our mom enjoyed ballet and theater. We couldn't really afford tickets, but she managed to take us to a show one time. It was quite interesting! Remember, Marcus?"

"I sure do," Marcus answers. "You fell asleep and was snoring through most of the performance. It's so embarrassing to have such a pig for a brother."

"Shut up," Dave groans.

"You shut up," Marcus grins.

"Boys, boys," Kitty scolds. "That's all very nice, but let's come back to the discussion. I'm still not sure what I wanna become. I can't dance. I can't sing or do art. And science bores me to death. I literally have no talents, except killing." She pauses, thinking. "Oh, that's it! I'll become a hitman."

"Great," I groan. "I'll have a hitman and stripper in my family. What's next?"

"Don't worry, Rex," Kitty says. "You'll become some kind of big boss in Elimination. Hey Chase, do you realize that my Rex could soon be your commander?"

Chase doesn't react, obviously exhausted with listening to all this nonsense.

Kitty continues joking and giggling. Everybody has a delightful mood, enjoying the quiet peaceful evening. For the moment, it almost seems like there's no war in the world. I can even pretend we're just having a family dinner. I only regret that Holtzmann and Rebecca couldn't join us. The crazy professor is still working with his subjects in the lab, and his cousin is busy helping refugees.

Vogel enters the room, an alarmed expression on her face.

"There's been a severe fire in the city," she informs us calmly. "A hospital filled with patients and medical workers has burned down. The few remaining survivors are said to be under hypnosis."

A deathly silence falls over the room.

My throat tightens. I immediately recognize the pattern. Bulldog and his gang used to burn buildings with hypnotized victims still inside. This fire can't be just an accident. Guardian's breakers must already be in the city. So this terrible act of terror must signal the beginning of a new wave of attacks.

CHAPTER 10

I sit on a curb, being completely worn out. It's dark outside, and the air smells of burnt human flesh. My hands and clothes are covered in the nauseating stench. My mind is restless, and I can't stop from hearing the agonized cries of the few remaining survivors.

It's unbearable.

Kitty stands a few feet away, covering her face and sobbing quietly. Jessie soothingly rubs her back, smoking her fourth cigarette in a row. I notice Jessie's hands are shaking. I've never seen her affected in this way before. Victor sits on the concrete, searching his pockets. He's already swallowed more than enough pills, but the drugs don't seem to have enough effect tonight. Dave paces in circles around us, wearing a blank stare. He looks like one of the hypnotized victims, but I know he's not under. This is just shock from the horrors we've all had to witness. His brother is still helping Elimination officers collect the bodies. We've all been helping with that for half the night.

The terrorists have burned down a large hospital with a few hundred patients and medical personnel inside. The hypnotized victims were left completely defenseless and couldn't run to safety. Only a handful of resistant people managed to escape the fire, some still receiving severe burns. The building finally collapsed, burying most of the victims under smoldering debris.

This is Guardian's doing, I think silently. He's sent in terrorists to heighten distrust and aggression towards breakers amongst the city's residents.

I look again at the scorched ruins of the crumbled hospital. I wish Guardian and all his terrorists were dead. I envision locking them up inside a building and setting it on fire. I sincerely wish them to experience the same terror and pain they've caused these innocent victims tonight.

A group of Elimination officers approach along with Chase. They stop several yards away, quietly speaking about something. Chase shakes his head negatively, but nobody seems to be listening to whatever he has to say.

"Are you happy now, breaker?" one of the officers asks me.

"What are you talking about?" I ask.

"You know exactly what I'm talking about, you terrorist!" he says, pointing his finger at me.

I get to my feet, staring back at him. The other officers stay back, just watching.

"What did you call me?" I ask.

"You heard me," the officer answers.

"I think your preference to fight with words makes you a coward."

"Did you just call me a coward?!" he exclaims. "Do you think I'm scared of you?"

He steps in closer. I remain motionless, feeling my blood begin to boil. I want to smash his face in, but realize I have to do my best to avoid conflicts with Elimination. I have to force myself to keep calm.

Chase grabs the officer by his elbow, trying to stop him. The officer shoves him away. The entire squad moves in closer, backing him up. Jessie, Victor, Marcus and Dave approach me from behind. Kitty steps ahead, curling her hands into fists, but I pull her back.

"Stay back," I command.

Jessie drags Kitty a few feet away. I understand that this could quickly turn into something really nasty. We have to do our best to avoid a gang fight.

"Do you know how many breakers like you I've killed?" the officer continues.

"Not this one," I say.

"You terrorist!"

"Don't try me."

He steps closer, getting into my face, and I push him away.

"Get the hell away from here!" I shout.

The soldier grabs my jacket, saying, "I know your breakers did this! You're all terrorists."

I can take it no longer. I head-butt the officer. He staggers backwards, cussing me. His nose is bleeding.

"You freak!" he spits. "I'll rip your head off!"

"Come get some more then!" I yell.

We move in toward one another, but Chase manages to get between us. Dave grabs me from behind, dragging me backward. Marcus grabs hold of the aggressive officer.

"Stop this!" Chase commands.

"Sir, we have to cooperate!" Dave yells at me as I shove him away.

"I'll kill you!" the officer continues shouting.

"Stand down," Vogel says. "What the hell is going on here?"

I don't anticipate anybody following her orders under these circumstances, but the officers become still. They hesitantly glance over at their commander. I stop wrestling with Dave, looking over at her as well.

Vogel approaches, frowning.

"What's going on here, soldier?" she repeats, glaring at my aggressor.

"The breaker started it," the officers answers. "He head-butted me."

"I don't care who started what," Vogel says. "Aren't you supposed to be helping collect the bodies? What are you thinking?"

The officers become silent, staring into the ground.

"I expect better from you," Vogel says. "Now get back to it."

The officers hurriedly pick up their rifles, jogging back toward the debris. Vogel shifts her glare to me.

"What was this all about, Rex?" she asks. "Why are you picking fights with my soldiers? I thought you'd come here to cooperate."

"He called me a terrorist and accused me of being responsible for all this," I answer angrily.

"He manipulated you. And you allowed him to, didn't you?"

I don't say anything.

"You had to know cooperation between Elimination and breakers wouldn't come easily," Vogel continues. "I believe you also realize that some insults and conflicts are unavoidable. So why did you allow this officer to provoke you into a fight?"

I remain silent. I know if I open my mouth I'll say something offhand.

"You have to be smarter," Vogel adds softly. "You need to set an example for others."

"Oliver's breakers had nothing to do with this act of terror," I finally blurt out.

"I'm aware of that," Vogel says. "All right, enough of this. Return to the facility and get some rest. You look exhausted."

I pick up my rifle, walking away and wondering why the heck I'm following Vogel's orders.

"Rex," she calls. I stop, turning to face her. "That was a nice head-butt by the way," she adds, smiling.

"Thanks," I say, smiling back.

My team and I return to the base, passing by a large crowd of raging protestors. They begin to whistle and shout, calling us terrorists. Elimination officers hold the group back, forming a perimeter around us.

"We're trying to help them and they hate us for it," Kitty sobs.

I put my arm around her, pulling her closer. When we arrive to our room, she falls flat onto the bed, weeping bitterly.

"I hate those terrorists," Kitty gasps. "Why are they doing these terrible things? They didn't even know those patients they killed!"

I sit on the edge of the bed, rubbing her back. Kitty continues crying. I don't know how to calm her.

"Why burn those people?" Kitty demands. "What did they do to deserve such horrible deaths?"

"I don't know, Kitty," I answer. "Terrorists aren't human. We can't understand them."

Kitty presses her face into the pillow. I lie down beside her, gently stroking her hair.

"Everything will be all right," I whisper softly, although I don't fully believe it.

Kitty finally calms down. We lie in silence awhile.

"Do you think Vogel will make us leave now?" she asks.

"No," I answer. "She knows we didn't burn the hospital."

"She'll try to kill us in the future, won't she?"

"Probably."

"Are you scared of her?"

I take a moment to think.

"She's just an Elimination officer," I answer. "I've never been intimidated by them before. Now, let's try to get some sleep. It's very late."

We crawl under the blankets, and I pass out almost instantly. I continue smelling the reek of burnt human flesh in my sleep. I dream of walking through a dark maze of prison passageways, stepping over bodies. I finally come to a small cell with no windows. Emily sits on the floor, holding a little girl.

"Please, take me away!" the girl pleads, reaching out her arms for me.

I grab her hand, pulling her away. Emily grips Marian tighter. My sister screams, pleading for me not to leave her.

"Let her go!" I shout at Emily.

She draws a handgun, aiming at my face. I notice movement in the darkness. A dark frightening shadow slowly creeps down behind my mother. I make out a large long head and an open mouth filled with sharp teeth. I continue trying to free Marian. Emily's grip is too strong, and I can't overpower her. The ominous shadow rises behind my mother, making a low growling sound.

"Watch out!" I yell.

The next moment the gigantic reptile lunges toward me, biting off my head.

I awaken, startled and confused. The nightmare felt disturbingly real. I wonder, what the heck was that? What was Vogel doing in my dreams?

I begin fantasizing about killing her, just to calm myself down. I visualize myself walking through a prison passageway at night, carrying a large pillow. I enter Vogel's room and approach her bed. I press the pillow into her face and hold it down until she stops moving. Then I suddenly realize where these thoughts are coming from.

Being eight years old, I awoke one night to find Emily standing by my bedside. She was holding a pillow above my face. I was sure Emily was about to smother me, but something changed her mind.

I decide to think of something more pleasant. I now envision Vogel and myself stand facing each other many yards apart, ready to draw guns. Just the way they did it in the Wild West. The image is soothing, but I'd probably have little chance to hit her first. My vision is too poor to aim well. The major would shoot me full of holes, unless I'd thought to place Jessie and her sniper rifle somewhere on a rooftop.

I wonder if this is normal behavior, to constantly have thoughts about killing someone.

I decide it's all just a result of all the stress from the terrorist attack. I close my eyes, willing myself to fall asleep. I remain awake till sunrise in spite of my most vigorous efforts.

***

Kitty and I often patrol the city during the night, walking through partially devastated neighborhoods. Several buildings were brought down during recent airstrikes. Shards of broken glass and empty bullet casings still litter the streets. The scenery appears oddly familiar and as I look around, I worry we'll find human corpses hanging from the lampposts.

Fortunately, there's only a few old posters hanging, with the same old calls to capture and kill mind breakers. "Kill a breaker, help save the world," one message reads.

One early morning our squad winds up on the city boardwalk, gazing at the ocean. The autumn sky is growing lighter. Everything seems too peaceful and ordinary, as if the war completely spared this part of the city. I can even briefly imagine there was never a war in the world.

We need to continue following our route, but can't help from lingering on the boardwalk. None of us speak, just listening to the sound of the surf. I breathe in the moist salty air, daydreaming about a normal life. I've almost forgotten what it's like to take an evening stroll or watch the ocean. I no longer remember much else, but endless war. I glance at Kitty standing beside me. I'm not sure there's a way back for me, but what about her? Would she be able to adapt to a civilian life after all this mess is over? Could she return to school and become an average teenaged girl?

Kitty smiles broadly, fascinated by the ocean waves under the pale sunrise.

"Look! There's a beach down there!" she exclaims, pointing into the mist.

I squint, looking in the direction she's pointing. I can barely see a large stripe of white sand off in the distance.

"We'll go swim there next summer," Kitty states. I'm not so sure we'll still be alive by the next summer, but nod anyway. "Dave, will you come with us?" she asks.

"May I?" Dave wonders, smiling. "I'll bring a fishing pole. I always wanted to try fishing off a pier. May Marcus come as well?"

"Sure," Kitty says. "We should all have a big party right here on the beach after the war."

I get an uneasy feeling. I wonder how many of us will actually make it to the end of this war.

***

A couple hours later Kitty and I return to the headquarters and run straight into an excited Holtzmann.

"There you are!" the professor exclaims, grabbing our arms and pulling us forcefully toward his lab.

"Holtzmann, we've just returned from a patrol," I resist. "We haven't slept the entire night. We can't be too useful for conducting experiments right now."

"Sleep deprivation can sometimes increase telepathic sensitivity," Holtzmann counters, cutting me off.

He pushes us inside a small windowless room with a bed.

"I want you to concentrate and try to locate the terrorists," the professor instructs, shutting the door closed behind him as he leaves.

There's no light in the room. I can't see anything in the darkness. I hear Kitty take a few unsteady steps before bumping into something.

"Ouch!" she cries out. "Well, I guess I found the bed. Come here!"

"I can't see anything," I say, standing motionless. It must be close to what blindness is, one of my greatest fears.

"Follow my voice," Kitty directs.

I take a few cautious steps forward and also bump into something. Kitty lets out a laugh, tightly gripping my jacket and pulling me onto the bed. I fall on top of her.

"Rex my love," she murmurs. "We're all alone in this small dark room. Do you think we can find something more interesting to do than telepathy?"

"Kitty!" I exclaim. "You should at least wait until we make it to our room."

"I was talking about telling scary stories, ghosts and zombies and such," Kitty says innocently. "What did you think I was suggesting? You have such a dirty mind!"

She begins howling and snapping her teeth, imitating monsters. I roll my eyes at her, but Kitty doesn't catch that in the darkness.

"C'mon, let's do some work," I say sternly.

"Gosh, you're so boring today," Kitty sighs. "All right, let's concentrate."

But we can't concentrate. After walking all night, we both immediately fall asleep. An hour later Holtzmann comes to check our progress and becomes furious.

"This is wholly unacceptable!" he exclaims, shaking his fists. "You must be locating the terrorists, not sleeping!"

"I wasn't sleeping," Kitty mumbles, wiping drool from her mouth.

"I sometimes see visions in my sleep," I say defensively.

The professor rages on for a good five minutes, before finally booting us out of his lab.

We head back toward our quarters. Passing Marian's room, I can't help sneaking a quick glimpse through the slightly open door. Her room is empty and her bed looks untouched. I know it's way too early for my sister to be up and around. She doesn't usually rise before noon.

Marian doesn't show up for the rest of the day. In the evening I become really worried. I realize my sister must have run away.

***

Elimination officers locate Marian two days later and bring her to me in the middle of the night. My sister laughs, pushing the officers away. Her clothes are torn and I can smell alcohol on her breath.

"Thanks, guys," I say to the officers. "Where did you find her?"

"You don't want to know," they answer before leaving.

Left alone, Marian and I stare at each other. She smiles. I envision smacking her head and yelling at her, but I know better. I begin calmly, "I was going crazy worrying about you. Where have you been?"

"What do you care?" my sister asks. "I can do whatever I want."

She lets out a mocking laugh, tilting her head backward.

"You're drunk," I say with disgust.

"So what?" Marian snorts.

"C'mon, I'll take you to your room," I say, grabbing her arm.

"Don't touch me!" Marian screams.

I grip her arm tighter, leading her into the corridor. She follows, whining quietly. As we enter her room, Marian finally frees her arm, moving away from me.

"Leave me alone!" she demands.

"I've been worried about you," I say, keeping my voice low. "You can't just disappear like that. You at least have to tell me where you're going. I thought something bad might have happened to you. There are terrorists in the city."

"Oh really?" Marian asks. "What can they do to me that I haven't already been through before?"

"They can kill you for one thing," I answer.

"Fine! I wish to be dead anyway. I'm sick of this miserable stupid life. I want them to kill me!"

Marian kicks the bed furiously, letting out a wild yell. She grabs a pillow and throws it against the wall, then begins kicking it too. I watch in a stupor.

"Stop that," I demand, grabbing her arm.

"Let me go!" Marian yells. "Help!"

I notice several old thin scars on the bare skin of her wrist.

"What's this?" I exclaim.

Marian follows my gaze and suddenly becomes motionless.

"Nothing," she quietly mutters.

I yank the sleeve up, staring at her damaged skin. Her entire arm is scarred.

"Goodness," I breathe out. "Did you do that to yourself? Are you a cutter?"

"Don't look!" Marian cries out, slapping away my hand. "I don't do that anymore."

She pulls her sleeve down low, seemingly embarrassed.

"Where else did you cut?" I ask.

Marian ignores my question, gazing at the wall.

"Where else did you cut?" I repeat. "Answer me, Marian!"

"My thighs," she confesses. "But nobody can tell even when I wear a skirt. That's it. I didn't cut anywhere else. And I quit like I said."

I don't believe her.

"Why did you hurt yourself?" I ask, making my voice sound softer. "It must've hurt. And it looks ugly."

My sister scowls, glaring at me.

"I want to feel the pain!" she shouts. "I want to look ugly! That's exactly what I need."

"Why?"

"Because that's how I am inside! I'm ugly and nasty. So I wanted to look this way. I'm just a filthy piece of stinking trash!"

"Seems so at the moment," I say.

"Do you really think you're any better? Maybe you actually believe you're a higher race because you're a breaker? You're worse off than me! You're nobody!"

I stare blankly at her. The image of a shouting Emily pops up in my mind. I will myself to stay calm, but become angry in spite of my effort. Marian obviously knows very well how to manipulate people.

"My mother never liked you," she says spitefully. "She hated you because she knew you were just a stinking freak. She loved me much more. I was her princess. And you killed my mother for that. Because you wanted to steal me away for yourself, you wanted to own me."

"Stop it," I say.

"I won't stop!" Marian shouts. "Don't you like me anymore? Do you hate me now? Well, enjoy it. This is who I've become. Or maybe you expected something different after everything you did to me?"

"What did I ever do?" I ask.

"You left me with her! You ran away like a coward. You didn't care one bit what might happen to me."

I stand unmoving, watching her. Marian continues yelling at me. Her face reddens, and she looks vicious and ugly. I think of Emily. It seems to me they're just about the same. Even Marian's voice sounds like my mother's. Ten years have passed, and I still have to listen to the same insults, now coming from her daughter's mouth. It makes me really angry. I get a strong urge to grab Marian and shake her violently, or else slap her hard across the face.

"I hate you!" she shouts. "And I'll always hate you! You're just a killer."

"Just shut up," I demand.

"Or what?" she asks. "What will you do if I don't shut up?"

"Don't try me, Marian."

My sister laughs, curling her lips into a challenging smile.

"Want to hit me?" she asks. "Go ahead, loser! I'm not afraid of you."

"I've warned you," I say slowly.

"C'mon, be a real man and hit me," Marian laughs, stepping closer. "Show me what you can do. I know you want to. You like hurting people."

I stand motionless, afraid of what I might do.

"Are you scared to hit your little sister?" she mocks.

"I'm not so sure you're my sister."

A moment later Marian slaps me hard across the face. I step away, staring at her in shock. I hadn't seen it coming, although I should have. I know she has a mean streak. But part of me still doesn't want to believe she could do something like that.

"Are you crazy?!" I ask.

Marian lunges forward, attempting to slap me a second time, but I catch her wrist.

"C'mon, do it!" she yells. "I know you hate me. I know you want to hurt me."

"Quit fighting!" I shout, restraining her arms. "I don't hate you."

Marian struggles to free herself but to no avail. Angered, she lets out a furious growl and spits right into my face. I release her, being stunned. I back away, wiping my face. Not even Emily has ever treated me this way before.

I turn to see my sister watching, waiting for my reaction. Our eyes meet and her expression becomes fearful.

"Do you hate me now?" Marian whispers.

Her hands begin shaking. I don't think she's only pretending. She must be truly frightened of me.

Why is she behaving like this? I wonder. Why is she literally begging me to hit her?

I suddenly remember Emily slapping my face, then holding me and asking for forgiveness. I remember her yelling insults and throwing books at me. Afterwards she was always so loving and gentle. That was the only way to earn my mother's love.

I finally get it. I realize why Marian is behaving so aggressively toward me. I don't understand why I couldn't see it earlier. My sister is trying to drag me back into the same vicious pattern of violence and forgiveness. She learned this behavior at our mother's feet. Emily must have abused and insulted her for many years. My sister now expects me to take Emily's role.

No way.

I quickly approach Marian and wrap my arms around her. She expels a terrified scream, weakly pushing me away. I tightly hold her, rubbing her back.

"It's all right," I say. "Everything is okay. I'm not angry."

She resists for a few more moments, then becomes still and begins crying. She presses her face into my shoulder.

"You can't possibly do anything to make me hate you," I say. "I love you and I want you to always remember that. But I need you to understand that you should never hurt the people you love, Marian."

"But that's what she did," Marian mumbles, still crying.

"She's gone," I say. "And we don't have to be like her."

I hold my sister for a long time, waiting for her to calm down. Marian finally becomes quiet, being completely exhausted. I help remove her boots and jacket, then put her to bed.

"She always said I was nasty and dirty," my sister mutters, as I pull the blanket over her. "She said I needed discipline. You have to keep me on a short leash, and yank it any time I misbehave."

"You're not a dog, Marian," I sigh. "Now go to sleep."

She looks up at me with a miserable expression. I kiss her lightly on her forehead and exit the room.

I don't sleep the rest of the night, thinking about my sister. I don't know how I can help her. How can I undo the harmful effects of an overbearing mother?

I also wonder whether Marian's suggestion concerning a lack of discipline has any bearing. My sister spends her days inside her room, mostly doing nothing. Perhaps bringing some discipline and schedule planning into her life could be helpful.

The next day I approach Rebecca, asking whether my sister could become a volunteer in the refugee center.

"She can be a little wild sometimes," I warn.

"I've no idea what you're talking about," Rebecca interrupts. "Your sister is a very sweet girl. I'm sure she'll be very helpful."

"Could you talk to Marian and ask her to help you at the center? I just don't think my sister will listen to anything I suggest."

"I understand," she says, nodding. "Of course I'll talk to her."

I thank Rebecca sincerely.

I decide I should also find some information about survivors of child abuse. Maybe it could help me understand Marian better.

The following evening, Kitty and I again attempt to locate the terrorists, spending hours in Holtzmann's lab. We don't succeed, leaving Holtzmann disappointed. Before falling asleep, I continue thinking about the burnt hospital and the terrorists responsible. I think about Guardian and his army. I wonder what they're planning to do next.

I wake up in the middle of the night, with my pulse racing. I look to my left and see Kitty staring wide-eyed back at me. Her eyes are filled with terror.

"Have you seen it too?" she asks.

I nod. I understand we've somehow just shared the same vision. We both saw aircraft dropping bombs on the city. We witnessed groups of soldiers marching along the highway. We saw Guardian and Hammer studying maps.

"They're going to attack the city, aren't they?" Kitty whispers.

"We need to inform Vogel," I say.

CHAPTER 11

I find the major in her office. She's studying reports behind a large cluttered desk. Although it's about 3:30 AM, Vogel still looks energetic and fresh, as if it's the middle of a working day. A half-conscious Chase sits on the floor amongst a pile of open paper-folders, staring stupidly at the documents. I wonder whether he can even see the text.

Vogel looks up at me.

"What's happened?" she asks calmly.

"Guardian's troops are preparing to strike the city," I blurt out, still breathing hard.

Vogel remains unimpressed.

"When?" she asks curtly.

"I'm not sure," I answer. "It seemed like night time. Maybe tomorrow night."

"Where did you obtain this information?"

I suspect she already knows the answer.

"Kitty and I had telepathic visions," I say.

"Could they be inaccurate?" she questions.

"That's definitely possible," I admit. "I've had false visions before. But this time Kitty and I both saw the same images. So it may increase the probability the visions were accurate. I don't know, Holtzmann understands these things better." I pause, collecting my thoughts. Vogel watches me warily. "I hope Kitty and I are mistaken," I say. "Otherwise, the entire city is in danger. It looked like a massive attack. Aircraft, bombings. Thousands of Guardian's soldiers heading toward the city."

I pause again, running out of breath. My pulse is still racing. Those visions have chilled me to the core.

Vogel doesn't answer, thinking on my words. I become worried that she won't heed my warning. I've no idea what's going on inside her head. Will she take action on the word of a breaker?

"We should prepare then," Vogel says. "Chase, go wake everybody. We'll have a meeting in twenty minutes."

I exhale a breath of relief. She believes me.

Chase obediently crawls away from the pile of documents and heads toward the door, slightly swaying. I wonder when he last slept.

Vogel becomes silent, gazing off into space. I remain standing in the middle of the room, thinking about the visions. I truly hope they were false.

I notice two framed pictures on Vogel's desk, one of a mid-aged man in a black uniform and another with a young guy about my age. Her deceased husband and son, I realize. Vogel catches me staring at the pictures. She suddenly seems thoughtful and tired, more human.

"I'm very sorry for your loss," I say.

"It wasn't your fault," Vogel answers. "A lot of people have recently lost their families."

There's no self-pity in her voice. I become quiet again, not sure what else to say. I've never been good at expressing sympathy. And I'm not sure whether it's appropriate or not for me to speak to Vogel about her dead relatives. Breakers killed her son as I recall.

"How many soldiers will Guardian throw into this attack?" Vogel asks.

"I don't know for sure," I say.

"Give me your best guesstimate."

"Three or four thousand. Maybe more."

Vogel nods, thinking.

"So they greatly outnumber us," she states. "Rex, can I rely on Oliver's breakers during the coming battle? Will they be willing to help us defend the city?"

"Sure," I answer. "Of course, you can rely on us. That's why we came, to help defend the city. We'll do our best."

Vogel smiles.

"Very well then," she says. "Have a seat, Rex. You're too wired. You need to calm down."

Simpler said than done. I take a seat, but can't keep still. I continue replaying the images of the coming attack in my mind. Bombs dropping directly into crowds of people. I imagine disfigured bodies and filling mass graves. I've already had to go through this before. I don't want to witness another massacre.

Vogel continues studying the reports. Nothing seems to affect her.

A few minutes later Chase returns with Oliver, along with my team and a group of officers. We have a two hour meeting, drinking strong coffee and developing a strategy for defending the city.

"They're going to smash us," Oliver says. "We currently have only two thousand soldiers, including new recruits. Guardian has ten times as many. They have aircraft with missiles and plenty of ammo."

"He won't be throwing all his troops into this attack," Vogel answers confidently. "His army is too strung out controlling multiple cities all over the country. They'd risk losing other positions, if they mass everything against us."

"And Guardian's soldiers are not professional," I add. "Most of them don't have any real combat training. I think his troops will be mostly used to test our perimeter. Guardian will want to see how strong our defenses are."

After the meeting we begin the vigorous preparations for a possible attack. Chase's media squad contacts the newspapers and TV stations, alerting city residents to the danger. They encourage any resistant people and breakers alike to join the city defense. Within a few hours, an enormous crowd of volunteers gather at the prison entrance. I doubt all of these people are truly resistant. Most likely they're just not willing to stand aside, with their families in imminent danger. I understand their desire to help, but only truly resistant individuals can be accepted. Vogel makes Holtzmann responsible for testing the fresh volunteers.

The officers and recruits build barricades across all main roads, to block incoming traffic into the city. They spread the few anti-aircraft guns around the city perimeter, although I doubt Elimination soldiers are trained to use these types of weapons. They had commandeered them from destroyed military bases during the first months of the war. They also acquired grenades and explosives, which we now use for setting traps all around the city borders. Other recruits mix crude Molotov cocktails in glass bottles, using gasoline and motor oil.

A major problem is that we don't have enough rifles to arm the volunteers. They'll have to use whatever they can find against Guardian's guns.

"They're gonna die," Chase states, looking over our new recruits.

"They'll only participate if troops break through our lines," I answer.

"I believe that's precisely what's going to happen," he sighs.

My team assists in building barricades. We use debris, junk cars and any large objects we can find. Dave and Marcus string rolls of barbed wire. We stay after it, working non-stop throughout the day. I ask Kitty not to carry anything heavy, but she doesn't listen. I'm also hesitant about letting her join the front lines of defense, but Kitty doesn't seem to care about my opinion.

"I have to be there with you," she says. "I need to make sure nothing horrible happens."

I begin to argue, but she only smiles back at me. I sigh, knowing that Kitty is going to participate in this battle, no matter what I say.

I haven't slept much, but still feel fully awake and energetic. I obsessively continue building the barricades, thinking about facing Guardian's soldiers. Some part of me craves blood, itching for revenge. But another part is still hopeful that the visions were false. It's going to be a massacre unwitnessed before. I've been in a few gunfights and even survived a bombing or two, but I've never participated in a battle of such magnitude as the one in the vision.

I suddenly remember Guardian's recruits wasting the prisoners in the Death Camp. I realize that these sadists would methodically murder all non-breaker residents in the city, should we fail to stop the attack. They'd also kill any breakers who refused to join their forces. We can't let that happen. We have to stop them, at any cost.

Somebody approaches me from behind and covers my eyes.

"Guess who!" I hear a girlish voice.

I instantly recognize her.

"Chelsey!" I exclaim, turning around. "Hey little one! How are you?"

We hug each other tightly, like old friends.

"I was missing you!" Chelsey says, giggling.

"You're wearing a uniform," I suddenly notice. "Are you a recruit now? Are you planning to fight?"

Chelsey nods, spinning around to model her new black uniform. She sure seems happy and excited.

"I'll be helping defend the city," she says proudly.

"Chelsey, you're too young for this one," I argue, becoming worried.

"All resistant people and breakers must do their part to help," Chelsey answers. "I volunteered because I truly want to do my duty and take part. I've told you how I hate Guardian. I wasn't joking. I really want to fight against him. And I've received some combat training recently. Jessie taught me to shoot as you suggested." She unholsters her handgun. "Look what I have! It's my trophy. I'm about to use it in real battle."

I now seriously regret having given this gun to Chelsey. I have to fight an urge to try talking her out of joining our defense. I realize that many teens will have to participate in this battle. We simply don't have enough resistant people in the city to exclude the kids.

Chelsey smiles broadly. Her smile is completely different from the one she flashed back in the Death Camp. She looks so joyful and full of life.

"I'll be worrying for you," I say. "Please, be careful."

"I'll be all right," Chelsey promises. "I'm not frightened. I've been through much worse in the Death Camp."

"How old were you when Elimination captured you?" I ask.

"I was seven," Chelsey answers. "They kept me in another facility before moving me to the Death Camp."

Goodness. She hasn't known anything else in her young life, except prison walls and various forms of torture.

"I'm so sorry," I sigh.

"It's fine. At least now I'm free."

Chelsey becomes quiet for a few moments, watching me with a hesitant expression.

"Rex, are we truly friends?" she asks.

"Of course we're friends," I assure her. "What's up, Chelsey? Do you need anything?"

"I just thought maybe you could help me locate my parents?" she asks. "I just really don't know how else I might find them. I've no idea where they are, and I don't have any telepathic abilities."

"Sure," I say. "Of course I'll try to help you. We should ask Kitty to help as well, because she's a much stronger telepath than me. I'll tell you what. Come find us after all this mess is over and we'll figure out something. Deal?"

"Deal," Chelsey says, smiling again.

She walks away, heading back to her squad. I follow her with my eyes. I don't want anything bad to happen to this brave little girl. I sure hope our visions were false.

In the evening, Vogel arrives to check progress. She expresses gratitude for our contribution, shaking my hand.

"You and Kitty along with a squad of recruits will be blockading this access road," Vogel informs me.

"Wait a minute," I say. "I thought my team was supposed to be on the front line of defense. We're strong breakers."

"That's correct," the major answers. "Jessie, Dave and Victor are welcome to join the main lines of defense. But you and Kitty will be staying behind."

I begin to argue, but Vogel doesn't bend.

"It's a direct order," she cuts me off. "Your primary duty here is to assassinate Guardian in the future. We can't afford to risk either of your lives unnecessarily."

I become silent. I have a strong desire to yell at her that she's not my commander and I won't follow her orders. But Vogel isn't the type of person you want to yell at. She'd simply order me locked up, should I continue to argue.

"Are we really gonna stay behind?" Kitty asks, after Vogel leaves.

I hesitate. I don't want to stay back like a coward while the others fight Guardian's soldiers. At the same time, this may be the only way to keep Kitty from joining the front line of defense.

"Vogel is right," Jessie says, looking at me and Kitty. "You two should stay back. Your lives are too important. Nobody else has a legitimate chance to kill Guardian."

Victor and Dave agree with her.

I still can't decide what Kitty and I should do. Not being an Elimination officer, I don't have to follow Vogel's commands. But I do realize that her decision to try to keep us safe is more than sensible. Should Kitty and I be killed, Holtzmann won't have any suitable subjects for his experiment.

"All right then," I say. "We'll help secure this road."

"We're gonna miss out on all the fun," Kitty groans, looking disappointed.

We continue building barricades.

"Vogel really appreciates all your help," Marcus suddenly says to me.

I don't answer.

"Did you know that she once worked closely with Wheeler several years ago?" Marcus asks.

"So I've heard," I say.

"They were rivals," Marcus continues. "They were competing for the same promotion, and Vogel won. Wheeler hated her for that. Vogel always caused him constant troubles. She once reported his excessive violence towards captured breakers. But in the public eye, they behaved like good friends."

I listen to Marcus attentively. I didn't expect Vogel to mind violence toward breakers. Empathy is an unusual trait in a high ranking Elimination officer.

"She was also investigating your case," Marcus says. "Not officially, of course. I guess she suspected that most of those acts of terror were organized by Elimination. She began collecting facts and asking questions. Right up until executives stopped her short."

Of course they did. Guardian controlled them. He couldn't allow an outsider to learn of his sinister plans.

"Vogel secretly continued gathering information," Marcus adds. "I think she figured out everything at the end, but it was too late. Guardian's breakers attacked us. I think Vogel even intended to contact Oliver's breakers, realizing they're not the real enemy. But you contacted us first."

Now I'm confused. Maybe I'm wrong about disliking Vogel? Maybe she isn't really plotting to kill us after the fact? I don't know what to think, because I'm too conditioned to seeing enemies in everybody. Too many people recently wishing me dead.

I decide not to jump to any more quick conclusions. After all, Vogel is an excellent manipulator. She has to be, otherwise she wouldn't be able to become a major with this outfit.

"How did Vogel come to join Elimination in the first place?" I ask Marcus.

"Her father was an Elimination general," he answers. "She followed in his footsteps, I suppose. Everybody knew Vogel would be a perfect fit for the job. She has the highest level of resistance to hypnosis. It simply runs in her family. Her mother worked for Elimination as well. Vogel didn't have to serve so much as a single day as a regular officer. Elimination promoted her to commander right after her training." He pauses, smiling. "You know, she could easily get a civilian job if she wanted. Most officers around here have only a high school diploma at best, so we don't have many options except serving Elimination. But Vogel has a law degree. She's from a wealthy family and could afford studying in college. So I don't really know why she chose Elimination. It's just probably something in her genes. She could have been a general by now."

"What stopped her?" I ask.

"She likes action," Marcus answers. "Generals don't participate in the missions to capture breakers. They mostly do planning and paper work. Too boring for Vogel."

I nod, thinking on his words. I can't figure out the major. I don't know whether she's evil or not. Does she really like capturing and killing breakers so much that she turned down a promotion? Or did she suspect that the Elimination generals were under Guardian's control, so she preferred to stay away from the Death Camp?

I can't tell. Maybe I'm just being overly paranoid. I decide I should at least stop fantasizing about killing Vogel. She hasn't done anything I can see to deserve that kind of thinking.

After dark, a mixed crowd of breakers and Elimination officers head off toward the city border. Everybody seems to have an upbeat mood, as if going to a parade. People laugh, whistle and yell slogans as they go. It reminds me of some kind of celebration. Kitty holds my hand, quietly murmuring a song.

"Kill a breaker, help save the world!" a few of the officers shout.

Oliver's recruits begin whistling and clapping their hands in agreement, instead of being offended for once. We may all have to kill a lot of breakers this night.

Jessie, Victor, Marcus and Dave leave to take positions along the front lines. Kitty and I along with a squad of recruits remain behind to guard the road.

Next comes the long hours of waiting. It's a crisp night, with shimmering stars and a full moon. I shiver from the cold, scanning the sky for any approaching aircraft. I can see none and it's unnaturally quiet. No sound of engines or falling bombs yet.

"Beautiful," Kitty says, gazing at stars. "Like Christmas night, isn't it?"

"Looks like," I agree.

Nobody else speaks, just somberly waiting for the night to end. I take a good look at our squad, assessing our chances. Most of our recruits are today's volunteers, untrained youngsters armed with clubs and knives. I don't think they've ever been in combat. I sincerely hope they won't have to fight.

Time drags by slowly. I finally become tired. I envision myself crawling into bed and getting a few hours of good sleep.

Just before sunrise, a missile strikes a nearby building, sending a shower of debris and dirt down on our heads.

CHAPTER 12

I cover Kitty, shielding her from flying debris. A thick cloud of dust enfolds us, limiting visibility. I can't see much, but hear startled cries nearby. A moment later I catch another familiar sound, the low menacing noise of approaching aircraft engines.

I quickly shake off my daze, scrambling to my feet. I help Kitty up, taking a careful look around at our surroundings. As the cloud of dust slowly settles, I can now see only a large smoldering crater where the building once stood. A former Elimination aircraft floats past us above, heading further into the city.

"Is everybody all right?" I ask, looking over our squad.

The recruits get to their feet, coughing and dusting off their uniforms. They appear startled, but uninjured. I'm sure most of the recruits have had to survive airstrikes before, although they were likely sheltering in basements. Facing the explosions right out in the open is a different experience altogether.

"What do we do, sir?" a young recruit asks.

I don't have an opportunity to answer. A cacophony of explosions and gunfire makes us all turn in the direction of the front lines.

"Gosh, what's happening out there?" another recruit whispers.

"A gunfight," I answer. "Come on, return to your positions."

The recruits obediently take cover behind the barricade. Kitty and I return as well, waiting. I think of my team out there engaging into a fierce fight. I suddenly feel like a coward, staying here behind fortifications. At the same time, part of me is relieved that Kitty isn't down there with them. At least for the moment, she's safer here with me.

"Shall we go join the battle?" a young girl asks, holding a knife in her shaking hand. "Shouldn't we help them?"

"Not yet," I answer. "We're staying here. Our primary objective is to hold this ground surrounding the road."

Nobody protests, waiting nervously for whatever may be coming next. The gunfire doesn't cease. I can't help but wonder whether my friends are still alive or not.

"We're going to miss everything," Kitty groans.

I don't answer. I only wish she was somewhere far away from all this mess.

"Are any of you breakers?" I ask the recruits.

A girl about Chelsey's age and young boy raise their hands.

"What level?" I ask.

"Professor Holtzmann said I'm level 3," the girl answers.

"Level 2," the guy says.

"Good, it means you can hypnotize other breakers," I say. "You two will help us hypnotize any attackers should they break through the lines. The rest are to toss the cocktails. I don't want you to break cover, unless it becomes unavoidable. Is that understood?"

"Yes, sir," the recruits answer.

"And try not to get killed," I add.

The recruits exchange glances, then a young girl says, "We're not afraid of dying, sir. We're not letting those breakers enter our city. If they come, we're going to stop them no matter the cost."

The others nod in agreement. They seem frightened, but determined to fight to the death.

"We're going to win this battle," Kitty says confidently. "Guardian's soldiers have nothing to fight for, while you'll be defending your homes and families. You'll be protecting your loved ones."

The recruits smile broadly.

"We're the good guys," one proudly exclaims. "And the good guys always win, right?"

He appears to believe in what he's saying.

I truly hope Guardian troops don't manage to break through.

More aircraft fly overhead. We watch them warily, listening to the distant rumbling explosions. An anti-aircraft gunner manages to score a direct hit on one of the gunships. There's a burst of orange flames and the aircraft begins rotating in the sky. It increases spin, until finally losing control and falling in a long fiery arc like a burning meteorite. It's mesmerizing. The recruits start whistling and clapping.

The aircraft flies low above our position and crashes on the opposite side of the street, damaging three homes along the way. I'm really glad that the residents have been evacuated from this section of the city. Kitty and I take a couple of recruits to check for any survivors. The hatch opens and somebody crawls outside, dropping to the ground. I keep my rifle on him. He's definitely injured. Lying on his side, the soldier in camo wipes blood from his face and raises an arm for help. He seems to be in shock. I pull the trigger. His head jerks to the side as the bullet takes him in the temple.

"Sweet," Kitty whispers.

The recruits stare at me in astonishment.

"He came to kill us," I say. "He got what he deserved. We're not taking any prisoners tonight. These are terrorists."

The recruits look shaken, but don't protest.

We light the cloth wick on a cocktail and toss the explosive liquid into the open hatch before returning to our positions.

Our squad continues waiting. The sounds of shooting sometimes grow closer, then distant again. More aircraft are hit from the ground, crashing into various sections of the city. I hope somebody will think to finish off any survivors.

At dusk, the gunfire suddenly becomes louder and more intense. I get really nervous, realizing that Guardian's soldiers may now be breaking through our front lines. I command the recruits to get ready. I see a few figures moving toward us through the mist. I raise the barrel of my rifle, waiting for their approach. It's Jessie and Marcus along with a few Elimination officers. I can also make out Victor and Dave amongst them. They jog toward our position, stopping only to take a quick shot at their pursuers. And further back, a group of men in camo stalking them. Guardian's breakers. All the recruits were ordered to wear black tonight, not to be mistaken for an enemy in the chaos of battle.

I realize we're losing this fight. My pulse rises for a moment, then an odd calmness settles over me.

My team joins us behind the barricade.

"Those bastards sent in hypnotized civilians to attack us," Dave says to me, still gasping after his run. "We had to gun them down."

I don't answer.

Using the darkness as cover, Guardian's troops slow their approach as they near the barricade. I command the recruits to begin tossing the Molotov cocktails. Kitty and I along with the others simultaneously project our thoughts, attempting to capture their minds. My head hurts. I don't know whether or not we're strong enough to break their wills. I know Guardian uses Holtzmann's drug on his soldiers, to increase their abilities. I hear explosions and a few anguished cries. A bright glow from the flames illuminates the street. I see several burning figures running in panic. Several others now stand unmoving, momentarily confused by our hypnosis. We open fire, instantly bringing them down. Now two large military trucks drive our direction. I've no idea how we can stop all of them.

"I'm empty," Marcus says, dropping his rifle. "Cover me!"

He jogs toward the nearest downed breaker. Kitty and Jessie cover him. Marcus quickly collects a few rifles and begins backing off. Rising from the shadows, a group of men in camo starts moving his direction. Jessie brings two of them down, scoring headshots. Marcus manages to drop to the ground, avoiding the line of crossfire as he puts to use one of commandeered rifles.

I close my eyes, focusing on trying to hypnotize the soldiers. Victor, Kitty and two recruits join me in the attempt. It's not having much effect. Most of Guardian's breakers are too strong for us.

Marcus has made it back behind the barricade and is now handing out rifles to the recruits. Dave runs out of ammo, but refuses to accept the last weapon from his brother. Instead, he tosses a flaming bottle at the nearest approaching truck. An explosion, and the vehicle catches on fire, flames bursting upward like a fountain. I hear screams and see soldiers scrambling from the back of the truck. A second blast, the impact knocking them down. Instantly assessing their disorientation, Dave rushes in. Pulling a knife, he quickly slits their throats before taking their guns. Kitty and I cover him.

Troops from the second truck somehow managed to flank our position in the darkness. The gunfire is now coming from all directions. Kitty keeps close by, covering me from the right. She must realize I'm half blind and can't see who's coming from the right side.

One of them has gotten too close. I empty my clip and drop the weapon to the ground. While Kitty keeps him pinned down, I pull a knife and spring out toward the guy. I have some ground to cover and he obviously sees me, but doesn't fire. As I close the distance, his expression changes to one of surprise. According to Guardian's propaganda, I'm proposed to be his commander. I stab the blade deeply into his stomach. The guy grunts, doubling over. The first cut is probably more than enough, but I can't stop. Hatred and rage overtake me. I withdraw the blade and repeatedly stab him in the chest, splattering blood. As he falls, I grab ahold of his rifle. With a furious shout, somebody charges into me from behind. I stagger a couple of steps forward, but manage to keep my balance. I grab an arm reaching for my throat, and throw my attacker to the ground. It's a young boy in camo, unarmed. He must have run out of ammo as well. I shoot him in the face then work my way back toward the barricade.

A man engulfed in flames runs past, screaming loudly. None of us wastes a bullet to end his agony. Kitty finally emerges from the darkness, firing her rifle as she jogs. I watch Dave as he crawls between unmoving bodies, collecting ammo. His face is smeared in blood, although I doubt it's his own. Another aircraft explodes in the sky, crashing down in a ball of fire. Guardian's soldiers aren't giving up their new positions easily. The fighting is intense. I've no idea how many we've already killed or how many of our people have gone down.

The battle rages on and on for hours. Everything mixes together: darkness, flames, gunfire, shouts. I lose track of time and any sense of reality. I suddenly can't understand where the heck I am or whom I'm fighting. Am I killing Elimination guards back in the prison during the riot? Am I fighting against Roger's criminals back at the camp? It doesn't really matter at all. All that matters is how I can survive and take as many lives as possible. My consciousness reduces into one single focus, the desire to draw blood. For the first time in my life I genuinely enjoy killing. I have no mercy left in me. No regrets and no doubts. I don't even care so much what I'm fighting for, simply craving to continue killing the people in camo.

This war has stolen anything good or kind left in me. I don't think I'm any better than our enemies at the moment. We're all the same, blinded by hatred and filled with a lust for violence.

At dawn Guardian's troops begin receding, leaving their dead and wounded soldiers behind.

***

The new dawn reveals the horrific ugliness of the battle just fought. Numerous bodies lie spread across the concrete. I stand motionless in the middle of the street, still tightly clutching my rifle. Dried blood covers my hands and uniform. I can't take my eyes off the dead.

Kitty runs toward me, laughing loudly.

"We won!" she yells, hugging me. "We've defeated Guardian's breakers!"

I don't react.

Kitty leaves me be and approaches Dave. She hugs him as well, shrieking in excitement.

"Victory!" Dave exclaims.

Marcus watches them blankly. I notice Jessie standing alone several yards away, also gazing upon the fallen. Victor sits on the concrete, nervously smoking a cigarette. So far, I count only three recruits left from our squad, each wandering about aimlessly with dazed looks in their eyes. I guess the other volunteers have been killed.

Chase arrives on the scene, issuing a command to help collect the bodies. We start the gruesome work, dragging the corpses to one side of the street.

A group of medics treat the injured, processing the more serious cases into the overcrowded hospitals. I try not to listen to their moans, focusing on the current task at hand. Kitty helps Dave and Marcus collect ammo. She has stopped laughing and is now quietly sobbing. Another girl outfitted in black weeps freely, kneeling beside a corpse. Nobody interrupts her grief.

I continue moving the bodies. Strangely, I don't feel anything at all. Neither sorrowful nor the slightest bit upset. I'm completely numb on the inside and my thoughts wander somewhere far away. This is war, and I simply can't allow myself to fall apart now. So I force myself to mechanically perform my work, without thinking about what I'm actually doing.

An hour into the task I bend over a dead girl, gripping her legs and pulling. I glance at her blood-smeared face and freeze. It's Chelsey. She's still holding the trophy gun in her stiffened hand.

I drop to a knee beside her body, checking her neck for pulse. I already know she's dead, but refuse to accept it. I close my eyes and sit unmoving for a few moments. I suddenly smell a whiff of chlorine from Carrel's lab, something I haven't experienced for a while.

I envision Chelsey bouncing around on one leg and giggling in anticipation of regaining her freedom. I remember her asking me to help locate her parents. I think of Chelsey fiercely slamming the gun into the head of a guard, helping me out in a desperate fight. She was a brave and funny girl, someone who just wanted to be free and return to her family.

I realize her blood is on my hands. If I hadn't given her that gun, she wouldn't have participated in the battle. If I hadn't included Chelsey in my plans, she may be still enslaved in the Death Camp, but she'd still be alive.

I remember Lena falling into my arms, after being hit by a bullet from Wheeler's gun. I get a flashback of the girl with a doll-like face bleeding to death back in the woods. I think of Jimmy shielding me with his body and taking my bullet.

It feels like I'm about to cry.

But I never cry, so I instead just stagger several yards off and plop down on the curb. I notice a rifle lying a few feet away from me. An image of a gun barrel pressed into my head comes to mind. I can almost hear the gunshot. I realize it's just a long-term effect after Drake's hypnosis. It seems I often think about shooting myself these days, especially when on the edge of losing my sanity.

"Are you all right?" Vogel asks, approaching.

I force myself to take my eyes off the rifle.

"I'm fine," I lie.

"Elimination is very grateful to you and Oliver's breakers," Vogel says in an official tone of voice. "You all fought very well last night."

"Thank you," I say.

Vogel sits down beside me. I sneak a glimpse at the rifle, thinking of Chelsey.

"Elimination now has approximately eight hundred officers," Vogel says. "Oliver has four hundred recruits left. We haven't yet counted how many city volunteers were killed, but I suppose we can both imagine the number."

"We won't be able to withstand another attack," I say.

"No, we won't," Vogel agrees.

"We can't win this war, can we?" I ask. "Do you still really believe we can win, major?"

"I absolutely believe we will prevail," she answers. "Many more good people will die, but at the end of the day we'll win this war. How about you, Rex? What do you believe?"

I don't answer.

"Rex, look at me," Vogel says softly.

I turn to face her.

"Are you sure you're all right?" she repeats.

I should probably pretend that I'm fine, but I'm tired of pretending.

"People around me keep dying," I blurt out. "No matter what I do or where I go, it always ends up with mass graves and burying somebody. I don't know how to stop it. No matter what decisions I make, it always turns out to be a mistake, and more good people get killed."

I begin telling her about burying the bodies of the recruits killed by Roger's gang. I suddenly catch myself, realizing whom I'm talking to.

"Well," I say. "I guess I don't need to be telling you all this. You've certainly seen enough ugliness in your life."

"I've seen my share," Vogel admits.

"Why did you return to Elimination?" I ask. "I heard you weren't even on duty when all this started. You could have just as easily stayed away."

"It's my job, Rex," she answers. "There was a thousand young boys with rifles, but no commander. They had no clue what to do. How could I leave them?"

I understand very well what Vogel means.

"Why did you choose to work for Elimination?" I ask.

"I followed my father's example," she explains. "I wanted to protect innocent people from criminal breakers. That's what Elimination was originally created for, before Guardian changed everything." She pauses, smiling slightly. "My entire family has served Elimination. I couldn't possibly think of choosing any other career. So it came as quite a surprise when my son chose to study medicine. He explained how he wanted to save lives, not take them." She looks at me sharply. "But saving lives is ultimately what we're trying to do here, isn't it?"

"I don't know," I say. "I'm afraid I've taken far more lives than saved."

"You really think so?" she wonders.

"I believe you realize why Guardian attacked the city," I answer. "He must know I'm here. He probably wanted to prove what he can do in case I disobey. All these people are dead because of me." I motion toward a pile of bodies. "If I hadn't shown up, they'd be still alive."

I continue speaking, although I'm not sure why I'm telling all this to Vogel. She frowns, saying quietly, "Please stop."

I become silent.

"Rex, you're just a very young man who had to go through too much in life," she says. "You shouldn't blame yourself for everything that's happened. This war is not your fault. You really need to quit thinking that way."

I remember Emily slapping my face and blaming me for anything she could come up with. I look straight into Vogel's eyes. They seem kind and worried.

"You're not planning to kill me, are you?" I suddenly ask.

Vogel lets out a laugh. "Do you really think I'd tell you, if I planned to kill you?"

I can't help from grinning. The question was ridiculous.

"I'm not your enemy," Vogel adds, and I believe her.

She looks at me with concern and touches my forehead in a kind, motherly gesture. Her hand feels pleasant and warm. I remain motionless. Emily has never done that for me.

"You have a fever," Vogel sighs.

I don't reply.

"You need to rest," she advises. "Return to headquarters and get a few hours of sleep. Tomorrow, we'll begin planning a mission to obtain Holtzmann's drug from the Death Camp. I'll provide you with an aircraft and support team."

Having spoken, Vogel gets to her feet, heading off toward a group of officers. I follow her with my eyes.

I no longer think about shooting myself. All my thoughts now focus on the coming mission. That is exactly why my team has come here, to gain use of Elimination resources for Holtzmann's experiment.

I smile widely. I choose to believe we can still defeat Guardian and win this war. And I still have a chance to fix some mistakes.

I rise to my feet to go look for Kitty and my team. We all need to get some rest. Tomorrow's a new day.

PART 2

CHAPTER 13

By the time Kitty and I return to our quarters, we can barely stand. I fall flat on the bed, thinking how I could probably sleep for the rest of my life.

Not today. I hardly begin seeing my usual nightmares before somebody starts banging on the door. I sit up, staring around blankly. The room is spinning. A few long moments pass before I realize where the heck I am and what the source of the bothering noise is.

"Who's there?" I ask, hardly recognizing my own voice.

"It's me," Victor answers. "Holtzmann requested your and Kitty's presence."

"Gosh," I groan, falling back down on the bed. My head hurts. I feel beaten up and unrested. I glance at the alarm clock, but can't focus my eyes well enough to see the numbers. "What time is it?" I ask.

"4 PM."

It means I've slept for 5 hours, but it feels more like 5 minutes.

"C'mon, champ," Victor calls. "Get a move on."

"No way," I answer. "We're too tired."

I turn over and press my face back into the pillow.

"Holtzmann needs you and Kitty to help hypnotize the injured," Victor says. "Doctors are running out of anesthetic and have to perform the surgeries without."

My mind suddenly clears.

"Give us ten minutes," I sigh. "We're coming."

"Hurry it up," Victor repeats.

I reach for Kitty who's curled up in a fetal position on the other side of the bed.

"Wakey-wakey," I say softy, touching her shoulder. "Holtzmann needs our help."

"No, please," Kitty sobs, wrapping her arms tightly around her pillow as if it's the most precious thing in the world.

"I'll be coming alone," I say to Victor.

"Holtzmann requested the both of you," he protests from behind the closed door.

"I don't give a damn what Holtzmann wants," I answer. "Kitty needs to sleep."

I sit on the edge of the bed for a minute, steadying myself. My head is still dizzy and I can barely will myself to keep my eyes open. I have to do something to snap myself out of this zombie-like trance.

Swaying and stumbling, I stagger into the bathroom, crawl into the shower and turn on the cold water. The shock takes my breath and I suffer a flashback from when Elimination guards sprayed me with cold water from a hose. At least I begin to wake up. Shivering, I return to the room and begin dressing.

Kitty sits up, gazing over at me. Her eyes are slightly crossed and her hair is sticking out in all directions, giving her somewhat of a resemblance to a scarecrow.

"Where do you think you're going?" she asks.

"To help out over at the hospital," I answer.

"Why didn't you wake me? Are you trying to slip away without me?"

I don't say anything.

"I'm coming with you," Kitty says decisively as she rolls out of bed, dropping to the floor.

"Careful!" I exclaim.

"I'm all right," she assures me. "I have to protect you."

I finish dressing and wait for Kitty to get ready. She struggles with her boots.

"Something is wrong," she complains. "It doesn't fit right."

"You're putting the left boot on your right foot," I explain, trying not to laugh.

"Really?" Kitty asks, staring at her foot in confusion. I don't think she fully comprehends what I've just said.

I kneel in front on her, help put her boots on and lace them up.

"You saved me," Kitty utters. "But I'm still not sure I can walk."

"If you can't walk, you can't help hypnotize patients," I say. "Why not just go back to sleep? I'll return in a few hours."

"No please, don't leave me!" Kitty complains, reaching out for me.

I end up having to carry Kitty all the way down to the main exit of the building.

"Be careful, don't drop me," she grumbles, as we're descending a staircase. "If you drop me, you'll be in really big trouble."

"One more complaint and I know somebody who will have to walk," I warn.

We pass by a crowd of protestors outside, ignoring their hateful shouts, and head toward the large Elimination SUV. We get in the back seat, and Victor settles in up front. I see Dave behind the steering wheel smiling in the rearview.

"Hey guys!" he exclaims. "I'm your driver today! Here you go, I brought sandwiches. Thought you might be hungry."

He hands me a paper sack.

"I feel sick and don't think I can eat anything right now," Kitty states, reaching for the sack. She ends up wolfing down two sandwiches without much chewing. After she finishes, Kitty throws a still hungry look my direction. I offer her half of my sandwich, which she promptly devours.

"I feel much better now," she says.

"Where's Jessie?" Dave wonders. "I thought she'd be joining us."

"She's only a borderline level 2 breaker," Victor answers. "Not strong enough for Holtzmann's task."

Dave seems disappointed. I feel sorry for him. I still don't understand why he chose Jessie for his love interest. She's at least 5 years older and hates Elimination officers. He has no chance.

We finally arrive at the overcrowded hospital and enter the hall, searching for the professor. We have to walk around the injured sitting around on the floor. This place simply doesn't have enough beds for this number of patients.

Holtzmann approaches our group, a joyful grin spread across his face.

"This is a significant step in developing trust between ordinary humans and breakers," he says. "Hypnotizing patients during surgeries is a perfect example of utilizing breaker abilities in a peaceful, productive way."

It might seem being in the presence of so many suffering people would distress the unstable professor. But I can't detect the slightest bit of worry in him. Holtzmann seems almost giddy. Maybe scientists don't react to tragedies the way as common people do.

We proceed toward the surgery rooms to assist the doctors. I begin hypnotizing the patients, trying not to pay too close attention to their wounds. I don't bother asking their names and don't look at their faces. I try to make everything as impersonal as I possibly can because I can't allow for any disruptions to my concentration.

Two hours later we take a break, walking outside to get a breath of fresh air. I hold a sobbing Kitty, rubbing her back and telling how everything will be all right. Victor nervously smokes several feet away. I have a splitting headache from hypnotizing so many people. I don't want to return inside, but what other choice do we really have?

Our group works in the hospital for three more hours, then Holtzmann sends us to the refugee center to check on patients recently arrived. Entering the building, we meet Rebecca and Marian in the hall. Kitty quickly cheers up, hugging my sister. She's so fascinated by Marian that she even forgets to express any jealousy toward Rebecca this time. Chuckling and whispering, my sister and Kitty walk to the opposite side of the hall and settle down into chairs.

I ask Rebecca whether they need our help with any injured.

"Not really," Rebecca answers. "The majority of these new arrivals only have cuts and bruises along with some stress related issues. Most lost family members and homes during the bombing."

We become quiet for a spell. I notice the dark circles under Rebecca's eyes. Her cheeks seem hollow.

"Are you doing all right?" I ask.

"I'm fine," she answers, smiling weakly. "We're working very long shifts, but it's nothing. I'm glad I can do something to help these victims." She pauses, giving me a strange look. "I sometimes wonder whether there's something wrong with me."

"What are you talking about?" I wonder.

"I'm not really sure," Rebecca sighs. "Seeing all these people suffering should make one upset. But I don't feel unhappy. I'm sorry for them, but at the same time being here makes me feel good. Caring about all these people feels like..." She breaks off, struggling to express herself.

"Like having family," I finish her phrase.

"That's exactly what I meant," Rebecca says in surprise. "How did you know?"

I shrug, unwilling to offer further explanation. Creating an illusion of having a family is a personal field of expertise.

"Has my sister caused any trouble?" I ask, changing the subject.

"No trouble whatsoever," Rebecca answers. "Marian has helped out a lot, taking care of injured and calming people down. She's very compassionate. She never complains or refuses to do the dirty work."

I find this surprising.

"Do you have any counseling in this center?" I wonder.

Rebecca confirms that they have a department of psychology for victims dealing with post traumatic complications.

"Do they have any literature I could borrow?" I ask.

"What kind of literature?"

"Something about survivors of child abuse. Maybe something about domestic violence also."

Rebecca looks at me in astonishment, then seems to understand.

"Is this for Marian?" she asks. I nod. "I think we may have something. I'd also recommend some therapy, but unfortunately our psychologists specialize in different areas and they're really busy."

"That's all right."

I don't think Marian would agree to work with any doctors anyway, although nothing can ever be certain with her. She's absolutely unpredictable.

"Good evening," somebody says from behind.

I turn to see a tall girl in her late twenties, with long brown hair and dark expressive eyes. She's wearing an old baggy sweater and poorly fitting jeans obviously provided by the shelter. I notice a large fading bruise on her neck.

"Rebecca, could you please introduce me to your friend?" the girl asks. She doesn't look directly at me, keeping her eyes downcast.

"Of course," Rebecca says. "Rex, this is my friend Cynthia. She lost her home recently."

"Nice to meet you, Cynthia," I say, extending my hand.

She blushes. Her handshake is very weak, and she still doesn't dare to make eye contact with me.

"It's a pleasure to meet you, sir," she mutters.

"How do you like living in the center?" I ask.

"I'm very thankful to have found shelter here," Cynthia answers. "Everybody has been very kind to me, especially Rebecca. I'd almost forgotten how genuinely kind and nice people can still be." Her large eyes suddenly fill with tears. "Guardian's soldiers destroyed my entire town. They burned homes and tortured innocent people. I still don't understand how I've managed to survive."

Her voice breaks, and Rebecca hugs her supportively.

"I'm very sorry," I say.

"I'm fine now," Cynthia answers. "We've all had to go through hard times during this war."

I become quiet. I suddenly feel ashamed for what Guardian's breakers have done to this girl and her family.

Rebecca leaves us, going to search for the books I requested. Cynthia blushes again, asking whether she could speak with me a little longer. I assure her that it would be fine. We sit, waiting for Rebecca to return. Cynthia smiles, remaining silent. I notice Kitty watching suspiciously from across the room. I wink at her.

"I'm really happy to meet you in person, Rex," Cynthia begins. "Shall I call you Rex or would you prefer I call you sir?"

"Whatever you like," I answer.

"I'll call you Rex then," Cynthia says. She moves in a little closer, stretching her full lips into a wide smile. "I used to imagine how I'd someday whisper your name into your ear."

It takes a moment to realize what she's just said.

"Pardon me?" I say.

"You're a hero to me, Rex," Cynthia says, now looking straight into my eyes. "Many residents in this city don't trust breakers, but I'm thrilled you've arrived. I know you're different from the rest. You want to stop this war and protect ordinary people like me. I admire your noble intentions."

"Well, thank you," I say.

"I used to watch TV documentaries about you," Cynthia continues. "And I collected every newspaper article I could find. The journalists wrote many bad things about you, but I never believed any of that. I could always feel in my heart how special you really are."

She pauses, blinking a few times and smiling. I have to admit she looks awfully cute doing so, but I'd prefer her to behave a little less enamored. I'm sure Cynthia is aware that I already have a girlfriend.

"You're such a fortuitous man, Rex," Cynthia sighs. "Life has provided you with such amazing opportunities. You're already a leader amongst breakers, and in the future you might even become leader of the entire country if you so choose. The possibilities are very exciting! I'd do anything to have what you have." She pauses, taking in a deep breath. "And I've also heard other interesting stories about you."

"Those stories are exaggerated," I assure her.

"I'd love to learn which stories are true and which are not. Maybe we could meet later and continue this conversation alone? I realize most ordinary people would be scared of being alone with a breaker, because you could so easily manipulate and take advantage of a girl. But I trust you, Rex. I believe you wouldn't use hypnosis to take advantage of me, would you?"

She gazes into my eyes, smiling charmingly. I really don't know how to answer. I don't want to hurt her feelings, but at the same time don't want to encourage her.

"I don't enjoy hypnotizing people," I say, although I realize it sounds stupid.

"I really wouldn't mind if you hypnotized me," Cynthia adds. "And I happen to have no resistance for hypnosis. You would be able to do whatever you pleased. So would you like to get together later, somewhere a little more private?"

Cynthia slowly runs her tongue across her lips, staring longingly into my eyes.

"Um, well," I say. "I'm very sorry, but I'm really busy. I don't think I could find the extra time."

She smirks, and for a split second her expression becomes angry.

"Who's keeping you so busy? That little girl?" she asks, motioning in Kitty's direction.

That's it, I think, I've had enough of this.

"I'd best be going now," I say coldly, getting up.

"Oh please, stay," Cynthia begs, grabbing my sleeve. "I'm very sorry if I said anything wrong. Please, don't be angry with me."

She quickly transforms back into an embarrassed, awkward girl. I sit down in the chair, watching her warily.

"I'm so sorry," Cynthia repeats, gazing away. "When life falls apart and all the people you care about start dying around you, you have to find something to hold onto. One needs to have some hope in life, otherwise you'll lose your mind." She turns to face me. "You've become my hope, Rex."

I don't answer.

"I'm sure we'll meet again and get to know each other much better," Cynthia adds. "Perhaps you don't fully appreciate all the opportunities life brings your way. Let's see whether I can help change that."

She quickly leans in toward me, grabbing me around my neck and placing her open mouth over mine. I push her away, being taken by surprise. I hadn't seen that coming. I get to my feet, moving away.

"Stop acting like that," I say. "I'm not interested, all right?"

Laughing cheerfully, Cynthia leaves, passing by Rebecca holding an armful of books and staring at me wide-eyed.

"Is she always like that?" I ask.

"I'm very sorry," Rebecca mutters, although she has no reason to apologize. "I've no idea what came over her. She's usually very shy and quiet. I've never seen her act that way before."

"It's fine," I say. "I'll survive."

"She's really been through a lot recently," Rebecca explains. "I understand a gang of breakers held her hostage for a few weeks. They were dangerous criminals. She still suffers anxiety and panic attacks."

I nod in understanding, once again feeling sympathetic toward Cynthia. She must be totally messed up.

Rebecca hands me the books and leaves, returning to her work. Kitty and I head toward the exit.

"It's unbelievable!" Kitty groans. "I can't leave you alone for ten minutes without women drooling over you."

"C'mon, Kitty," I say, laughing. "It was just one confused and messed up girl."

"I don't like her!" Kitty snorts. "You'd be better off continuing your little affair with Rebecca. At least she's classy."

"Kitty, there's nothing between Rebecca and me."

"I know," she admits, giggling. "But I like to imagine there is. It's just so much fun bringing you into trouble."

I roll my eyes. Kitty punches my arm, making a silly face.

We return to our quarters around midnight. I crawl into bed, instantly passing out. I continue seeing red-stained bandages and smelling chlorine in my sleep. Cynthia suddenly approaches and presses her lips into mine. Tasting blood in my mouth, I understand she bit me.

I wake at dawn, Cynthia still on my mind. I have a strong hunch that there is something deeper to her words and behavior, something I couldn't quite understand. It bothers me a while longer until I fall asleep again.

***

During the day my team, along with Marcus and Chase, meet in Vogel's office. We discuss the details of our new mission, figuring out who will be going to the Death Camp to acquire the drug. Holtzmann volunteers, but I protest.

"We can't risk you, professor," I say. "You're our lead scientist."

"I'll remind you of my participation during two previous riots," Holtzmann argues. "I'm more than capable of taking part in a mission of this nature."

"This mission will be like nothing we've done before," I disagree.

We argue for a few minutes, and Holtzmann finally proclaims that he's the only one who is capable of identifying the drug. I hesitate. He's got a point on one hand, because determining the correct drug might be problematic without him. But on the other hand, allowing the unstable professor to take part in such a dangerous mission could be setting ourselves up for disaster. What if he has one of his fits?

Vogel finally authorizes Holtzmann's participation in the mission, assigning Dave as his personal bodyguard. Dave seems very proud. My participation raises more doubts in her.

"I don't want to stay behind while others risk their lives," I persist stubbornly.

"Rex, you're the Beta subject in Holtzmann's experiment," Vogel reminds me.

"I'll be all right," I assure her. "It's not my first song and dance, major."

"Your last dance ended with a bullet in the head and a subsequent four months imprisonment," she adds.

"All the more reason I should go," I say. "I spent four months in the Death Camp. I know that prison inside and out."

Vogel hesitates, looking me over carefully. I smile back at her. I wonder whether her unwillingness to send me on this mission isn't actually more personal. I remember her unexpected kindness toward me after the battle. I can't help wondering whether I remind Vogel of her deceased son, although I fully realize the utter weirdness of having such thoughts.

"All right," she finally gives in. "Marcus will be assigned to protect you during the mission."

"What?!" Kitty cries out. "I'm his protection! That's my job!"

Kitty and I spend the next ten minutes fighting over her participation in the mission.

"I'm going on this mission no matter what you say!" Kitty yells. She turns to Vogel and says in a trembling voice, "I have to be there to protect him. Every time we separate, he always winds up getting shot or captured. If you let Rex enter the Death Camp without me, you're likely to lose your Beta subject."

There's sense in her words. Any time I leave Kitty behind, I get myself into trouble. Still, I'm not willing to allow her to participate in what may turn out to be a suicide mission.

Unfortunately, Vogel doesn't care much what I think. She authorizes Kitty's participation. I try to protest, but I'm not the commander.

Chase remains silent during the entire discussion. Vogel finally requires him to provide us with his opinion about the plan.

"Nothing's wrong with the plan," Chase answers. "But I don't care for the idea itself."

"Please elaborate," Vogel requests.

"It's just not doable," Chase says. "It's like playing around with a hornet's nest. If anything goes wrong, there will be hundreds of guards coming after them. It's just plain crazy."

"Yeah, but we're the psycho team!" Kitty exclaims. "That's our one advantage. Nobody will expect us to do something this crazy."

"I think you're committing suicide," Chase sighs.

"Can you offer any better ideas how to obtain the drug from the Death Camp?" Vogel asks. Chase remains quiet. "Then we have no choice but to accept some risk," she adds.

The major is about to say something more, but an officer bursts into the room, wearing an alarmed expression. I realize something unusual must have happened because nobody would interrupt Vogel's meeting otherwise.

"Ma'am, one of our patrols have reported suspicious activity in an abandoned factory," he informs. "We believe this location to be where the terrorists are holed up."

My heart begins beating faster. I hope his information is correct. I think about the scorched hospital and all those innocent victims who died in the fire. I'd like to personally kill as many of those terrorists as I possibly can.

CHAPTER 14

I don't get the chance to kill any terrorists. Vogel refuses to let my team participate in the bust. According to her, we're to continue preparing for the Death Camp mission. So we remain stuck inside headquarters, waiting anxiously for Vogel to return.

I pace around the dining room, while the others chat nervously over tea and coffee. I approach the window and watch a growing crowd of protestors walk carrying posters outside the prison fence. I drink a cup of coffee, angrily staring at the clock. Time seems to freeze, as the clock's hands appear glued on the same spot.

Dave and Kitty pass time amusing themselves with choosing a new name for Elimination.

"Elimination sounds too aggressive," Dave says. "Things have changed around here, so we need a new name. I think Defense sounds much better."

"It doesn't really fit," Kitty disagrees. "Just listen. Elimination, Retaliation and now Defense. No, it wouldn't do."

"How about Protection?" Dave offers. "Or Salvation."

"We need something cooler," Kitty says. "Something like Elimination, but only more positive."

"Illumination," Dave suggests. "It's like we're bringing light to the world, fighting the dark forces of evil."

"And perhaps even changing light bulbs for free on our days off," Marcus comments. "Do we really need a new name? I don't think Vogel would approve anyway."

"A new name is essential," Kitty insists. "How can we win this war without a cool name? Rex, what do you think?"

I can't concentrate on their naming troubles at the moment. All my thoughts swirl around the terrorists, mixed with flashbacks of burned corpses. I decide to go check on Marian to distract myself, although it may not be the best idea right now. My current state of nervousness combined with Marian's spitefulness may prove an explosive mixture.

I walk through the long prison passageway, knock on the door and enter. My sister is sitting on the bed, wrapped in a blanket and reading a thick book. She looks sleepy, so I guess she's just woken up.

"Hey Marian," I say. "How are you doing?"

She gives me a blank stare.

"Rebecca was telling me how you helped her out at the center," I add, smiling. "So you like working there?"

My sister scowls, throwing the book at me. I duck and the book hits the wall, dropping to the floor.

"What do you want from me?!" Marian shouts. "Why are you always sneaking around?"

Surprisingly, her outburst raises no emotion in me.

"Marian, I know exactly what you're doing," I say softly. "But it won't work. No matter what you say or do, you can't make me hurt you."

"We'll see," she growls, throwing her pillow.

I catch the pillow and pick up the book from the floor. I approach Marian, and she screams.

"C'mon, knock it off," I say, placing the pillow and the book beside her. "We both know you're not really scared of me."

Marian doesn't answer.

"Rebecca had a lot of good things to say about you," I say. "I was very proud of you. I still am."

My sister stares intently into space.

I return to the dining room, thinking about her. I wonder whether she will ever heal. Emily used to pour out her violence and hatred on me, while I was around. She must have turned on Marian after I left.

A couple hours later Chase enters the dining area, looking rattled. We all turn to face him.

"The information was correct," he announces. "We found and confronted the terrorists. They're all dead."

"You killed all of them?" I ask in surprise. I don't mind, but I expected Vogel to spare a few for interrogation.

"No," Chase answers. "They shot themselves before we had a chance to capture anybody."

***

"I don't get it," Marcus says during supper. "Why would they do that?"

"They might have been programmed to commit suicide in case of capture," Victor suggests. "Guardian could have used hypnosis for that particular deed."

I get a sensation of déjà vu. I recall an officer blowing his brains out a moment before I could corner him.

"Hypnosis doesn't work that way, does it?" Dave wonders. "You can't program somebody to kill himself."

I remember fantasizing about killing myself, pressing the gun barrel to my head.

"It's possible," I answer. "Hypnosis can have lingering after-effects."

"I think those terrorists were hiding something," Chase says. "They preferred killing themselves to being taken alive. Perhaps they didn't want to reveal information about a second group of terrorists active in the city. Vogel subscribes to this theory."

I realize it's a likely scenario. Guardian could potentially have planted several terrorist cells in the city. It means nothing is over. We may have to deal with additional acts of terror.

"I still don't get it," Marcus repeats. "Why bother with all the conspiracy and sending in terrorists. Guardian has more than enough soldiers to take this city, doesn't he? Why not just overrun us?"

"He's a sadist who enjoys the process," I answer. "He perceives this war as a grand play, one he's staged. I guess he doesn't want everything to be over too quickly. In addition, he's a mega control freak obsessed with leadership. He likes to put people on their knees. So if he just marches in and kills everybody, he won't have anybody to torture and submit to his will."

Marcus frowns, a puzzled expression on his face.

"Maybe Guardian still entertains hopes that you'll join him," Chase says, looking at me.

"Maybe so," I answer. "But it's not happening."

"I wonder why not," Chase questions.

I turn to him. "What do you mean?"

"Why didn't you join him?" he wonders. "He offered you a pretty sweet deal."

"Would you make such a deal?" I ask.

"Of course not, but I'm not a breaker."

I become silent for a while, not quite sure whether to punch Chase or let it slide. Is that what he really thinks about me?

"Jerk," I answer.

I expect him to snap back, but Chase doesn't reply. The room becomes quiet, and I can now distinctly hear the protestors shouting outside. We now have two different groups of people raging out there. The first group consists of our traditional haters, ones who throw rocks at the windows and demand all breakers to leave. The second group arrived just this morning, supporting us and expressing gratitude for helping defend the city. The protestors became more active, confronting the supporters. So we now have to listen to their shouting and whistling all day long.

"Stinking terrorists!" I hear them yell. "Go home, breakers!"

Kitty groans, approaching the window. She opens it up, sticks her head outside and yells back, "We don't have a home!"

"Stop it, Kitty," I say. "Get away from the window."

She's not listening. She continues shouting at the protestors, and they shout right back, getting more agitated. Dave joins her.

"These breakers are good!" he yells, sticking his head out. "They're friends! They help us!"

"Traitor!" somebody shouts at him.

"What did you call me?" Dave bursts out.

"Get away from the window, idiot!" his brother commands.

"They're insulting my friends!" Dave snaps back at Marcus.

I get to my feet, intent on dragging both Kitty and Dave away from the window. But I'm too late, as they both rush out of the room, shouting how they're going to straighten out those protestors. I run after them, commanding them to stop. Marcus follows, loudly cursing his brother. We all exit outside, facing the protestors.

Only a few officers hold the ground between the prison entrance and the crowd. Upon seeing Kitty and Dave, several people lunge forward, quickly overwhelming the guards. Dave jumps in against one of the overly aggressive protestors, knocking him down. Others grab him along with Kitty, throwing them to the ground. Most of these people probably don't intend to cause any real harm to anybody, but their current state of agitation pushes them overboard. I don't think they fully realize what they're doing at the moment.

I charge into the people swarming over Kitty. I kick and push them off while simultaneously projecting my thoughts, but manage to put only a couple of them under.

"Get back!" I yell. "Let her go!"

Somebody throws a stone. It smacks me squarely in the forehead. I don't feel any pain, but somehow end up lying on my back. Multiple arms grab hold and begin dragging me off.

A cold blast of water knocks the protestors off. They let out yells of surprise, and begin to recede. I scramble to my feet, looking around. A squad of officers led by Vogel carry hoses, shooting water into the crowd. The protestors and supporters alike quickly disperse.

Kitty sits a few feet away, dazed. I help her up and lead her back inside. Once we pass the entrance, I grab Kitty by her shoulders, yelling, "What the hell were you thinking?!"

Kitty stares back at me in utter horror.

"Your head is bleeding," she says.

I touch my forehead and look at my fingers. They're stained with blood. I sit down on the floor, overcome by dizziness. The wound suddenly begins hurting, and a bit of nausea rises in my throat.

"I'm so sorry," Kitty sobs, kneeling beside me.

"I'm fine," I say. "I've been through worse."

Marcus enters the building, dragging his brother in tow and smacking his head. Dave mumbles something incoherent, having the look of a whipped dog.

Vogel and Chase approach. Kitty lets out a whimper, taking cover behind my back. Vogel glares at me.

"What were you thinking, Rex?" she asks, repeating my own question. "Were you really going to take on that raging crowd of protestors? I believe you know better than that. There's a certain protocol to follow in such cases."

I don't answer. Vogel sighs, looking me over.

"Chase, lead our Beta subject to the infirmary," she commands.

Chase tightly grabs my elbow, helping me up. "Easy now, breaker."

He leads me along the passageway. Kitty doesn't follow, probably being too ashamed to face me.

A doctor examines my wound and provides several stitches.

"Just like the good old days," Chase comments, laughing. I'm getting really tired with him.

The officers managed to restrain and lock up some of the more aggressive protestors, so I decide to pay one a visit. I wonder whether I can change his mind about hating breakers. Chase shakes his head in obvious disapproval of the idea, but doesn't argue. As we proceed down toward the cellblock, Marcus joins us.

"What does Elimination intend to do with the new inmates?" I ask.

"Vogel will probably order them shot," Chase answers.

"What?!" I exclaim.

"I'm just joking," he says, laughing. "We'll send them to clear debris. Have them do something useful besides all that yelling."

Chase seems surprised that I fell for his joke. But what else can I expect from Elimination? Executing prisoners is something they've been doing for a long time.

The handcuffed protestor begins shouting insults as soon as we enter the cell. He's a young guy about my age, filled with anger and hatred. I remain silent, letting him say whatever he's got on his mind. The guy rages for ten solid minutes, mostly repeating the same stuff. He believes all breakers to be merciless killers and terrorists.

"I agree that there are plenty of evil breakers in the world," I say calmly after the guy finally quiets down. "But not all breakers are the same. Our group came to help defend this city from Guardian's army."

"I'll never trust any breaker," the guy blurts out. "You're all terrorists!"

"The first acts of terror were organized by ordinary people," I protest. "Warden Browning and Captain Wheeler were responsible."

"That's a lie!" he shouts, and begins with another round of outrageous insults. I listen for a while before deciding that I'm wasting my time. No matter what I say, I won't change his mind. He's a hater.

We leave the cell, walking back in gloomy silence.

"So what do you make of all this?" Chase asks me.

"Nothing," I answer.

"All those insults don't bother you?" he wonders.

"Why should they? I actually agree with him on a few matters. I think it would be a much better world if breakers never existed."

Chase and Marcus both stare at me, open-mouthed.

"Well, I must admit I've never heard a breaker say anything like that before," Chase says.

"Well, enjoy it," I answer.

"Rex, you're a true Elimination officer," Marcus comments.

"Breakers aren't freaks," Chase says. "It's just you, Rex. I think you're the main problem. Remember the day I captured you?"

I nod. It would be a hard day to forget.

"If I could travel back in time, I'd let you slip away," Chase says. "All this crap started right after Elimination captured you."

He smiles, obviously joking. But I wonder whether there's not some grain of truth in his words. I'm the one who organized Retaliation and executed the Elimination leaders. Although I'm not a terrorist as the protestor claimed, the blood of too many people are on my hands.

***

The night before our mission I see Chelsey in my dreams. We're back at the parade, pushing through a crowd of breakers. I tightly grip her wrist, dragging her toward safety. But no matter what I do or where we go, Chelsey always winds up dead. I repeatedly find myself dragging her stiffened corpse along behind me. I look into her deadened, glazed eyes and Chelsey suddenly whispers, "Alex."

I can't understand how she knows my real name.

I awaken to a light knocking at the door and a soft girlish whimper. It's still dark, and Kitty sleeps peacefully beside me.

"Alex," Marian sobs from outside the room.

Worried, I jump off the bed and approach the door.

"What's happened?" I ask.

"I feel bad," she answers, crying.

I get a flashback of our speaking through the closed door years ago. Marian was begging me to stay, and I promised to come back and steal her away from Emily.

"Just a second," I say. "I'm coming."

I hurriedly put on my pants and open the door, walking into the corridor. My sister is sitting in the hallway on the floor, like a broken doll. Her head lolls to the side and her face is wet from tears. She's barefoot and wearing only underwear with a t-shirt. I notice several old scars along the top of her thighs.

"I feel bad," she repeats, shivering.

"You'll catch cold," I sigh.

I grab my jacket and wrap it around her.

"C'mon, let's get you back to your room," I say, pulling her up.

Marian can't walk. She must have completely worn herself out from crying. I have to carry her the entire way. She whimpers weakly. I put her to bed and cover her with a blanket. I wet a washcloth and wipe her face. My sister stares back at me with big empty eyes.

"I'm just like her, Alex," she whimpers miserably. "I'm the same way sick."

"You're nothing like her," I say.

"What's wrong with me?" Marian questions. "Why do I always have to be so obnoxious and nasty?"

"Nothing's wrong with you," I say, stroking her hair. "Relax now. Get some sleep. You'll feel better in the morning."

She clutches my wrist, holding on tightly.

"Don't leave me," she pleads like a scared five-year-old. "Please, stay here at least until I fall asleep. I'm still afraid of the dark. Monsters are hiding there. Don't you believe me?"

I think about Wheeler and Browning. I remember Roger and his gang.

"I believe you," I say. "I think I've even met a few of them."

"Are you frightened of them, too?"

"Nah. I kill monsters."

"Have you killed all of them?"

I think about Guardian and Hammer. I envision soldiers shooting the prisoners back in the Death Camp.

"There's a few still left," I admit.

Marian becomes quiet, still holding onto my wrist. I sit on the edge of her bed, watching over her and waiting for her to fall asleep. Just as I always did when she was little.

"Alex, do you ever feel like killing yourself?" Marian asks.

"No," I lie. "Never.

"I feel like that all the time."

I don't know how to answer. I look at her bare arm, covered with multiple old scars.

"It's ugly, isn't it?" Marian asks, frowning.

"Nah, it's all right," I answer. "I have much worse scars."

"I'm a fake cutter," she says. "I didn't do it because I wanted to cut or hurt myself. I did it because I wanted to hurt... her."

"Why?"

"Emily wanted me to be beautiful and sweet. So I made myself nasty and ugly. I wanted her to hate me, because I couldn't take her love anymore."

I remember Emily throwing me against the wall. Falling, I hit my head, smearing the wall with blood. Then I had to go beg her for forgiveness.

"She once shoved me outside into the cold and locked the door," Marian says. "I was only wearing a nightgown. I spent all night outside by the door, crying and pleading for her to let me in. I was about ten."

"I'm very sorry," I whisper.

"I hated her," my sister says. "And I couldn't get along without her. I was always running away and coming back." She looks at me, puzzled. "Why do I miss her so much, Alex? How can you hate and love somebody so much at the same time?"

"I don't really know," I admit.

Marian stares into the dark, still and quiet again. I watch her. She catches my gaze and our eyes lock for a few moments.

"I'm so sorry I left you," I suddenly say. "But I'm back now. Just tell me how I can help. Is here anything at all I can do to make you feel better?"

"Tell me a story," she says.

"What story?"

"You know. The one about dinosaurs."

I can't help from smiling. My sister really is full of surprises. One day she fantasizes about becoming a stripper, and the next she wants to hear a childish fairy tale. I begin telling our made up story about a magic land with dinosaurs. It's the same one I used to tell her when she was little.

Listening, she closes her eyes and her face relaxes. She finally calms down enough and falls asleep. I watch her for a few more minutes before quietly leaving the room.

Back in our quarters, I find Kitty sitting on the bed. She's fully awake and worried.

"Is Marian all right?" she asks.

I nod, although I doubt that any of us are fully okay.

"She's sick, isn't she?" Kitty asks in a sad voice.

"A little, I guess," I answer, getting back into bed. "She's been through a lot."

"We've all been through a lot," Kitty sighs. "You know that your sister loves you, don't you?"

"I hope so."

"Of course, she does. That's why she's so mean to you. She's just scared."

"Scared of what?"

"That she's not good enough for you."

I remain silent for a few moments, thinking about Emily. Letting her hurt you was the only way to receive her love. That's the life my sister got used to.

"That's nonsense," I say.

"Sometimes I worry about the same thing," Kitty confesses.

"That's even more nonsense," I assure her.

"I'm also worried for you," she adds.

"Let's quit with all this worrying and go to sleep," I suggest. "We'll have to be ready for the mission in a few hours."

Kitty frowns, gazing up at the ceiling. I expect her to say something else, but she snuggles in close and quickly falls asleep.

I remain awake, holding her and looking at the window. It's almost dawn. Today, I'll be returning to the Death Camp.

CHAPTER 15

Our aircraft flies steadily toward the Death Camp. After two hours in the air, we're getting very close to our destination. Everyone on board remains quiet, waiting to land.

Our plan may be just bold enough to have a chance at being successful. We're to land a couple of miles away from the prison. Victor's agents, already planted in the camp, are to create an explosion and fire at the ammunition dump as a diversion. The explosion will be the signal to begin making our way inside the Camp. Our squad is dressed in Retaliation camo, so we hopefully can blend in and pass through unnoticed in the confusion. We'll locate the lab, obtain the drug and leave the same way we came in.

Although the plan seems more than feasible, I can't shake my doubts. There are too many unknown variables. What if they're expecting us? What if the guards recognize our faces?

I become so nervous that I can't keep still. I take a deep breath to relax, telling myself that everything will go according to plan. As long as we get in undetected, things should go smoothly. We'll obtain the drug and an hour later we'll be flying back to Elimination headquarters, safe and sound.

I almost manage to persuade myself of a quick return to the city, when a loud explosion shudders the aircraft. We go into a sickening spin. Everything turns upside down, and I can no longer understand which way we're flying. I become completely disoriented. The lights flicker off and on.

I can hear nothing except explosions mixed with the sounds of breaking metal. Cables tear apart overhead, sending a shower of electric sparks down on top of us. It all happens so fast that I don't even have time to become startled. Kitty screams, grabbing my hand. The aircraft suddenly drops, rotating a few more dizzying times, before we begin flying more steadily. We are still rocking and losing altitude, but we've at least stopped spinning.

I turn to check on our team. Everybody looks dumbfounded and rattled, but nobody seems to be injured. A white-faced Kitty stares at me.

"What the heck was that?" she asks.

I can hardly hear her. The sound of explosions has ceased, but the engines produce a lot of abnormal rattling and screeching.

"I don't know," I yell. "Something's majorly wrong."

I unfasten my seatbelt and fall to the floor. The turbulence is still severe enough that I struggle to find my feet. Jessie crawls toward me along the aisle.

"We need to check on the pilots!" she shouts.

Together, we crawl on our hands and knees toward the pilot cabin. We find the pilots inside desperately trying to gain control of our battered aircraft. I stare stupidly at the panels with numerous buttons and monitors, attempting to understand what's happening. I glance into the front window, but see nothing except a pitch-black darkness.

"What the hell is happening?" Jessie asks.

"We got hit with a rocket," one of the pilots answers. "Two fighter jets are still on our tail."

Both Jessie and I become speechless. These must be Guardian's aircraft. But how could they have known about our mission?

"Can we make it to the Death Camp?" I ask.

"I don't know," the pilot answers. "We're still losing altitude."

"Are we able to land?" Jessie asks.

"We can't land," he says. "Three of the four engines are gone. As soon as the last one goes, we're going down."

I realize how screwed we are. We won't be sneaking into the Death Camp unnoticed because Guardian is obviously aware about our mission. We can't fly much further and we can't even land. And even if we are lucky enough to survive the coming crash landing, we'll be immediately captured.

"Then crash it into the Death Camp," I command.

Both pilots turn to face me, confused.

"Try to make it to the Death Camp and crash right on top of their heads," I repeat. "There's no going back now."

"Roger that," a pilot says. "We'll do our best."

Jessie and I crawl back to our seats.

"Are we gonna continue the mission?" she asks.

"Do we have a choice?" I answer. "We have to obtain the drug."

I get back into my seat and fasten the seatbelt. The aircraft continues rocking and shaking. I suddenly realize that we're about to fall out of the sky.

Jessie informs the others about the change in plan. Everybody stares at her wide-eyed, but nobody speaks. I look at Holtzmann, becoming worried that the professor might throw a fit. His hands tremble and his face is as pale as death. Dave attempts to calm him. Kitty grabs my hand again, and I feel her sharp fingernails piercing my skin.

I hear another explosion and experience a nauseating sensation of weightlessness. I realize that we're in a free fall. The rattling and screeching become louder. I attempt to calm myself that this aircraft isn't like a regular plane. This particular model was designed with reinforced steel to help withstand crashes and explosions. But I can't quite persuade myself on the idea of a safe landing. I suddenly realize that we're all going to die. As we continue falling, my fear grows into stark horror. And at some point I become so terrified that I stop worrying and thinking altogether. Things are so out of control that there's simply no use in being worried. I close my eyes and relax, just waiting for impact with the ground. The sickening noises become even louder and then everything turns dark.

I must've lost consciousness, because the next thing I know is that somebody is slapping me across my face. I can hear rifle fire and smell gasoline. As I open my eyes, I find myself lying on the floor inside the crashed aircraft. Marcus kneels beside me, shaking me and shouting, "Are you all right?! Can you hear me?!"

"I can hear you," I answer.

"Thank God!" he exclaims. "I thought you were dead."

"I'm fine," I say, although I'm not too certain about that.

I finally realize that at least some have survived the crash.

"Where's Kitty?" I ask.

Marcus helps me up, assuring me that Kitty is all right, too.

"We've lost three officers and the pilots," he adds.

I stand unmoving, steadying myself. Looking around, I notice dead bodies lying on the floor.

"C'mon, we gotta help the others," Marcus says, pulling me toward the open hatch. "Can you hypnotize anyone?"

"I think I can," I answer. "Where are we?"

"Inside the Death Camp. We crashed onto the roof of the prison building. We went straight through it."

I become glad that I was unconscious.

Marcus and I jump out of the hatch, dropping to the floor. It's very dark inside the prison. Gunfire comes in from all different directions. I scramble to my feet, turning back to take a quick glance at the aircraft. It lies on its side like a huge beached whale. The aircraft destroyed the ceiling and took out a few walls of the building. I look up and see the night sky through the giant hole in the roof. I can't believe we're still alive.

Kitty and Jessie along with the survived Elimination officers fire at Guardian's soldiers, keeping them off us. Victor attempts to hypnotize our enemies. Holtzmann lies on his back, semi-conscious and foaming at the mouth. Dave is giving him some assistance. Marcus joins the shootout, and I help Victor hypnotize the guards. Together, we manage to put most of them under. Marcus tosses a few gas canisters into a passageway.

Elimination has run out of sleeping gas so whatever it is won't be knocking anybody unconscious. But it should at least provide cover, besides serving as a threat to the guards. They must believe that the gas is toxic, because they begin receding. We carefully walk through the passageway, shooting down any guards already immobilized by hypnosis. Dave supports Holtzmann, helping him walk. The professor gives us instructions as to what direction we should move. My bad vision in addition to all the smoke doesn't permit me to recognize the place. Kitty has to lead me, tightly holding my hand. I walk, staring straight ahead and feeling blind. Marcus walks beside me, keeping his rifle ready. Jessie, Victor and what's left of the squad of Elimination officers follow closely behind.

We finally make it outside, and I realize why only a small number of Guardian's soldiers confronted us. The rest of them are busy dealing with the fire. The huge building utilized for ammunition storage is entirely enveloped in flames. Heat has caused the massive stock piles of missiles and ammo to detonate, and multiple rockets shoot up overhead into the dark sky. They collapse back onto the prison, exploding and smashing everything in their path. It looks surreal and reminds me of a giant fireworks display. Hundreds of guards run around the prison yard in complete panic. I guess some of them haven't even noticed our crash.

Our team stops for a moment, stunned by the scene. I finally recognize the place, and help Holtzmann navigate our group toward the lab. We move carefully across the prison yard, but don't run into any resistance. The guards are too consumed by the fire to pay any attention to our small squad. It's dark, and they can't make out our faces. We blend in with the crowd, and continue walking toward the lab.

I look around anxiously, worried about running into Guardian. He's not supposed to be inside the Camp tonight, which is the primary reason we planned our mission today. But how can we be certain of his absence since he was obviously tipped off about our plan?

Entering the lab building, we confront a squad of guards.

"Stop!" they command, aiming their weapons at us.

I step forward, letting them see my face.

"What the hell are you doing?" I ask arrogantly. "Move out of our way!"

According to Guardian's previous announcements, I'm their leader. Only a small group of his personal security knows the truth concerning my situation.

The guards stare at me in confusion. The Elimination officers use their moment of hesitation to bring them down. Our squad enters the lab, which consists of many interconnected rooms filled with monitors, medical gurneys and drug storage. Holtzmann now leads us, becoming excited and energetic upon returning to his former lab. He checks the storage, tossing vials of other drugs to the floor while searching for the correct tray. Elimination officers secure the entrance. I look around, suffering a flashback from the time spent in Dr. Carrel's lab. I try to shake off my disturbing memories, but a sharp odor of disinfectant makes it problematic. This place looks and smells exactly the same.

A burst of gunfire makes me turn toward the entrance. The officers along with Jessie fire their rifles at somebody trying to break into the lab.

"Hurry Holtzmann," I say, approaching the officers. Kitty and Marcus stick with me like glue. Dave remains beside Holtzmann, acting as bodyguard during the mission.

"There are too many of them," Jessie says.

Victor, Kitty and I attempt to use hypnosis, but it doesn't affect this group of guards. They continue shooting as they move in closer. I suddenly feel trapped, realizing that there's only one exit to this room and it's now blocked.

Guardian's guards cease fire, and I recognize Hammers' voice yelling, "Hey Rex! Are you in there? All this mess outside and on the roof is your doing, isn't it?"

He pauses, waiting for a response. I remain silent.

"Very impressive!" he shouts. "But you should have simply used the main gates. We'd have welcomed your return home."

I realize this standoff can't last forever. Hammer has many more men. They could easily overwhelm us, should he give the order to storm the lab.

"Last chance, Rex!" Hammer yells. "Come out now and we'll spare your life. Guardian is still interested in your services."

I remain quiet, thinking. Jessie watches me suspiciously. I don't understand why she has any doubts in me.

"If you don't come out now, we'll use grenades," Hammer threatens. I have no doubts concerning his willingness to kill all of us.

Holtzmann signals that he's finally found the right drug, showing a plastic bag filled with white crystals. Unfortunately, we have no way out of this room.

"Stupid fool!" Hammer shouts. "You don't fit the role of leader. You never appreciated what Guardian offered. He should have chosen me as leader of this army. I'd serve him well."

I recall how much Hammer is obsessed with leadership. I might try to use his desire for control to manipulate him.

I clear my throat and say loudly, "That's the exact reason why Guardian didn't choose you, Hammer! You have no pride. True leaders don't serve anybody higher. They dominate and rule."

My statement must make Hammer furious. He shouts, "Shut up, traitor! You're serving Elimination. You've betrayed your own kind."

"Are you so sure about that?" I ask. "What do you know about my motives, Hammer? I'm not serving Elimination. I'm just using them. As soon as I get what I want, I'll rid myself of them."

My words sound awfully fake even to me.

"Elimination won't let you out," Hammer replies.

"Not until I kill their leader," I continue. "Don't you get it? That's why I chose to cooperate with them. I'm using Elimination resources to fight Guardian, and then I'll assassinate Vogel. Have you ever heard of her? Do you really think I'd let some stupid woman pretending to be a commander give me orders?"

I pause, waiting for his reaction. Marcus along with a few Elimination officers stare at me.

"Careful now," Hammer says. "You have a few Elimination dogs in there with you. They might hear."

"They're all in," I answer. "They work for me."

"You're bluffing!" he shouts. "You've always been such a liar."

"It's true!" Marcus helps me. "Rex promised to spare our lives as long as we go along with his plan."

"I don't believe a word you're saying," Hammer answers.

"I don't care if you believe us or not," I say. "But I hope you at least realize you'll never be the commander as long as you serve Guardian. He is just using you for a puppet in his show. You have no real control. That's why I left. I don't want to follow anybody's commands. I'm going to be a true leader."

"What are you talking about?" Hammer asks.

"You still don't get it? You think I escaped from the Death Camp because I care about ordinary humans? I don't give a damn if they all end up dead. I just can't tolerate anybody controlling me." I pause, catching my breath. "I'm planning to assassinate Guardian and take his place!" I yell.

Hammer doesn't answer for a few moments. Come on, I think, swallow it. I'm articulating your dream. We both know you'd like to take Guardian's place.

"Nobody can kill him," Hammer finally says.

"Who told you that?" I ask. "Holtzmann works for me now. He has a way to bring Guardian down."

Jessie aims her rifle into the darkness. I look at her. She shakes her head, letting me know she can't get a clear shot at Hammer.

"You've chosen the wrong commander," I say, letting out a short laugh. "Do you really want to remain Guardian's puppet? We both know he doesn't give a damn about his soldiers. He could waste you any time he pleases. I could make you a real leader, Hammer! You could have as much power as you wish."

"Why would you do that?" Hammer asks.

I have to admit it's a really good question.

"I need strong soldiers," I assure him. "And you're a natural commander, Hammer!"

I don't know what else I can say.

"C'mon, Hammer," I continue. "Stand down. I'll allow you to join my team."

"You're lying!" he repeats. "You've never cared about leadership."

"Are you crazy enough to believe that?" I ask. "Power is everything! I have been concealing my true ambitions to fool Guardian and Vogel."

I'm trying so hard to convince Hammer that I almost begin believing it myself. I suddenly realize that there's no reason why my lies couldn't possibly be the truth. Hammer must realize this as well.

"I'm coming out now," I offer. "Let us pass."

"Hold your fire," Hammer commands.

I let out a breath of relief. He believes me. I carefully step into a dark passageway.

"Order your soldiers to lower their rifles," I direct.

Hammer hesitates. His soldiers look at him, puzzled. Most of them are still teens. I imagine they've no idea what's going on.

"How can I trust you?" Hammer asks me. "How do I know you won't gun us down?"

"You have my word," I answer. "C'mon, Hammer. You've known me for a long time. Would I order the killing of a squad of kids?"

Hammer takes another long moment in hesitation, then orders his soldiers to lower their rifles. They look surprised, but obediently follow his command. As soon as it's safe, my squad steps out from cover ahead of me.

"Fire!" Jessie commands, shooting her rifle.

The Elimination officers join her. I watch as Hammer and his soldiers fall. I don't feel any regrets for what has taken place. These teens chose to join Guardian's force by their own free will, and they were ready to kill us.

We proceed down the passageway, stepping over the bodies. I stop beside Hammer, looking down at him. He lies on his back, dying. He's making gurgling, incoherent noises as he fights to breathe. A bullet took him in the throat. Jessie approaches and we exchange glances.

"He's yours," she says. "You deserve it."

I pick up a rifle from a downed soldier and place the barrel on Hammer's forehead. Feeling no hatred, I pull the trigger. I'm just doing what needs to be done.

Our squad moves toward the main exit. Taking advantage of the continued confusion outside, we cross the prison yard again and approach a group of military trucks. A few of Guardian's soldiers finally notice us. We hardly manage to climb inside and start the truck, before they open fire. The main gates are locked, so Dave accelerates the vehicle, smashing into the gate. The gates give, and we drive away. Several trucks follow in pursuit. We open fire in attempt to slow them down. Holtzmann protectively presses a bag containing the drug to his chest, as if some sort of treasure. His face is whiter than snow, but he appears stable enough for now.

As soon as we gain a little distance between us and our pursuit, one of the officers commands Dave to stop.

"What are you doing?" I ask in surprise, watching as the Elimination officers jump out of the truck.

"We'll try to buy you some time," an officer answers.

I stare at him. I realize these officers likely tortured and killed innocent breakers before. They used to be our enemies, but now they're willing to sacrifice their lives for us.

"Thank you," I simply say.

"Get going, breaker," he barks at me. "Now!"

I climb back inside the truck and we drive off, leaving the officers behind. Most likely, we'll never see them again.

Dave drives until we run out of gas in the middle of nowhere, with little ammo and no communication whatsoever with headquarters.

CHAPTER 16

Our group walks under the cover of darkness along a dirt road leading through the woods. We've been traveling for hours, trying to distance ourselves from any possible pursuit. The night is unusually warm and I can make out the low rumble of ominous sounding thunder. I realize we risk getting caught in a storm.

"You're not really planning to kill Vogel, are you?" Marcus asks me. "You were just bluffing back there, right?"

His voice sounds goofy, as if he's just joking. But I can still make out a bit of hidden unease in his words.

"Of course I was bluffing," I answer.

"You sure sounded convincing," Jessie says. "I almost bought it."

She gives me a meaningful glance. I realize I haven't informed Jessie about my change in plans concerning Vogel.

"Fortunately, so did Hammer," I answer, grinning.

Jessie frowns. We both understand we can't freely discuss the matter around Marcus or Dave.

We walk a little further, exiting the woods to cross a field. A large farmhouse soon comes into sight. We decide to check whether we can use it for a temporary shelter. Approaching the house, we pass an ancient gnarled oak growing in the front yard. I look up and freeze, staring up at three corpses hanging from a thick branch. My night vision is poor, but I can still tell these are the bodies of a young man, woman and child.

I can't help from shivering. I've seen abused corpses many times before, but never gotten used to facing them. I know exactly who killed this family. Guardian's breakers have developed a taste for mutilating corpses and hanging them from the nearest streetlamp or tree.

We spend a few moments in silence, gazing up at the bodies.

"Let's bring them down," I finally say.

Dave quickly climbs the tree and pulls a knife. He cuts the ropes, dropping the corpses to the ground. Marcus and I drag them to the back yard, leaving them lying there unburied. We simply don't have strength left to be digging any graves tonight.

"Who could do a thing like that?" Marcus mutters.

I don't answer. We both know who it was that likely did it.

We enter the house. The rooms are in shambles, everything ripped apart and smashed. I can vividly envision Guardian's soldiers trashing the rooms, then torturing and killing that family. I have to fight back a sudden strong desire to smash something as well.

We settle down in the living room, thinking over our predicament. We have sparse ammo, no communication with headquarters and no food.

"I'm certain Elimination will utilize their team of telepaths to locate our squad," Holtzmann assures. "Perhaps, Kitty and Rex should attempt sending a message."

Kitty and I get busy following Holtzmann's suggestion. I close my eyes, focusing my thoughts on Elimination. I don't know whether this will work or not. We're too exhausted to concentrate effectively. Additionally, the Elimination telepaths don't have much experience in locating anybody. Holtzmann only recently created the team and didn't have enough time to train them properly.

As I reopen my eyes, I notice everybody watching us attentively.

"I can't tell for sure," I say. "But it doesn't appear we can get through right now."

Kitty sits on the floor with her eyes closed, wincing from the effort. I repeat my attempt to make contact, but don't believe I succeed.

"Is there anything you have to tell us, Victor?" Jessie asks.

Victor looks over tiredly at her, remaining quiet.

"I think you probably have something to say," she insists. "We're all aware that somebody informed Guardian about our mission. I've been wondering who that might be."

Everybody turns their attention toward Jessie and Victor. I realize nobody else knew about our mission, except Vogel, Chase and the team in this room.

"What did Guardian promise you, Victor?" Jessie asks.

"Are you out of your mind?" he blurts out. "Why do you think it was me who betrayed us?"

"You've always been a rat," Jessie states.

They glare at each other with unhidden disgust. I ready myself to get between them.

"Fess up, Victor," Jessie continues. "We all know it's you who ratted us out."

"Are you so sure?" Victor asks.

"Who else could it be?"

"I wouldn't know. Perhaps it was you. Everybody knows how you hate Elimination."

The accusation throws Jessie off kilter. She instantly springs to her feet and rushes across the room, charging at Victor. Luckily, I manage to get between them wrapping my arms around Jessie in a tight bear hug.

"Stop it, Jess," I say. "Calm down."

"Let me kill this rat!" Jessie demands.

She tries to push me away, but I continue holding her tightly. Our faces are now very close and I suddenly become concerned that Jessie may head-butt me.

"Please, Jess," I plead. "Just stand down."

"Do you really believe this traitor?" Jessie growls.

"I'm tired of this crap!" Victor exclaims.

Marcus helps me restrain Jessie. The others silently watch the unfolding scene. Dave stands aside, as if he can't decide whom exactly he's supposed to be helping.

"Get your hands off me!" Jessie finally shouts. "I'm calm, alright? Let me go."

We release Jessie, although I'm not convinced it's such a good idea. She looks furious. I'm quite surprised she hasn't attacked me yet.

"I didn't inform Guardian," Victor says in exasperation. "For your information I quit switching sides a while back."

"I know," I answer. "I believe you."

"Really?" he asks.

Victor seems astonished. Jessie rolls her eyes at me.

"You're crazy," she comments.

"Think about it, Jess," I say. "Guardian obviously didn't know the exact time of our mission. Otherwise, he would have been waiting for us in the Death Camp, and he'd have increased the number of soldiers securing the lab. He must have known that we were planning something, but wasn't sure what to expect. Had Victor betrayed us, he would have provided all the details."

"It must be somebody who knew about our plan, but didn't know any of the details," Marcus says thoughtfully.

"Nice deduction," Victor agrees. "So instead of blaming me, you'd better think of whom all you told about this mission. There must be an outsider who knew our basic plans."

We all become silent, trying to figure out the source of the information leak. It sure wasn't me. My sister wasn't even aware of our plans. I look over at Kitty, and she shakes her head negatively.

"Rebecca knew I'd be participating in this project," Holtzmann mutters. "But my cousin wouldn't betray us."

"Of course not," I agree.

The storm arrives outside and I hear the heavy rain pounding the rooftop. The wind howls like a wild animal. It looks like we're stuck here for a while. I'm at least thankful we don't have to be outside during such weather.

"I'm going to smoke," Jessie announces angrily, looking at me. "Would you care to join me, Rex?"

Her offer doesn't sound friendly whatsoever, which can't be good. Jessie is most likely fixing to bring me into some sort of trouble. But I'm in no mood for more fights tonight.

"Nah, not really," I answer.

"I really think you should come smoke with me," Jessie persists.

She leaves, motioning for me to follow. I sigh tiredly and rise to my feet. We step into another room, illuminating the way with a flashlight. Jessie lights a cigarette, never taking her eyes off me.

"Do you really trust Victor?" she finally asks.

"I trust him enough," I answer.

"Appears Victor isn't the only one who's recently gained your trust," she adds.

"What are you talking about?"

"Did you really change your mind about killing Vogel?"

"Well, I think we were wrong about her," I admit.

"Are you mad? She'll order all of us shot as soon as we get rid of Guardian."

"Vogel wouldn't do that," I protest. "She's not like Wheeler. She's actually more like the opposite of him."

"So you're out," Jessie states coldly. "Fine then. I'll do Vogel on my own."

"I can't let you do that," I say.

"Do you really think you can stop me?" she asks, grinning.

"I think I can if I have to."

We both become silent, glaring at each other. There's something definitely challenging in Jessie's eyes. I know her temper all too well and realize I'm risking her friendship.

"Listen, Jess," I sigh. "I believe Vogel sincerely wants to change Elimination for the better, and she's a great commander. Everything would fall apart without her."

"You're an idiot," Jessie interrupts. "Vogel is probably plotting your demise at this very moment, while you're standing here defending her like a doofus."

"I seriously doubt that!" I snap. "She actually likes me, unlike some supposed friends."

Jessie remains quiet for a few moments.

"Rex," she says, smiling. "Answer honestly. Are you crushing on Vogel?"

"What?! Are you serious?"

"You're always staring at her like she's a juicy steak."

"Come on," I groan. "She's twice my age. She's old enough to be my..." My voice trails off. I was about to say that she could be my mother, but something doesn't let me articulate the thought. "I understand you hate Vogel because she's an Elimination commander," I say instead. "But she didn't kill your parents, Jess. You shouldn't hold her responsible."

Jessie looks away. I know she'd love to kill Guardian out of revenge for her relatives. Unfortunately, that is something she can't pull off as she's only a level 2 breaker.

"Please, promise not to do anything," I say, worried that she'll go ahead and waste Vogel.

"I won't make any promises," Jessie answers.

"You're making a mistake," I warn. "You should listen to what I'm saying."

"Give me one good reason why I should ever listen to you," Jessie says.

"I'm your friend for one," I answer.

"You're not my friend," she snaps. "I don't even like you!"

I realize that Jessie is just angry, but her words sting anyway.

"Sorry," she mutters. "All right. I promise not to do anything, at least for the time being."

"Thank you, Jess," I say sincerely.

"You're trusting her too much," she sighs.

I shrug, not saying anything more. Jessie was right in that I truly like Vogel, but not quite the way she thinks. I realize that the major may very well be faking her kindness. I could be completely wrong about her, but it doesn't matter now. Because in spite of my best efforts to remain cautious, I can no longer perceive Vogel as the enemy. She could probably walk right up and put a gun to my head, and I wouldn't be able to stop her. And everything would go down the same way it did with Emily, when she pointed a gun at my face and I could do nothing. I just didn't want to believe my own mother could pull the trigger. I couldn't believe she'd ever try to kill her own son.

Jessie and I go back to the living room.

"What were you talking about?" Kitty asks.

"Nothing really," I answer. "We just smoked."

Kitty sniffs at my hands and face, frowning.

"You didn't smoke," she states.

I don't bother to reply. Marcus and Dave watch intently. I just grin back at them, acting like everything is all right.

The storm continues raging outside, so we decide to get a few hours of much needed sleep. Marcus volunteers for watch duty. I close my eyes and my mind quickly slips off into the usual nightmares filled with human corpses hanging from trees.

I awaken at dawn, unrested and worried. Kitty lies beside me on the floor, curled up in a ball and dreaming peacefully. I glance over the room. Everybody is asleep, except Marcus. He sits close by a window, holding his rifle, looking like an actual Elimination officer on duty.

"Go back to sleep," he advises. "The storm hasn't passed yet."

"I should replace you," I offer, rising to my feet and taking a look outside. It's still raining, although the wind has lessened.

"Nah, I'm all right," Marcus says.

He approaches a still slumbering Holtzmann and removes the bag containing the drug from his hands. The professor mumbles something incoherent but remains asleep. Marcus stares curiously at the white crystals.

"Are you really going to inject this stuff?" he asks. "I've heard it's highly toxic."

"So Holtzmann says," I answer. "Yeah, Kitty and I will be injecting that garbage."

Marcus sighs, returning the bag to the professor's hand.

"Why are you doing all this?" he wonders.

"It's the only way to kill Guardian," I say. "If Kitty and I don't take him out, he'll be coming after us."

"I understand that. But I was talking about your decision to cooperate with Elimination. Why did you contact us?"

"To further the same purpose. And to gain use of Elimination resources."

"Will you continue working for us after the war ends?"

I take a moment to think. Working for Elimination used to be something unimaginable for me.

"Possibly," I answer.

"It'd be great," Marcus says, smiling. "I'd like for you and the rest of the team to remain with us."

He becomes quiet for a few moments, watching his brother sleep.

"I'm still not sure whether it was the right thing to do, bringing Dave into Elimination," he adds.

"The job seems to fit him," I say.

"I don't know," Marcus sighs. "Dave wasn't so tough when he was little. He was just a really nice kid, one who always shied away from trouble. He didn't even like to fight. Mom always thought Dave would be the one to go to college. She never had a chance to go herself, so she hoped that at least one of us would earn a degree." Marcus smiles at the memory. "One time when Dave was about five or six, I took him along fishing. We caught a big catfish and he got so scared that he began crying. I must have spent a good half an hour calming him down. He sure didn't want to go back to the lake after that."

We both laugh quietly. I glance at Dave and suddenly remember Jimmy, the harmless, awkward kid who once saved my life. There's also something childish and naïve in Dave's appearance. Then I remember his eager killing of Guardian's soldiers during battle. He never had a second thought, brutally slicing their throats.

"After mom died, there was nobody left to look after Dave," Marcus continues. "I was working for Elimination, so I didn't have time to help him with homework or make sure he attended classes. Once he began skipping lessons, I decided it was time for him to find a job. After passing the resistance test for hypnosis, he became an Elimination officer. He was barely fifteen at the time."

"How old is he now?" I ask.

"Seventeen," Marcus answers. "Last two or three years have changed him a lot. He's a professional killer now. It's just crazy."

I look at Kitty, having the same thoughts. I still can't believe how much she has changed.

Kitty suddenly opens her eyes and sits up. She stares around in a near panic.

"Rex," she mutters. "I saw them coming!"

"What?" I ask. "You had a vision?"

"I don't know for sure," Kitty answers. "Everything was blurry. I saw a truck filled with Guardian's soldiers heading this way."

I approach Kitty and wrap my arms around her, soothingly rubbing her back. Kitty lets out a sob, pressing her face to my chest. She's on the verge of tears. Getting telepathic visions can be awfully unpleasant at times.

Marcus hurries to wake our team. Jessie approaches a window, staring at the road. It's getting lighter.

"I see a military truck in the distance," she reports. "We have to leave the house."

I suddenly realize it's already too late for us to leave. We'd have to cross a hundred yards of open space between the woods and the house.

"We'll have to split up," I say. "We can't let them capture Holtzmann."

Jessie instantly understands.

"You and I can draw their attention," she says. "The professor and the others will remain inside the house, and leave as soon as it's safe."

"I'm going with you guys," Marcus offers.

"Me too!" his brother exclaims.

"You're not going anywhere without me," Kitty objects, grabbing the sleeve of my jacket. I realize I'll have to let her join our group. We simply don't have time for arguing.

Victor doesn't mind staying behind.

"You're Holtzmann's bodyguard on this mission," I say to Dave. "You're to remain with him and make sure nothing happens to the professor."

Dave opens his mouth to argue, but I cut him off, "That's a direct order, Dave!"

"C'mon, guys," Jessie says, glancing through the window. "They're getting close. It's time to leave."

"Wait, Jessica!" Dave exclaims.

Jessie turns to face him. Dave takes in a deep breath, approaching her. He hugs her carefully and lightly places a kiss on her cheek.

"I'll be thinking of you, Jess," he mumbles. "Please, be careful."

Embarrassed, he quickly backs off. Jessie stares blankly at him. I can't believe she didn't break Dave's jaw.

"I apologize for my brother," Marcus says to Jessie.

"Let's go!" she commands.

We leave the house, firing at the quickly approaching truck as we run. The vehicle stops and soldiers in camo jump outside. They return our fire. I focus on running toward the woods. It's hard to move very fast because the field is flooded. We stumble through the mud and puddles. It's still raining and my uniform instantly soaks through.

We enter the woods, continuing to run. The soldiers give chase, firing their rifles above our heads. I realize Guardian must still intend to capture me alive. I suddenly think it may be better to be killed than recaptured.

Kitty runs along beside me, breathing heavily. I'm out of breath as well, but we can't slow down. Jessie and Marcus follow.

A second squad of soldiers wearing respirator masks suddenly emerge from behind the trees just ahead. They toss small containers, and I hear loud hissing. I understand what's happening, but it's too late to do anything.

White gas fills the space around us. My eyes begin tearing and my throat burns. I hear Kitty coughing loudly. I take a step forward but somehow wind up on my hands and knees.

Elimination may have run out of sleeping gas, but Guardian's soldiers apparently still have a good supply. I can't resist the overpowering urge to sleep.

I hope Holtzmann, Dave and Victor will use any opening to slip away. I hope Guardian won't recapture the professor. As long as he remains free, there's a chance to win this war.

I worry for a few more seconds before everything becomes dark.

CHAPTER 17

I awaken to a splitting headache and dizziness. I strain to look around and understand I'm inside a large basement. The air down here is stale and dusty. Meager lighting comes in through a small window near the ceiling. I can hear the steady rumbling of thunder outside.

Kitty, Jessie and Marcus remain unconscious on the floor, confined along separate walls of the basement. We're all handcuffed in front to long metal pipes running alongside the walls.

"What the hell?" Jessie groans, waking. She glances around, frowning. "What's this place?"

"A basement," I answer. "They must've brought us back inside the house."

"Holtzmann and the others," Jessie says. "Did they get away?"

I shrug. I've no idea what happened to the others. I can only hope they managed to slip away.

Marcus opens his eyes as well and sits up, swaying.

"Damn," he blurts out. "Looks like we're in trouble."

"It could've been much worse," I assure him.

Kitty moves her head, letting out a weak whimper.

"Are you all right?" I ask worriedly.

"I feel sick," she complains.

Kitty has low body weight, so the gas must have hit her even harder than the rest of us. Her face is sickly pale and her eyes hazy. My chest aches for Kitty. I shouldn't have allowed her to participate in this mission. What was I thinking?

"All right then," Marcus says. "Let's try to think how to get out of this mess. Does anybody know how to unlock handcuffs?"

"I do," Jessie says. "But I need a safety or hair pin. Does anybody have one?"

Nobody answers. We obviously won't be able to unlock the handcuffs.

"Darn!" Kitty groans. "From now on I'll never leave my room without a few hairpins in my pocket!"

I understand her exasperation. We were completely unprepared for capture. It's useless to now begin having regrets.

"Rex, your pipe looks old and rusty," Jessie says. "Try to break it."

I get busy attempting to break the pipe. I manage to make it to my feet, standing in an awkward half-bent position. I grab the pipe tightly by both hands and pull. Nothing happens. I continue trying. I hold the pipe, working it back and forth, but it doesn't give.

"Damn it!" I groan in anger. "C'mon! Break already!"

No matter how hard I shake the pipe, it remains intact.

I hear voices and heavy footsteps upstairs. Somebody's coming. I stop my idle attempts to break the pipe and sit back down on the floor. A group of five soldiers in camo enter the basement. A big muscular guy about my age approaches. A single glance at his face is enough to convince me we're in really big trouble. He pulls a long sharp blade, smiling sadistically.

"Remember me?" he asks.

"Hello Butcher," I answer.

I met Butcher a few months ago back in the Retaliation camp. He's a hardened criminal, one who acquired his nickname for his psychotic tendency to cut his victims into pieces.

I relax my face, concealing any emotion.

"Where's the drug?" Butcher asks.

I now know they haven't yet captured Holtzmann.

"What drug?" I ask stupidly.

"The one you stole from us," Butcher says.

"I've no idea what you're talking about," I answer. "I don't use drugs."

"You were gonna use this one. So where is it?"

I remain quiet. Butcher grins, crouching down beside me and flashing the knife. His soldiers silently watch the scene unfold, each of them wearing a nasty smirk. I'm sure they're all itching to torture and kill me. I project out my thoughts toward them, but it has no effect. They're too strong.

"Come on, Rex," Butcher says. "Answer me. Did the psycho professor take the drug with him? Where is he?"

"I've no idea," I answer honestly.

"Really?" he asks, putting his blade close to my face. "Do you realize I'm a level 4 who can read your memories?"

"Go ahead," I offer. "I'll just block you. Victor attempted to read my memories once and failed. But I believe you've heard that story. And you must be aware how Victor is a much stronger memory reader than yourself."

Butcher angrily glares at me. He must realize very well that he can't read my memories.

"I've never liked your ugly face," he says. "But I've always wanted to cut it."

I feel the sharp blade slowly slicing across the skin on my chin, leaving a trail of blood. I remain motionless. I won't let him intimidate me.

"Leave him alone, freak!" Kitty shouts.

Butcher doesn't bother to acknowledge her.

"Do you remember when I promised to cut out your tongue?" he asks me, licking the blood clean from the knife. "Now seems like a really good time."

"You definitely wouldn't be hearing any answers from me in that case," I answer calmly.

Butcher punches me in the face. My head snaps back from the hard blow. I hear Kitty yell.

"Where's Holtzmann and the rest of your squad?!" Butcher shouts.

"I don't know," I mutter.

He hits me again and the room swirls in front of my eyes.

"Do you realize what I could do to you?" Butcher asks. "Do you know why everybody calls me Butcher?"

I spit out blood onto the floor, steadying myself.

"I've heard some stories," I assure him. "But we both know Guardian ordered you to deliver us alive and in one piece."

"I don't really care much for taking orders," Butcher answers.

"I think you must," I say. "Otherwise, he'd simply kill you along with the rest of your gang."

"How can you be so sure about that?" he asks, smiling.

"I'm sure you know nothing about Guardian's plans," I answer. "Do you really think he'd allow someone to destroy half of his headquarters and steal the drug?" I pause, forcing a grin. "It was all staged."

"Don't make me laugh," he snorts.

"Well, you won't be laughing when Guardian learns that you captured my team," I add, although I've no idea what I'm talking about.

"He ordered me to capture you," Butcher says.

"That only means he chose the wrong guy for the job," I answer. "You're too stupid to understand the meaning behind his orders. You obviously can't read between the lines. Your squad were never meant to actually capture us. It was all just supposed to be staged for Elimination."

"What?"

"Guardian ordered me to join Elimination. My objective was to gain their trust, so it would be easier to assassinate their leader. It's all part of Guardian's grand plan."

I pause, unsure what more to add. Butcher begins laughing.

"Do you really think I'm such an idiot?" he asks.

"I was actually hoping you're not," I say. "I hope you understand that you're about to screw up Guardian's plan."

"Why steal the drug then?" Butcher wonders.

I don't have an explanation to offer. There's simply no sensible explanation.

"That is privileged information," I say. "Details I'm not allowed to share with outsiders."

Butcher watches me warily. Come on, I think, buy it and let my team go. I realize I can't affect his mind. Butcher is too resistant.

"Liar!" he exclaims, punching my face. Blood drips freely from my nose and the cut on my chin.

I quickly understand Butcher won't be believing my ploy. He grabs me by the hair, tilting my head back and looking straight into my eyes.

"Remember Roger offered you to join our gang?" he asks. "I'm glad you declined. You could never become one of us. We respect only strength and power. And you're miserable and weak. I despise you. Do you know what we did with cowardly boys like you in prison?"

For a split second I consider spitting in his face, but realize that would only lead to further beatings. I regain my composure and say calmly, "Do you know what I do with guys like you Butcher? I killed your former leader. And I'm going to kill you as well."

Laughing, Butcher slams the back of my head against the wall. The room spins.

"Your stubbornness won't do you any good," he says. "I'll capture Holtzmann on my own. He couldn't have gotten away too far. And then I'll come back and give you and your little friends a time to remember."

I don't buy into his threats. If Guardian wasn't interested in capturing us, we'd already be dead. I'm quite certain he ordered Butcher to bring us in alive and unharmed. I've no idea why though. Maybe Guardian wants to personally torture each of us, relishing every moment of our pain.

Butcher commands the other four soldiers to stand guard, while he takes the rest of his gang go to search for the escaped professor.

"Snake, you're in charge," he says to a big heavy guy. "Don't touch the prisoners. We need to keep them in somewhat presentable condition."

After he finally leaves, the four soldiers go upstairs. I continue trying to break the pipe, becoming ever more frustrated at my failure. No matter what I do, the dang pipe remains intact. Marcus also attempts to free himself with no avail. I plop down onto the floor, exhausted from the effort and having no idea what else we might try to ease the situation.

The guards return a couple hours later. They speak too loudly now and walk somewhat unsteadily, which gives one the impression that they're drunk. I also notice they've left their guns upstairs. If we could only free our hands, we might knock them out and escape. The problem is that we can't free ourselves.

The biggest guy, Snake, takes a long lingering look at Jessie.

"Recognize me?" he asks, breaking into a nasty smile. Jessie remains silent. "I saw you back in Hammer's camp. Always liked you. But I think you were too uptight to notice. You probably thought I wasn't good enough for you." He pauses, staring down at her. "You don't seem so good and proud now," he adds.

Jessie doesn't answer, gazing coldly back at him.

"You're sure a pretty thing though," he says. "Like to have a little fun, bashful?"

"Leave her alone!" Marcus shouts.

I become really anxious suddenly realizing what Snake has on his mind.

"Butcher gave you an order not to harm us," I firmly say.

"Shut up," he answers. "We don't care about his orders. We do whatever the hell we want around here."

I watch as he steps closer toward Jessie, the same broken smile spread smugly across his face. She remains silent, watching him without emotion. She's got to be one of the bravest people I've ever met.

"All right," I say, grinning. "I don't really care what you'll do with her. I'll just sit back and enjoy the show."

Snake looks over at me, obviously surprised. Seems he wasn't expecting such a reaction.

"I think you care a lot," he insists.

"Why should I?" I say, continuing to smile. "That nasty, arrogant girl never noticed me either. I tried to be nice to her, but she always thought she was too good for me. She's not even a friend. To tell the truth, I kind of despise her. So I won't mind in the least if you teach her a good lesson. She really deserves one."

"You jerk!" Jessie yells back at me. "I've always hated you. And I've always known you're just as bad as these stinking criminals."

I realize Jessie must have caught on and is now helping me confuse the soldiers. I've no idea whether it may work or not.

"Shut your mouth, stupid girl!" I shout back at her. "I'm really sick of your uppity attitude. Somebody needs to put you in your place. I'm glad these guys are about to straighten you out. Come to think of it, I'd kinda like to have a turn with you myself." I look up at Snake. "What do you think, boss? Butcher wouldn't have to know."

I pause, waiting anxiously. If they were only silly enough to unlock my handcuffs, I would… do what? How would I fight the four of them? I don't know, but it's our best shot anyway.

"Do you think I'm that stupid?" Snake asks, smirking. "I admit it was a nice little act you two just performed. But we all know she's your best friend."

I almost groan in frustration. Damn it! I can't fool anybody today. Looks like it's time for plan B.

"Guardian will kill every one of you, should you so much as lay a hand on her," I say. "I can guarantee that."

Snake ignores my threat, grabbing Jessie by the hair. The situation is becoming desperate.

"That's a really bad choice," I comment. "You're practically committing suicide this very second. Have you ever seen a head explode? Guardian is gonna blow your head into a thousand tiny pieces. He'll break every bone in your body. You must not be aware of what he's capable of."

The guy remains oblivious to my threats. He begins undoing his belt. Jessie rolls her eyes, demonstrating just how unimpressed she is. The other soldiers laugh, watching the scene develop. I feel sick. I have to do something, so I take a deep breath and begin cussing Snake. I can't free my arms, but can at least try to divert his attention. Kitty stares at me open-mouthed. She never heard anything so obscene coming from me.

"Shut the hell up or you'll take her place!" Snake snarls, turning to face me. He releases Jessie.

I become stunned for a split second, having never received a threat of this nature before, but then continue the insults even louder. Angered, Snake quickly approaches and kicks me viciously in the stomach. I lose my breath.

"Don't touch him!" Kitty screams.

"Leave him alone!" Jessie demands. "I'm not finished with you yet!"

"You're a dead man," I say. "You hear me? I'm gonna kill you."

Snake kicks me again. I groan. The pain is intense, but it's still better than letting him attack Jessie.

"You coward!" Kitty yells. "I said, don't touch my Rex!"

"Shut your hole, fleabag!" Snake commands.

"Why don't you come over here and shut it yourself?!" she continues. "Do you think I'm scared of you? You're just an ignorant freak, one who obviously thinks way too much of himself. You can do nothing to me!"

I know precisely what Kitty is doing. She's trying to divert his attention away from me as I did for Jessie.

"Kitty, be quiet!" I exclaim.

"I've warned you, girl," Snake threatens.

"I'm waiting," Kitty says, grinning. "Or maybe you're the one afraid?"

"Shut the hell up!" Snake growls. He approaches Kitty and slaps her hard across the face.

"Don't touch her!" I yell, frantically jerking my arms. The pipe remains solid.

"Is that all you've got?" Kitty mockingly asks. "I could hardly feel that little slap."

Snake snarls, punching her in the face. Kitty lets out a moaning sound, becoming slack. I shout more insults, continuing to pull at the pipe. Nobody pays me any attention. I hear Marcus also begin to yell something. Kitty curls her split lips into a challenging smile, staring down Snake.

"You hit like a little girl," she says, laughing.

A moment later she kicks his leg. He cusses furiously, punching Kitty again. I become desperate. I yank my arms so hard that the cuffs begin to rub the skin off my wrists. I yell at Snake to leave her alone, but he's not listening.

"I'm fed up with you, little one," he says, pulling a set of keys from his pocket. He turns to face me, grinning. "I understand she's your girlfriend, right? I'm gonna borrow her for a little while."

Kitty becomes quiet. Snake unlocks her handcuffs, grabbing her around her waist. He quickly raises Kitty up, throwing her over his shoulder. He's at least twice her size.

"Stop!" I shout. "Don't do it Snake! I'll kill you! You hear me?!"

"Beat the hell out of that fool," Snake commands the others as he heads out the door.

"No, please. Let me go," Kitty whimpers, although she doesn't seem to be putting up any real resistance. Her face is strangely determined and calm. She catches my gaze and winks at me a moment before Snake carries her out of the basement.

"Come back, coward!" I shout so loud that my throat hurts.

"Don't worry, hero," one of the soldiers says. "Your gal will enjoy this. She needs a real man to help settle her down."

I desperately grab the pipe with both hands, pulling as hard as I can. I begin kicking at it, cussing angrily. The three remaining soldiers laugh loudly, enjoying my predicament. I continue with the effort, ignoring them. I have to free myself and somehow rescue Kitty. The pipe suddenly gives. I stagger backward, almost falling, now holding a large section of rusted pipe in my hands.

"Damn it!" a soldier cusses, charging at me.

I turn to face them, swinging the piece of pipe around. I slam a sharp, jagged end into the face of the closest soldier. He cries out in surprise, backpedaling and covering his gouged bloody face. The other two quickly close the distance. I hardly manage to cover before they begin raining punches.

One soldier steps around and grabs me from behind, squeezing me in a bear hug. The second lunges for my throat, pressing his face close to mine. I head-butt him. He stumbles backward and I deliver a hard kick to his thigh as he goes. He falls, landing on his back beside Marcus. Marcus instantly grabs him around the neck with his free hand, choking him violently. The guy grabbing me raises me into the air and slams me heavily onto the floor. I roll to my back as he throws a heavy punch at my head I just manage to slip. I reach for his face and dig my fingers deeply into his eye sockets. He screams out, flinching backward. I punch him in the jaw, knocking him off. He scrambles to his feet, moving a step away. I lunge for the guy, but the soldier with the pipe wound comes at me again. His face is a bloody mess, but he's apparently still not out of the fight. I sidestep and back away. They now come for me together, grabbing and punching. As we move past Jessie, she kicks one of the criminals in the knee, knocking him off balance. He stumbles and falls, landing in front of her. Jessie kicks him solidly into the head, knocking him out cold. The last soldier tackles me to the floor. I land on my back with the guy on top. I'm now too exhausted and beaten up to continue fighting well. All I can do is cover, trying to block the punches raining down, as he relentlessly pounds away at my head. Jessie and Marcus begin yelling encouragement.

I hear a door slam, quickly approaching footsteps and then a gunshot. The soldier's head jerks forward, a bloody hole appearing on his forehead. He falls on top of me, limp and unmoving. I shove his body off and sit up, trying to regain my senses. Kitty stands before me, panting and holding a handgun. Her entire face is covered in fresh blood. I'm disoriented and can't fully understand what's just happened.

"Rex, honey! Are you all right?" she exclaims, kneeling down beside me. "Did they hurt you? I'm sorry it took me so long. I came as fast as I could."

"You're bleeding," I mutter, wiping at her face.

"Stop that!" Kitty exclaims, pushing away my hand. "I'm fine. It's not my blood."

"Where's the guy?" I ask, slowly rising to my feet. "Where's the one who carried you off?"

"Snake? I left him upstairs," she answers. "Dead."

I stare at her in astonishment. She didn't even have a weapon.

"I hate to interrupt your lovely reunion," Jessie says, "but could somebody please free us?"

"Oh darn!" Kitty blurts out. "I forgot to search him for keys."

Kitty and I run upstairs, entering the living room. Snake lies on his back in a large puddle of blood, his eyes still wide open. A large chunk of flesh has been ripped from his neck. I can't believe my eyes. It looks like a wild animal attacked him.

"I guess I tore an artery or something," Kitty says innocently, as I hurriedly search his pockets. "I enjoyed watching him squirm and groan as he was dying."

I shiver, getting a mental image of the shocking scene. Kitty smiles at my reaction. We suddenly hear a truck engine outside. I realize Butcher and his squad are returning to the house. Kitty and I gather the three handguns left in the living room, and hurry back to the basement. We uncuff Jessie and Marcus, handing over the weapons. We rush outside, leaving the house through the back and head toward the woods. Butcher's men notice us and begin giving chase.

I get a sense of déjà vu. Here we go, running through the rain again, trying to avoid capture. I only hope our pursuers have used all their canisters with gas. Nobody will care to spare our lives a second time, should we be recaptured.

Entering the woods, we split up, heading off in different directions. Kitty and I run together, aimlessly returning fire as we go. There's simply no time to take aim. A thick white veil of fog greatly limits visibility. Everything looks surreal, as if we're in some kind of dream world. We quickly run out of ammo.

Butcher along with two soldiers suddenly emerge from the fog directly ahead. I realize we're surrounded.

"Freeze!" I yell, pointing the now empty gun at Butcher.

He raises his handgun.

"Go!" I direct Kitty.

She rushes off into the fog, as two of Butcher's soldiers give chase. I leap forward, charging into Butcher. He pulls the trigger, and the bullet slams into my vest. Off balance, I grab his arm with the gun. He lands a haymaker to my temple. I fall into a puddle, still tightly gripping his arm. He drops down on top of me, sticking his gun into my face. I jerk his arm away from my head. He hammers at my head with his free fist, while simultaneously pulling the trigger. The bullets slam into the mud inches away. He finally manages to muscle the barrel back onto my forehead. He pulls the trigger again, but the gun only makes a clicking sound. Empty. I release his arm, punching him into his ribs. Snarling, Butcher slams the gun at my head. I realize he's the better fighter. I'm losing, taking too many blows. By the time I finally manage to dislodge the gun, my head is swirling and I'm close to blacking out.

Butcher transitions smoothly, now pulling his knife. He stabs at my throat, but I cover. I feel his long sharp blade slicing deeply into my arm. I cry out in pain, blood flowing freely from the fresh wound. Butcher stabs again, this time at my face. But I manage to catch his arm, trying to grab hold of the deadly flashing steel. He grips my throat with his free hand. I begin choking. He leans in, bringing the blade a couple inches closer to my face. I can't breathe, again feeling myself losing consciousness, still pushing his knife away from me.

"I promised you I was gonna slice you up," he growls.

Kitty suddenly springs from the fog onto his back, fish-hooking Butcher and pulling him backward. He releases my throat, swinging an arm around at Kitty. His hard punch knocks her off as if she's a rag doll. I suck in a precious breath of air while slamming a fist into Butcher's chin. He falls back, releasing the blade. I grab the knife and begin stabbing Butcher in the neck. He emits gulping sounds from his throat as he stares at me in wide-eyed shock. I quickly stab him in the chest a couple of times, then finish the job of cutting his throat. Butcher's body twitches a few times and becomes still. I roll onto my back to try and catch my breath. My head is woozy. Blood still gushes from my wounded arm. Kitty lies unconscious on her back in a puddle of mud.

A dozen soldiers in camo suddenly emerge from the fog, taking us in a circle. I understand Kitty and I are about to be executed.

I dive on top of Kitty, shielding her and closing my eyes.

CHAPTER 18

I hear the sound of an approaching helicopter slicing through the air. Gunfire and angry voices fill the space around us.

"Freeze!" somebody shouts from a speaker above. "This is Elimination!"

A couple of bullets slam into the back of my vest, but I remain unmoving. I can't chance rising up.

"What's happening?" Kitty utters, finally waking and trying to look around.

I place a hand on her forehead, pushing her head back down.

"Keep still," I whisper. "Don't move."

"Get them all!" a firm voice commands. "Don't let anyone slip away!"

I lie motionless, waiting for the situation to resolve one way or another. It seems like an eternity passes before somebody asks, "Are you all right?"

I realize it's relatively quiet now. Only a few random gunshots still sound in the distance. I raise my head, staring around in a daze, and see Chase kneeling down beside us. Several officers in black run past. I never thought I would be so happy to see Elimination.

"Chase!" Kitty blurts out, sitting up. "You've found us!"

"Damn!" Chase exclaims, looking us over. "You two are really messed up."

I sit on the ground, gazing off into space. I feel weak and worn out.

"You're bleeding," Chase states, checking the knife wound on my arm.

"It's just a scratch," I answer as I pass out, falling back down into the puddle.

When I come to, Chase and Dave are carrying me.

"I can walk," I mutter.

"The hell you can," Chase says angrily.

"How did you find us?" I ask.

"Our team of telepaths received Kitty's message a few hours ago," he explains. "We didn't know your exact location and located Holtzmann, Victor and Dave first."

I ask Chase if the professor is okay, and he assures me that Holtzmann and Victor are safe and sound. They must already be back at headquarters.

"I refused to return with them," Dave says. "I wanted to help put a stop to Butcher's breakers. I believe we've killed all of them!"

"Look what I found!" Kitty exclaims, walking beside us and stabbing Butcher's knife at the air. "A trophy! Like to have it?"

"I don't want his knife," I answer.

"C'mon, it's a really good blade," she protests. "I always wanted it."

Chase and Dave deliver me to a waiting Elimination helicopter perched along the edge of the woods. I see Jessie and Marcus standing nearby, grinning and speaking to the officers. I feel a huge sense of relief.

"You just can't stay away from trouble, can you?" Chase asks, patching up my wounded arm during liftoff.

I ignore his grumbling. Kitty sits beside me, pressing a pack of dry ice to her face while still admiring the knife. I look over at Jessie and Marcus. I think of them helping me bring down the three criminals during the fight in the basement. I recall Jessie demanding that Snake leave me alone. I think of Kitty diverting his attention in a reckless attempt to protect me. I suddenly realize why we all managed to survive and escape. We all worked as a team, each one selfless and offering ourselves as a target. And it's not me, Kitty or anyone else in particular who saved us back there. It was friendship and teamwork that got us through, something completely foreign to guys like Butcher and his gang.

I smile, it almost feels like we're a family. Then I look at Jessie and my cheery mood disappears. I recall another image from that basement: Jessie cuffed to the rusty pipe and Snake grabbing her by the hair with bad intentions.

"What are you staring at?" she asks upon noticing my prolonged gaze.

"I was worried for you, Jess," I answer. "Are you all right?"

"I'm not the one with the cut veins here," she reminds.

"Jess, you knew I was bluffing with the comments back there, right?" I suddenly ask. "Please, tell me you knew what I was doing."

"Don't be so dense!" she exclaims. "You couldn't even convince those stupid criminals. Do you really think you could fool me?"

"Thanks Jess," I say. I move in closer and hug her gingerly. She rolls her eyes, but doesn't protest. I've long thought of Jessie as my trusted friend, but this is the first hug we've shared.

"All right, enough!" Jessie finally demands, pushing me away. "What's going on? Why is everybody trying to hug and kiss on me today?"

She shoots an angry look Dave's direction. His face reddens and he turns away, embarrassed. Kitty begins chuckling and also scoots down to hug Jessie, causing her to groan. She obviously appreciates her personal space.

A couple hours later the helicopter lands in front of the Elimination prison. Holtzmann, Vogel and a squad of officers are waiting anxiously for our arrival. The professor almost throws a fit upon seeing my and Kitty's faces.

"Look what those monsters did to my subjects!" he cries out.

Vogel commands Chase and Dave to take us to the hospital. Kitty and I are subjected to multiple x-rays to make sure our skulls weren't fractured. Luckily, we haven't sustained any severe injuries. A doctor injects anesthetic before stitching my arm along with the nasty cut on my chin.

"I thought you ran out of anesthetic," I comment.

The doctor assures me that they've put back a little for emergencies. I argue that my case is no emergency. Chase reminds me that Kitty and I will be participating in Holtzmann's experiment, so special treatment has been authorized. I sigh heavily, giving up. Although I realize somebody with more severe injuries could have used that shot, a more selfish part of me is thankful for the anesthetic.

It's already getting dark when we return to our quarters. I fall flat onto the bed, too tired even to turn. The painkiller has stopped working and my arm begins to throb. My entire body feels sore and I'm suffering a worsening headache.

Kitty lies beside me, unmoving. Her black eye has already swollen shut. She looks battered and exhausted.

"My face hurts," she complains. "My stomach hurts as well. And my back doesn't feel right. How about you, honey?"

"About the same," I answer.

She crawls toward me and wraps her arms around my neck.

"My poor Rex," Kitty sobs. "They've beaten you up so badly."

Kitty tries to kiss me, but instantly yanks her head backwards.

"Gosh, that hurts!" she exclaims, touching the stitches on her lips. "All right then. Let's just go to sleep."

"I think that's a wonderful idea," I admit.

But we can't just go to sleep. Regardless of her level of exhaustion, Kitty is still too wired. She suddenly sits up and says, "I was so terrified! I knew you wouldn't be able to sit tight and wait for me to return and shoot down those guys. I knew you'd find a way to start fighting all of them. I was so afraid they'd kill you before I could make it back and rescue everybody."

"Is it what you were worried about?" I ask.

"What else would I worry about?" Kitty says, laughing.

"Goodness, Kitty!" I exclaim. "Don't you know? He could have killed you."

"Snake? No way. He was too stupid. I knew I could take him. It was actually my plan all along."

"What?!"

"Didn't you catch me winking at you?" Kitty wonders. "You see, I knew I had to do something to get us out of that basement. I needed to free my arms and then get hold of a weapon. So how could I accomplish all that? I decided to separate Snake from the others and then kill him." She pauses, chuckling. "It was really kind of brilliant, wasn't it?"

"It was stupid," I say. "You shouldn't have done something like that."

"Snake would have beaten you to death," Kitty says. "I should have done him much earlier, while we were still in the Retaliation camp." She pauses, frowning. "He was trying really hard to be friendly with me back then. But I always knew he was a jerk. Sometimes he would say some really dirty things to me."

"What?!" I exclaim. This conversation is becoming crazy. "Why didn't you tell me?"

"Why would I?" She smirks.

Of course. She always prefers to deal with her problems on her own. I don't know what I can do about that. Although I have no doubts in her fighting and killing abilities, I sure wish she'd exercise a little more caution.

"C'mon" she sighs. "Snake was an easy kill. It wasn't hard to manipulate him. He did everything exactly as I expected him to." Kitty grins, gazing off into space now. "He brought me into the living room and threw me on the floor. He didn't even beat me, which was stupid of course. Instead, Snake went ahead and got on top of me. And it was exactly where I needed him to be. I had to be really close for the plan to work. So I locked my feet behind his back and tightly wrapped my arms around his neck, so he wouldn't get away. And then I began biting at his throat like a pit-bull!"

She snarls, growling and shaking her head in a not too shabby imitation of a vicious dog.

"Quit that," I say, barely recognizing her. "You're freaking me out."

She smiles again, shrugging her shoulders.

"I'm a good biter," Kitty states. "But don't worry, I'll never bite you."

Come to think of it, she has bit me on a few occasions during arguments. Those attacks were apparently just child's play.

"Why are you looking at me like that?" she asks. "Do you think Snake didn't deserve what he got? He had it coming. Nobody can be so ignorant and mean, and expect to live for too long."

"I have no problem with your killing him," I answer. "I'm just worried for you. You're too reckless. What if he simply shot you? Or what if all of them came after you?"

"I'd figure something out," Kitty insists.

She lies down beside me, gazing at the ceiling. I don't know what else I might say. No matter what I tell her, Kitty will do as she pleases.

"Do you want to know the biggest difference between you and me?" she asks. "I enjoy hurting and killing those who are deserving. I learned very early in life that we live in a world where you have to kill or be killed, and I'm fine with that. But you are a little different. You're too kind and nice. That's one reason why everybody comes after you. And that's also why I have to protect you from those who may hurt you."

I remember relentlessly stabbing Butcher, even after he'd already died. I don't know why Kitty believes I'm so nice.

"You're just tired," I say. "You're talking nonsense."

"You don't understand!" she exclaims. "Why are you bringing me into trouble for what I did? Why can't you simply be grateful that I rescued you? You always say how I shouldn't risk my life, but what other choice did I really have? Snake was beating you and wouldn't have stopped until he'd killed you!"

I don't know how to answer. My head still aches and I just want to sleep. Unfortunately, I know only too well that this conversation will continue as long as Kitty wishes.

"I owe my life to you," she states solemnly. "I'd be long dead by now, if you hadn't saved me five years ago. Remember that night I first came to your place?"

I nod. It's something I'll never forget.

"That was my time," Kitty continues sadly. "I was supposed to die that night. I was very sick and had nobody to help me. And I didn't trust you back then. I spent hours sitting behind dumpsters, deciding whether I should go to your place. It was cold and raining. And I suddenly realized that I wouldn't survive till morning, should I choose to remain outside. I remember staggering toward your apartment building, thinking that I wouldn't make it. I did fall a couple of times, but managed to get back to my feet."

She pauses, letting out a quiet sob.

"You saved me," Kitty says. "And then you took care of me. You became my only friend and family. I still remember your reading books to me and helping me with homework. I remember when you taught me to swim and later took me to a meadow, just because I wanted to pick wild flowers. And whenever I got ill, you spent hours by my bedside, telling me stories or bringing water and medicine." She becomes silent for a few moments, looking away. "So how can it be any different, Rex? How can I not feel protective toward you? Aside from you, I have nothing good in my life. You're all I have!"

She suddenly begins crying. She throws her arms around my neck and presses her lips against mine, wincing in pain.

"Don't hurt yourself," I say, gently pushing her away.

"I don't care," she sobs. "I love you so much."

"Well, I have some stitches too, Kitty," I say, stroking her hair. "Just go to sleep. It's been a long day."

"Tell me a story," she demands.

"I'm really tired, Kitty."

"Please."

I sigh, giving in.

"All right, listen," I say. "Once upon a time there was a girl with red hair and sharp teeth. She once went into some dark woods and ran into bad guys. And she killed them all. The end."

"That's too short!" Kitty exclaims, laughing. "You forgot the dinosaurs. What was T. Rex doing while she was killing those bad guys?"

"He was busy taking a beating in the basement," I answer. "Go to sleep now."

Kitty yawns and finally closes her eyes, drifting off quickly. I remain awake for a few more minutes, thinking over her words. I don't know whether I should take it too seriously. Her thinking that she owes her life to me could become a big problem. With a false belief like that she might do something even more outrageous. She could decide to sacrifice herself for me, if need be.

I suddenly think about Lena and Jimmy. I remember Chelsey and the unknown recruit who sacrificed his life for me during my escape from the Death Camp.

I feel an unsettling premonition that something bad may now happen to Kitty. I'm afraid that we won't both make it to see the end of this war.

***

A few days later, Kitty and I arrive at the hospital for our first injections. Chase, Marcus and Dave tag along to assist.

Smiling, Holtzmann informs us that there's no need to worry about anything. The intensive-care unit is prepared for any emergencies, and the best medics around are on standby to take care of us, should anything go wrong.

All this preparation is making me nervous. I look over at two recliners with matching IV stands and plastic bags filled with a whitish liquid.

"Looks like milk," Kitty comments. "That's what we can call it."

"What kind of drug is it?" I ask. "How exactly does it affect the brain?"

"The substance significantly intensifies activity within certain sections of the brain," Holtzmann answers, "thereby temporarily expanding the potential of the mind."

"Wait a minute, professor," I say. "Don't tell me that we were risking our lives for a bag of LSD."

Holtzmann frowns and begins a long tiring lecture, explaining that this drug has little in common with LSD. He even makes sure to write out the chemical formulas, but I can't comprehend half of what he says.

"Considering the aforementioned ingredients utilized in synthetizing the substance, you may have already realized the inherent risks you'll be taking during this experiment," Holtzmann says. I nod stupidly. "Fortunately, both the positive and negative effects will only be temporary. During injection, you may experience a few unpleasant sensations such as weakness, pain, seizures or restlessness. It will take a few hours for the drug to begin to induce an alteration of your brain. In approximately 12 hours the effects will peak, hopefully enabling you to practice telekinesis. In the case you receive no additional injections, the effects should desist within two or three hours. That's why we'll need to perform multiple injections, allowing the drug time to safely accumulate in your body."

"What other kinds of side effects are possible?" I ask.

Holtzmann explains that the range of afflictions is wide and unpredictable, as nobody before has ever received such a high dosage. He expects Kitty and I to experience nausea, weight and hair loss, weakness, anxiety and likely even some moderate level of depression. The drug also decreases the immune system which subsequently leads to higher risks for infection. And it may cause blood thinning, which can result in nose and gum bleeding along with bruising all over your body.

After the professor finishes speaking, the room becomes deathly quiet for a while.

"So you've never conducted this type of experiment before, have you?" I ask.

"Not to this degree no, the other subjects were receiving lower dosages," Holtzmann admits.

"Why do both of us have to go through this?" I wonder, still not fully understanding his concept of using two telepaths.

"The drug will also increase telepathic sensitivity," he says, "letting both subjects connect with one another's minds and act as one, especially when using telekinesis. It will also permit me to use only half of the needed dosage, thereby lowering the health risk for each of you."

I nod again, still having incomplete understanding. All this science is too complex for me.

After Kitty and I verify our agreement to be his subjects, Holtzmann requests Chase and Marcus to strap us into the recliners. Kitty willingly lets the officers restrain her. I suffer flashbacks from Dr. Carrel's lab, where I was strapped to the chair and approached by a lunatic with a drill in his hand.

"I don't need to be strapped down," I begin protesting. I don't feel safe when my hands aren't free.

Holtzmann and I spend a good ten minutes arguing before I finally allow Chase to strap me down. Holtzmann inserts a needle into my vein. I nervously watch as the white concoction flows through a long plastic tube into my body. It reminds me of the supposed lethal injection I once had to go through.

Ten minutes later I understand the necessity for the straps. Sharp pain pierces through my muscles, and I suffer a seizure. The last thing I see is Kitty foaming at the mouth in her chair, before I wake on a medical gurney. A doctor injects something else into my arm, asking how I feel.

"I've been through worse," I mutter, sitting up. "Where's Kitty?"

"I'm here," she answers weakly, lying flat on another gurney. Her face is sickly pale.

Holtzmann arrives, apologizing for the complications during the injection and promising to decrease the dosage of the drug. After numerous head scans and blood tests, he finally lets us return to headquarters.

The next morning, I awaken to an intense headache. I'm dizzy and nauseated. I realize these are the first side effects of the drug.

"I feel like I'm about to throw up," Kitty whimpers. "And my head hurts terribly. I don't usually suffer any headaches."

We somehow pull ourselves together, heading toward the hospital for another injection. It goes much smoother than the first time. Holtzmann uses muscle relaxant in combination with an anesthetic, to prevent us from having more seizures. We don't experience the pain this time around, remaining awake. Chase and Marcus stand aside, watching us with sympathetic expressions.

"I think you're heroes," Dave says.

During the next several days Kitty and I receive daily injections, doing head scans and blood tests afterwards. We haven't suffered any severe side effects yet, outside of frequent headaches, nausea and some postinjection weakness. Holtzmann perceives that to be a positive sign.

One morning he invites us to his lab inside Elimination headquarters. It's time for the first experiment. He places monitors on our heads, directing us to sit at the table. We follow his request as the professor places matches, a pen and a thin book in front of us. He explains that while Kitty and I are breakers of almost the same strength, she is able to use her abilities much better at the moment. He claims that I'm still blocking myself, refusing to fully accept being a breaker. That's why Holtzmann believes Kitty will develop an ability for telekinesis quicker. But I'll still have to help, combining my effort with hers.

Jessie, Marcus and Dave arrive to witness the experiment. My jaw drops upon seeing them. They all wear helmets, safety glasses and bulletproof vests, along with metallic shields. Holtzmann also places a helmet on his head, backing off into the furthest corner.

"Are you sure Kitty and I shouldn't wear protective gear as well?" I ask.

"You have nothing to worry about," the professor assures us. "It's a mere precaution. Telekinesis shouldn't hurt the subjects."

"How can you be so sure?" I blurt out. "You haven't conducted this type experiment before."

After a few agonizing minutes of arguing, Holtzmann allows us to wear vests and safety glasses. He refuses to give us the helmets because they may interfere with his monitors.

"What do we do?" Kitty asks impatiently.

"Try to move an object on the table, using telekinesis," Holtzmann instructs.

"How exactly are we supposed to do that?" I wonder.

"It should come natural to both of you," he answers. "Just believe in your abilities."

"Thanks for nothing, professor," I groan. What else can we expect from this guy?

During the next hour Kitty and I obsessively stare at the objects, willing them to move. We wave our hands above them, but it doesn't help. No matter what we try, we can't move the darn objects a single inch.

"It's not working," I finally say, giving up.

"Then try harder," Holtzmann suggests, watching the data from his laptop.

"I was trying as hard as I could," I protest, watching Kitty making funny faces in futile attempt to move a match.

"It's all your fault, Rex," the professor states matter-of-factly. "You don't believe in your abilities, thereby subsequently blocking Kitty. You should connect with her mind and work together as one."

"Don't blame me for your experiment not going the way it should," I answer, becoming angry.

"Holtzmann is right," Kitty says. "You never believe in us."

"Where did that come from?" I ask, raising my voice.

"You know it's true!" Kitty blurts out. "You always try to hold me back!"

Word by word, we end up having an ugly argument. As Kitty and I shout at each other, Holtzmann continues peering into his laptop. He now has a curious expression on his face.

"You're talking nonsense, Kitty!" I shout.

"I'm sick and tired of your excuses!" she yells back furiously.

"That's excellent!" Holtzmann suddenly exclaims, still watching the monitor, a wide grin spread across his face.

A moment later the entire room explodes.

CHAPTER 19

Every window in the room implodes, raining down shards of glass. The table and chairs simultaneously rise upward into the air, lifted by some unseen force. Jessie, Marcus and Dave are thrown against the wall, their shields torn from their hands, the metal bent as if made of paper. Holtzmann is slammed to the floor as his laptop flies across the room.

Kitty and I drop down low at the beginning of the chaos. Kitty cries out, covering her head. I realize we have to get away from here. I scramble to my feet, grab her arm and pull her toward the exit. As we run along the corridor, all the doors to the offices fling open. Lamp bulbs explode above our heads.

"What's happening?!" Kitty yells.

"A scientific breakthrough!" Holtzmann exclaims, running behind us.

One of the doors ahead suddenly comes unhinged and flies toward us, missing by only a couple of feet. I tackle Kitty to the floor, covering her from shards of airborne glass and splintered wood.

"Please calm down," I whisper, realizing that we're the cause of all this commotion.

Kitty finally manages to gain control of herself. The explosions cease and everything becomes quiet. A few startled Elimination guards emerge, shining flashlights into the now dark corridor.

"What the hell was that?" one of them asks.

"Telekinesis!" Holtzmann exclaims joyfully.

Kitty and I are still laid out across the floor, too shocked to move. My ears are ringing. I'm surprised we're still alive.

"Damn you, Holtzmann!" I say. "You said it wouldn't be dangerous."

"You haven't been injured, have you?" he asks. His question sounds more like a statement. "Telekinesis doesn't affect the subjects. You two managed to create a protective field around yourselves."

I have no idea what he's talking about.

Jessie and Marcus approach, cussing loudly. Dave silently follows them, wearing a dazed expression.

"So Rex and I will have to argue every time we need to use telekinesis?" Kitty asks, puzzled.

"It'd have to be a last option as using spontaneous emotions to initiate the telekinesis lends to uncontrollable outcomes," the professor explains. "You must learn to consciously manipulate the telekinesis."

"Will everything now start exploding every time Kitty and I argue?" I ask.

"Possibly, but not necessarily," Holtzmann answers. "Although you should learn how to better control your emotions in any case."

He orders Kitty and I return to the hospital for head scans. As we walk toward the prison exit, Marcus clears his throat and says uncomfortably, "Rex, Kitty... Well, you be careful, all right? Don't do anything else too exciting during the night."

Kitty blushes, turning away.

"Just shut up," I say.

"I'm not joking," Marcus answers defensively. "I'm worried about everybody's safety. I don't want you two to blow up our entire headquarters."

"He actually has a point," Jessie admits.

"Not likely," Holtzmann says. "Telekinesis is more of a defense mechanism. It's best triggered by a survival instinct such as in a case of imminent danger. As we have witnessed today, fear and anger can also possibly trigger this ability."

"Good to know, but how can we use telekinesis in a time of need without killing the wrong people?" I ask, changing the subject. "How do we control it once it starts?"

Holtzmann assures us that the ability will come naturally over time. Kitty and I just have to telepathically synchronize our effort and get accustomed to the effects. I sigh, thinking that time is one thing we don't really have much of.

The next three weeks Kitty and I perform multiple telepathic exercises under the wary supervision of the professor. Our goal is to be able to maintain a solid connection, to act together as one, while practicing telekinesis. Holtzmann places us in separate rooms and requests I visualize in my mind what photographs he shows to Kitty.

"I can't see anything," I report. "I don't have any connection at the moment."

"Rex! As I've already explained, it's impossible to turn a telepathic connection on and off," Holtzmann protests. "You have a strong connection with Kitty, permanently sending and receiving information."

"Why isn't it working then?" I ask.

"You still don't fully believe in your telepathic ability, thus preventing yourself from having visions," he states matter-of-factly.

I realize that Holtzmann may actually be right. Being inside somebody's head isn't something I exactly wish for. I know most non-breakers often perceive telepathy as something romantic or otherwise desirable, like reading each other's thoughts. But in reality, there's nothing enjoyable or pleasant in having telepathic visions. It simply messes with your head, making you feel dizzy and disoriented. You may even forget yourself for a few moments and not remember where or who you are. On top of everything else, telepathic ability usually increases when the subject you're connected to is frightened or in pain. And being a connected telepath, you suffer through the same range of sensations. So it's just not something I'd like to fully experience again.

Unfortunately, Kitty and I don't have much of a choice.

We spend hours in Holtzmann's lab every day, practicing our telepathy. I sit alone in a dark room, trying to visualize what Kitty is doing at that exact moment. I wear a headset, so that Holtzmann and Kitty can communicate with me.

"Beta! Beta! Do you copy?" Kitty asks in an official tone of voice. "What am I doing now?"

"Standing by the window?" I guess.

"Not even close!" Kitty exclaims. "I'm eating at the table. Now tell me what I'm eating."

"A sandwich?" I offer.

"I'm eating a tomato!" she blurts out. "What sandwich are you talking about?"

I sigh. I just can't see anything today.

"Let's try again with a more intense stimulation," Holtzmann informs me. "Get ready and focus."

"All right," I mutter, closing my eyes again. I suddenly remember Dr. Carrel directing the officers to burn Lena's hand, while testing my abilities. It takes a few moments to shake the disturbing thought.

I continue concentrating, focusing on Kitty's image. Suddenly, something begins to burn my mouth and throat. My eyes begin tearing. I gasp, feeling like I've just swallowed something extremely hot.

"What are you doing in there?!" I exclaim. "Stop!"

"Did you receive the transmission?" Holtzmann asks. I hear Kitty giggle. My mouth and throat are on fire. I can no longer take it.

"Quit whatever it is you're doing!" I demand, taking off the headset and running for the door.

I find Kitty and Holtzmann in the dining room. I somehow knew they'd be there. Kitty is smiling, holding a half-eaten red chili pepper. Her eyes are watering and her face is an even brighter shade of red than the pepper. She laughs upon seeing me.

"Stop eating that! You're killing me!" I exclaim, grabbing a bottle of water. Washing out my mouth doesn't help a bit. These are not my sensations, but Kitty's.

"Drink it for God's sake!" I command, shoving the bottle of water into her hand.

Other days Kitty and I have to play hide and seek, using telepathy to find one another. She has no problem locating me, but I often have to search the entire prison to locate her. The other exercises include guessing words and numbers. We also practice telekinesis, but still can't move the objects whenever we wish to.

Every day, Kitty and I receive our daily injections. The feeling of sickness increases a little each time, but nothing too outrageous happens yet. We also frequently feel light-headed and suffer regular headaches. Studying our blood work, Holtzmann advises us to take vitamins and go on daily walks.

Kitty and I decide to walk to the Elimination training facility, to visit Jessie. She's there coaching a fresh group of recruits, teaching marksmanship. Heading toward the exit, we run into Marian. Turning away, she shyly asks my permission to join our stroll.

"Of course you can walk with us," I say.

Marian doesn't answer, now purposely ignoring me. She's been distant and cold since our last conversation, when she was hysterical. So I'm glad I can at least spend some time around her.

Smiling and whispering, Kitty and my sister walk ahead together. I don't interfere, following a few steps behind.

We find Jessie at the shooting range and she soon sends her students on a short break. It's cold outside, so we walk inside the gymnasium. Kitty and Marian momentarily leave us. There's a small obstacle course, where officers usually practice storming techniques. A few metal poles support a weird-looking contraption, and my goofy sister heads straight toward them.

"Time for me to start preparing for my future," she announces, gripping a pole and trying to swing around it. I let her do whatever makes her happy.

Jessie and I discuss Holtzmann's project for a while.

"I wish I could find a way to help you kill Guardian," Jessie sighs.

"I wish so too," I admit, remembering our time hunting Wheeler together.

"Would you like to know what I've been wondering about?" she asks. "The traitor. I wonder who could have informed Guardian about our plans."

"Vogel and Chase are checking backgrounds on all breakers recently arrived in the city," I say. "But they haven't come up with a list of suspects yet."

"I'm pretty sure, it was one of us that leaked the information," Jessie says. "If it wasn't Victor, I don't know who else it could be."

"Alex! Watch what I can do!" Marian yells.

I turn to the sound of her voice and see my crazy sister hanging upside down, gripping the pole by her arms and legs about 6 feet above the floor. I realize she'll likely land on her head, should she slip.

"Marian!" I shout. "Get off that thing before you break your neck!"

"But I saw it done in the movies," she answers.

"We're not in a movie," I remind her. "Now get down. I don't want you to hurt yourself."

"Well this is interesting," she says, pausing. "I don't really know how to get down. I'm kind of stuck here."

Sighing, I go to rescue my sister from her predicament.

"You see? Maybe this career choice is just not for you," I say, wrapping my arms around her shoulders. "You'll just have to pick another profession. Now let go of the pole."

"I'm afraid of falling," she whimpers.

"I'm holding you," I assure her.

Screaming, Marian finally releases the pole, kicking at the air and swinging her arms around in a wild panic. She somehow knocks me off balance. We both fall onto the floor, Marian landing on top of me. Upon seeing my angry face, she smiles guiltily and mutters, "Don't kill me, all right? I'm sorry."

"Rex! Look how well I can climb!" Kitty exclaims.

Expecting to observe something else outrageous, I glance over at her. Kitty's swinging from a climbing rope, close to the top near the ceiling. And she's holding the rope with only one hand. They're going to give me a heart attack today, I think with exasperation.

"Kitty! What are you doing up there?!" I yell, approaching the rope. "Get down right now!"

I secretly hope she's not stuck there, because I really have no desire to climb that rope. Marian stands beside me, watching Kitty with admiration.

"I'm leaving now," Jessie announces, walking back toward the range. "God help you, Rex."

I spend a good ten minutes persuading Kitty to come down.

"You never believe in me," she complains, finally descending. I decide to be really angry with her. But as soon as Kitty smiles, I have to give up on the act. I can never seem to remain angry at her for too long.

Heading back toward headquarters, we run into Dave. He's holding a bunch of flowers, looking like he's just seen a ghost.

"Is Jessie still at the range?" he asks in an unsteady voice.

"I guess you finally decided to reveal your true feelings!" Kitty exclaims happily.

Dave simply nods, wearing an expression as if he's on death row.

"Remember Dave, girls like confidence," Kitty instructs.

"I'm confident enough," he mutters sheepishly.

"Good luck," I say, smiling. "You'll really need it."

Dave thanks me, not picking up on the intended sarcasm, and heads toward the range.

"If she rejects you, come see me!" my sister yells. "I'll help soothe your feelings!"

The officer doesn't seem to hear. As soon as he disappears from sight, I burst out laughing.

"How can you be so insensitive?" Kitty asks, frowning. "Love is a very serious thing! What if Jessie breaks his heart?"

"I'd be more worried about his jaw," I answer. "Jess might just kill him. It's horrible. We already have too few soldiers, and we're about to lose one more."

"You don't know Jessie," Kitty interrupts me. "At times, she can be very nice and sweet."

I realize that Kitty may be right. Besides Jessie being an excellent shooter, I know little else about her.

***

The next morning, I awaken to find Kitty sitting on the edge of the bed, fully dressed and very angry.

"Did you sleep well?" she asks through gritted teeth.

"Yeah, I guess," I answer. "Is anything wrong?"

"Nothing's wrong. I'm very happy for you," Kitty says spitefully. "I stayed awake the entire night because of nightmares. I saw dead bodies, your mother and long dark corridors. I was waking up every five minutes or so, until I finally gave up on sleeping."

"Wait a minute!" I exclaim. "You saw my dreams?"

"I wouldn't exactly call them dreams," she answers. "It looked more like a horror movie. Gosh, what's happening inside your head?" Kitty groans, rubbing at her eyes. "I'm so tired now!" she whimpers pitifully.

This must be another side effect of Holtzmann's drug, I realize.

Arriving at the kitchen for breakfast, we run into the professor, Chase, Victor and Marcus.

"Where are Jessie and Dave?" Kitty wonders out loud. "They must've overslept. I'll wake Dave, and you go find Jessie," she suggests.

I realize it should actually be the other way, but don't argue. After walking through a long corridor, I approach Jessie's room and knock on the door. A few moments later Dave opens up. We stare at each other in surprise.

"Dave?!" I exclaim.

"Rex!" he blurts out.

"What are you doing here?" I ask stupidly, knowing precisely what he's been doing even as I ask the question.

"I don't know, just visiting," Dave answers, becoming embarrassed.

"Rex, is that you?" I hear Jessie's voice. "Come on in."

I brush past Dave, walking inside the room. Jessie is sitting on the bed, wrapped in a blanket and yawning. I gawk at her, still in a stupor from the shock of seeing them together. She waves a goodbye to Dave as he hurriedly leaves.

"What?" Jessie asks.

"Oh, nothing," I answer.

"He's a really nice guy," Jessie says defensively. "And he could be killed at any time. So I just decided to bring a bit of happiness into his life."

"Too much information," I say, trying not to smile. "I just came to wake you for breakfast."

As I head toward the door, she says, "Rex, I'd be very thankful if you kept your mouth shut about all this."

It sounds more like a warning than a request.

"Oh c'mon," I say. "You know I don't gossip."

I return to the dining room, thinking that I truly don't know Jessie very well. Perhaps I only see her tough side.

"I couldn't find Dave anywhere," Kitty says worriedly.

I assure her that he's all right and will be coming down for breakfast soon.

Jessie and Dave arrive together a few minutes later, taking seats on different sides of the table. They pretend to ignore one another. While I don't really understand such a conspiracy, I'm not one to judge.

During breakfast, we speculate on who might have possibly informed Guardian about our mission. Chase begins telling about Vogel's effort to identify any possible spies. A loud snoring suddenly interrupts his report.

I turn to look at Kitty. She has fallen asleep and her face is almost in her plate of food. I nudge her gently, waking her back up.

"I see somebody isn't too interested in catching the terrorists," Chase comments mockingly.

"It's all Rex's fault," Kitty mumbles angrily. "He kept me awake till sunrise."

The room becomes deathly silent for a moment, then everybody bursts out laughing. Victor gives me a thumbs up. Kitty's eyes widen in panic, as she realizes exactly what she had just said.

"It's not what you think!" she exclaims. "His nightmares kept me awake! I was seeing his nightmares all night."

Only Holtzmann remains stone-cold, instantly understanding what Kitty's referring to. He says that sharing dreams is a good sign. Our telepathic connection is obviously growing stronger.

"What can we do about it?" I ask him. "I don't want Kitty to suffer from my bad dreams."

Holtzmann repeats how it's impossible to turn the telepathic connection off. I realize that this could become a problem, and unfortunately, I happen to be right.

Kitty can't sleep during the next several nights. She often wakes up crying and shivering. She soon becomes too frightened to even try to fall asleep.

"Kitty, they're just bad dreams," I say softly. "They can't hurt you."

"It feels so real," she sobs. "How can you sleep, seeing such things every night?"

"I don't know," I admit. "I guess I just got used to it."

I finally decide to stay awake, letting Kitty get some needed rest. I just can't watch her suffer any longer. Kitty protests a little, but soon gives up and closes her eyes. I watch her for a few minutes, before grabbing a book from a stack on the floor and leaving.

I sit in the corridor, trying to read, but it's just too dark. My good eye quickly gets tired. I give up, shutting the book and walking along the lonely passageway. I step outside and wander around the building. A few dedicated protestors notice me, and begin calling me a terrorist. I wave at them, ignoring the insults.

I return back inside the prison, wandering along the corridors in an attempt to pass time till morning. Around 3 AM, I somehow wind up in front of Vogel's office. The light is still on, which means the major must be awake. I hesitate a few moments, wondering what the heck I'm doing here. I raise my hand and freeze, hesitating to knock. I realize it's just not appropriate. Vogel is probably busy checking lists of recently arrived breakers in search of any possible terrorists. And if even she's not busy, what would I say to her? How would I explain a sudden night visit?

I realize I know well enough what I'm doing here. I simply want to see Vogel and have a chance to speak to her. Vogel's image lures me, because I can't stop wondering what it would be like to grow up in her family. I can't help thinking what kind of life Marian and I would have had, if Vogel were Emily. And why couldn't things have turned out that way?

I decide I'm just too tired and thinking nonsense. I turn around and leave, giving up on the idea to see Vogel. It was a really ridiculous thought.

I continue walking the corridors. I keep myself busy thinking about Guardian and his possible plans. His terrorists may be still concealing themselves within the city. Hopefully, Vogel and Chase will soon establish a list of suspects.

I suddenly think how the last weeks have been too peaceful and quiet. It reminds me of the silence before a thunderstorm. Maybe Guardian and his breakers are preparing for another violent attack. Or maybe I'm just being too paranoid.

***

Weakness, nausea and nightmares are not the only side effects of the drug Kitty and I have to cope with. Late one evening Kitty screams from the bathroom.

"What happened?" I ask, knocking on the door. It's locked.

Kitty lets out another terrified shriek instead of a reply.

"Are you hurt?" I ask. "Open the door!"

"No! I don't want you to see," she mutters. I don't know what possibly could have happened to her, but it must be something terrible. She sounds very upset.

"Kitty! Open the damn door or I'll break it down," I demand.

Sobbing, Kitty finally gives in, letting me in. Her face is wet from tears and she's holding a long thick lock of hair in her fist.

"What did you do?" I ask.

"Nothing," Kitty whimpers. "I was just brushing my hair and it started falling out."

I look Kitty over carefully. I realize that her hair seems very thin and I can almost see her scalp in a few places. I hadn't noticed this before.

Kitty is crying miserably.

"C'mon," I sigh. "It's just hair."

"I'm growing bald!" she yells.

Her emotional outburst causes a lamp bulb to explode overhead, sharp pieces of glass crashing against the floor.

"I'm sorry," Kitty sobs quietly.

"Don't move," I order, realizing that she's barefoot and may cut her feet.

I quickly put on my boots and carry Kitty out of the bathroom. I place her on the bed and carefully run my fingers through my own hair. I stare at the small pile of dark hair left in my hand.

"What do we do now, Rex?" Kitty asks.

"Well," I say. "I guess we'll just have to shave our heads."

Kitty covers her mouth, looking at me in near panic.

"I'm sure it will grow back after we stop using the drug," I add.

"It's all right," she says calmly. "I'm not some silly girl who cares so much about her hair."

The next day Kitty makes a whole production out of shaving our heads. She invites Marian, Marcus and Dave to witness our transformation. She makes Jessie responsible for performing the procedure. I go first, trying not to think about the time Dr. Carrel tried to implant electrodes into my skull. The haunting memory still makes me uncomfortable.

"You look like an inmate," Kitty comments, after Jessie finishes.

"Well, we are inside a prison, aren't we?" I say.

Kitty smiles uneasily as Jessie shaves her head. Afterward, Kitty looks at her reflection in the mirror, and her lips begin to quiver.

"I'm ugly now," she sobs.

"It's fine, Kitty," I say, realizing that she's about to break down. "You always look beautiful to me."

"But I want to look beautiful to everybody else too!" she exclaims.

She starts crying bitterly. I attempt to calm her down. I assure her that losing hair isn't the end of the world. I suggest that she wear a wig, if it bothers her so much. My words aren't helping. Kitty only mumbles how I'm a guy and can't possibly understand.

It's not me, but my sister who finally soothes her feelings. Marian hugs Kitty, smiling broadly and saying, "Well, you don't look so girlish now. And so what? You look very tough. Just like a real warrior."

"Really?" Kitty asks, momentarily stopping her crying. "Rex, do I look tough?"

"Very tough," I hurriedly lie. Kitty actually looks very vulnerable and somewhat alien-like without her hair.

She grins, studying her new reflection in the mirror.

"I think I'm even beginning to like it," she proclaims. I glance at Marian and silently mouth a thank you. My sister shrugs, offering me a cold smile. She soon leaves for her work at the refugee center. The others head toward the dining room.

I can't stop thinking about my sister. I can't understand the rapid changes in her mood.

A short time later an officer marches into the room.

"There's a large fire at the children's hospital a few blocks from headquarters," he reports. "Vogel and Chase are awaiting your team outside."

CHAPTER 20

I instantly understand that the fire at the children's hospital isn't just some accident. I'm pretty sure Guardian's terrorists are behind it. But a part of me still doesn't want to accept this likelihood, because it's too nasty and brutal. Why target sick children, for God's sake?

Upon arrival at the hospital, I watch as two Elimination officers carry a teenaged girl away from the building. She's screaming non-stop, kicking and clawing at her rescuers. The girl is only about thirteen, but she fights so furiously that she nearly manages to knock the officers off balance. It takes a supreme effort to immobilize the girl and get her inside the truck.

I now realize what's happening. Before setting the hospital on fire, the terrorists must have put the patients under. They probably directed their victims to do whatever it takes to remain inside the burning building. Under hypnosis, the patients would feel neither fear nor pain. They could break a bone and continue fighting. They won't stop until completing the task placed in their minds.

Vogel with a squad of officers are already inside the building evacuating victims from sections of the hospital not ablaze. I look around anxiously, realizing that nobody is here to fight the fire. Chase explains that the firefighters haven't received a salary since the beginning of the war, so they are all currently on strike.

Great timing, I think grimly. That means there's nobody else coming to help rescue the victims. And we don't have any special protective gear or equipment to deal with the fire. Elimination does possess respirators for protection from sleeping gas, but those masks wouldn't adequately protect us from this suffocating smoke.

Time is of the essence, so our team along with a few of Oliver's breakers quickly proceed inside the hospital. Our primary objective is to snap the patients out of their hypnosis and fighting mode. It's not an easy assignment because it's incredibly hard to manipulate subjects whose wills are already under somebody's control.

We walk from room to room, searching for any hiding children. Upon seeing us, they begin to growl and come out fighting like wild animals, resisting any attempts to help them. They bite and claw as the officers try to grab hold of them. They scream and kick furiously, their minds filled with some pointless rage. Our hypnosis often fails, so we're unable to snap many out of their aggressive trances.

I'm becoming desperate. The fire is spreading terrifyingly fast, and we have only minutes left to complete this evacuation. My head feels ready to explode from pain, and I'm constantly choking. It's impossible to concentrate and use my hypnosis as effectively as the situation requires. I almost begin to hate these stubborn kids who fight so hard against us as we're trying to rescue them.

I notice a little girl lying under a gurney inside one of the rooms. Her face seems relaxed and her eyes are glazed. As I approach, she hisses like a stray cat, lunging at me. I pin her to the floor, while she's shouting and clawing at my eyes. Concentrating as best I can, I project my thoughts into her perplexed mind. Stop fighting, I direct, let me help you. My hypnosis slows her aggressiveness down enough for the officers to carry her outside.

A teenaged boy attacks me inside another room. He comes through the smoke before I can see him. He grabs my throat, trying to choke me. I don't have time to use hypnosis, so I punch him hard into his temple, knocking him out cold. I only hope I haven't injured him too badly. I drag him toward the doorway where Chase and another officer carry the unconscious boy outside.

The evacuation seems to last forever. But I know that in reality it can't be longer than fifteen minutes, because of the rate in which the fire is spreading. We simply don't have time to get all the patients outside. The children still inside are being burnt alive, unable or unwilling to get to safety. The thought makes me sick, and I have to force myself to remain calm. I can't allow myself even a moment of weakness now. I have to concentrate on the task at hand.

Kitty and others are also helping assist officers in evacuating patients. Together, we manage to lead at least half of the kids outside. The smoke is becoming thicker with each passing second. It's time for us to leave, but we stubbornly remain inside. There are still too many kids trapped inside this building. We have to try and save as many of them as we can.

I continue hypnotizing the afflicted children as long as is possible. I soon find myself stuck inside one of the rooms. Kitty is crouching beside me, rubbing at her eyes and muttering something incoherent. My eyes are tearing. I'm becoming disoriented, and have trouble understanding what we need to do. I finally grab her arm and begin crawling toward an exit. Kitty suddenly collapses in a doorway, quiet and motionless. Grabbing her by the arms, I stagger down the passageway, dragging an unconscious Kitty toward the main doors. My lungs seem to burn. I sway and feel myself starting to pass out, no longer knowing where exactly I'm going. It's getting really difficult to understand anything.

"Rex!" I hear somebody's shrill voice. "Where the hell are you?"

"Here!" I yell.

Jessie approaches, saying something, but I can't comprehend her words.

"Take her!" I plead, pushing Kitty into Jessie's arms.

She doesn't protest, tightly gripping Kitty by her wrists and dragging her away. I realize I should follow them, but instead plop down on the floor. I have no strength left to follow anybody. Kitty is safe and that's what matters most.

Some part of my consciousness realizes that I have to get out of this building. I begin crawling on my hands and knees along the corridor. I can't see anything, with my good eye watering profusely. I'm becoming weaker. I bump into a wall and freeze.

I understand I won't be getting out of here on my own.

I spend a couple of moments, trying to find an air pocket to relieve my burning lungs. Suddenly, two strong arms grab my jacket, pulling me forward.

"Get up!" Vogel commands. "Walk!"

She throws my arm over her shoulders, supporting my weight. I still can't see a damn thing, and I've lost coordination for walking. Vogel tries to lead me out, but I'm too weak.

"Rex!" she barks. "Stay with me! Come on, move!"

Despite of my best efforts, I fall back down onto the floor. The major angrily curses me, pulling me up again. I realize there's no chance she can carry me outside. I'm too heavy for her.

"Go on," I mutter. "Get out."

Vogel continues barking commands at me, gripping my arms so tightly that it hurts. She's choking on the thick smoke as well, but refuses to leave me. I realize we're both about to suffocate and then be burned alive. But I don't become overly worried by the fact, because I'm only half-conscious now. I weakly attempt to rise to my feet one more time, before everything fades.

***

When I come to, somebody is splashing water over my face.

"Wake up! Please wake up!" Kitty sobs.

I open my eyes, but can't see anything. I begin to panic.

"Where are you?" I blurt out. Becoming permanently blind is one of my worst fears.

"I'm right here," she says. "Calm down. You're safe."

I attempt to sit up, but somebody pushes me back down. I continue mumbling about my lost vision, as an oxygen mask is placed over my nose and mouth.

"It's unacceptable!" I hear Holtzmann's hysterical voice. "Help him immediately!"

Another voice assures him that his subject will be fine.

I inhale several deep breaths, almost getting high on the pure oxygen. My eyes are still burning, but my vision slowly normalizes. I find myself sprawled across the pavement outside of the hospital. I must have been out for several minutes, because the entire building is now in flames and beginning to collapse. I notice row after row of small bodies laid out across the concrete. I've no idea whether these patients are still alive or not.

Kitty is beside me, holding my hand and sobbing. Two paramedics check my eyes and pulse. They pull me up, leading me away toward an ambulance.

"Vogel," I say. "Where is she?"

"She's already been taken to the hospital," Chase answers flatly, walking alongside.

"Will she be all right?" I ask. He remains silent. "Will she be all right?" I repeat.

He ignores me, returning to the other officers to help carry more unconscious patients. Paramedics shove Kitty and me inside the ambulance and we leave. They deliver us to another hospital for examination. Holtzmann arrives a few minutes later to check on us. He looks distressed.

I can't stop worrying about Vogel. Kitty informs me that the major passed out a moment after dragging me out of the burning building. I'm amazed by the fact that Vogel somehow managed to get me all the way to an exit. I've no idea where she found the strength to do so.

After the medics are done with me, I go look for Vogel. Holtzmann informs me that the major is in intensive care. Medics are doing their best to revive her.

"Wait a minute, professor," I say. "Vogel and I spent the same amount of time in there, breathing that smoke. Why does she require intensive care, when I'm perfectly fine?"

Avoiding my stare, Holtzmann explains how my breathing was much slower since I was already unconscious, therefore I inhaled less smoke than Vogel. Another complication is that she suffers from heart disease. The medics informed Holtzmann that the major had a difficult surgery several months ago, and it didn't go quite as well as it was supposed to.

I suddenly feel ill. I recall what Marcus told me about Vogel. I asked him why the major didn't get killed by Guardian's breakers during the initial massacre. She wasn't on the duty, he had explained, she was on sick leave.

I spend the next hour in front of the intensive care unit, waiting for any news on Vogel. Kitty sits beside me, clutching my hand. We don't exchange a single word while waiting. There's simply nothing to be said.

The surgeons finally come out, and by the looks on their faces I can already tell what kind of news they're bringing.

Vogel didn't make it. She sacrificed her life, rescuing me from the fire.

Kitty sobs quietly, covering her face. I listen to the doctors, hearing only some of their words. Vogel wasn't supposed to be put under any stress or excessive physical exertion after her surgery. She needed complete rest, and almost any sort of complication could cause her heart to stop.

I gain control of myself and proceed into the intensive care unit, leaving Kitty in the corridor. I stand beside the gurney, looking down at Vogel's lifeless body. She's covered with a white sheet. I cautiously grip the sheet and pull it down a little, revealing her head and chest. I see a rough, fresh scar spread across the right side of her rib cage.

"Gosh, Erica!" I breathe out. "I'm so sorry."

I want to say something else, but my throat clenches, and I can't utter another word. I pull the sheet back over her and sit down on the floor, gazing off into space.

I can easily envision Vogel learning the news about Guardian's breakers taking over the country several months ago. She was still in the hospital and not fully recovered from her recent surgery. She pulled on her black uniform, even while her scar was still bleeding. She holstered her gun and left the hospital, knowing full well that she could die at any moment.

Vogel could have easily stayed away, letting Guardian destroy the world. But she didn't. She fought as long as her health allowed, trying to save the rest of us.

I mentally add her name to the growing list of people who have died because of me. Although I gave up on any senseless plans to assassinate Vogel, I indeed became the one who caused her death.

It takes a few minutes for me to fully comprehend that Vogel is gone forever. I won't ever get a chance to speak to her again. I'll never again experience her support and kindness. And I suddenly feel as if I've just lost a great friend.

There was always something about Vogel that made her special. She always acted as if she had all the answers. She possessed an exceptional inner strength and calmness, which made everybody want to follow her. She was a true Elimination officer, a brave fighter, and at the same time a genuinely good person. And although I never really expected her to replace Emily, I always felt she could teach me some things I naturally lack.

I'm still sitting on the floor, when Chase, Marcus and Dave enter the room. They all stare at their dead commander, no one speaking for a long time.

"We're all screwed now," Chase finally utters. "There's no point in continuing to fight. There's zero chance we can win this war without her."

"Are you so ready to give up now?" I ask, looking up tiredly.

"What else can we do?" he asks, letting out an inappropriate laugh. "Elimination no longer has its leader."

"It's gotta be you," I say.

Chase frowns, not understanding what I'm getting at.

"You have to lead Elimination now, Chase," I inform him. "You'll fill in for Vogel."

"You must be kidding," he answers. "I don't have the qualifications for such a job. I didn't even go to college."

"Think about it, Chase," I say. "Try to figure out why Vogel was always asking your opinion. Why did she make you deal with all the documents and take you along with her everywhere? Vogel was obviously coaching you for something big."

"You're insane," he states. "I'm just a regular officer."

"Vogel believed in you," I protest. "She knew she could die at any moment, so she groomed you to become her replacement."

"I can't lead anybody," Chase answers stubbornly.

"You led other officers during the prison riot. You're a natural leader. Vogel must have seen it in you and chose you for this special role. She also realized that you're tolerant to breakers. No matter what you think, you'll make a perfect commander, Chase."

He doesn't answer.

"Rex is right," Marcus says. "It really does seem like she was developing you all along."

Chase shakes his head.

"We'll follow you," Dave quietly adds.

"Cut the nonsense!" Chase says, wincing. "Just look at us. We're standing before Vogel's still warm body, discussing who'll take her place. It's sick. Show a little respect for God's sake!"

"You know this is something that Vogel would approve of," I say calmly.

"I'm not Vogel!" Chase suddenly shouts. "Now get the hell out of here, now! Leave us alone!"

Marcus, Dave and I head toward the exit. Passing by Chase, I quietly repeat, "She always believed in you."

He turns away, ignoring my proclamation. I know Vogel's death has completely demoralized Chase along with all the other officers. Unfortunately, we don't have the luxury of time to properly mourn.

Back outside the hospital, we meet Holtzmann, Jessie and Kitty. Everybody is already aware of the bad news. Upon seeing my expression,

Jessie lights two cigarettes and hands one to me. I snatch it from Jessie's fingers and smoke nervously. I don't know what we're going to do.

An Elimination truck stops a few feet away from us. Oliver and a couple of officers jump out, seemingly troubled.

"We just received a phone call from one of the refugee centers," Oliver informs us. "Somebody claims that the Army of Justice has taken over the building. It looks like a hostage situation."

I swallow hard and ask, "Which refugee center?"

"The city's northeast location."

I get a sensation as if the ground is shifting beneath my feet.

That is the refugee center where Rebecca and my sister work, and now they've become hostages. This fire was possibly only a distraction, while Guardian's breakers were preparing for another vicious terrorist act.

CHAPTER 21

Twenty minutes later my team and a squad of Elimination officers arrive at the square in front of the refugee center. A few dozen bystanders have already gathered outside, and the crowd is growing. I also notice a group of overly excited journalists present.

"So what's the plan?" Chase asks, gazing at the building. Everything looks absolutely ordinary, as if nothing unusual is happening inside.

"I don't have one," I answer. "You're the commander."

Chase sighs, obviously disliking the idea of leadership. We watch him expectantly.

"All right then," he finally says in an assertive voice. "Set up a perimeter. Don't let anybody approach the building."

The officers hurriedly execute his command.

Chase requests Oliver to repeat what the terrorists said during the phone call to Elimination headquarters.

"A male's voice proclaimed that the Army of Justice has taken over the north-eastern refugee center," Oliver answers. "He said nobody should try to go inside the building or even so much as contact their group. They'll begin shooting hostages, should we disobey."

So there must be about six hundred hostages inside the center, including my sister and Rebecca, I think grimly. And there's no telling whether or not they're still alive.

"This place looks weird," Chase notes, staring at the building again. "What was here before it became a refugee center?

"My sister said it was a theatre," I answer.

"The terrorists must be keeping the hostages inside the auditorium," Kitty guesses. "Marian told me it's the biggest room in the building."

"I wonder whether we should go ahead and break in," Chase offers.

"The terrorists said the building is set with explosives," Oliver reminds us. "They promised to blow the entire center should we try anything."

"How can we be sure they have explosives in there?" Jessie asks. "Maybe they're just bluffing."

"Maybe," Chase says. "But we don't want to find out the hard way. So we just have to assume that all their threats are genuine."

He sends Marcus to examine the main entrance of the center, without actually going in. We watch anxiously as he approaches the large glass doors and takes a careful look inside. We all realize he could be shot at any moment.

"There are several large bags left out in the hall," he reports, after safely rejoining our group. "Could be explosives. I also noticed video cameras on the walls."

An hour later the phone rings in a nearby office building, and a male's voice informs us that five journalists may safely enter the center.

Chase hesitates, then allows the journalists to go on inside. It's an opportunity to collect some needed information. Having returned, the journalists report that there are about twenty terrorists inside controlling the hostages.

"They're keeping everybody in the auditorium," one correspondent advises. "They have plenty of ammo and bags filled with explosives."

"Do they have any requests?" Chase asks.

It happens that the terrorists demand Kitty, Holtzmann and me to walk inside the center, unarmed.

"Don't even think about it," Chase barks before I can open my mouth to say anything. "You're not going anywhere."

"Guardian must know why we stole the drug," Kitty says. "That's why he wants the three of us inside the building. He's aware we're planning to assassinate him."

"I may go in there alone," I offer. "I could try to negotiate with the terrorists."

"Are you crazy?" Chase exclaims. "Don't you understand why they really want to lure you inside? It's not for any negotiations."

I understand everything better than Chase probably thinks. Guardian needs to kill Kitty, Holtzmann and me, before we can complete our mission. It may be the singular purpose behind this terrorist act.

We discuss the possibility of storming the building. The problem is that the officers would have to walk through long corridors and pass a large open space, before reaching the terrorists. There's no chance of getting inside the auditorium unnoticed. The terrorists would either start killing hostages or blow up the entire building. We can't take such a big risk, at least not yet.

An hour later, an officer reports that the terrorists have called again and request to speak to Chase. We proceed inside the office building. Chase puts them on speaker, so that we can all hear the conversation. One of the terrorists assures us that hostages will begin to die, should his demands remain ignored. Holtzmann, Kitty and I must enter the building immediately.

"We can't agree to that," Chase says. "Adjust your demands and free the hostages. I personally guarantee to spare your lives if you let the hostages go. We will allow you to safely leave the city."

"Cut the crap," the terrorist answers, breaking off the connection.

Chase plops down on a chair, holding his head in exhaustion.

"They're gonna start shooting people," he states. "And I don't have a clue what we can do about it. I keep trying to think what Vogel would do in this situation. But I'm not Vogel, and can't know what she would do."

"It's all right," I say. "You're doing fine, Chase."

He pulls himself together and assigns Oliver responsible for checking out different scenarios for storming the center.

"Find a similar building," he instructs. "Take a few officers and run simulations to see if there's any possibility of killing the terrorists before they could activate the explosives."

Oliver leaves with a squad of officers.

We wait for the terrorists to contact us again, but the phone remains silent.

"Do you think you possibly could hypnotize those breakers?" Chase asks.

"I seriously doubt it," I admit.

Guardian certainly must have chosen the most resistant breakers to carry this out. And we can't be taking any chances, because the current situation doesn't leave any room for mistakes.

Nobody sleeps that night. Oliver, along with his squad of officers and recruits train for the possible storming of the building. My team and I help evacuate patients from a nearby hospital, clearing beds for expected new patients. The city Department of Transportation provides a few buses, so we're able to transport about three hundred patients into city schools. Surprisingly, most patients don't protest, being very understanding. Everybody realizes this is war.

The second day begins with another phone call from the terrorists. Their leader repeats the demand for Holtzmann, Kitty and I to walk unarmed inside the theater. He breaks the connection before Chase has time to respond. An upset Oliver enters the room and reports that he's run all possible variants of storming the center, and there's no way to do it before the terrorists shoot hostages or blow the building. The spacious floorplan of the former theater simply doesn't allow enough time. There's no cover on approach to the auditorium. So we'll have to find another solution.

"What about using sleeping gas?" Jessie asks.

"We ran out several months ago," Chase reminds her.

"The hospitals may have some other gas available to use," I insist.

Chase shakes his head, patiently explaining how doctors have run out of most types of anesthetics and tranquilizers.

"What about veterinarians?" Kitty asks.

It seems like a good idea at first, but Holtzmann assures us that usage of these types of tranquilizers may be too dangerous for humans.

"Any other suggestions?" Chase asks. Nobody answers. "We should try and gasify the animal tranquilizers then. Right now it's our best shot. Holtzmann, you'll coordinate with the veterinarians. Try to find some sort of acceptable drug."

"They're all unacceptable," Holtzmann mumbles angrily before leaving.

The rest of us pass time observing the refuge center from out on the square.

Around 3 PM, we hear gunfire coming from the inside. A window on the second floor suddenly breaks and somebody jumps out, falling into some bushes growing on the side of the building. I immediately recognize her hysterical girlish scream.

"Marian!" I yell.

I lunge forward, but Chase tightly grabs my jacket and holds me back.

"Cover her!" he shouts.

The Elimination officers open covering fire toward the windows, preventing the terrorists from shooting down onto my sister. She quickly scrambles to her feet, continuing to scream, as she sprints across the square. Marcus and Dave run forward and drag her back toward our group. Marian is limping and her hands are cut from the glass. She looks around blankly, then shoves away the officers and gives me a hug. I squeeze her in my arms, still not believing she's safe.

"I'm alive!" she cries.

"You're hurt," I say, looking her over.

"It's just a small cut," Marian answers, smiling.

Medics pull her away from me and lead her toward one of the waiting ambulances. Kitty and I follow. The doctors assure us that my sister is all right and hasn't sustained any life threatening injuries, only cuts and bruises. They clean her wounds and bandage her hands.

"I've never seen anything like that before," Chase says. "I don't understand how she didn't get herself killed during an escape like that."

"She's my sister," I answer proudly.

"Yeah that sounds about right," he laughs. "You two seem to specialize in all the crazy stuff."

He asks Marian what's happening inside the building.

"Gosh, Chase!" I exclaim. "Let her recover first."

"It's okay," Marian says. "I want to help."

She begins telling us how the terrorists are holding the hostages in the auditorium without food or water. They walk amongst the rows of terrified people, constantly threatening them with rifles and knives.

"They're lunatics," Marian states. "They promised that nobody would be leaving that building alive."

Listening to her story, I become really worried. I realize the hostages won't last for too long without food or water. The clock is ticking, and we still don't have an actionable plan.

"How did you escape?" I ask Marian.

"It was Rebecca's idea," she answers.

"Is she all right?"

My sister nods.

"She's busy keeping people calm and trying to negotiate with the terrorists," she answers. "Rebecca persuaded them to allow the hostages some water. They provided only one bottle for every five people, but it was still better than nothing."

I'm dumbfounded. I've no idea how Rebecca managed it. How did she find a way to reason with those crazies?

"Rebecca and I were together," my sister continues. "She pointed at the window and said that it was my only chance. She began speaking with the terrorists, diverting their attention. And I was thinking how I'm gonna screw it up for sure. Because I can't do anything right. The terrorists will

240

see me and then shoot me down. That's what I thought, and of course I was absolutely correct. I did screw up, by trying to sneak too cautiously and slowly toward that window. Of course the terrorists noticed me. I heard gunfire, and thought I was a goner for sure. So I freaked out and just ran as fast as I could, and then," Marian pauses, catching her breath, "just slammed full speed into that damn window and fell. I still don't understand how the terrorists didn't manage to hit me. I mean, they were firing from close range."

"That's the craziest story I've ever heard," Chase says, looking at me. "You know, she really is related to you. It definitely sounds like something you'd do in a similar situation."

I can't decide whether it's intended as an insult or a compliment.

"Why didn't Rebecca try to escape as well?" I ask.

"She chose to stay inside to look after the other hostages," Marian answers. "Cynthia truly seems to like her. Rebecca thinks she may possibly influence her."

"Cynthia?" I mutter. "What does she have to do with all this?"

"You really don't know?" Marian asks as her eyes widen in surprise. "Cynthia is the leader of those terrorists."

My jaw drops. Everybody stares at my sister.

"Who's Cynthia?" Chase asks. "Where does she come from?"

"She's just an ordinary girl," I answer.

"She's a powerful breaker," Marian insists.

"Will somebody just answer my question?" Chase wonders.

I tell him what I know about Cynthia, which is definitely not too much.

"A gang of breakers were keeping her hostage," I add. "She also had to leave town after Guardian's soldiers destroyed her home."

Chase says that he needs to conduct some research. He leaves, returning to headquarters to check files. We remain inside the office building, sitting by the phone and waiting for the terrorists to call.

Chase comes back an hour later and places a photograph on the table in front of me.

"Is this your Cynthia?" he asks, grinning.

I stare at the photograph, realizing it's a mug shot of Cynthia. She looks much younger in the photo, probably in her late teens, and her head is shaved. Nasty-looking electrodes protrude from her skull, giving me a flashback of little Lena.

"It's Cynthia," I say.

"She's a level four breaker," Chase says, still smirking. "And a gang of breakers didn't torture or hold her hostage. She was actually their leader. Elimination captured her while she was still a teen. She initiated several riots in prison and killed plenty of officers. Even after being transferred to a more secure facility, Cynthia managed to start a riot there as well. She finally escaped with a group of dangerous criminals and quickly became their leader. Then her gang began robbing and killing ordinary humans. We recaptured her a few months before the war started and kept her in the Death Camp. That's likely where she met Guardian."

I listen to Chase, not really hearing his words.

I remember Cynthia being shy and blushing, then suddenly becoming aggressive. I think about her telling me how I didn't appreciate the opportunities I had been provided. I remember her saying that she'd do anything to have a life like mine. I also recall Cynthia vigorously insisting on meeting me somewhere alone.

How stupid can you really be? I ask myself. I finally understand everything.

Guardian must have promised to make Cynthia some sort of leader, should she manage to assassinate me. And it seems like I always suspected there was something a little off with her. If I'd only chosen to trust my gut feeling, if I'd only thought twice about everything she'd said…

"Gosh," I groan out loud. "I could have stopped her!"

Everybody looks at me in confusion. I quickly explain what kind of conversation Cynthia and I had.

"Whoa!" Chase exclaims. "You're lucky you didn't go on a date with her. It was obviously a trap. That chick would simply have killed you."

"I realize that now," I answer flatly.

"Did you really think she had a crush on you?" Jessie asks. "You actually believed that she would just immediately fall for you, after being tortured by other breakers? Rex, are you really that naive or just retarded?"

I don't have anything to say. I did swallow all the ridiculous lies Cynthia fed me. I only now realize how I could have prevented two acts of terror. I could have told Chase or Vogel about Cynthia, and we could have captured her. Many people would be still alive, including Vogel. And now, it's just too darn late.

The phone suddenly rings. The familiar male's voice begins saying something, but Chase cuts him off, "I know your leader is Cynthia. I won't speak to anybody except her."

The terrorist curses and hangs up on him.

"I hope I haven't just killed any hostages," Chase sighs.

A few minutes later we receive another call.

"So you now know the truth," Cynthia states.

"We know who you are, Cynthia," Chase assures her.

"Shut the hell up," she interrupts. "I won't speak to any Elimination swine. The next time I call, I want Rex to answer. Is that understood?"

She breaks the connection before Chase has time to utter another word.

"You heard her," he says, looking at me. "You'll have to be the one to negotiate with Cynthia."

"Are you joking?" I ask. "How in the world am I supposed to do that? What do I say?"

"She often asked Rebecca questions about you," Marian mutters thoughtfully. "It sure seemed Cynthia is really interested in you."

"Do you remember Jack?" Kitty asks me. I nod because it'd be hard to ever forget Jack, who tried to kill me. "What if Cynthia is just like him?" Kitty continues. "What if she used to look up to you before becoming disappointed in you?"

I doubt Kitty's conclusion and I also doubt I could be any good at negotiating with Cynthia. Unfortunately, the other members of my team share a different opinion. They continue trying to persuade me on the most effective ways to influence her.

"Just try to get her to free the hostages," Chase instructs.

"How?" I ask.

"Gosh, just do what all guys normally do," Marian answers. "Lie to her. Say you were an idiot and you regret having rejected her. Tell her you didn't realize how special she was."

"C'mon, Rex," Kitty says. "We believe in you. You're a great liar."

I open my mouth to protest, but the phone suddenly rings. Chase presses the button for the speaker, as Jessie simultaneously shoves me over closer to the phone. I take a breath, readying myself mentally, and say, "Hello?"

"Hey darling," Cynthia answers. Her voice sounds annoyingly friendly. "I thought you were too busy to find any time for me. Have you finally changed your mind?"

I linger for a moment, realizing that the lives of hundreds people depend on my words.

"You have my full attention," I say.

"Well," Cynthia sighs. "That's not exactly what I want."

"What do you want?" I ask.

"You," she answers, "along with your girlfriend and the professor. Walk inside the refugee center and I might decide to spare the hostages."

I look at Chase. He shakes his head no.

"That's not happening," I answer calmly.

"Listen to this then," she offers as the ominous sound of gunfire fills the room.

"No! Stop!" I blurt out, envisioning her gunning down hostages.

Cynthia hangs up. I stand unmoving, staring at the phone. I realize my hands are shaking. I look helplessly around at the members of my team. Everybody seems astonished. Nobody speaks.

Cynthia calls back a few minutes later.

"Will you be more agreeable now?" she asks, still using the same pleasant voice. "Drop your crappy attitude and be a good boy, or I'll kill more hostages. So make it easy on everybody and just bring yourself in."

I steady myself and say, "I have to do what Elimination orders me to do. I'm not a free man."

I've no idea what I'm talking about. But there's a long pause and I don't hear any more gunfire. Cynthia must be at least thinking over my words.

"You mean they're keeping you prisoner?" she asks, letting out a laugh. "Well, it's your own doing, you stinking traitor. Guardian offered you everything a human being could wish for. And you spit in his face, rejecting his generous offer." She curses and adds with spite, "You didn't even have to do anything in order to acquire his attention. Do you know what I had to go through to achieve my current position in his army?"

"Tell me," I suggest.

"I won't tell you anything, you piece of trash. Even hearing your voice makes me want to vomit!"

"Why do you hate me so much, Cynthia?" I ask. "You don't even know me."

"I know you well enough, traitor," she assures me. "You chose to betray your own kind."

I look around, motioning for my team to somehow help me. Marian scribbles down something on a piece of paper and shows it to me. Apologize, her scribbling suggests.

"Sorry, I've made a lot of mistakes," I say. "I just couldn't stay in the Death Camp. I had to return to my sister."

"She isn't even a breaker," Cynthia snorts.

"You're right," I say. "And I regret leaving the Death Camp. It was a bad decision, because it turns out my sister doesn't even like me. I should have accepted Guardian's offer. I truly regret that I refused to cooperate with him."

"I'm getting tired of this," Cynthia says. "I think I'm gonna kill a few more hostages now."

"Wait! Don't do that," I plead. "Talk to me. Please."

"Come on in and we'll talk face to face," she suggests. "Do you remember how I offered you the opportunity to meet with me alone? We can still arrange that."

She's bluffing. No chance she would meet me alone.

"How do I know you wouldn't bring back up?" I ask.

Cynthia begins laughing. "Do you really think I'm so scared to meet you alone? You still believe that you're the stronger breaker, one who could overpower me?"

"I don't know," I answer. "I guess we won't find out unless we meet."

"And what exactly would you do being left all alone with me, with no guards for your protection?" Cynthia asks.

I'd break your neck, I think, but instead I say, "Cynthia, let's just quit with the nonsense. You know Elimination won't permit your full request. It's just not gonna happen. You can't have Kitty or Holtzmann. But you may still get a chance to capture me. I'll bring myself over if you'll agree to free the hostages."

"Careful now," Cynthia says. "You may anger me."

"There's no reason to be angry," I answer. "I'm offering you a deal."

"Six hundreds lives in exchange for one? I wouldn't exactly call that a fair exchange. Holtzmann, Kitty and you must walk in together. I won't accept anything less."

"Do you realize that Elimination won't let you escape, should you kill the hostages?" I ask.

"Is that what you think about me? That I'm scared of Elimination?"

"No, I guess not," I sigh.

"Would you really sacrifice yourself for ordinary people?" she asks.

"Yes, I would," I answer. I'm not sure whether I'm lying or not. What would I do if Cynthia agreed to make a deal with me? Would I enter the refugee center and then... what?

She doesn't answer right away. I hold my breath. Come on, I think, agree to do this.

"You're even more an idiot than I originally thought," Cynthia says.

I hear a burst of gunfire before she breaks the connection. I take a step away from the phone. I wonder whom it was she killed this time. I hope it wasn't Rebecca or any children. My stomach suddenly churns. I stagger out of the room, double over and throw up in the corridor. I don't know whether it's the result of Holtzmann's drug or stress from my conversation with Cynthia. It's probably a combination of both.

"It's not your fault she didn't believe you," Kitty says, handing me a bottle of water. "Everybody knows you did your best."

I wash out my mouth, return inside the room and stare at the phone, waiting for it to ring. Thirty minutes later we receive another call.

"Listen up, traitor," Cynthia says calmly. "I want you, Kitty and Holtzmann to turn yourselves in before sunset. I'll begin systematically shooting hostages, should you fail to execute my request. Every hour after dark will cost you twelve hostages. These deaths will be on you."

She breaks off the connection before I can answer.

"Looks like we have no other option available, but storming the building," Chase states.

CHAPTER 22

It's 4 AM and I'm standing in front of the refugee center, waiting for the lights in the building to be shut off. As soon as officers cut the electricity, my team along with a group of Elimination soldiers and Oliver's recruits will go inside.

Thirty minutes ago, two officers managed to climb unnoticed to the rooftop of the center and have already piped the sedative gas into the ventilation system. It's a strong tranquilizer which veterinarians usually only use on large animals such as horses or cows. Holtzmann says using it on humans may cause severe side effects and possibly even death. It looks like we're going to have plenty of casualties amongst the hostages. But this tranquilizer is the best Holtzmann could come up with on such short notice. We simply couldn't wait any longer, because Cynthia has already begun gunning down hostages, a dozen at a time, at the end of each hour. So people are dying anyway.

I look toward the entrance of the refugee center and can see a pile of unmoving bodies through the glass doors. Wasted lives. The terrorists brought them down to the hall, so that we'd fully realize where our failure to satisfy their requests had led.

I force my eyes away from the dead, although doing so brings no relief. Because all I can see now is a crowd of crying and hysterical people. These are the relatives and friends of the hostages. Medics already had to hospitalize somebody's mother who had a mental breakdown, as well as an old man who suffered a heart attack from all the stress.

The officers finally contact Chase on the radio. He exchanges a couple of words with them, breaks the connection and says, "One minute to go time. Get ready."

We pull on our breathing masks. The lights inside the building go off and our squad carefully proceeds toward the entrance.

The next thirty minutes become a blur.

The gas apparently didn't reach every section of the building, because we run into a group of terrorists on the first floor. They're fully awake, and begin firing their rifles upon noticing us. We shoot back. It's very dark inside, and hard to see anything. I get a sensation that I'm back in the Elimination prison, fighting guards during a riot. I also remember our night battle with Guardian's breakers. It seems that I always wind up in the same situation. There's an attack in the darkness and I'm killing somebody, while trying not to get gunned down myself.

When we finally make it inside the main room, I can see hundreds of motionless bodies spread across the floor. Hostages. It's hard to tell whether they're dead or just sleeping. A few terrorists in camo uniforms move unsteadily toward the center of the room, where the canvas bags with explosives are placed. Two of them fall unconscious, knocked out by the still present gas. We fire, killing the others before they can activate the explosives.

Some of the hostages try to sit up, but quickly fall back down. I see several unconscious guys in camo lying on the floor. More of Guardian's terrorists. The officers quickly handcuff them and place blocking collars around their necks.

We need to remove these hostages from the building as soon as possible. They seem to be in very bad condition, and there's still the threat of explosions. Unfortunately, we can't help anybody just yet. It's necessary to capture or kill all the terrorists first. A few of them could have escaped the auditorium. It'd be virtually impossible to monitor who enters and exits the center once evacuation begins. So there's no choice but wait until we clear the entire building.

"Cynthia isn't here," Chase states after the officers check all the unconscious terrorists in the main room.

I wish I had time to locate Rebecca amongst the victims, but we can't spare any time. Although all the exits are blocked by our men and there's no way Cynthia could get outside, she may still be able to activate concealed explosives.

My team leaves the auditorium, searching for Cynthia. We find her hiding in a doorway on the first floor. She was obviously heading toward a back exit. I realize Cynthia is dressed in civilian clothing, wearing the same poorly fitting sweater and jeans as I remember. She probably planned to slip away during the evacuation, mixing in with the hostages.

"Freeze!" Chase yells, pointing the barrel of his rifle at her.

Cynthia suddenly tosses a small round object under our feet and runs for the door. A grenade, I realize. And there's no place to take cover. We all drop onto the floor, although doing so won't protect us from an explosion. I fall on top of Kitty, shielding her from the coming blast. I hear a muffled explosion, but no fragment of grenade hits us. I raise my head and see Dave spread across the corridor where the grenade landed. He lies motionless on his stomach and a puddle of blood spreads slowly beneath him. I realize Dave has just saved our lives. He sacrificed his own, throwing himself on top of the grenade and covering it with his body.

Kitty lets out a horrified scream, shoving me away and approaching him. Marcus also runs toward his brother. He kneels beside Dave, shouting something. I watch them for a moment in some sort of daze, then rise to my feet, picking up my rifle. Chase and Jessie have already exited the building, searching for Cynthia. I follow them outside, leaving Kitty and Marcus behind.

Once outside, I see Chase and Jessie standing beside the bodies of five officers spread across the concrete. They're lying on their backs, staring into space with wide open, glazed eyes.

"She's put them under," Chase states.

Apparently, Cynthia is an extremely strong hypnotist. I doubt I would be able to hypnotize these officers. Only the most resistant soldiers serve in Elimination.

"Where did she go?" I ask, receiving no answer.

Chase contacts headquarters, requesting a helicopter search of the area. He commands the officers to blockade all roads surrounding the block. Then we begin desperately searching for Cynthia, walking along the dark empty streets. We have to find her before she takes more hostages or kills someone else.

I concentrate on her image. I try to imagine where I would go if I was in her place. My head hurts and I can't focus well enough. I haven't slept for two nights, and the shootout with the terrorists back in the hall sapped most of the strength left in me.

Squadrons of Elimination officers march through the neighborhood, knocking on the door of every house, methodically searching for Cynthia. They can't find her anywhere. I become worried that she could have already broken through our perimeter. What if she managed to hypnotize those officers as well?

I can't let her escape, I think. I can't let her go on living. She's a dangerous, vicious terrorist.

I somehow wind up standing in front of a large building. It was probably supposed to become a mall or business center, but remained unfinished due to the financial collapse. I take a long look at the building, staring into the black holes of windows with no glass. Something tells me to go inside. She's here, I suddenly realize.

I don't know whether it's just intuition or I actually have some sort of telepathic connection with Cynthia. But what I do know is that I have to check it out, by going inside.

"What are you staring at?" Chase asks, approaching.

"She's here," I say.

"How do you know?"

I shrug, not having an answer.

"All right," Chase says. "Let's check it out."

We proceed toward the entrance. Inside the building, I can't hear anything aside from our own footsteps. We move slowly along a wall.

"We need to take her alive," Chase whispers. "She's their leader and may know something important."

I nod.

"Remember when you wondered who leaked the information about the mission to obtain the drug?" he continues. "Rebecca probably complained to Cynthia about Holtzmann going on a mission and…"

"Quiet," I whisper, worried that Cynthia may hear us.

My worries about being heard are probably pointless. She likely already knows we're inside the building. No matter how cautiously Chase and I attempt to move, we produce too much noise. The floor is strewn with broken glass, so it's impossible to walk silently.

We stop ever so often to spend a few moments listening. Nothing. No telling where Cynthia is.

Chase and I continue further into the building. We climb a staircase, entering the second floor, when somebody fires at us from the darkness. Chase groans in pain, falling. I return fire, catching a glimpse of Cynthia running along the passageway. I turn to check on Chase. He's pressing a hand against a wound in his thigh, blood seeping between his fingers.

"Go!" he yells.

I take off after Cynthia. I pass through the corridor and stop at a staircase, hesitating. Should I go up or down? I climb the stairs, coming to the third floor. I stop again, listening attentively. I can hear footsteps, but can't discern the direction from which they're coming.

Holding my breath and trying to be as quiet as possible, I proceed down the hall. I carefully check each room, anticipating to be shot at any moment. Suddenly, I'm hit with an odd dizziness and the floor begins to sway. I recognize the sensation, but can't place it yet.

I see Cynthia standing a few feet away from me. She's aiming a gun at my face. I raise my rifle and fire. She backs off, still holding her weapon on me. I pull the trigger again, but I'm out of ammo. I drop the rifle and charge into Cynthia, trying to tackle her. My arms grab nothing but air. I fall onto the floor, realizing that something is terribly wrong. I hear gunfire, but the bullets don't hit me, even though she's firing almost point blank. And my shot didn't hit Cynthia.

I'm hypnotized, I finally realize.

As soon as I come to understand the situation, Cynthia's image disappears. I stare at the place where she just stood, but now can't see anybody.

Nice job, I think, feeling like an idiot. She's fooled me again. My rifle is now empty and I don't have another weapon. And I know for a fact that Cynthia is armed. The memory of Kitty offering me Butcher's knife as a souvenir haunts my mind. Damn it, I think, I should have taken it. I'd at least have a knife to take into the coming gunfight.

I understand I can't just walk away, although right now I really want to. I can't give her a chance to escape again.

I walk a little further into the darkness, projecting my thoughts. Give up, I repeat in my mind, drop your weapon and surrender. Nothing happens. Cynthia is obviously too strong to be put under, unlike myself.

I stop again, listening and trying to concentrate. I feel disoriented. Only now, I can fully realize how much my blind eye and loss of hearing limit my abilities.

I force myself to remain calm, telling myself that a gun is the only real advantage Cynthia has over me. I'm much stronger physically. I just need to grab hold of her weapon and then I can easily bring her down. I only have to take care she doesn't hypnotize me again.

"We're finally alone, aren't we?" I hear her voice. "Just you and I. I've been waiting for this moment."

She's somewhere nearby. I carefully back into a room, concealing myself inside the entrance.

"You're out of ammo, aren't you?" Cynthia asks. "Come on out, Rex. Let's see who is better. I'm unarmed."

Nice try, I think, though I know she's lying.

I realize she's walking along the passageway, slowly approaching. I ready myself. I suddenly think about Vogel, Dave and all those children burnt alive in the hospital. Hatred fills me. I want to kill Cynthia.

A moment later she comes to the doorway, but hasn't noticed me yet. She's holding a handgun. I leap out from my cover, tightly grabbing her gun hand with both hands. Dropping her weapon, Cynthia reaches for my face with her free hand. Her fingernails dig into my good eye. I flinch, instinctively letting go of Cynthia. She knees me into the stomach and I double over. She instantly slams the same damn knee into my face. I lose balance and fall. My left eye is burning and watering. Cynthia dives for her gun, but I grab her ankle, stopping her progress. She kicks me in the head. Bleeding, I manage to lunge forward, landing on top of her. Cynthia is flat on her stomach, squirming underneath me and still reaching for the handgun. Her hand is only inches away from the weapon. I grab the back of her head and slam her face into the floor. Cynthia groans, but remains conscious. She tries raising up to create distance for a head-butt. But I happen to know this little trick very well. I lower my face out of harm's way and chop at her elbow, bringing her back down. I then begin smashing her face into the floor until her body becomes limp and stops moving.

I pick up the gun and feel her neck for a pulse. It's steady. I keep a knee on her back, taking a moment to collect myself. The desire to kill Cynthia is almost overwhelming. I want to shoot her in the head. I'm tempted to grab her chin and break her neck.

Not just yet, I remind myself, she may know something important.

I raise her up by the neckline of her sweater and drag her toward the staircase. I watch attentively in case she awakens. I'm sure Cynthia will begin fighting again whenever she comes to.

CHAPTER 23

I sit behind Vogel's desk, studying Cynthia's file while waiting for Chase to return from the hospital. I carefully read the documents, although I'm not sure exactly what I'm looking for.

I learn that Elimination initially captured Cynthia when she was in her late teens. She hadn't committed any crimes and had only been suspected of being a breaker. The officers transported Cynthia to a research facility where scientists implanted electrodes into her skull. They utilized various forms of torture, including burning her hands and electroshock while conducting their brutal experiments. Cynthia often misbehaved and attempted to escape, so the guards frequently would beat her and throw her in solitary confinement without food or light.

Reading her file gives me vivid flashbacks from my own incarceration in a different research facility.

I close the file and spend a few minutes thinking. Something is bothering me. Cynthia was a falsely accused and tortured inmate who initiated a riot and escaped from Elimination. She's embittered, manipulative and violent. It sounds all too familiar. Although I hate to admit it, Cynthia's story closely resembles my own. Only she chose a different path.

I can't feel sorry for her and won't bother trying to justify her actions. There's simply no justification for what she's done. Terrorists don't deserve any forgiveness or sympathy, period. What I'm hoping to understand is why Cynthia chose to become a terrorist at the first place. Why did she start killing innocent people? How much hatred does it take to be able to commit such heinous crimes?

Could I ever pour my anger and hatred out against the innocent? Could I ever justify the killing of children?

The problem is that I don't know for sure. I want to believe that I'm somehow different than her, but how certain can I be of that? There's just so much similarity between us. And what if at some point I make a bad choice and become a hater like her? What if I turn into a full-fledged criminal, murdering ordinary humans just because they're different?

I need to get some answers from Cynthia. I have to learn why she chose such a path, so that I might choose a different one.

***

Kitty enters the office and informs me that Chase has arrived. We head toward the cell where Cynthia is being kept. Chase, Marcus, Jessie and Victor wait for us in the corridor. Everybody looks gloomy. Chase has bandages around his wounded leg and is supporting himself with a crutch.

"Let's go have a talk with Cynthia," he suggests.

"I'd better wait for you guys here," Marcus says. "I can't face her. I'd likely kill her on sight." His voice breaks as he turns away, so we wouldn't see him cry. "She killed my brother," he adds.

We enter the cell, leaving Marcus in the corridor. Cynthia is sitting on a chair in the middle of the room. She's handcuffed and chained down, and a blocking collar is placed around her neck. Her nose is obviously broken and her face swollen and bruised after our encounter. Fortunately, I only have a black eye after Cynthia kneed me in the face.

"Listen up, breaker," Chase begins. "I guess you fully realize where you are and what we can do. So make it easy on yourself and answer our questions."

Cynthia looks away, her expression blank. Chase asks whether there's another group of terrorists in the city, but she ignores the question. He demands her to tell us about Guardian's plans, but receives no response.

That's how I behaved during my interrogation with Wheeler, I suddenly think. This association makes me very uncomfortable.

"C'mon, breaker," Chase says. "Answer the questions. You know we have other methods of extracting information from you. Let's not go there."

"Not interested," Cynthia answers.

"Let's just kill her," Jessie offers.

"We should torture her first," Kitty suggests.

Cynthia smiles. "Is that supposed to scare me? I'm getting bored."

"No," Chase says. "We're not trying to frighten you. There's no need for this because as I said, Elimination has other means to get what we need. Have you met Victor?"

Victor grins, waving to Cynthia.

"The infamous junkie and memory reader," she says.

"I'm aware that memory scanning can be somewhat unpleasant," Chase assures her. "So just cooperate and maybe you won't have to go through that particular procedure."

"Officer, you may not be aware of the fact you're speaking to a level 4 breaker," Cynthia reminds him. "And as a memory reader myself, I know very well that the scanning will mess up Victor's head much more than my own. You wish me to talk because you're trying to spare poor Victor, aren't you? Is that more correct?"

Chase seems a little surprised. Cynthia has surmised everything correctly. I have to admit she's really clever. Chase continues asking questions, attempting to intimidate Cynthia. But she's been through numerous interrogations before and knows the drill all too well.

"All right," Chase finally says. "I give up. Victor, she's yours."

"Wait," I say. "I need to speak with her first. Leave us alone for a bit."

Nobody moves. Cynthia watches me intently.

"What exactly are you planning to do with her?" Jessie asks me.

"For goodness sakes, Jess!" I exclaim. "I said I just want to speak with her."

"Well, speak then," she says. "We'll just listen."

I give her a hard look. I know Cynthia won't answer my questions in their presence. I have to speak to her alone to have any hope of getting her to open up.

"All right," Jessie groans after a long pause, proceeding toward the door.

"Just don't do anything too crazy," Chase says passing by.

They all think I want to get Cynthia alone to kill her. I did feel that way an hour ago, but there's no desire to do so at the moment. I'm empty and tired. I just want to learn her side of the story before we waste her.

Cynthia and I are finally left alone. I take a moment to collect my thoughts, wondering what I should say. Cynthia watches me curiously.

"I should advise you that there's nothing you can do to make me talk," she says.

I remember myself saying almost those exact words once to an Elimination captain.

"I realize that," I assure her.

"Why don't you remove these handcuffs?" Cynthia asks, grinning. "My wrists hurt."

"C'mon Cynthia," I answer. "That's not even a good try."

"I guess we finally figured out who's the better fighter," she suddenly says. "Remember our phone conversation? You were wondering whether you could overpower me. I hate to admit it, but you did come out on top. Congratulations."

"Thanks," I say. "Although you almost killed me."

"Almost wasn't good enough. I made a mistake. I shouldn't have dived for the gun. I should have kept kicking you in the head or just scratched out your eyes."

"We all make mistakes," I state.

"I won't give up any information," she warns. "I won't betray Guardian. So don't bother wasting your time."

"I'm not here to speak about Guardian."

"Oh, really?" She looks up, now interested. "Now that's intriguing."

"Why did you kill all those innocent people, Cynthia?" I ask. "How did you make such a decision?"

She becomes quiet.

"C'mon," I say. "Tell me."

"And what exactly are you planning to do should I not tell you?" Cynthia asks, stretching her bruised lips once again into a wide grin. "Will you beat me? I've already told you there's nothing you can do to impress me. You can't make me talk."

"You don't have to answer," I say. "I'm not gonna beat you."

"Well now, that's a really unique method of interrogation," she says.

"I'm not interrogating you, Cynthia. I'm mostly just curious, I suppose. I want to understand what made you become a terrorist. And I do hope to get an honest answer from you. I think I deserve some small consideration from you, after everything you've put me through."

Cynthia seems perplexed. It looks like I've somehow managed to impress her after all. She remains silent for a couple of minutes, thinking and studying my face.

"Ah, hell with it," she finally says. "Why not answer your question? It seems harmless enough." She pauses, sighing. "You ask why I killed those people. Well, it's because they deserved to be killed. They're non-breakers."

"They didn't do anything to you," I remind her.

"I hadn't done anything bad to them either until Elimination captured me," she counters. "Do you have any idea what those non-breakers put me through?"

"I think I may have a hunch," I say.

"Don't pretend to understand. How long were you incarcerated? A few weeks? I spent half of my life locked up for no reason. Do you really want to hear what Elimination did to me?"

I nod.

Cynthia smiles, then calmly begins telling me how Elimination scientists drilled holes in her skull. She tells how officers captured and murdered her relatives who had tried to protect her. How the guards broke her ribs while beating her. How they kept her without food for days on end, all just to break her spirit.

I offer no comments, just listening to her story. After she finishes, we both remain silent for a while. I realize that right now she doesn't look much like the girl who approached me in the refugee center a few weeks ago. She's not even the ferocious killer with whom I earlier spoke on the phone. Perhaps I'm seeing the real Cynthia, the way she used to be before Elimination ruined her life.

"I'm really sorry for everything that's happened to you," I say. "But you shouldn't have made the innocent pay for what Elimination did. That was wrong."

"Do you actually think I killed those people out of revenge?" She lets out a laugh. "C'mon, Rex. You're smarter than that. It's never been about vengeance. I just hate ordinary people. I treat them the same way they treat us. And I kill them simply because I can. They're completely helpless against us."

I take a moment to consider her words, trying to view the world through Cynthia's eyes.

"I don't think I could ever understand such pointless violence," I say.

"Too bad," she sighs. "You're a good soldier. I'm sure I could find a place for you in my squad."

"I don't really think it would work out, Cynthia."

"Well, perhaps you're right. I probably wouldn't keep you alive for long. You're too dangerous."

"As are you," I say.

"Thank you. That's really sweet." She smirks.

"What did Guardian promise you?" I ask. "Did he promise to make you the leader of his army, should you kill me?"

"You said we wouldn't be speaking about Guardian."

"Well, I don't think answering that particular question could possibly hurt him."

She remains silent for a moment, then says, "You've guessed correctly. I'd become the leader of the Army of Justice, as long as I proved that I was a better candidate for the role. In doing so, I was to cut off your head, along with the heads of Kitty and Holtzmann, and deliver them to Guardian." She smiles broadly, looking straight into my eyes. "Any more questions?"

I don't have any other questions in mind, so I open the door and inform the team that Victor may now read Cynthia's memories. I exit the cell and wait in the corridor, while he's conducting his business.

Fifteen minutes later, the team returns and Victor explains that there shouldn't be any other terrorists in the city. Which is good news. But the bad news is that Guardian's army is preparing for another attack on the city. They're planning a massive strike toward the end of the month.

I realize that we won't have time to complete our project.

"Inform Holtzmann," Chase commands. "And bring him in here."

After Victor leaves, he asks who wants to finish off Cynthia. Marcus, Kitty and Jessie all volunteer.

"Let's pull matches," Jessie suggests. "Whoever gets the long one is the lucky winner."

She finds a pack of matches in her pocket, pulls out three and breaks two.

"Make it four," I say, joining the contest. Although I no longer have any desire to kill Cynthia by my own hand, I simply don't want to make the others do all the dirty work.

We draw matches, and I pull the long one.

"Lucky you," Jessie comments. "So how are you gonna put her out of her misery?"

"Do her slowly," Kitty says. "Make her pay for Dave's death."

I don't follow her suggestion, because there's no point in torturing Cynthia any further. Doing so wouldn't bring back Vogel, Dave or any of her other victims. It would only serve to make me like Butcher and other hardened criminals. And that's precisely what I hope to avoid.

I borrow a rifle from Marcus and lead Cynthia out into the prison yard. My team follows behind. I command Cynthia to turn around, standing with her back to me.

"No," she answers. "I want to look into the eyes of my killer."

"All right," I agree. "Any last words?"

"Go to hell," she says, smiling.

"Ladies first," Chase replies.

I aim the barrel of my rifle toward Cynthia's forehead. There's no fear whatsoever in her eyes. I have to admit she's very brave if misguided. I pull the trigger and watch as her body falls.

"Nicely done," Kitty comments.

Chase directs his officers to remove Cynthia's corpse. We return inside the prison to speak with Holtzmann. The professor seems to be in total distress. He says that the only way to complete the project before the coming attack is by increasing the dosage of the drug. Although doing so would subsequently worsen its side effects. Up until now, Kitty and I have been receiving only minimal amounts of the drug to minimize health risks. There's no way to predict how our bodies might react to an increased amount.

"Are you sure there's no other option?" I ask him.

Holtzmann shakes his head negatively. I don't know what we should do. I hate endangering Kitty's life any more than we have to, and that's just what would occur by letting her inject larger amounts of the drug. But if we don't stop Guardian, his army will certainly kill every resident in this city, including Kitty.

"Let's do it," she whispers, taking my hand. "Please. You know we have to cut the head off the snake."

"All right," I sigh. "We've agreed to having the dosage increased, Holtzmann. Looks like we don't have a choice."

PART 3

CHAPTER 24

The refugee center takeover cost more than two hundred lives. The terrorists gunned about half the victims down, the rest being killed by the tranquilizer gas.

I have no idea whether the decision to use toxic gas inside the building was appropriate or not. Perhaps there was a better solution. But I don't want to think about it, because what's done is done. It seems that no matter what choices we make, we always have to face the same consequence. We wind up burying people. People continue dying for no reason. That's our reality in the harsh world in which we live. And I don't know whether there's anything we might do to change that. How to stop all this mindless killing? How to change an outcome seemingly set in stone?

Two days later, our team gathers with a few dozen Elimination soldiers at the city cemetery to bury Vogel and Dave. It's wartime, so we don't really follow any official protocol. Nobody has much to say. We stand gathered around the graves, solemnly watching as dirt is shoveled over the coffins. Each deeply immersed in our own thought.

I try not to think about the deceased. I try to keep my mind busy, thinking about ways to survive the injections, the mission of Guardian's assassination and a possible looming attack on the city. But just being here, looking over the hundreds of freshly dug graves isn't helping my task. This cemetery has recently become significantly larger. And my thoughts continually revert back to the very images I'm consciously trying to avoid. I envision Vogel lying on a gurney in the hospital, pale and motionless, a nasty scar across her chest. I remember Dave covering the grenade with his body. I wonder why it was him, and not me, to do something like that.

Distracting myself, I turn to find Jessie. She's keeping her distance, away from the others, casually smoking a cigarette. Her face is unconcerned as always, and I can see neither regret nor pain in her eyes.

I approach her at the conclusion of the funeral to express my condolences. Jessie sighs, saying, "I'm not like the rest of you, Rex. I never fall in love, and no, I didn't love Dave. But I just hate thinking that one more good guy has been killed. It's too bad."

I'm not sure whether I believe Jessie or not. But I don't force her to continue the conversation. No matter what she says, I know she's upset and it's better to leave her be for a while.

Regardless of the need to conserve ammo, the officers fire off three volleys to pay respect to the deceased. Then we all take a last lingering look over the graves before heading back to headquarters. Time for mourning is over, now it's time to finish this war.

***

Later in the day, I stop by Rebecca's quarters and she lets me in. I haven't had opportunity to visit her in the hospital because we have been too busy evacuating the victims and then collecting the dead. Rebecca looks a little thinner than usual, and she's pale as a ghost. I ask how she's feeling, worried about possible side effects of the tranquilizer gas. Rebecca assures me that she's fine.

"I still can't believe that Cynthia orchestrated all that," she says after a long pause. "How could I have been so mistaken about her? And even after learning the truth about Cynthia, I still thought I could somehow influence her. She did treat me a bit differently than the others. I begged her to free the children and allow us to have some food, but she wouldn't listen."

"You did great, Rebecca," I assure her. "You helped my sister escape, and convinced Cynthia to provide some water to the hostages."

"It was you who captured and killed Cynthia, right?" Rebecca asks.

I nod. She offers no further comment.

"Egbert wasn't too worried about me, was he?" she wonders.

"Of course he was," I answer, keeping secret the fact that Holtzmann never expressed any concern for his cousin during the entire situation.

"He really only cares about his science," Rebecca sighs.

I begin speaking in Holtzmann's defense, but she quiets me with a sharp look. We share a few moments of silence, then I leave to return to my team.

***

Kitty remains glum for the rest of the day and finally breaks down at night. She lies across the bed, pressing her face into the pillow and weeping. I sit beside her, patting her shoulder.

"Why did Dave have to die?" Kitty sobs. "He never did anything bad in his life. And remember the party we planned to have on the beach after the war? Dave won't be going with us now… And he was looking forward to going so much, because he'd never been to a beach party before."

I remain silent. I very much want to say how everything will be all right, but I know it just isn't true.

"All the good people are dying," Kitty states. "I hate this war! I can't take it anymore!"

"There now," I whisper, holding her close. "Calm down. Please don't cry."

My words aren't helping much and Kitty continues crying. I look over helplessly at her. The door to our quarters opens and my sister enters the room. Her eyes are still swollen from the funeral. She approaches and sits on the edge of the bed. Kitty lets out another sob and throws her arms around my sister. Holding her, Marian glances at me, then toward the door. I nod in understanding, pick up a book from the stack and quietly exit the room.

In the corridor, I sit down on the floor and begin reading to distract myself. I can still hear Kitty crying, but her sobs seem to be lessening. The book I picked up is about survivors of child abuse and those who had to witness domestic violence in their childhood. I'm reading it to hopefully gain some understanding of my sister, although I don't know whether it's going to help.

The book is written in an official language. But I can vividly make out familiar, disturbing images behind the words. I remember my sister and me hiding under the blanket, listening to the commotion going on in the next room, scared to raise our heads. I recall our living in a state of constant turmoil and aggression. It seemed Emily was constantly fighting with her boyfriends. She frequently changed them out, always finding new ones, but nothing in our situation ever seemed to change.

The book suggests that children exposed to domestic violence and abuse may become fearful and anxious. They become guarded, always watching and waiting for the next event to occur. The range of problems for these children can include anxiety, fear, shame, self-blame, guilt and even thoughts of suicide. Growing up, they're at higher risk for alcohol and drug abuse, self-harm and becoming runaways.

I stop reading for a moment. I remember seeing scars on Marian's arms and legs. I recall her outburst of anger toward me and her questioning whether I ever thought about killing myself.

As for myself, I remember fantasizing about smothering or gunning down Vogel. And I continued stabbing Butcher's corpse, even though it was obviously overkill. I had always thought I was unaffected by Emily's hatred. But why then is it so easy for me to kill people? And why don't I seem to have any regrets?

***

My sister approaches, distracting me from my thoughts.

"She is asleep," she utters softly.

"Thank you," I answer.

Marian shrugs, smiling slightly. She plops on the floor beside me and places her head on my shoulder.

"What are you reading?" she asks.

"Just a book," I say, quickly putting it away. But Marian snatches up the book and glances at the cover.

"Oh, you're worried about your little sister, now are you?" she asks. "That's so sweet." She pauses, thinking, "It was a history book about the twentieth century."

"What book?"

"The book I threw at you back in Oliver's camp when you asked what I was reading. It was a book about the history and culture of our country before the Eruption."

"You like history?" I ask.

"I'm curious as to how things were before," she answers. "Want to know what else I'm really curious about?"

"Sure," I encourage, happy to learn something new.

"The human brain," she says. "That's what I'm currently obsessed about. I've read how all the different parts of a brain work. I'd like to study it further. And I'm also interested in learning about mind breaker phenomena. I'm very curious about your kind."

I remain quiet, listening attentively. I can't quite figure her out. She's cruel yet kind, rude yet compassionate, shallow yet intelligent. I admit I'm fascinated by this strange, messed-up girl.

Marian misinterprets my astonishment.

"Yes, I truly love science," she says defensively. "I'm not as stupid as I look."

"I never thought you were stupid."

"Holtzmann often spoke about his research back in the camp," Marian continues. "And he didn't seem to care whether anybody was listening or not. Typically, a few recruits would come to hear his lectures, and I was always amongst them." She frowns, averting her eyes. "You think I could assist Holtzmann in his research in the future? I'd love to work in his lab. And I swear I'd behave decently around him. I know he's a no-nonsense type of guy."

She looks at me hesitantly, as if fearful that I may begin laughing.

"Why not?" I say. "He could probably always use another good assistant."

Her eyes sparkle as she flashes a wide, pleased grin.

"Let's do something together, Alex," she suddenly offers. "It's late, but I don't feel like sleeping. Let's go for a walk just like the old days."

"It's already dark outside," I remind her.

"So what? You used to tell me that you're a breaker and could protect us from anybody. Remember? So let's go! Please!"

Gripping my wrist, Marian leads me toward the exit doors. I follow. Outside, we walk side by side along the dark empty street. I gently hold Marian's bandaged hand.

"Thank you again for calming Kitty," I say.

"She's my friend," my sister answers. "I never had a friend like her before. I mean, there was always lots of girls around me at school. And I was their leader. But they were happy to stab me in the back the first moment I slipped up. Kitty isn't like that. She's genuine and loyal. Sometimes I wish I could be more like her."

"That's funny," I comment. "Kitty wants to be more like you."

"Oh really?" Marian smiles. "Well, I guess we'd better remain ourselves in that case." Her eyes suddenly grow distant. "Like to know who I'd really like to become?" she asks. "Myself. The way I used to be when I was little. Remember? What about you, Alex? Who would you like to be?"

"Myself as well, I guess," I say. "The way I was a year ago."

"Why?"

"Well, I used to be really nice. Never robbed or killed anybody."

"Do you think you're so bad now?"

I don't answer. I've done a lot during this war.

"You happen to be the nicest guy I've ever met," Marian insists. "You haven't so much as slapped me even once, although I suppose I've truly deserved it."

"C'mon," I say. "You haven't done anything so terrible."

"I spit in your face!" Marian reminds me.

"It was far better than shooting me in the face," I answer.

We both fall into an uncomfortable silence.

"I still can't believe she did that," my sister finally whispers.

"Me neither," I admit.

We continue walking, passing through debris left from the bombing. It's a cold and cloudless night. Moonlight illuminates the street, making everything appear unearthly. I get the sensation of being in a dream world.

"Do you think I'm like our mom?" Marian asks. "I do. I'm always looking for trouble, you know. Because if you let someone hurt you, they'll love you for it. Nobody would punish someone they didn't care about, right? You know what I'm trying to say?"

"No, not really."

"Do you like hurting people, Alex?"

I linger with my answer. I recall enjoying beating Dr. Carrel. I think about killing Guardian's soldiers during the attack, and smashing Cynthia's face into the floor.

"Not the people I love," I say.

"All my boyfriends beat me," Marian states. "It was the same way with Emily. Remember how she was? It was impossible for that type of guy to not beat the hell out of her. She'd act all sweet and nice with her new guy for a couple of weeks, and then she'd open her big mouth. And I imagine you still remember the kind of crazy crap she would say when she lost it."

"They could have just left her," I suggest.

"Well, they didn't," my sister answers. "They must've enjoyed all that stuff. I guess Emily liked it as well because she always put herself in the same situations."

"There was nobody to help her," I argue. "And she was still very young."

"But aren't we the same?" Marian asks. "Can't you see how it works? Your father hurt Emily, so she in turn hurt us, and now we're going to hurt somebody else. And it will just go on and on, forever."

"We're going to break the pattern," I say.

"You think we can?"

"We have to."

"Did you really believe her story?" Marian asks. "You know, the one about her uncle. She told you something different, didn't she?"

"I believed her," I answer.

"Do you forgive her?"

"I was never really angry at her."

"She began hurting me right after you left."

My sister starts telling me about those ten long years of living alone with Emily. She goes on how our mother would lock her up in a dark closet whenever she misbehaved. She informs me how Emily hated it when she began transforming from a child into a young woman. How she continued to make Marian wear childish dresses. How Emily slapped and yelled at her.

"She wanted me to wear stupid ribbons in my hair," Marian says. "And when I told her I wouldn't do it, she grabbed a handful of my hair and cut it short. I was only twelve."

"I'm very sorry."

"I loved her anyway," Marian sighs. "Sometimes she could be so loving and wonderful. We'd crawl into bed and pillow talk for hours. She'd tell me how great I was. I guess, you didn't get to see much of that side of her. But I always knew she had a lot of love in her. And she offered all this love to me. But in return, I'd have to let her control me. I'd have to give up my own free will. She wouldn't tolerate anybody else in my life accept her. No friends, no boyfriends, not even you."

My sister pauses, looking away. I remember Emily holding me tightly, crying and sobbing. She'd slap or shove me, only to afterward express her love.

"I ran away once at thirteen," Marian continues. "I met a guy who had a house, so I went to live with him. After three weeks he began beating me. So I had to leave him for another, but it wasn't much better. After a couple of months I returned home. Emily was furious. She slapped my face and called me these horrible names. I ran away a few other times as well, but always returned. I could never strike back at her. I begged her for forgiveness and swallowed the humiliation. And it's weird, because I could easily get in a fight with others, but never Emily. I could never protect myself against her."

I remember freezing up myself, letting Emily do as she pleased. I could never put up much of a fight against her either.

"I'm very sorry," I repeat.

Marian shrugs.

"I guess I deserved it," she says quietly. "I know I'm a horrible person."

"Everybody around here thinks you're very nice," I protest.

"Only because they don't know the real me," she interrupts, turning to face me. Her lips tremble. "They have no idea of the things I've done."

"What could you possibly have done?"

"Everything!" she exclaims. "Everything you might imagine. I even experimented with drugs a few times. And when I was living on the streets..." She gives me a piercing stare. "Just imagine what I did to pay for my drinks and drugs. Just think about it, Alex."

"How does any of that make you a bad person?" I ask calmly.

"What?"

"Have you ever killed anybody? Have you tortured or gunned down falsely accused inmates? Have you burned kids alive in hospitals? Gosh,

Marian! You've no idea what bad really means. You didn't hurt anybody, except maybe yourself. So how could you possibly be a horrible person?"

Tears begin rolling down her face.

"Thank you," my sister whispers, hugging me. I wrap my arms around her, burying my face in her hair. "Do you truly love me, Alex?"

"Of course I do," I sigh.

"No matter what?"

"You're my sister."

"But you do realize how I can be mean and nasty sometimes, don't you?" she asks.

"You can be as mean and nasty to me as you wish," I answer.

I'm not lying, because I fully accept Marian the way she is. She's no longer that funny five-year-old who used to be my best friend, but it doesn't matter. What does matter is the fact that my sister loves and needs me just as much as I love and need her.

"Thank you," she repeats.

We continue walking, keeping quiet. We somehow wind up on the boardwalk. I point at the beach and tell Marian that's where we're going to celebrate our victory after the end of the war.

"Cool!" she exclaims. "I love parties. But I should warn you how I usually get so drunk I can't remember what I did afterwards."

She winks at me, chuckling. Holding my hand, she leads me toward the beach where we sit on the wet sand, watching the waves. It's peaceful and quiet. Suddenly, my sister shrieks and falls flat on her stomach, grabbing something off the sand.

"I caught it! Look!" she exclaims, holding up a large frog. "I love frogs," Marian states. "Remember how you made me kiss a frog one time, telling me that it would turn into a prince?"

"Well," I say, averting my eyes. "I honestly don't recall that."

Marian kisses the frog and carefully puts it back down on the sand.

"It never works," she sighs. "I guess I'm not a real princess. I think I need a real kiss to turn into something good myself. What do you think, Alex? Would it work on me?"

"Let's check it out," I offer.

"Okay," Marian agrees, closing her eyes.

I lean into my sister and kiss her lightly on the forehead. "That was a true love kiss, Marian."

"Did it work?" she asks. "Do you notice anything different?"

"It might take some time," I answer. "It's a slow process. And you're not a frog anyway."

We both start laughing. She shoves me and I push her back. She stick out her tongue, and I yank her hair, pretending to be angry. It's the same silly games we used to play as kids.

Then Marian and I walk back toward headquarters. This night will soon end and another day will come. Day one of a new stage in Holtzmann's project, where Kitty and I will begin injecting the dangerous drug in ever larger quantities.

CHAPTER 25

Kitty and I stare intently at the box of matches inside Holtzmann's lab. Developing our skill with telekinesis is tiresome work. A good hour passes before the box finally flips onto its side and moves a few inches toward the edge of the table. Kitty lets out a shriek of excitement. Holtzmann assures us that we've achieved an excellent result.

"Oh sure," Kitty says, laughing. "Moving matches could definitely help us kill Guardian. We can probably stick a lit match right in his eye."

Holtzmann hypothesizes that moving matches is only the beginning. Developing a more advanced skill level will take time.

Kitty and I return to the exercise. I still don't fully understand how telekinesis works. I just gaze at the box, trying to synchronize my thoughts with Kitty's. And at some point I can almost physically sense how I'm touching the box of matches without actually touching it, as if some invisible thread is attached from my mind to the object. And when I can concentrate hard enough, the object begins to move.

Unfortunately, it's really hard to concentrate for long on the task. I feel woozy and nauseated. My joints ache and I'm suffering from a pounding headache. These are all side effects of the drug injections. We've been receiving an increased dosage for the last five days and our health has subsequently worsened. We now have to deal with decreased immunity, blood thinning and permanent weakness. My throat is sore and I suffer the symptoms of a moderate cold. Kitty isn't doing much better. I know this well enough. Being so telepathically connected, I'm usually able to tell exactly how she feels.

I share my concerns about Kitty's health with Holtzmann. The professor assures me that according to our blood test results we're both doing fine.

"But she's not eating," I protest. "She feels nauseous and lightheaded. How can that be fine?"

Holtzmann mumbles something about the importance of our experiment and saving humanity. He can't seem to comprehend that Kitty is much more important to me than all the rest of mankind.

Fortunately, our health struggles aren't the only effects of the injections. Our abilities for telepathy and telekinesis have increased significantly. We're as close to reading one another's thoughts as possible. That may appear to be something interesting and good in theory, but in reality it causes us some trouble. Because whenever I now suffer a flashback, Kitty sees the same images in her mind. Whenever she feels depressed, I feel down as well.

Another side effect is our unconscious use of telekinesis. There are instances when we walk together along a prison passageway and all the doors begin to swing open. Light bulbs occasionally explode above our heads. We accidentally break a few windows and even turn a table upside down in the dining room.

"I don't get it," Kitty says with exasperation. "Why can we do so much damage unwittingly, but struggle to so much as move a box of matches when we consciously try to?"

Holtzmann offers us a long, scientific explanation. He theorizes that we are subconsciously preventing ourselves from using telekinesis. The ability isn't natural for us, so it will take a while to fully unlock our full potential.

That is of course, if the drug doesn't kill us beforehand.

***

I wander the prison passageways after it starts getting late. Kitty and I can't stay on the same sleep schedule because she still suffers my nightmares whenever we dream at the same time. The nights are long and boring. It's too dark to read out in the corridors. My good eye quickly becomes tired when trying to read anyway.

I wonder why in the world Elimination prisons are so dark. Are they trying to reduce their usage of electricity? I descend the staircase, approach the main exit and go outside. I stroll around the prison grounds, breathing in the cold air while passing by a dozen or so protestors. They immediately begin calling me a terrorist, although they don't sound quite as enthusiastic these days. It's winter now and the temperature drops below freezing. The protestors are obviously cold, but continue their watch well into the night.

I approach their group and invite them inside for a few minutes to warm up.

"Come on, guys. Take a little break," I offer. "It's warm inside."

The protestors hesitate, watching me suspiciously.

"I know you," one of them says. "You're the level 5 breaker, aren't you?"

"Not really," I answer, not wanting to make the effort to fully explain Holtzmann's experiment.

"Can you really read thoughts?" another protestor asks curiously. "Can you make heads explode with just your stare?"

I sigh tiredly. I'm sick of hearing this same nonsense over and over again.

"Don't you even bother to read the newspapers?" I ask. "There are plenty of articles about all that stuff."

"We don't believe Elimination propaganda," they answer emphatically.

I assure them that although Elimination had manufactured a lot of lies in past, the more recent articles are factual. The protestors nod their heads in understanding, but continue staring at me as if I'm some sort of freak. And I soon begin feeling like a freak.

The protestors finally do follow me inside the prison, continuing to pepper me with questions. I patiently explain whatever I can. I realize they actually know very little about breakers.

Thirty minutes later we come to an agreement that not all breakers are evil incarnate, and not all protestors are overly aggressive and mean-spirited. They assure me that their hatred of breakers isn't personal.

"We just don't believe breakers and ordinary folks should live in the same place," their leader says. "We don't feel safe around your kind."

Having warmed up, the protestors leave, returning to their unenviable duty. I have no doubts that by tomorrow they'll be back to calling me a terrorist.

I sit on the floor for a while, trying to read my book. My eye soon begins to water and I get a dull, annoying headache. I shut the book and once more proceed on down the prison passageway.

Passing by Jessie's room, I notice a light coming from under the door. She must be awake, although it's only about four in the morning. I approach her door and stop, hesitating. Would a visit at this time be appropriate? I don't know and am becoming too tired to think clearly. The lack of sleep has me perceiving everything through a hazy fog. What if Jessie just forgot to turn her light off? She'll be furious, should I wake her.

I spend a few moments listening for any sound coming from her room. I hear nothing, so I cough loudly a few times and pause, listening again. I begin wondering whether my deaf ear may be the reason why I can't hear anything. I step closer toward the door, pressing my left ear against the surface. My common sense still detects that my behavior is off, but I'm too exhausted to care about protocol.

Jessie suddenly opens the door and I almost fall into her room.

"What the hell?" she asks, laughing. "Have you decided to begin stalking me now?"

"I just saw the light and assumed you were awake," I answer, grinning stupidly. "I thought maybe you would like some company."

Jessie offers no comment, staring blankly at me.

"May I come in?" I ask. "It's awfully lonely out here in this dark corridor."

She remains silent for a few more moments.

"Rex, do you even realize how awkward this situation is?" she asks.

I think about it for a second and realize that my intentions could be easily misunderstood.

"C'mon, Jess," I plead. "It's just me."

"True that," she admits. "Come on in, stalker."

I step into the room. It's brightly illuminated. She gestures toward a chair and I plop down. Jessie sprawls out across her bed, lying on her stomach and opening a book.

"What will Kitty think when she learns that you spent part of the night in my room?" Jessie asks mockingly. "She's a telepath, you know. You can't keep secrets from her."

"Kitty likes you, Jess" I state. "And she trusts you. She knows you wouldn't try to take advantage of me."

Jessie rolls her eyes.

"Read your book," she commands.

I stare into my book, but can't focus on reading for too long. This psychological material is too complicated. Instead, I begin thinking about the night Kitty and I spent in Jessie's apartment. We were on the verge of despair, being hunted by both police and Elimination. And Jessie offered her friendship and help, even though she didn't know us.

"I like you too, Jess," I say sincerely.

"You're becoming creepier with each passing minute," Jessie comments, smiling.

"I'm just trying to say that I'm really grateful for everything you've done for Kitty and me," I add. Jessie doesn't answer. "But why?" I ask. "Why help strangers?"

"Well," Jessie says. "Probably because I'm an idiot. I admit I shouldn't have gotten involved in your trouble. Although if I had to do it over again, I'd probably do the same thing."

She returns to her book. I watch her carefully. Her face still bears scars from the beating she took back in the Elimination prison. If she hadn't helped us, Wheeler wouldn't have captured her and Jessie's parents would be still alive.

"I'm sorry for everything you've gone through on our behalf," I say.

Jessie shrugs, remaining silent.

"Why did you leave your parents?" I ask. "Did you reveal your breaker abilities?"

"If you don't shut the hell up and let me read, I'm kicking you out of my room," she threatens.

I don't bother her with any further questions. Several minutes later she closes her book and says, "I had to leave home because I killed four people."

Her voice sounds unemotional and her expression doesn't change. She sits up on the bed, sighs, and tells me her story. It's the first time Jessie has opened up about her past with me.

"My parents had a small farm in the south," she says. "We weren't rich, but we were getting by. They knew I was a breaker, but they didn't seem to care. I was their only child and they both truly loved me. My dad often took me hunting. It was he who taught me how to use a gun."

She pauses, smiling at the memory. I remain silent, recalling my own time living on a farm.

"One day while I was away, four guys broke in our home," she continues. "I don't know why they chose our house, because we were far from rich. They didn't take anything, just trashed the rooms and hurt my parents. They almost beat my dad to death and broke my mom's skull when she tried to run away. I returned in the evening and took my parents to the hospital. The next day I asked our neighbors to look after them. We had some really nice neighbors. And then I took my dad's rifle and followed after those criminals. It wasn't too hard to track them down." She gives me a sharp look, adding, "I killed all of them."

"How old were you?" I ask carefully.

"Sixteen," she answers. "That was six years ago, although it seems like yesterday. I had to leave home after that, because everybody knew who gunned those guys down. And regardless of their being criminals, it was still considered homicide."

Jessie returns to reading her book. I sit in silence, thinking.

"I'm very sorry," I finally say.

"Yeah, me too," Jessie sighs.

I want to add something more, but nothing comes to mind.

"What are you reading?" I ask, changing the subject.

"A sci-fi novel," Jessie answers.

"Is it any good?"

"It's interesting. A lot of fighting and killing. I believe it was written before the Eruption, but somehow reminds me of our world. People going around shooting and killing each other. It's the normal everyday way of life for them." She pauses, staring at me. "Like to know what they call that type of way of life in this book? A kill culture."

"What?" I ask, not fully catching what she said. I haven't slept the entire night and my brain is functioning slowly. "What the heck is that supposed to mean?"

"It's a setting where murder is normalized and accepted by society," Jessie explains. "The more you kill, the better person you're believed to be."

"What does that have to do with the real world?" I ask. "Murder is not really accepted in our society now."

"Really?" Jessie grins. "And just how many people have you killed?"

I can't answer, having lost count long ago.

"Mine were mostly done in self-defense," I say.

Jessie continues looking at me, still wearing the same knowing grin.

I recall Rebecca feeling ashamed of the fact she had never killed anybody. I think of Kitty admitting to how she enjoys hurting people. I also think of myself and everything I've done.

"I don't know," I say. "You think we might still change things somehow?"

"I doubt it," Jessie answers.

She returns to her reading. I think over her words. I wonder whether killing Guardian would actually help to alter the current situation. Will our world be able to change, should this war end? Will I ever be able to return to normal life and stop being a killer?

I see no easy answers to these questions. We'll just have to do our best and see what happens.

***

I return to my room around seven in the morning. Kitty is sleeping and it's still too early to wake her. I sit on the edge of the bed, reading Jessie's book. Suddenly, I'm overcome with dizziness. A moment later Kitty sits up, gazing at me with unfocused eyes.

"Rex," she mutters. "I feel sick."

I understand that my sickness isn't real. Kitty and I just telepathically shared the same sensation.

I steady myself and help Kitty into the bathroom. She throws up, kneeling in front of the toilet.

"Just try to relax," I say, holding her by her shoulders.

She finally stops vomiting and plops down on the floor, leaning back against a wall. I wet a towel in the sink and wipe her face. Kitty remains silent, shivering and looking at me with a miserable expression. My heart aches with pity. She seems so helpless and ill. Her shaved head gives her more than a passing resemblance to a cancer patient. She's only wearing a t-shirt and underwear, and her legs and arms appear too thin. Only now I realize how much weight Kitty has lost the last few days.

"You'll be all right," I say soothingly, wiping her face. "We'll take you in to see a doctor today."

Blood begins flowing from Kitty's nose, dripping onto her shirt. She touches her nose, looks at her stained fingers and says calmly, "Rex... I think I'm dying."

I become truly scared.

"Just hold on," I say, running into the bedroom. I snatch a blanket from the bed and return to the bathroom. I quickly wrap Kitty in the blanket, pick her up and carry her into the corridor. I approach the door to Marcus's quarters and kick it a few times.

"What's happened?!" Marcus exclaims, opening the door.

"Kitty is very sick!" I shout. "Where's Holtzmann?"

"He must be over at the hospital," the officer answers, staring at Kitty. "He is probably preparing everything for your next injections."

"Take us there!" I command. "Now!"

Five minutes later I'm in the back seat of Elimination sedan, holding Kitty in my arms. Marcus drives, heading toward the hospital as fast as morning traffic allows. We run a few red lights. Kitty's eyes roll up inside her head.

"Stay with me, Kitty," I say, slapping her cheeks lightly. "Please, stay awake."

She mumbles something incoherent, before passing out cold. I don't know what to do. What if she doesn't make it to the hospital?

No more experiments, I think desperately. I won't let Kitty inject any more dangerous drugs.

"Can't you drive any faster?!" I yell at Marcus.

"I'm driving as fast as I can!" he shouts back.

We finally arrive at the hospital. I run inside, frantically calling out for help. The alarmed doctors take Kitty from my arms, placing her on a gurney. They head further into the hospital, Marcus and I follow. Holtzmann arrives, demanding an explanation for all the commotion.

"Your drug is killing her!" I yell. "That's what is happening."

Holtzmann's expression becomes startled and he chases after the gurney, following them into the examination room. The doctors allow him to assist, but they require Marcus and I to wait in the corridor.

"What the hell?!" I shout, completely losing it. "I want to know what's wrong with her. I'm not gonna wait out here!"

"C'mon, Rex," Marcus says. "We should follow their instructions."

"I don't give a damn about their instructions!" I answer, trying to brush past the medics blocking the doorway.

Marcus grabs me by the shoulder, saying something. I push him away. The next moment he takes my arm, quickly twisting it behind my back.

"Calm down," he says. "You can't do anything for Kitty at the moment. The doctors will take care of her."

I stop resisting. My shoulder hurts and I suffer a quick flashback from a time I struggled with Elimination guards back in the research facility.

"I'm all right," I say, gaining control of myself.

Marcus momentarily releases his grip.

"Sorry about that," I add.

"No worries," he answers. "I understand how you feel."

We sit down outside her door, remaining quiet and waiting for any news on Kitty. Waiting is the only option left.

CHAPTER 26

A couple hours later, Holtzmann walks out of the examination room and proclaims that Kitty's health isn't in danger.

"Her condition has stabilized," he states. "Her blood test results are good and reflect no reason for concern."

"What?!" I exclaim. "Do you even realize how sick she was?"

Holtzmann states confidently, "Vomiting and nose bleeding are expected side effects from the injections. I'm certain I've warned you both in regards to these complications. The reaction wasn't unusual and isn't of itself any cause for alarm."

I don't have anything else to say. I realize fully that the professor must know what he's talking about. Yet I can't help but be worried for Kitty. And I can't know whether I'm overreacting or not.

"All right then," I say finally. "Where is she? I want to see her."

I move toward the examination room, but Holtzmann quickly steps in front of me, blocking my path.

"Kitty is under heavy sedation at the moment," he informs me. "She needs time to recover. You may visit her later."

"What the heck?" I ask. "What's going on, Holtzmann? Why can't I see her now?"

Marcus stands a few feet away, watching me warily. No doubt he'll try to restrain me again, should I disobey Holtzmann's instructions.

"You'll be allowed a visit as soon as practical," Holtzmann assures me. "But prior to doing so, it's necessary to have a few simple tests run on you."

"What are you talking about?" I ask.

Holtzmann ignores my question, insisting on performing tests on me. I give up. It's simply a waste of time to argue with this crazy scientist. He won't tell me anything unless I do whatever it is he requires.

We proceed into an examination room, where doctors take my temperature, blood pressure and weight. They insert a needle into my vein to get a blood sample.

"Rex, I have to inform you of a developing situation," Holtzmann says after the medics leave. I sense he's more anxious than normal, and his expression is dire.

"Just spit it out for God's sake," I demand, beginning to panic. "What's wrong with Kitty?"

I have a gut feeling he's about to tell me something horrible.

"Kitty's health isn't what I'm concerned about," Holtzmann says. "It's your condition that has me alarmed. According to the test results, your condition is much more serious than hers."

"I'm not the one who just became very sick," I remind him. "I'm perfectly fine, Holtzmann."

He questions whether I still have symptoms of a lingering cold.

"What does that have to do with anything?" I ask, still confused.

The professor patiently explains that Kitty's immune system is still resisting, rejecting the invading chemicals on a cellular level. Her body was simply trying to cleanse itself as she was vomiting. On the flip side, my immune system has almost completely shut down. Therefore I don't suffer similar side effects. And the larger problem is that the slightest infection could now kill me.

"That sounds like AIDS," I state after a long pause.

Holtzmann assures me that it's only temporary condition and my immune system will begin recovering as soon as I stop taking the drug.

"As I've said professor, I don't really feel sick," I persist.

"Your blood pressure is dangerously low," Holtzmann comments. "And you have lost nearly ten pounds."

"Kitty has lost more weight," I say.

"Only three pounds," he answers, staring into some papers.

"Three pounds for her is like thirty for me!" I counter.

"Not quite," the professor argues.

He informs me that it will be necessary for Kitty and I to relocate into the hospital. We'll have to continue the experiment under 24 hour medical supervision.

"We're not a couple of lab mice professor," I interrupt. "No more experiments. We're out."

"Rex, the future of the entire human race may well depend on the successful completion of this project," Holtzmann says. "I'm certain you're aware that it's the only way to stop Guardian's genocide. As long as he's alive, there can't be any lasting trust or peace between mind breakers and ordinary humans. The war will therefore continue until both species are extinct."

"I don't much care about Guardian or this war," I answer. "Kitty is more important to me than the rest of humanity combined."

"This project is quite possibly the most important work of our generation," Holtzmann continues. "Similar experiments have never been conducted, therefore any data we collect is precious."

"Gosh!" I exclaim. "You remind me so much of Dr. Carrel. Kitty and I are only lab rats to you for scientific experiment, aren't we?"

"I do realize that while assisting in this project your health is at considerable risk," he says. "And I'm extremely grateful for your contribution to science. While I won't force you to continue being subjects, I..."

"The hell you won't," I interject. "What do you think you're doing right now?"

Holtzmann ignores my comment. He continues, "You must come to realize that the lives of thousands of individuals carry more value than the lives of two."

I can't believe my ears. Is he suggesting that our lives mean so little to him?

"Go to hell, Holtzmann," I say. "You'll have to find another Alpha subject. I agree to continue with your experiment, but you'll have to replace Kitty."

"She's irreplaceable," Holtzmann answers. "There's no time to find perfectly matching Alpha and Beta replacements for this project."

"Well, that's just too bad," I say. "But it isn't my problem."

Holtzmann attempts to argue further, but I quickly cut him off, "We agreed to stop everything on my say so. This is it, Holtzmann. We're out."

I exit the room, leaving the distressed professor behind.

I wonder whether I'm being too selfish in refusing to continue with Holtzmann's experiment. He's right in saying that the lives of thousands depend on the assassination of Guardian. But how can I care about the future of the human race, when Kitty's life is being put directly in harm's way? Nobody else loves or needs her as much as I do. Holtzmann simply can't understand. Kitty is only an experimental subject and scientific curiosity for him.

I enter another examination room, approaching the gurney where Kitty lies. She's not awake yet. I stand nearby, leaning against a wall, and watch her sleep. Wearing a patient's gown makes her appear even more ill.

A few minutes later Kitty opens her eyes, and smiles broadly upon seeing me. I smile back. She sits up on the gurney, yawning.

"I feel fine, don't worry," she utters. "I'm sorry to have scared you."

"That's all right," I say, giving her a careful hug. She seems very fragile.

"Rex, I know what you're thinking," Kitty suddenly says in a firm voice. She pushes me away, frowning angrily. "No!" she exclaims. "We can't give up now! Not when we're so close to the completion of this project!"

Darn, I think. She seems to be able to literally read my thoughts, although I always believed that to be impossible. Or perhaps she just knows me so well that she can easily guess what I'm thinking.

"We can't continue the project," I answer. "It's becoming too dangerous for you."

"Please! I'm sure Holtzmann told you that I'm perfectly fine!" Kitty groans. "So why do you continue insisting that I can't hack it? Why can't you just believe in me, Rex? You realize that it's up to us to kill Guardian. It's our destiny!"

"I don't believe in destiny!" I say, becoming irritated.

"Well, I do!" Kitty argues, raising her voice. "And I want to achieve something really great in my life!"

"Poisoning yourself and needlessly risking your life isn't so great!" I answer.

"Stop it! I can't listen to any more of this! Why do you always have to try and control me?"

"How do you say I control you when you always wind up doing whatever you please anyway?"

"I said stop!" she yells.

The next moment a large window breaks behind our backs. We both flinch from the sound of crashing glass, turning to examine the damage we've caused.

"Oops," Kitty says quietly, chuckling. "Was that you or me?"

"I'm not sure," I answer. "Probably both of us."

Kitty giggles, wrapping her arms around my neck.

"You see how strong we are together, darling?" she murmurs. "We've already achieved so much! We've almost learned how to harness the telekinesis. We just need to work on it a little more." She pauses, smiling sweetly. "Please, believe in us," she pleads. "I know we can kill Guardian together. We have to get revenge for everything he's done."

I become vaguely aware she's trying to manipulate me.

"Kitty…," I begin, but she quickly interrupts.

"Think about what Guardian's soldiers did to Chelsey," she whispers. "Remember Vogel and Dave. Don't forget about all those people Guardian has ordered killed. And how many more people will he murder in the future, should we give up right now? What will happen to the world, if we allow it?"

I don't answer. Kitty looks deeply into my eyes, her expression sad yet hopeful.

"Please," she begs. "You know we can do it. We're strong enough together. And my health isn't in danger. You're the one who's really sick."

I know this is going to be a mistake. I realize I'm going to regret my decision later. But what other choice do we truly have besides continuing the project? Guardian's army will soon destroy the entire city, should we quit now. There are only a couple of weeks left before his army attacks. And I suddenly remember Guardian's ominous promise to kill everybody I love or care about.

I guess, there's no going back for us now. We have to continue.

"All right," I concede. "Perhaps I'm overreacting."

Kitty lets out a happy shriek, kissing me. She obviously doesn't share any of my concerns.

***

Kitty and I spend the next several days in the hospital. Morning injections then follow up testing. They take blood samples, measure our body temperature and make us go through a multitude of head scans. Holtzmann carefully monitors the results. We soon begin feeling like guinea pigs serving scientific research.

Our health progressively worsens. We both now have to deal with painful sores in our mouths, frequent nose bleeding, coughing, dizziness and occasional blackouts. It's exhausting. The mild cold I was trying to ignore transforms into a full blown flu. I suffer from a running nose, watering eyes and a constant fever. Kitty continues to lose more weight, becoming all skin and bones. I'm also getting noticeably thinner. Holtzmann orders additional meals for us, although the nausea makes eating really hard. We have to constantly swallow vitamins along with other pills, in attempt to support our weakening bodies. Medics also administer daily IV injections of glucose. Dark purple bruises soon cover our arms, and our veins begin to disappear. They now sometimes have to insert the needles into our hands.

After completing all the injections and tests, Kitty and I practice telekinesis. We are now able to move chairs and close doors, using only our minds. We sometimes compete whose chair can move quicker. Holtzmann scolds us for doing so. He insists that we shouldn't compete with one another, but work together as a team. But we don't really worry too much about his objections. I believe we're entitled to have a little fun in our lives, considering everything else we have to suffer through.

In the evenings, we go for a short stroll around the hospital. We read books or just lie in bed, often not saying a word for hours. And I think that perhaps Kitty and I have never been so close before. It's a miserable, yet somehow pleasurable time. We no longer have any real arguments or disagreements. We entertain ourselves by guessing each other's thoughts. And despite my poor health, I somehow begin feeling almost happy. Because why should I care about being sick, when I can spend each waking minute with Kitty? As long as she's safe and nearby, I don't care much about anything else.

One day Chase drops in for a visit. He informs us that Elimination is planning to attack Guardian's troops before they can strike the city.

"We've located a few other squads of resistant soldiers, currently fighting Guardian's troops in different parts of the country," he says. "They're willing to join us in future battles."

"Why is it taking Guardian so long to prepare for this attack?" I ask. "Why doesn't he just go ahead and destroy the city before we can complete the project?"

"He simply can't," Chase answers. "His army is in much worse condition than we had previously thought."

He explains that according to Victor's agents, Guardian currently has about four or five thousand recruits. His army lacks discipline and fighting skills. Many soldiers are ready to desert, no longer willing to risk their lives.

"I doubt they'll be too eager to fight," Chase concludes.

I ask him how he likes his new role as the leader of Elimination.

"Well, I guess I'm doing all right," Chase sighs. "But I really hate being commander. I now have to think and worry about too many things at once. Being a regular officer suited me much better."

"Well, maybe you should take a day off," I advise.

"And who exactly would replace me during that glorious day?" he asks. "And what would I do with a day off anyway?"

"You could visit your family," I suggest, causing Chase to frown. After a long pause, I carefully ask, "Is your family all right?"

"They're fine," he answers flatly. "They're actually living here in the city."

"And you never visit them?"

"Why would I? I told you once before they don't really care about me. I'm not being paid and can't help them. So I don't think they would be overly excited upon seeing me."

"What about your brothers and sisters?"

Chase shrugs.

"You should go see them before we attack the Death Camp," I conclude.

Kitty and I receive a few more visitors. One day Marcus arrives to check on us. We discuss the project and preparations for the coming mission. Kitty keeps quiet during our conversation, intently watching Marcus. Then she suddenly covers her face and runs out of the room, sobbing. I realize that the officer must remind her of Dave.

After a few quiet moments Marcus says, "I still can't understand why I allowed him to do that. Why couldn't I have covered that darn grenade myself?"

He has an absent expression, as if thinking out loud. I remain silent.

"I promised our mother to take care of Dave," Marcus adds. "She'd asked me to look after my brother right before she died."

"I'm very sorry," I say.

"Others say that I should be proud of the fact that my brother died a hero." Marcus sighs. "But is there really any difference in how he died? How can his death make me proud? He was the only relative I had left."

I don't answer. We spend a couple of minutes in silence before returning to our discussion concerning the coming attack on the Death Camp.

Rebecca and Marian stop by for a short visit. My sister ignores me, heading straight for Kitty. She's been cold and indifferent toward me since the night we went for our walk. She behaves as if nothing has changed, but I don't worry over that stuff anymore.

Rebecca and I speak for a few minutes. She informs me how the northeastern refugee center is almost ready to receive new homeless.

"Marian and I will become volunteers again," she says happily.

One late afternoon, Jessie pops in for a visit. Kitty becomes overly excited upon seeing her. We update Jessie about our progress in telekinesis and even manage to move a chair several inches to demonstrate our newly developed skills. Regardless of our best efforts, Jessie remains unimpressed.

"Are you really sure you will be able to take down Guardian with that?" she asks, grinning.

"Well, we don't have much choice, now do we?" I answer.

"I'll be part of your support group, by the way," she adds.

"That's the best news I've heard all day," I say.

"Perhaps I won't be able to gun down Guardian," Jessie continues. "But I'll do my best to help somehow."

I don't doubt a bit that Jessie will be very helpful during our mission. I tell her as much.

"We'll see," Jessie mutters, turning away. She must be still disappointed by her inability to personally shoot down Guardian. We share a few minutes of silence before she leaves.

The days pass quickly, and I secretly wish for time to slow down a little. I want to enjoy this temporary reprieve as long as we can. Because a part of me realizes that this may very well be only an ominous silence right before a thunderstorm. Once again, I feel a strong premonition that something horrible will soon take place.

Unfortunately, the premonition proves correct.

An enemy aircraft strikes the hospital during the tenth night of our stay. We don't get a chance to carry out the mission or complete Holtzmann's project. All our plans and hopes are put to an early end.

CHAPTER 27

I have a strange dream the night of the airstrike. I'm inside an old apartment, one we used to live in many years ago. My mother is sitting on the floor in the middle of the room. She's holding a little redheaded girl on her lap, brushing her long curly hair. I watch them for a few moments before Emily feels my presence and turns to face me.

"You can't have her," my mother says. "She's mine."

My sister outstretches her tiny arms toward me.

"Take me away!" she cries.

Her voice sounds desperate and while I feel sympathy for the child, I don't do anything to help her. Because anytime I try to take her from Emily, she overpowers me and then something really nasty occurs. So I just continue standing there motionless, watching them, and then leave the room.

I next find myself trapped in a dark corridor. I guess this must be an Elimination prison. Still I'm not too worried about being here, because I somehow understand that everything is just a dream.

Somebody touches my arm. I turn to see Lena and Chelsey holding hands and smiling at me. I realize they're both dead, although nothing indicates it in their appearance.

"Won't you join us?" Lena asks. "We're waiting for you."

"I need to stay with Kitty," I answer. "I can't leave her alone."

"She may join us soon too," Chelsey offers.

Lena takes my hand, pulling me deeper into the darkness. She has a very strong grip for such a small girl. I somehow realize that there won't be any returning, should I follow her.

I open my eyes and find myself half-sitting in a chair inside a hospital room. It's dark and quiet here. An opened book lies across my lap, one I recently borrowed from Jessie.

Kitty sits up in bed.

"Gosh," she groans. "That was a really weird dream. Did you accidentally doze off?"

"I guess so," I say. "Sorry about that. Go back to sleep."

"Wait a minute," Kitty mutters, frowning. "What's that noise?"

"What noise?"

Kitty doesn't answer, just continues listening intently. Her expression becomes worried and her eyes widen in fear. A moment later I too hear the familiar roaring of aircraft engines.

"Could that just be an Elimination aircraft?" she asks.

"I don't know," I answer truthfully, getting to my feet.

I approach the window to take a look outside. I can't see anything. The street is empty and dark. The noise becomes louder. Kitty jumps off the bed and hurriedly pulls on her Elimination uniform and boots. I'm still standing by the window. I can't decide what we should do. Should we remain inside the building or get outside?

A missile hits the hospital and the floor begins trembling under our feet. Kitty lets out a short startled scream. I realize what must be happening. Guardian's telepaths must have learned that Kitty and I are inside this building. He's sent his soldiers to take us out.

I grab Kitty's arm, pulling her out into the corridor. It's filled with panicked patients and doctors. People run blindly, attempting to get out of the building. We join the mass exodus, jogging along the corridor. We soon have to slow to a fast walk, and then stop along a wall. Weakened from the injections, we're completely out of breath. My head spins, and I can't understand what we need to do or where we should go. I get the eerie sensation that I'm still stuck in a bad dream and can't wake up.

I hear another explosion and the ceiling starts crumbling. Kitty grips my arm, pulling me forward. We walk slowly, heading toward a staircase. People run past, sobbing and screaming. Somebody falls. The lights flicker on and off several times, then the corridor becomes pitch dark.

We make it into the hall area and locate the exit doors. Outside, I see a large aircraft hovering above the hospital. It fires more missiles causing the remnants of the building to collapse. The surrounding space fills with clouds of dust and multiple explosions. People stagger along the street, crying and calling for help. I hear a burst of automatic rifle fire, and watch as several patients fall to the ground, blood staining their hospital gowns. I'm in a state of shock and can't fully comprehend the situation yet. What's happening? Where's the gunfire coming from?

I notice a smaller aircraft with an open hatch on the opposite side of the street. Soldiers in camo move toward the crowd, raising their rifles and firing into the people. I understand they're here to kill Kitty and I. We're the primary targets, although they haven't spotted us yet. So they kill the other patients, hoping that we're mixed in with the crowd.

Kitty and I drop to our hands and knees, crawling back toward debris left from the destroyed hospital. The assassins continue gunning patients down. I hear the anguished pleading of those still alive.

Elimination troops arrive, and we find ourselves stuck in the middle of a violent shootout. Elimination trucks approach the aircraft. Several officers in black now exchange fire with the soldiers in camo. I attempt to project my thoughts toward our aggressors, but they're too resistant. My hypnosis doesn't affect them at all. Perhaps these breakers are on the same drug as Kitty and I.

I recall Guardian stopping bullets merely by the power of his mind. Damn it, I think, why can't we do that? What's the use of telekinesis if we can't protect ourselves when we need to? Why is it taking us so long to develop our skill?

A soldier in camo approaches, bringing up his rifle. I tackle Kitty to the ground. Several bullets thud into debris close by, then blood suddenly sprays from the soldier's head as he falls. A stray bullet must've hit him. I crawl toward the body and pick up his rifle. Taking cover behind debris, I fire into the direction of our attackers. I can't see whether I hit anyone or not. My vision is blurry and I still can't think clearly. Worse yet, I quickly run out of ammo.

Suddenly, Kitty lets out a shriek and jumps on me, shielding me with her body. We both fall to the ground. I hear another burst of gunfire coming from our right. Guardian's soldiers must have flanked us from that side. I hadn't seen them because of my blind eye.

The sudden, hammering impact leaves me unconscious for a few moments, as everything fades. Sharp pain pierces my entire body. I open my eyes and realize I'm lying on my back. I feel blood pulsating from my neck and oozing from wounds in my chest and stomach. I realize I've been shot multiple times. My mind is foggy. I can't breathe correctly. Balancing somewhere between a dream world and reality, I manage to press my palm against the wound in my throat, trying to lessen the bleeding.

Something is wrong.

I can't find the wound where the bullet penetrated. I look at my fingers and realize there's no blood. My breathing slowly normalizes and the pain begins to recede. I stare at my hand in confusion for a few more moments, then it dawns on me.

I haven't been shot. These are not my sensations.

Terrified, I sit up and look around. I find Kitty lying on her side beside me. Her eyes are opened wide and glazed over. A large puddle of blood spreads slowly beneath her bullet-riddled body.

She took my bullets, I realize. Horrified, I close my eyes and for the slightest moment I'm just not here. We're far away in a safe place. This can't be real, I think, I must be still dreaming. This must all just be a really bad dream from which I need to awaken.

Kneeling beside her, I press my hand against the large wound on her neck. I feel her warm blood oozing between my fingers.

"Hold on Kitty," I mutter. "Please, stay with me."

I don't know whether or not she can hear me. Her eyes hold no expression and her face is deathly pale. Listening closely, I can just make out her shallow, labored breathing. I realize she is dying.

I begin to panic, scared out of my mind. I don't know what to do.

"Hold on, Kitty," I repeat. "Please don't leave me."

How could she have done that? Why did she take bullets intended for me? I didn't ask for this. This can't be happening.

"Silly girl," I whisper. "What have you done?"

My throat clenches. I can't speak. I continue my desperate attempts to slow her bleeding. It's not working out too well. I can still hear gunfire and shouting nearby, but don't bother to look around. I don't care what's happening out there. I can't worry about anything, except Kitty.

Marcus and Chase approach, saying something. I don't comprehend their words. I realize it's quiet now. I notice several more officers in black walking toward us.

I carefully pick up Kitty's limp body from the ground and stagger a few steps toward the Elimination trucks. I feel very weak and my legs are wobbly. Marcus takes Kitty from my arms, continuing to speak softly. His eyes look concerned. Chase grabs me by an elbow, pulling me forward and following Marcus.

The trip to the hospital seems torturously long. Kitty lies across two seats inside the truck, her eyes still open but unfocused. Blood continues dripping from her wounds. I kneel on the floor, clutching her hand. She moves her lips, emitting a hissing sound from her throat.

"Hold on, Kitty," I say. "Please don't leave me."

"I saved you," she whispers. "I repaid my... debt."

She manages a weak painful smile.

"Just stay awake," I beg. "Stay with me, Kitty."

I have some odd thought that Kitty may be able to pull through all this, should she only remain conscious.

"Please, stay with me," I repeat, gently touching her cheek. My hands are shaking.

Her eyes close as she passes out.

***

I'm sitting on the floor in front of the intensive care unit. I'm looking off into space trying to steady my still shaking hands. I've been waiting for some news on Kitty for four full hours. Those coming out have told me that they couldn't offer any prognosis yet. I feel like they are concealing the truth from me. I tried to stay with her, but the doctors forced me out of the ICU. They offered me a sedative, which I refused to take. I have to stay focused and be able to understand everything.

Don't leave me, I repeat over and over in my mind. Don't you dare leave me, Kitty. I won't be able to survive, if I lose her.

My team, along with Rebecca and Marian, arrived a short time ago. They all sit nearby, keeping quiet. There's simply nothing left to say or do. My sister is crying, covering her face. Rebecca gives her a supportive hug. Tears roll down her cheeks as well, but she's not sobbing. Holtzmann paces the corridor, talking to himself. He looks devastated. I guess he's the one needing to be sedated. He seems to be on the verge of one of his epileptic fits.

Jessie approaches and motions for me to follow. I rise unsteadily to my feet, walking behind her. She opens a window, and offers me a cigarette. I believe it's going to be my third smoke within the hour.

Don't leave me, I repeat in my thoughts. Please, stay with me, Kitty.

I have no idea whether she's still even alive or not.

Doctors finally emerge from the intensive-care unit. I toss the cigarette butt out the window and head toward them. My pulse races and legs become wobbly again.

They still refuse to offer a prognosis. Kitty remains critical and in a coma, one with no guarantee she'll ever be able to come out of.

"Will she live?" I ask in a hollow voice.

They don't answer. After a long pause one of the doctors says, "Doesn't look good, she's sustained considerable damage to almost every vital organ. Her lungs have collapsed and her heart may fail at any moment."

He continues speaking, avoiding looking directly into my eyes. I can't comprehend half of the words he's saying. What I do understand is that Kitty is in terrible shape. One of the bullets crushed her spine. It's impossible at this point to know whether she'll be able to survive such severe injuries. And even if Kitty does survive, she would likely remain paralyzed for the rest of her life.

"Just keep her alive," I say calmly.

After the doctors leave, I sit back down on the floor to begin waiting again. What does it really matter to me if she's paralyzed? Why worry about such things when her life is in danger? Invalid or not, all I want is for Kitty to live. I'll never give up on her. I'll never leave her. I'll always do my best to take care of her. We can handle it. Everything will be all right, if only she survives.

Only now I'm fully understanding that Kitty may actually die. Up till now I was trying to block such thoughts, but it suddenly hits me.

I begin praying. I've never prayed before, so I don't know how to do it right. I just repeat quietly the same words, "Let her live. Please, let her live. Don't take her from me."

I don't know whether anybody is listening or not.

***

Several hours later a doctor approaches, announcing that Kitty has come out of her coma.

"You should see her now," he suggests.

"Is she going to live?" I ask, rising to my feet.

The doctor doesn't answer, looking into the floor.

"You should see her now," he repeats.

I proceed inside the intensive-care unit. There are machines and tubes all over the place. One machine produces a monotone beeping sound which fills the room. Kitty lies on her back on a gurney in the middle of the room, covered with a thin white sheet. A tube has been inserted into her neck, hooked up to a machine ventilating her lungs. Slowly, I approach her gurney. Her face resembles a waxen mask, her eyes only slightly open.

"Hey sweetie, how you feeling?" I say. I want to add something more, but my throat closes. I can't speak for a few moments.

"Rex, is that you?" Kitty manages to whisper. "Where are you?"

"It's me," I say, taking her limp, cold hand. "And I'm right here."

Kitty remains silent for a while.

"Are you holding my hand?" she asks in a weak voice. "I can't feel anything."

I experience a sudden wave of dizziness. I steady myself and say, "You'll be all right. Just stay with me."

I squeeze her fingers tightly, as if afraid she may die should I release her hand.

"Rex, I'm sorry but I think I won't make it this time," she says calmly. "I'm so tired."

"You'll make it all right," I answer. "You'll recover in time. I've been shot in the head and I'm perfectly fine. And you'll be fine, too."

I don't know whom I'm trying to persuade more, Kitty or myself.

"Are you proud of me?" she whispers.

"I've always been proud of you, Kitty."

"Do you love me?"

"I love you more than anything in the world."

My voice cracks and I become quiet. I feel a strong urge to do something, help her somehow, but there's nothing I can think of to do.

"Promise me something," she mutters.

"What's that, Kitty?"

She manages to focus her gaze and look up at me.

"Promise to survive," she says. "Promise to live and be happy for both of us. And never forget me."

"Please don't say those things," I plead. "You'll recover. You'll be all right."

"Don't be sad," Kitty whispers, smiling. "Everything is okay. You'll be fine."

She fades out again. I stand beside her, still gripping her hand. A moment later the machine begins beeping loudly, and doctors rush back into the room. Somebody grabs me by the shoulders and leads me toward the exit.

In the corridor, my legs give and I sit down hard on the floor. I can't hear or see anything. I start praying again.

"Please, let her live," I repeat. "Please, don't let her die."

Rebecca approaches, saying something. I stare at her blankly and turn away. She leaves me alone. I continue whispering my prayers. And at some point I manage to persuade myself that everything will be all right. Kitty will survive, because she just can't die. It'd be too pointless and cruel. She's young and has her whole life ahead of her.

I hear somebody's voice. I look up tiredly. It takes a moment to realize that a doctor stands before me. He must have said something, but I couldn't understand.

"What?" I ask.

"I'm very sorry," the doctor repeats. "We did everything we could."

CHAPTER 28

This can't be right. She can't be dead. There must be some kind of mistake.

I stare vacantly at the doctor, without actually seeing him. He continues speaking, but I can't hear his words. Why listen further to anything he has to say? He must be talking nonsense, because Kitty can't be dead.

I brush past the doctor, heading toward the ICU. He says something else, probably directing me to stop, but I ignore him. I have to see Kitty. I have to prove to everybody, including myself, that all this is just a stupid mistake.

I enter the intensive care unit. I approach the gurney where Kitty lies. She is covered by the same white sheet, now stained red in a few places. She's motionless and pale, but doesn't necessarily look dead. She may just be sleeping or still in a coma. I refuse to believe that she could be actually gone.

I reach toward Kitty's face, but hesitate to touch her at the last moment. My fingers linger an inch away from her skin. I suddenly become afraid that this one single touch could destroy my last hope. What if Kitty happens to be stiff and cold, like all those corpses I've seen over the past several months? I'd have to accept the unbearable truth that Kitty is dead. But as long as I don't have such undeniable proof, I might be able to push the unimaginable thought aside. I'm able to block and ignore it. But if something indicates that she's truly dead, one unquestionable thing…

I touch Kitty's face and her skin is still soft and warm. I feel a flood of relief. She could very well be just asleep or in a coma. And sooner or later Kitty should definitely wake up.

***

Another part of me realizes that Kitty is gone. That everything is over. And nothing will ever awaken her from her sleep.

She really left me.

Kitty was always afraid that I'd leave her, but in the end it's her who's left me.

This is all wrong, I think suddenly. Everything is so messed up. Her death doesn't make any sense. It's so meaningless. I was supposed to be the one protecting Kitty, not vice versa. I mean, protecting her is the whole purpose behind anything I do. Providing her a chance for freedom was the singular reason I allowed Elimination to capture me and agreed to work for Warden Browning. Protecting her is the reason I chose to take part in Holtzmann's experiment in the first place. Everything was done because I wanted to save Kitty. And after all that, she took the bullets meant for me. She gave her life for me.

There was something she said. *Promise to live and be happy for both of us.*

Her final request. But how am I supposed to continue living, let alone be happy? What am I supposed to do in this world without her?

"For God's sake Kitty," I groan. "What have you done? How could you leave me now?"

Of course, she doesn't offer an answer to my questions.

I gently caress her cheek, looking down at her face. I tightly squeeze her fingers in my hand. Kitty has a calm, relaxed expression in death. I quietly hope for her to yawn, open her eyes and smile at me.

But Kitty remains asleep.

I watch her for a few more moments, then lean in closer and kiss her lips. They're soft. I wait for Kitty to awaken, but she doesn't. I place my good ear next to her chest, listening intently. I can't hear a heartbeat nor feel a breath. She's lifeless. And no matter what I try, it won't bring her back.

***

Somebody enters the room. I turn around, startled. I've almost forgotten that there were other people in this hospital, besides Kitty and myself. It's Chase. He mutters something about medics and the body.

"What body?" I ask stupidly, not understanding.

Chase repeats what he said. I realize that doctors have asked for me to leave the ICU, so that they might take away the body.

"Damn you Chase!" I exclaim. "Don't call her a body. This is Kitty! And she's just sleeping!"

"Rex…," he begins uncertainly.

"Get out," I say firmly. "I won't let anybody touch her."

Chase's expression becomes worried.

"Rex, I'm afraid you're losing it," he says.

"Get out," I repeat. "There must be some sort of mistake. The doctors have misdiagnosed her. Kitty can't be dead. Her death wouldn't make any sense. No, she's just sleeping or in a coma."

Chase continues staring at me. I smile broadly, to show that everything is all right. It's odd to see him so dumbfounded and worried. When Kitty awakens, I'm sure we'll all laugh over this ridiculous situation.

Holtzmann, Rebecca and Marian linger in the doorway, hesitating to approach. I wonder whether they overheard our conversation. They probably did, because they all share the same concerned looks on their faces.

Chase requests for me to follow him out into the corridor. I shake my head no, still smiling. He suggests how we'll eventually have to bury the body.

"Damn it!" I exclaim. "Here you go again. Stop calling her a body."

Chase moves closer to me, taking me by an elbow. I slap him hard, just to distract him. As Chase stares at me in astonishment, I snatch the gun out of his holster. I point the barrel directly into his face.

"Now get out," I repeat calmly.

The officer freezes, staring point blank down the barrel.

"Easy, breaker," he says.

The others begin speaking all at once. I ignore them.

"Leave us be," I command.

He stands unmoving, probably calculating whether he should risk attacking me or not. I thumb the hammer, demonstrating my willingness to use it. Chase slowly backs away.

Rebecca and Marian continue speaking. Holtzmann remains quiet, his expression one of shock. I wave the gun at them, commanding them all to leave. They finally do so, leaving me alone with Kitty in the ICU.

I touch Kitty's cheek, smiling down at her. I won't let anybody take her from me. And I certainly can't let them bury her. Because it's not too late, and I might still find a way to fix everything. There must be a way out. Her precious life can't just end like that.

I gently lift Kitty up off the gurney, wrapping her in the blood-stained sheet. I sit down on the floor, holding her tightly in my arms. I softly explain to her how much I love her. How happy I am to have her in my life. Her eyes remain closed and her body is limp and motionless. Her face is gradually getting a bit colder. But none of this bothers me.

Chase reopens the door, stepping in the doorway. I raise the gun.

"Rex, calm down," he says. "You're stronger than this."

"Get out," I say, "before I shoot you in the face."

Chase decides not to test my willingness to shoot him, and likely find out the hard way, so he closes the door.

I begin telling Kitty soothing stories. These are the same stories I told her when she first came to me. Retelling them brings an avalanche of warm, happy memories. I smile, continuing to whisper to her.

Rebecca is the next one to try and steal her away.

"Rex, please," she pleads, standing by the door. "Allow the doctors to come in and help you."

I train the gun on Rebecca.

"Don't try me," I warn.

Rebecca's eyes widen in shock. She opens her mouth to add something more, but can't utter a sound. She looks really surprised. I like Rebecca a lot, but I'm likely to gun her down without a second thought should she attempt to take Kitty. Kitty is mine, and nobody will take her from me.

"Please," Rebecca repeats, almost crying now.

"Just leave," I command, "and be sure to tell everybody that the next one entering this room will be shot on sight."

Rebecca quietly sobs as she goes. I lower the weapon.

Kitty and I will be always together. I won't allow those fools to bury her while there's still a glimmer of hope.

***

The night has fallen. I'm still sitting on the floor, holding a now stiff and cold Kitty in my arms. She hasn't awakened.

The door opens. I flinch from the sudden noise, instantly raising the gun. It's Jessie this time. She doesn't try to say anything. I continue holding the gun on her.

After a long pause, she begins walking toward me, as if the barrel aimed at her forehead isn't reason enough to keep away. She approaches and carefully takes the weapon from my hand. I let her have it. She sits down beside me, remaining silent.

"We'll have to bury Kitty," Jessie finally says. "She's gone."

"No," I answer stubbornly. "You don't understand, Jess. She can't be dead. It wouldn't make any sense."

"She's dead as dead gets," Jessie assures me.

I shake my head.

"Rex, if you don't stop freaking out, Chase and a squad of officers will break into the room," Jessie warns. "You'll be sedated and locked up."

I nod in understanding.

"Come with me," she continues.

I nod again, rising to my feet. I place Kitty's body back onto the gurney.

"I'll be back soon," I promise, kissing her lightly on the forehead.

Jessie watches me warily. She motions for me to follow and we walk into the corridor.

Chase, Holtzmann, Rebecca and Marcus meet us in the doorway. I notice a couple of concerned-looking doctors standing behind them. Jessie returns the gun to Chase.

"Sorry about that," I say to him. "I guess I just overreacted."

"It's all right," Chase answers, still watching me carefully.

Holtzmann mumbles something about getting medical attention and having me sedated.

"I'm okay, professor," I sigh. "And I won't be needing a sedative."

"Are you completely certain that you're all right?" Holtzmann asks.

"Of course," I answer, smiling. "Why wouldn't I be?"

***

The remainder of the night and the next day pass in a haze. I don't remember many details.

I do vaguely recall Rebecca and Marian trying to feed me. I remember them being very upset. My sister cries non-stop, but I don't bother with trying to soothe her. I eat whatever food they bring, so that everybody will finally leave me alone.

Jessie and I dress Kitty in a black Elimination uniform. I notice fresh stitches covering Kitty's body. It looks like maybe seven or eight bullets had hit her. I hope she didn't suffer too much the last hours. It's probably good she had passed out almost instantly and then medics quickly sedated her.

In the evening, we all stand around Kitty's gravesite in the cemetery. We decided to bury her under the shade of a large old oak. I actually think Kitty would prefer to lie under a palm tree, because she always seemed fascinated by them. But there are no palm trees in this city, so the oak will have to do.

It's winter and the ground is close to becoming frozen. This worries me, because Kitty never could stand to be cold. What if she gets cold under the ground? What if the Elimination uniform doesn't keep her warm enough?

We don't have an official ceremony. Holtzmann asks whether I'd like to say any special words. I shake my head because I've no idea what to say.

Marcus, Chase and I lower the coffin. Then we all spend a few more minutes in silence, standing around her grave. Marian breaks down completely and sits on the ground. Rebecca hugs her tightly, sobbing as well. Marcus turns away, looking over in the direction of his brother's grave.

I have no tears to shed and don't even feel like crying. My only concern is that Kitty may get cold. I can't stop worrying about that. Maybe I should have wrapped her in a blanket? Maybe I should have dressed her in a warmer coat?

***

Back at the headquarters, I leave everybody in the dining room, heading back toward our quarters. I sit on the edge of our bed till late at night, staring off into space. This room seems awfully silent and empty now. I envision Kitty smiling and laughing. I think of her wrapping her arms around my neck and kissing me.

I realize I'll never be hearing Kitty's laughter again. I'll never again see her smile. Never again hold or kiss her.

It hurts so much that I want to yell. I want to fall down onto the floor and cry my eyes out. But I remain motionless and silent. I have no tears in me.

This is all wrong, I think. I should be the one under the tree instead of her.

Her blood is on my hands.

Of course I didn't pull the trigger of the rifle that shot her. But I put my Kitty in harm's way.

I'd already gotten Lena killed... and Jimmy, and Chelsey. Vogel died on my behalf, rescuing me from the fire. That nameless recruit died, diverting the guards' attention away from me back at the parade. Too many deaths. Too many sacrifices.

It feels like I've been staggering through an endless cemetery these past several months.

I suddenly realize I might have saved Kitty. If not for my sightless eye, if I could only see as those soldiers approached... I could have shielded her.

As I look back, I also realize that there were numerous other opportunities to avoid her death. I should have done so many things differently.

If only I'd prohibited Kitty from taking part in Holtzmann's experiment. If only I'd actually died during the lethal injection. If I hadn't allowed Kitty to fall in love with me. If only I'd never revealed my breaker abilities a year ago...

It's too late to change anything.

Kitty is gone and I have no reason to continue living. Nothing should keep us apart, even death.

***

I find Kitty's forty-five right where she hid it in the closet. I sit back down on the bed and place the barrel in my mouth. I hold a finger on the trigger. And then I make a really stupid mistake. Instead of shooting myself, I hesitate, as if waiting for some miracle to happen. No matter how much I wish to die, some small part of me still holds onto life, although doing so makes no sense. Some kind of damn survival instinct.

"Are you trying to eat your gun now?" Jessie asks, entering the room.

I quickly remove the barrel from my mouth, embarrassed.

"Leave me be, Jess," I say quietly.

"You were doing it the wrong way," Jessie explains, grinning. "You have to press the barrel toward the rooftop of your mouth. Otherwise, instead of blowing out your brains you might just make a big hole in the back of your throat."

"Well, thanks for the advice," I say. "Now leave, please."

Jessie remains in the doorway.

"I don't really mind your committing suicide," she proclaims. "But do you really think that's what Kitty would want you to do? She saved your life, Rex. So she obviously wanted you to live."

"It doesn't matter much now what she wanted, does it?" I say. "She's no longer with us."

"What about Guardian?" Jessie continues. "Would you leave him unpunished? I imagine you know very well who ordered Kitty shot."

"So what?" I ask.

"Don't you want a little payback before offing yourself?"

"His death won't bring Kitty back. So what's the point?"

Jessie slowly approaches and sits down beside me. I become a little tense. I'm not so willing to let her take my gun away a second time.

"Rex, I'm not here trying to talk you out of committing suicide," Jessie explains. "We just have to take care of Guardian first. You must realize I can't kill him on my own. I hate to admit it, but I do need your help."

"It's over, Jess," I answer. "There's no way to kill Guardian without Kitty. She was the Alpha subject."

"There has to be a way!" Jessie exclaims. "And we have to find it!"

"Well, go ahead and find it," I suggest. "Consult with Holtzmann. He must have a few ideas. But I'm out."

She turns to face me. Her eyes become angry.

"That's just being selfish," Jessie says.

I shrug.

"You can't just walk away. Guardian will destroy the entire city. He'll kill everybody here, including your sister and Rebecca. Did you even bother to stop and think what might happen to them?"

I shrug again.

"Fine," Jessie snorts, rising to her feet. "Then go ahead and do as you please."

She turns to head toward the door, but I suddenly grab her wrist. Jessie stops, glancing back at me.

"Stay awhile," I say. "Please."

I know very well I won't survive till morning, left alone.

I squeeze her wrist tighter, as if afraid that Jessie may run from me. She hesitates for a few moments, but then seems to come to understand everything.

"Let's go to my room," Jessie offers. "I have some whiskey there."

We walk together through the long lonely corridor, heading toward her quarters. I'm still holding her wrist, but Jessie pretends not to notice. Inside her room, she pulls out a full bottle from her closet.

"I was saving it to celebrate our victory," she explains.

We both sit on her bed, passing the bottle and taking long pulls. I quickly become drowsy, but continue drinking. I want to knock myself out so that I can't think about anything.

At some point, Jessie begins crying silently. It's so shocking to see that I even stop fantasizing about shooting myself. I never imagined that she could actually cry.

I wrap an arm around her, pulling her closer. We sit side by side and head to head for a few moments, sharing our grief. I'm not sure whom she's crying for. It could be Kitty, her parents or even herself. Or maybe she's crying for all of us.

Jessie wipes her eyes, finally calming down. She snatches the bottle from my hand, takes another slug and passes it back.

We finish off the entire bottle, and we're still not drunk enough yet. Jessie slides off the bed and rises to her feet, swaying.

"Wait here," she commands in a slurred speech.

I nod, watching as Jessie stumbles toward the door. Left alone, I fall onto my back on the bed and lie unmoving, gazing up at the ceiling. It's spinning. I feel nauseated. But I'm not sure I'd be able to pass out yet.

I continue thinking of Kitty. She's actually dead, the thought swirls in my mind, Kitty's really gone.

Jessie returns, raising a bottle filled with some unidentifiable liquid.

"Where did you... what...," I mumble, unable to finish a sensible phrase.

Jessie mutters something back, but the meaning of her words slip outside of my consciousness. She hops onto the bed and we continue drinking.

I pass out somewhere about half way into the second bottle. No more worries or sad thoughts this night.

***

I awaken to a monstrous hangover. The sun is coming up and the room is growing lighter. I'm lying on my side across the bed. My head is pounding. I feel nauseated and ill. I can't remember where I am or how I ended up here. This place doesn't resemble my quarters at all.

My memory suddenly returns. I remember drinking with Jessie. And I also recall the precise reason why we were getting drunk.

I shut my eyes, hoping to pass out again.

But I remain conscious. I finally sit up, wincing from the sharp pain inside my head. I feel like I'm about to vomit, so I crawl off the bed almost stepping on Jessie. She's lying on the floor, an empty bottle still tightly clenched in her hand. She's sound asleep.

I step carefully around Jessie, heading into the bathroom. I kneel in front of the toilet and begin throwing up. Afterward I wash out my mouth with cold water and return inside the room. I sit on the edge of the bed, thinking of what to do next.

Jessie mutters something incoherent. I remember our hunting down Wheeler together. It was Jessie who finally got him. I look at her sniper rifle propped against the wall. I think about Guardian raising me up into the air, using telekinesis. I remember him losing his concentration when Kitty, Oliver and Chase opened fire on him. He had dropped me, being momentarily distracted.

I finally understand what must be done.

The lethal injection. That's when things started going completely wrong. I was supposed to die that day, but didn't. So it's time to make things right.

I kneel down beside Jessie, shaking her awake.

"Wake up, Jess!" I exclaim. "Please, wake up!"

She groans, pushing me away.

"Come on!" I shake her harder.

"Leave me the hell alone," she mumbles.

"Wake up!" I insist.

Jessie finally opens her eyes, wincing. She must be suffering a terrible headache as well.

"What do you want from me now?" she asks.

"I know how to kill Guardian," I answer. "But I will be needing your help."

CHAPTER 29

"What are you talking about?" Jessie asks, sitting up unsteadily and rubbing her head.

"You and I will kill Guardian together," I state, grinning like an idiot.

"Fine," Jessie answers indifferently, falling back down onto the floor. Her unfocused eyes close again as she goes back to sleep.

"Damn it, Jess!" I exclaim, shaking her. "Wake up! Can you hear me?"

She pushes me away, groaning.

"Come on!" I persist.

"Please!" she exclaims. "Stop pestering me, my head is killing me!"

I continue shaking her. She sits up, finally understanding that getting rid of me is simply not going to happen.

"My head," she complains. "I need a drink."

Jessie looks disappointedly at the empty bottle still clenched in her hand. I find a glass and fill it with cold water. I hand it over and she drinks half.

"Where are my cigarettes?" she asks.

I find a pack, light one and stick it between her lips. She takes a deep drag.

"Better?" I ask.

"Not really," Jessie mutters, coughing.

I begin telling her about my new plan on how to assassinate Guardian. Jessie raises her hand, motioning for me to stop. I stop talking. I realize I have to let her recover first. I doubt she's able to comprehend much of what I'm saying at the moment.

After Jessie finishes her smoke, I suggest she take a shower. Hopefully, it will help to revive her. Jessie mumbles something incoherent, neither in support nor opposition to my idea. I grip Jessie under her arms, pulling her up. I lead her toward the bathroom.

"You're such a jerk, do you know that?" Jessie grumbles. "Why can't you just let me sleep it off?"

She's becoming more aggressive and rude. I'm thankful because it's a sure sign of her recovery.

I shove her on inside the bathroom.

"A shower will help you wake up a little," I say, smiling. "And then we must have a serious talk."

"Will you just close the damn door already?" Jessie asks angrily. "Or were you planning to watch?"

I hesitate a moment. I have a thought that she could fall in the shower, and wonder whether it's safe to leave her alone in her current condition.

"Just don't fall down, all right?" I say finally. "Please be careful."

Jessie rolls her eyes.

"Fifteen minutes," I add. "If you're not out in fifteen minutes, I'll know that something bad has happened and I'll come in."

"Good grief!" she exclaims. "You're a real creeper!"

Jessie pushes me out of the bathroom and shuts the door. Well, perhaps I am overreacting a little. But what should she expect, when everybody seems to be dying on me?

I sit on the edge of the bed, watching the clock. I hear water running in the bathroom. I think of Kitty and the cold, dark grave we buried her in.

A few minutes later Jessie returns to the bedroom, drying her short hair with a towel. She looks much better, her eyes now more focused and attentive.

"All right," she says. "Spit it out."

I tell her about my plan. Jessie listens intently, frowning and assessing the odds for success. I know it seems crazy at first, but I'm sure Jessie will agree to everything I'm suggesting. She won't be able to resist an opportunity to personally gun down Guardian.

I explain how Elimination should attack the Death Camp and destroy it, instead of passively waiting for them to strike the city.

"I'm sure we can handle that part," Jessie says. "I can see how Elimination with Oliver's recruits might overpower Guardian's troops and destroy the Camp. But what about Guardian? Who'd kill him?"

"You," I answer. "He's yours."

"He can stop bullets," she reminds me.

"Not when he's distracted."

I explain to her how Guardian lost his concentration after being distracted, and dropped me onto the floor. She never had a chance to witness all that, having been shot in the stomach.

"I was right there," I tell her. "I saw everything with my own eyes. So I believe that Guardian won't be able to stop your bullet, provided we divert his attention. The problem is that you'll have to make the shot from pretty far away. And you'll only get one try, Jess. Otherwise, he'll realize what's happening and kill us both."

"I suppose you're planning to be the one to distract him, aren't you?" Jessie asks.

I nod.

"How?" she asks. "He may explode your head on sight."

"Not if I have the same level of telekinesis."

"But you don't... Wait. Are you going to...?"

Jessie's voice trails off. I catch a new glint in her eye, an understanding mixed with something similar to respect. She grins.

"I'll have Holtzmann inject me with a mega dosage of that drug," I say.

"That much will kill you, won't it?"

"It probably will. But hopefully I'll have time to take care of Guardian first."

"Sounds like a very extravagant method for committing suicide," she comments.

"Not so much. It's just a lethal injection."

Jessie takes a moment to think things through.

"It may actually work," she concludes.

"It just might," I agree.

"Damn!" Jessie exclaims. "What are we waiting for? Let's go find Holtzmann!"

***

Holtzmann doesn't particularly like the plan. After all his mumbling about saving humanity and willingness to sacrifice a couple of subjects for such a noble cause, he's suddenly grown reluctant to assist me with any further injections.

"I can't condone your taking the full dosage at one time," he says. "Uncontrolled risk taking is against my principles. There's a probability that you wouldn't survive the injection. And even if you did, I'd estimate an approximate ninety-five percent chance that your heart would fail within the following twelve hours."

"So what?" I ask. "I only need enough time to distract Guardian. And twelve hours is more than enough."

Jessie and I are sitting at Holtzmann's desk inside his lab. It's around ten in the morning. We've been arguing back and forth now for an hour.

"I won't knowingly participate in your suicide," Holtzmann answers as his eye twitches annoyingly.

"C'mon, professor," I sigh. "Consider the probability of saving this city. Consider possibly saving all humanity. Just think about possibly stopping the war between ordinary humans and mind breakers once and for all. Remember, it was you who told me that the lives of two individuals is not too high a price to pay for the future of the entire human race. Well, you were absolutely right all along professor. And now you have only one life left to sacrifice in order to save thousands. The possible reward justifies the risk. Let's follow our destinies and save this world."

I smile broadly, hoping for the professor to get on board. I know well enough how obsessed he is about saving humanity and preventing an apocalypse.

"I never said that the lives of two individuals are not valuable," Holtzmann mutters. "You either misunderstood or purposely misinterpreted my words. Every human life is precious. Additionally, considering your current mental state and the undoubtedly devastating effect of the alcohol you consumed last night..."

"Humanity is screwed if we don't do this," Jessie interrupts.

"She's right," I say. "You must realize that, professor."

He remains silent, frowning.

"We have to do it," I persist.

"It's insanity!" Holtzmann exclaims.

"Maybe so. But the world in which we live is insane, so it seems reasonable enough to me to try insane methods to save it."

"Even having successfully received a large enough dosage of the drug to acquire the ability for telekinesis, you still won't be able to defeat Guardian," Holtzmann argues. "As the Beta subject, you simply don't have the required skills to effectively utilize the telekinesis. Guardian would easily overpower you. You'd be barely capable of defending yourself in a best case scenario."

"Listen, professor," I say firmly. "You know it's our only chance to stop Guardian and protect the city's residents. We're going to do it with or without your assistance. I'll inject the drug myself if I have to, should you refuse to assist. But considering how I know nothing about proper dosages, it's likely I'll just needlessly kill myself. So will you help us or not? We're doing it either way."

"He's right." Jessie grins. "Your refusal to help won't change a thing."

Holtzmann argues for a little while longer. But eventually he does agree to go along with the plan. Holtzmann is a true scientist after all. It's virtually impossible for him to resist the temptation to conduct such a unique experiment.

**

Chase is much easier to persuade. He realizes that Elimination won't be able to withstand a second attack.

"How exactly are you planning to kill him?" Chase asks. "He's naturally a much stronger breaker than you. I can't see how a drug would help you overcome that obstacle."

"We'll use his weakness against him," I answer.

"He doesn't have a weakness," Chase interrupts. "He's as powerful as they come."

"Exactly," I say. "And within his strength lies his biggest weakness. Guardian thinks that he's invincible. He won't think to be careful. He won't believe we'd be crazy enough to attempt shooting him."

"And what if Jessie misses?" he asks.

She rolls her eyes, annoyed.

Chase becomes silent for a spell, thinking. We all wait for the idea to sink in.

"Let me get this right," Chase says to me. "So if even you survive the injection and Guardian doesn't kill you, you'll eventually die anyway. Am I correct?"

I shrug.

"How tragic," Chase concludes.

An hour later Holtzmann, Oliver and Victor join us to discuss planning for defeating the Army of Justice and taking over the Death Camp.

Our plan is a simple one. Victor's spies will inform us of Guardian's precise location. They'll also help set up a few diversions, such as starting fires inside the prison. Elimination's troops and Oliver's recruits will simultaneously attack the Camp, confronting the remnants of Guardian's soldiers. Jessie and I, along with our support team, will be waiting inside an aircraft until a direct path to Guardian has been cleared. The primary objective of the support team is to get me near Guardian. I'll lure him out into the prison yard where Jessie will gun him down from half a mile away.

***

Preparations for the mission take about twenty-four hours. I spend the afternoon in bed. I try to think of Kitty and how proud she would be, but can only imagine her lying alone in that cold, dark grave in spite of my best efforts to block those thoughts.

Marian and Rebecca knock on the door, but I don't answer. I don't feel like having company. Fortunately, they're both quick to give up their attempt to see me. Nobody else bothers me for the remainder of the evening.

I have trouble sleeping during my last night. After tossing and turning in bed for over an hour, I finally doze off only to wake twenty minutes later. I'm exhausted and need sleep, yet restless at the same time. I start becoming paranoid. I begin wondering why it's so dark inside this room. Maybe I'm not in my quarters, but in a grave? Maybe I really did die during my execution a year ago? Perhaps Drake or Emily managed to gun me down after all. Or maybe I died shielding Kitty, and it's me instead of her, lying under that oak? The thought makes me smile.

I realize I'm losing my mind. But I can't allow myself to go insane just yet. I have to keep it together until Jessie and I can kill Guardian. And then... then it won't really matter whether I'm sane or not. I'll be dead for real. Then, I can join Kitty in infinite sleep.

I lose my sense of reality, get it back, only to lose it again.

I continue pondering what's really happened to me. When a man is actually dead but continues walking amongst the living... well, nothing good comes out of it. The world becomes unbalanced and the wrong people get hurt.

I snap out of my paranoia with the first beams of sunlight. I dress and sit on the edge of the bed, drowsy and feeling ill. A few minutes later, somebody knocks on the door.

"Injection time, hero," I hear Jessie's voice.

"I'm coming," I answer.

I suddenly become aware of one more thing I need from her.

"Jess, wait!" I exclaim, opening the door. "Come on in for a sec. I need to talk to you."

Jessie enters the room and I shut the door.

"What now?" she asks.

"You realize why I'm doing all this, don't you?" I wonder.

"I have an idea," she answers. "What's wrong? Spit it out."

"Those five percent," I say. "There's still a small chance that the drug won't kill me. So I may need your help, because I'm not sure I'd be able to do it on my own."

Jessie looks up at me, frowning. "Are you seriously asking me to shoot you?"

"It wouldn't be murder," I say. "It'd be an assisted suicide."

She becomes silent.

"C'mon," I say. "Just one extra shot for old times sake. It's really that simple. So, can I count on you?"

Jessie doesn't answer.

"Please, Jess," I plead. "Promise to finish me off in case I survive. I have nobody else to ask."

She remains speechless.

"Please," I repeat.

"Oh all right," she sighs. "I promise."

"I love you, Jess," I say, smiling.

"Shut your mouth!" she snaps.

We leave my quarters, heading toward the main exit of the building. I have a surprisingly upbeat, delightful mood.

Rebecca meets us in the corridor.

"Rex, please don't do this," she begs, walking beside us. Jessie and I don't slow. "You know what will happen. You're going to die!"

"I'm already dead," I say.

"Why are you doing this?" she asks. "Are you doing it to get revenge for Kitty?"

"I'm not sure," I answer. "Maybe I'm just doing what I've always tried to do. I hope to make things right."

"What about Marian?" Rebecca asks. "Did you forget about your sister? She won't survive without you."

"She's survived ten years without me," I counter. "I don't think my death will actually upset her too much."

"You're so wrong! Marian loves and needs you! Jessie, please stop him. Are you really willing to let Rex kill himself?"

Jessie and I exchange glances, both smirking. Rebeca doesn't know anything about our little agreement.

"I just want to see Guardian dead and save the city," Jessie states. "Why should I focus on what might or might not happen to Rex? I've never really liked him anyway."

Rebecca follows us all the way out to an Elimination truck. Jessie and I hop inside, and Marcus drives off. Twenty minutes later, I'm sitting in a recliner, watching the deadly needle being inserted into my vein.

The mega dosage of the drug doesn't go down smoothly. There's a lot of vomiting, dizziness and weakness afterward. As soon as I'm stable enough to speak, Holtzmann explains that my symptoms should disappear within the next twelve hours. Then the drug will kick in, and I should temporarily acquire the abilities of a level five breaker. The effect will last for about an hour before my heart fails.

He hands me over a syringe with a needle, filled with a colorless liquid.

"Antidote," Holtzmann says. "It's supposed to be injected intravenously. But I wouldn't expect you to be able to perform an intravenous injection without prior experience. So you should simply insert the needle into your thigh and inject the antidote as soon as Guardian is terminated. It'll increase your odds for survival by up to ten percent."

"Thanks professor," I say, putting the syringe inside my pocket. I'll toss it later.

Marcus transports Jessie and I back to headquarters. I spend five torturous hours inside my room, making trips to the bathroom for vomiting every thirty minutes. My pending death seems more and more appealing after each trip.

Jessie stays with me, helping me deal with my increasing sickness. When it's time to leave for the mission, she helps me walk to the aircraft. She manages to support most of my weight, although I'm a little too heavy for her. We don't exchange words, but I guess words aren't necessary. Jessie and I have always been able to understand each other well enough without the necessity of speaking. And I suddenly realize how similar the two of us are. We've both lost everything, everybody we loved and cared about. And nothing is left for us in this world. We're both hardened, revenge-driven and violent people. We've lost the ability to love, now only being capable of hating and killing.

Marian is waiting for me at the aircraft.

"Please don't leave me again!" she cries, throwing her arms around my neck. "Please, Alex! Stay with me!"

I push Marian away. Why should I care about this girl? She's more of a stranger to me now than a sister.

"You'll be all right," I say coldly, proceeding toward the opened hatch.

"I love you, Alex!" Marian sobs. "Please don't leave!"

I don't bother looking back.

Jessie and I along with our support team take seats inside the aircraft. A few minutes later we leave for our final mission. I now have only seven or eight hours before I die.

CHAPTER 30

The aircraft lands a mile away from the Death Camp. The team remains inside, while Elimination troops and Oliver's recruits confront Guardian's soldiers. They attacked the Camp a few hours ago, and it doesn't take much imagination to envision the ferocious battle raging not far away.

Everything will be over by tonight, I think silently. I just have to wait five more hours and then I can join Kitty.

I don't mind dying. There's not too much left to live for. And when a guy is as far gone as I am, there's just no sense in keeping him around.

Symptoms from the injection increase gradually. My head spins. I'm still nauseated. I take several deep breaths to steady myself. I feel like I'm already dying. And while it's true the drug is killing me, it also simultaneously rewires my brain. It builds new connections as it destroys the old ones, eventually turning me into a level five breaker. It seems as if I've stopped being human altogether, transforming into the product of some deranged scientific experiment. I'm becoming a strange and dangerous creation, one that should never exist.

I check my watch. Four hours to go. I only have to hold on a little longer.

In spite of my best efforts, I begin drifting in and out of consciousness for the rest of my wait. Stuck in some kind of limbo, being neither fully alive nor completely dead. The ill effects finally begin to lessen and my nausea recedes. I realize that the effects of the drug must be reaching its high. It means the transformation of my mind is almost complete.

Kitty. I'll be seeing you soon. This is the one thought that keeps me going.

I don't have any regrets. I'm done with this world. It seems I've always been walking on the edge of a cliff, afraid to stumble. And now that I'm finally falling, there's nothing more to be afraid of. It's actually relieving in a morbid sort of way.

"It's go time," Chase finally says, after making contact with Oliver over the radio.

Our group exits the aircraft under the cover of darkness, hiking toward the Death Camp. We have fifteen officers, including Chase and Marcus. Jessie helps me walk, supporting part of my weight. The glare of flames illuminate the night sky. I can now hear the gunfire and explosions of the pitched battle ahead. I distract myself, remembering Kitty. I don't want to think of what we're about to witness. I wouldn't want to guess how many people have already died tonight.

Approaching the Camp, our team splits off into two groups. The first group will be tasked with protecting me while the second will assist Jessie. She's to take a position on the rooftop of one of the prison blocks approximately a half mile away from Guardian's bunker. I'm confident Jessie will be able to make such a distant shot.

Before separating upon entering the prison yard, Jessie and I stop for a few moments. I guess it's the last time we'll see each other.

"Don't forget your promise," I remind her.

"I remember," Jessie answers.

"Well, goodbye then," I say. "And thank you for everything."

Jessie nods, avoiding looking directly into my eyes.

"Rex," she says. "I guess you're all right after all."

I smile. It's the first compliment I've ever received from her.

We shake hands.

My group enters the prison yard. Marcus helps me along. The other officers move to encircle us to lower the risk of my getting shot. I see signs of death all around, sights I've seen many times before, images I don't want to witness again. I lower my head, concentrating on thoughts of Kitty. I try to block out rifle fire and cries from the fallen.

We have to step over corpses stretched out over the ground. We take cover as we go until we have to jog between prison buildings. There's a sudden burst of gunfire. Somebody gets shot in the head. Before the circle can close back around me, I take a couple of stray bullets in my vest. I'm not sure who's still alive on this team or who is already lost.

My mind suddenly clears. I find myself standing before a bunker door. It must be locked. Marcus and Chase with a couple other officers are right behind me. They're firing steadily into some approaching soldiers in camo. I understand we're outnumbered and boxed in.

Time seems to slow down. I feel relaxed and calm. I turn to face our attackers. I suddenly realize that I can feel their heartbeats. We're somehow connected. I look around and understand how everything in this world seems to be connected. Everything is indivisible and we all affect one another. And I suppose by concentrating hard enough, I can control any object or person.

I guess I'm now officially a level five breaker.

I finally know what it's like to be Guardian. It's almost scary to possess such power. Taking lives becomes so easy. There's nobody to stop you. You can submit or destroy anybody. And I guess there wasn't much choice left for a man like that, besides becoming what he became.

But I'm not Guardian. I need the ability for telekinesis strictly for killing him.

So I turn to face our attackers and a moment later they all freeze in place. An invisible force rips the rifles from their hands. Their bodies simultaneously rise into the air. Then I drop them down, smashing them into the ground. It's too easy.

Chase and Marcus stare at me, open-mouthed.

"Holy cow!" Chase exclaims.

"Was that you?" Marcus asks. "How did you do that?"

I offer no explanation. I've no idea how I did it.

I look at the metal door and it begins trembling. A moment later the metal buckles and breaks by the same invisible force.

"Don't follow me," I say to Marcus and Chase.

I enter the bunker, leaving them behind.

I walk slowly down a long dusky corridor, the same passageway I'd walked several months ago. It's the same bunker where Guardian captured me before. It's the place Hammer ruthlessly gunned down the leaders of our former government. And the place where I saw my mother for the last time, right before she shot me in the face.

This is where everything will end, I think. It seems logical and somehow fitting.

I run into squads of Guardian's soldiers along the way. They open fire, trying to shoot me on sight, but their bullets veer harmlessly away. I continue walking ahead, as their flailing bodies ascend into the air. Their heads explode as I pass, flesh and blood splattering against the walls and ceiling.

I guess I'm truly some sort of monster now. And it's unsettling to say the least. No one possessing this level of power should be allowed to live.

I enter the main office area, instantly recognizing the place. This is the room where everything happened. Guardian trapped me in here, pressing me against a wall to watch as Hammer killed the leaders of our government. I remember like it was yesterday.

I take a look around and suddenly, there he is. Casually sitting behind a large desk. It looks like he has been waiting for me. We face each other. This is the very man who's destroyed our world and ruined my life. He's also the one who ordered Kitty shot.

"So you finally made it, did you?" Guardian asks in his soft voice. "Bravo, my friend. You haven't disappointed me after all."

I remain silent. I hate the sound of his voice. I'm disgusted by seeing his face. And I'm not scared.

Guardian smiles mockingly. He rises to his feet, walks around his desk and stops right in front of me. I become tense. I know I can't manipulate him in the same manner as I have with his soldiers. He's probably still much stronger than me. His ability comes naturally. So it may be wise to wait until he makes the first move.

"So what now, Rex?" Guardian asks. "Why have you come? Have you finally returned home?"

"I'm here to kill you," I answer.

Guardian laughs. "Do you really think you have the slightest chance to take me?"

"We'll find out soon enough," I say.

"Such arrogance!" He grins. "Do you remember asking why I chose you? Well, there's a good reason. You've always been so disgustingly arrogant and stubborn. You always had to do things your own way. You amuse me. I immensely enjoyed watching your struggles. You realize of course, how most human beings are far too easy to subdue. But you, along with your little redhead friend, offered real challenges." He sighs, adding, "I'm very sorry for your loss by the way. It must be terribly hard on you."

He pauses. I don't speak.

"Her death was accidental, you know," Guardian continues. "My soldiers were directed to terminate you, not her. I'd never condone having such a unique breaker like Kitty destroyed. Her death is a tragedy."

Guardian pauses again, waiting for my reaction. I remain quiet.

"You shouldn't continue to waste energy blaming me for her death," he adds. "It's your own fault. Had you only accepted your destiny, she'd be still alive. Had you ceased resisting, you'd be leader of the Army of Justice by now. And Kitty could have become one of our top notch soldiers. Perhaps even a commander in time."

"She would never have agreed to serve you," I answer.

"How could you know that?"

I shrug.

"So let me ask you again. What happens now, Rex?" Guardian says. "Let's consider the remote possibility that you kill me, ridiculous as that notion is. What then? Do you think breakers and non-breakers would then learn how to coexist in peace? Did the crazy professor convince you to believe in his fairy tales?" He lets out a laugh, looking at me with condescension. "We can never coexist in peace. And saying we, I mean all humanity. Hatred coupled with an innate desire to kill are part of our nature. It's not love or friendship driving us to further development and progress. Our enemies make us strong and we have to have them in order to move forward. Were there no breakers left in this world, human beings would simply create another foe. They would find somebody else to hate, anyone with some slight variation from the norm. It may be those handicapped, or even people with a different color of eyes or hair. Don't you agree?"

"Honestly," I say, "I don't give a damn."

Guardian ignores my comment, continuing with his philosophical onslaught.

"Our hatred toward non-breakers is justified," he states. "It's the natural outcome of evolution. Out with the old, in with the new. That's precisely what all animal species do."

"We're not animals," I remind him.

"You're still emotionally attached to the non-breakers, aren't you?" Guardian asks.

I don't answer.

"I respect your stubbornness," he declares. "And I admit I enjoy our conversations. It's difficult to find a person who's willing to speak to me as an equal. It's not easy being me, Rex. My soldiers are scared of me. And they all perceive me like some kind of God. It seems that you're the only one who fully realizes that I'm just a man."

"You would be mistaken," I say. "I think you're a freak."

"You're not intimidated by me, are you?" he asks, smiling. The table and chairs begin trembling behind him.

"No," I answer. "And tonight, we're both going to die."

"You'll be the one who dies this night my misguided friend," he counters. "You're a dead man and it's time to put you in the grave for good."

The table and chairs fly upward, ripped into pieces by an invisible force. Something hits me hard in the chest, knocking me across the room. At the same time, an unseen force also hits Guardian. It raises him off his feet and plunges him down hard. We're on opposite sides of the room now, each trying to recover. Guardian is first to rise back to his feet.

"Not too shabby," he says, laughing. "Holtzmann obviously did a great job with you, but did he instruct you on how to properly manipulate the telekinesis? I imagine you have no idea what you're doing."

Lamp bulbs explode above both our heads, sending shards of sharp glass raining down. I scramble to my feet and run toward the door to lure him outside. It shuts closed right in front of me.

"Coward!" Guardian yells. "You miserable, weak coward!"

The floor and walls begin vibrating. He's going to kill me, I realize. I don't mind dying, but I have one more thing to do first.

I concentrate harder. I manage to rip the door from the doorway and hurl it at Guardian. It doesn't manage to hit him.

I run down the long passageway. The main exit, I think, I have to make it to the main exit. My heart is racing and my heartbeat is unsteady. I see everything only through a blurry red haze. The drug is beginning to kill me now.

Something grabs me from behind, forcing me down hard onto the floor. I look back and watch as Guardian walks toward me. He moves his feet slowly, because he has no reason to hurry. I'm the one running out of time.

"Do you really think you or anyone else can stop me?" he asks. "You can destroy my headquarters and kill all my puppets, but guess what? I don't mind. I'll rebuild everything only to allow it to be destroyed again."

The force holding me abruptly raises me up into the air, smashing my body against the ceiling. I fall back down, hitting the floor hard. Sharp pain pierces through my left arm. I think it's broken.

I mentally strike Guardian. I slam him against a wall, but can't concentrate hard enough to keep him pinned down. He quickly blocks the attempt. I can hardly affect him at all.

"Very impressive," he comments dryly. "But not quite good enough."

I get to my feet, continuing to move toward the main exit. I'm limping badly and can't move my left arm.

An invisible force strikes my head, knocking me down once again. Blood gushes from my nose, pooling on the floor. I realize Guardian is intent on tearing me into pieces. I find I'm still able to resist him only a little.

"Stop trying to block me," I hear Guardian's voice from behind. "You must realize there's no use in it."

I begin crawling toward the main exit. There's about hundred yards between myself and the door, although it feels like a hundred miles.

Guardian laughs loudly.

"You're like a worm," he comments. "It's so entertaining to watch."

I don't react, continuing to crawl and leaving behind a blood trail along the way.

"After you die, I'm going to kill all your friends as promised," Guardian states, following after me. "Let's see who we have on the list. Rebecca, Marian, Marcus, Chase, Victor. Or maybe Victor isn't you friend? Well, I'll terminate him anyway. Did I forget anybody? Oh, of course… Jessie. I shouldn't forget her."

Finally approaching the exit, something invisible grips my legs, dragging me back a few feet into the building. I concentrate, trying to fight it off. I hear Guardian's derisive laughter. He's not fighting with me, not really. He's just toying with his victim in the same manner as a cat plays with a mouse before killing it.

I finally make it outside. It's dark. I still hear gunfire in the distance. I look around, wondering where Marcus and Chase are. Hopefully, they're still alive. They've probably taken cover, because Guardian will kill them on sight.

"It's a beautiful night," Guardian sighs, standing beside me now. "I'm actually glad Elimination has destroyed this place. It was a prison after all. It never really befitted serving as my headquarters."

He tosses me up into the air again, only to smash me against the concrete below. I cry out in pain. I feel like every bone in my body has been broken. I lie on my back, watching Guardian watch me. He has a wide grin spread across his face. Something begins pressing me harder into the concrete. I concentrate, trying to stop him from crushing me. I reach back for anything that's left in me and focus on resisting his will. Guardian winces in his effort.

"It's all over, Rex," he says. "Stop resisting. Make it easier on yourself."

I continue concentrating, ignoring the pain. I have to distract Guardian as much as possible. He mustn't focus on anything else, besides killing me.

Doing so seems to amuse him.

"Did you really believe you could kill me?" he asks. "Did you think you could overpower me, being all alone? You're nothing in comparison to me. You're just a drugged boy, one with no idea how to use his skill. I don't even have to kill you myself. I could simply wait until the drug finishes you off." He pauses, looking straight into my eyes. "Any last words, Rex?"

I don't answer, concentrating.

A moment later, a bullet smashes into Guardian's temple. Blood sprays from his head. His body remains standing for another instant before collapsing a few feet away. He has an astonished look on his face in death.

"I'm not alone!" I exclaim, kicking his corpse.

That's it, I think, this is where everything ends.

I begin laughing. Guardian is dead and Jessie has gunned him down.

"Thank you," I whisper, still laughing. "Thank you so much, Jess."

I lie motionless on the ground, waiting for the drug to finish me off. My head and arm hurt, but the pain won't be bothering me much longer. I'm about to join Kitty. I'm about to leave this violent, crazy world behind.

I smile. My heart begins to beat faster and faster, then slows. I can't feel my legs. It's getting difficult to breathe.

I think of Kitty. I want her image to be my final thought.

My vision darkens. I close my eyes, embracing death. It feels good and relieving, almost like falling asleep.

***

I awaken on my back in tall green grass. I sit up and find myself in the middle of a large beautiful meadow, colorful flowers blooming all around. I can't understand where the heck I am or how I ended up here. The blue sky is impeccable. The temperature is neither hot nor cold. I feel a light pleasant breeze on my face. I can see some sort of farmhouse across the meadow and some dark shady woods on the horizon.

My jaw drops. Where am I?

I slowly rise to my feet, realizing that my left arm now seems perfectly fine. I don't feel any pain anywhere. And on top of everything else, my right eye is no longer blind, and I can hear!

I stand unmoving, unable to comprehend everything.

"Rex!" I hear Kitty's voice from behind.

"Kitty!" I exclaim, turning to face her.

Kitty falls right into my arms. I hug her tightly. She's laughing and crying at the same time. She kisses my face and lips.

"Kitty!" I breathe out. "Are you real?"

"Of course I'm real!" she laughs. "I've been waiting for you! What took you so long?"

"I'm sorry, sweetie," I say. "I had work to finish, I came as fast as I could."

Kitty gives me another hug. She's dressed in a summer dress, her long red hair flowing behind her back.

"What is this place?" I ask. "Is it heaven or just some hallucination?"

"I don't really know," Kitty answers. "But it doesn't make any difference now, does it?"

"No," I say. "It doesn't matter a bit."

She takes my hand, pulling me in the direction of the farmhouse.

"Come with me," Kitty says. "I'll show you around."

We walk across the meadow, holding hands and smiling. I can't stop staring at her.

"It's so great here!" Kitty exclaims. "I'm sure you'll like it. Everything is exactly the way you described. There are dinosaurs in the woods. We can hunt them later. The weather here is perfect year round. And the best thing about this place is that everybody is here. Chelsey, Lena, Jimmy, Vogel… everybody! Even Dustin and Christina."

"Wheeler," I say. "Is he here as well?"

"I don't think so," Kitty answers. "But if he ever shows up, we're gonna kick him out. What can he do to us now? We're already dead."

"I guess you're right."

"I'm always right. Come. Marian must be waiting for us."

"Marian? What is she doing here?"

"I don't know. Is something wrong?"

Something bothers me for a second, but then I look into Kitty's eyes and the worrisome thought disappears. I don't care about anything else as long as I'm together again with Kitty.

"You'll never leave me again, will you?" she asks.

"Never," I answer sincerely. "I promise."

Kitty smiles broadly, holding my hand and pulling me forward. I willingly follow, leaving all my worries and painful memories behind. I'm happy and there's no other place in the world I'd wish to be.

CHAPTER 31

I hear voices and irritating beeping noises. I sense bright light through my closed eyelids. I realize I'm lying on my back on some sort of hard, cold surface. My entire body is hurting and I can't move.

"We've brought him back," somebody says in a firm voice. "He's stabilizing now."

What?! They brought me back? I don't want to be brought back. I want to return to that wonderful, beautiful place where Kitty is waiting.

I'm desperate. I want to order the medics to let me go. I want to push them away, but remain motionless. No matter how hard I try, I can't move. I can't speak. I'm not even breathing on my own. There's a plastic tube inserted into a hole in my neck, hooked to a machine that steadily pumps oxygen into my lungs.

Despite my weakness, I manage to collect enough strength to raise my right arm. I grab the plastic tube and rip it away from my throat.

Doctors begin fussing over me. Somebody tries to unbend my fingers, but I hold onto the tube as tightly as I can. I'm not about to stay in this world. I'm returning to Kitty. I promised her I'd never leave her again, and that's a promise I must keep.

A needle pricks my skin and the drug knocks me out. I don't have any dreams this time, I'm all alone in pitch-black darkness.

***

When I next come to, I'm lying in bed inside a hospital room. I can hardly breathe and my hands are shaking. I attempt to sit up, but instantly fall back down.

A few minutes later, several doctors barge in. They shove a thermometer into my mouth. They take my blood pressure and shine a light into my eyes. I'm so confused and woozy that I can't comprehend their words. But what I do pick up is that I've just spent the last five weeks in a medically induced coma until my condition stabilized. My heart didn't fail after all, I only stopped breathing. Fortunately, Chase, Marcus and Jessie found me in time. They performed resuscitation until the medical team arrived. My body is now clean of Holtzmann's drug and my prognosis is positive. The only complication is that my muscles have atrophied due to being totally incapacitated during the past few weeks. As soon as I regain my strength, I'll be allowed to leave the hospital.

I'm obviously in that darn five percent the drug didn't kill! And I'm going to kill Jessie.

The doctors say I'm extremely lucky. They call me a living miracle. I remain silent as I don't share in their enthusiasm.

After the medics leave, a furious Holtzmann marches in.

"Why couldn't you follow simple instructions?!" is the first thing I hear from him. "Why didn't you inject the antidote?!"

The professor rages for a good ten minutes before finally calming down enough to update me on our current situation. The war has ended. Most of Guardian's troops quickly surrendered after their leader's demise. The majority of them are awaiting trial, locked away in prison. Of course they all deny their crimes, insisting that Guardian forced them to serve in his army against their wills.

Our Republic will soon be split into two states. The northern section will be for ordinary humans and the southern for mind breakers. Residents of both states will be allowed to travel across the border only after receiving special permission. Elimination will be closely monitoring the relationship between both states and imprison any rule breakers, now functioning strictly as a defense mechanism.

Holtzmann holds very enthusiastic prospects for our future. He thinks that we've finally begun to learn how to cooperate with one another and coexist in peace.

"It's only the beginning," he explains. "Of course, some conflicts will be unavoidable, but I believe humanity will be able to overcome any further issues and learn from our past mistakes."

I don't say anything. I don't really give a damn what happens to humanity going forward.

"Someone else is here to visit you," Holtzmann adds, smiling.

He leaves, then a moment later a hysterical Marian runs into the room.

"Alex!" she exclaims, hugging me tightly. "I've missed you so much!"

I don't react.

"How could you do that to me?" Marian exclaims. "How could you leave me again?"

She grips my hand, pressing it against her face.

"I thought you wouldn't make it," she sobs. "I was afraid I'd lost my brother forever."

Marian finally calms down and explains how she stayed with Chase and Rebecca while I was in coma. They looked after her.

"Chase and Rebecca?" I ask, a little confused. "Wait, you mean they're living together?"

"Well, yeah," Marian answers, smiling. "Didn't you know? They've been dating for a while now."

"No."

"You're kidding!"

Marian giggles. She begins telling me about her work in the refugee center, but I'm not really listening. I no longer feel anything special toward this odd girl. She remains more of a stranger to me than sister.

I need to find Kitty. I promised to stay with her.

***

I remain in the hospital for the next three weeks. My muscles gradually strengthen. Doctors provide a cane so I can now go for slow tiresome walks along the hospital's corridors. I eat whatever the nurses bring. I do all the physical exercises they direct me to do. I speak when spoken to and remember to smile, faking a positive attitude. I can't allow anybody to learn my true thoughts and intentions.

I'm plotting an escape. I somehow have to return to Kitty. They can't force me to continue living against my will. Unfortunately, I still haven't decided just how things should go down. I currently don't have access to a gun, and the medics are doing a good job of keeping away any sharp objects. They've even mounted video cameras on the walls inside my room, so I assume I'm under constant watch now.

It's frustrating.

I finally decide to wait to make my escape after I'm allowed to leave the hospital. As soon as I'm out of here, I'll get hold of some sort of weapon and then…

Marian remains nearby all the time. She returns to headquarters only late at night, and every sunrise she's back in the room by my side. She helps out a lot during walks, bringing me water and telling entertaining stories. She clings to me and is constantly holding my hand, always trying to catch my gaze. Most of the time though, I simply ignore her.

Jessie drops in one day for a visit. She sits across from me in a chair as I'm lying in bed in near total exhaustion after a three hundred yard stroll. We don't speak for a long time.

"What the hell happened, Jess?" I finally ask. "You made me a promise."

"Well, guess what?" she answers. "I lied."

"Damn you!" I exclaim. "I thought I could trust you."

Grinning, she shows me a finger.

"I'll make you regret you didn't kill me," I threaten.

She lets out a laugh, obviously perceiving my threat as a joke. It's not easy to scare Jessie.

"Seriously, Jess," I say. "I counted on you."

"Stop whining," she interrupts. "You're such a wimp! It's me who should be complaining. I had to perform resuscitation on you for a solid twenty minutes. It was disgusting! Marcus and Chase refused to help me out because you know… you're a guy."

"But why?!" I ask. "Why did you do it?"

"What else could I do?" Jessie's expression becomes serious. "What would you do if you were in my place? If I'd asked you to kill me?"

I don't answer.

"I know you, Rex," she says. "You'd have done the same thing."

She spends a few more minutes in my room, then pats me on the shoulder and leaves. Although Jessie certainly didn't keep her promise, she remains a trusted friend.

Chase visits me another day. We speak about Elimination's new executives including our freshly elected governmental leaders.

"What about you, Chase?" I ask. "Will you remain Elimination's leader?"

"No way!" he blurts out. "It's too much of a headache. No, I prefer being a regular officer."

"Thanks for looking after Marian," I say.

"No big deal," he sighs. "But listen, can you explain to me how you manage to deal with that girl? I mean, she's completely off her rocker."

"Yep," I agree. "What has my sister done now?"

"I really don't want to go into specifics," Chase mutters. "But she's just like you. She's nothing but trouble. So please do me a big favor, get well quickly and come take your Marian the heck away from me."

I grin, amused by Chase's frustration. I know firsthand how nasty Marian can be at times.

Rebecca is the next one to drop by. I thank her as well for taking care of Marian.

"Oh, it's been my pleasure," Rebecca assures me. "Your sister is my best friend. And she's such a sweet girl! I'll miss her terribly after she leaves."

I don't comment.

Rebecca tells me about her future plans.

"I'll continue working in the refugee center," she says. "They're going to make me some kind of supervisor there. I will also continue assisting Egbert in his lab part time. He's creating a new department in Elimination, one where telepaths and memory readers will be working together. And I've also been thinking about going to college in the future. Maybe I could become a child care specialist or something else along those lines. What do you think?"

"I think that's a great idea," I answer, smiling.

Rebecca lowers her eyes, seemingly embarrassed.

"Marian told you about Chase and I, didn't she?" she asks.

"She did," I answer. "And I'm very happy for you and Chase."

"Truly? I was a little scared to tell you."

"Gosh, Rebecca! What's to be scared about?"

She shrugs, still avoiding looking at me.

"I'm really very happy for you two," I say sincerely. Rebecca smiles.

Marcus comes for a visit one afternoon. We discuss Elimination and captured Guardian soldiers. Then I ask carefully, "Are you getting along all right, Marcus?"

He frowns, instantly realizing what I'm referring to. His brother. Marcus hasn't been quite the same after his loss.

"Well, I guess I'm doing okay," he says. "I was thinking about leaving Elimination. I thought maybe I should go to study. I remember telling you how our mother had always wanted for at least one of us to get a degree." He smirks, sighing. "But nah, I can't imagine myself being anything but an officer. You know once you begin working for Elimination, there's no going back. This job kinda sucks you in."

"I do know," I say.

Oliver and Victor come for a visit. They both plan on staying in Elimination for a while as well. Oliver may become one of the commanders, although he's not too thrilled about his offer. Looks like he's also getting tired with the idea of leadership.

Victor claims that he'll remain in Elimination only until they manage to find a suitable replacement for him. As soon as that happens he's planning to head south, find some kind of gravy job where he can be whoever he wants to be. Which happens to be a junkie. Well, what could anyone ever really expect from Victor?

My days pass slowly with the same monotonous routines. Visitors come and go. I eat, sleep and continue walking and doing exercises. I slowly recover and get stronger. And I constantly think about my escape.

They won't be able to keep me here much longer. They can't separate me from Kitty. I've always been pretty good at escaping, and I won't fail this time.

***

A few days after Victor's visit, Chase drives Jessie, Marian and I to the city cemetery. We walk between the rows of fresh graves. We find the place where Dave and Vogel are resting. We spend a few minutes in silence, standing near the graves. And then we walk toward a large, tall oak and stop at Kitty's grave. Marian instantly begins sobbing, clutching my wrist and shivering. Jessie quietly puffs on a cigarette, looking away. Chase watches me intently, probably concerned I'll freak out as I did in the intensive-care unit. I remain silent and calm. None of us has anything to say.

"Well, let's get going," Jessie whispers finally.

"I'll catch up with you guys," I say. "I want to spend a few more minutes with her. You can wait for me in the car."

"Alex," Marian utters.

"Give him some space," Jessie says, grabbing hold of my sister's elbow and leading her away.

Left alone, I sit on the ground and begin crying. I weep like I've never wept before.

Perhaps not only for Kitty, but crying for everybody that died during this pointless war. I remember our fallen. I remember all those people who gave so much and got so little in return. All those whose deaths were so meaningless, unnecessary and tragic. Little Lena. Chelsey. Jimmy. Erica Vogel. Christina and Dustin. Dave. Frank. Rebecca's parents. Jessie's parents. Vogel's son. Emily.

But most of all I cry for her. I cry for Kitty. And when I finally stop weeping, I realize that I'll probably never cry again in this lifetime. There are no tears left in me now. I've used them all.

I wipe my face and rise to my feet.

"I love you, Kitty," I whisper. "And I miss you so much. But I have to stay here for a little bit longer. I still have one more thing to do. Just know I'm always thinking about you. And I'll never forget you."

Then I turn and walk slowly toward the main gates of the cemetery. Jessie, Marian and Chase wait for me outside the car. We get in and drive away.

Driving, Chase clears up his throat and says, "Well, maybe it's not the best time to speak about it, but anyway... Elimination is currently recruiting breakers. You and Jessie are welcome to join our team."

Jessie and I exchange glances.

"You'd be working with me, Marcus and Holtzmann," Chase adds quickly. "And you can actually ask for any kind of compensation you wish. So what do you think, guys? Are you ready to help hunt down evil breakers?"

Neither of us says a word.

"Hello," Chase says. "Elimination is offering you two a job lest you weren't listening. It's okay to speak up."

"No, thanks," Jessie answers. "I'm sick of Elimination. I'm planning to head south and become a bartender."

"Are you kidding?" Chase groans. "What about you, Rex?"

"Sorry, but I'm out as well," I say.

"Well, you don't have to decide anything right now," Chase adds. "Considering your contribution to our victory, you both can take as much time to think things over as you please. This is an open-ended offer with no expiration date."

"We'll see," I answer curtly.

I don't know whether I'm going to accept Chase's offer or not. Maybe I'll just follow Jessie's example and head south, leaving Elimination behind. Or maybe I'll join Chase's team and go hunting evil breakers. But for the moment, all I really want to do is take care of my sister. She's still young and vulnerable. And there's still some innocence left in her because she has never killed anybody. Her hands are clean of blood. I need to make sure she remains this way. I must help Marian find the right path in life and live better and happier than her brother. I have to make certain she doesn't repeat my mistakes.

My sister is sitting beside me, lightly brushing her fingertips against my sleeve, thinking I don't notice. I turn to look at her. She catches my gaze and smiles shyly. I hesitate for only a moment before returning her smile.

ABOUT MARINA EPLEY

Marina is an indie writer from Yaroslavl, Russia, where she grew up on and was influenced by American movies like Terminator, Rambo and Aliens. She studied journalism at Yaroslavl University and worked as a journalist for the local newspaper.

No stranger to a blank piece of paper, Marina had begun writing stories to share with classmates by the age of 12, and won district poetry competitions while still in school. Later, she became a laureate in a Russian National Contest for Young Writers Debut. Her two prize winning novellas were subsequently published in a Moscow literature magazine.

Besides having a great passion for writing, Marina loves to read, travel, study martial arts, and has developed quite a taste for tex-mex since relocating to the Houston area. She enjoys nature, animals, long walks with her husband, and competes in 5K and 10K runs as time allows.

Always a natural story teller, Marina has already come a long way since her modest beginnings, both figuratively and literally. From her first serious study of English in 2007 to starting her first novel upon arrival to Canton, Ohio in 2011, Marina demonstrates very well what one can achieve with a strong imagination and hard work no matter the obstacle.

She mostly writes YA dystopian, with plenty of action and adventure, but is a great fan of all good stories containing lots of twists and turns and surprise endings.

Stay updated with Marina's new releases at:
https://www.facebook.com/writerdystopian/
https://twitter.com/MarinaEpley
email: epleymarina@gmail.com

Made in the USA
Columbia, SC
19 November 2018